‖‖ ‖ ‖‖‖‖‖‖ ‖ ‖‖‖ ‖ ‖‖‖‖‖‖‖‖‖‖‖ ‖

W9-BMQ-401

Advance Praise for *Playing by the Book*

"There's so much to admire in S. Chris Shirley's debut novel, but the most remarkable thing may be its voice. Jake Powell is both earnest and skeptical, curious and guarded, and he tells his story with an endearing humility that–somehow–avoids the sarcasm that has become the norm. *Playing by the Book* reminds us of how rewarding it can be to climb into someone else's head."

—Patrick Ryan, author of *Send Me* and *Saints of Augustine*

"In *Playing by the Book*, S. Chris Shirley tells a story I loved curling up with, featuring one of the most endearing teen protagonists I've read in years."

—Alex Sanchez, author of *The God Box* and *Boyfriends with Girlfriends*

"S. Chris Shirley's *Playing by the Book* is winning, witty, touching, and full of life. Jake Powell's journey from wide-eyed innocence to self-actualization is a pleasure to witness. What's even more pleasurable is being in the hands of a writer who knows how to tell a story, who knows how to create complex characters, and who brings honesty and love to every page of his debut. Bravo!"

—Martin Wilson, author of *What They Always Tell Us*

"In the ideal world, S. Chris Shirley's *Playing by the Book* would be made into a teenage romantic comedy to play at your local Cineplex. A classic coming of age story with a queer twist, *Playing by the Book* manages to be both poignant and lighthearted at the same time as young Jake navigates the currents of first love to a realistic but still happy ending. Shirley finds the truth in Jake's story and gives it to us in clear and accessible prose. A thoroughly enjoyable read that should be on the shelves of every school library as well as the bed stands of anyone who wants to understand what it feels like to grow up gay."

—Kevin Jennings, Founder, The Gay, Lesbian and Straight Education Network (GLSEN)

"In this heartfelt and moving coming-of-age story, S. Chris Shirley has given us a Holden Caulfield for a new generation."

—Geoffrey Nauffts, Tony-nominated playwright of *Next Fall*

"S. Chris Shirley's *Playing by the Book* is beautifully written and vividly conveys a journey of self-discovery. This moving, funny, and sexy young adult novel also illuminates how combining Christian fundamentalism and a gay love story can produce another very Good Book."

—Bob Smith, author of *Openly Bob, Selfish and Perverse*, and *Remembrance of Things I Forgot*

3 4170 08192 1653

PLAYING BY THE BOOK

A NOVEL

S. CHRIS SHIRLEY

This is a work of fiction. Names, characters, places and incidents are either products of the author's imagination or, if real, are used fictitiously.

Copyright © by S. Chris Shirley

Magnus Books, an Imprint of Riverdale Avenue Books
5676 Riverdale Avenue, Suite 101
Bronx, NY 10471

All rights reserved. No part of this book may be reproduced or transmitted in any form or by any means, electronic or mechanical, including photocopying, without permission in writing from the publisher.

The Holy Bible, New International Version®, NIV® Copyright © 1973, 1978, 1984, 2011 by Biblica, Inc.™ Used by permission. All rights reserved worldwide.

Printed in the United States of America

Cover design by Tal Goretsky with photographs courtesy of Richard Gerst and Jonnie Miles

Digital and Print Layout by www.formatting4U.com

Print ISBN: 978-1-62601-071-0
Digital ISBN: 978-1-62601-072-7

www.magnusbooks.com
www.riverdaleavebooks.com

For Mom and Dad

"If you desire to be good, begin by believing that you are wicked."

—Epictetus (55 AD - 135 AD)

CHAPTER 1

KABAM!

I popped up in my seat, not knowing if we'd landed or gotten shot down.

"I'd like to be the first to welcome you to New York," the pilot announced.

Some welcome. Sounded more like a warning shot (N y 4 y)

I quickly stuffed my New York travel guides in my backpack and capped my highlighter, not believing that I was spending half a summer at the most prestigious high school journalism program in the world? The Columbia University Summer in Journalism program is limited to high school newspaper editors and has an acceptance rate that probably rivals their undergraduate program. As far as I could tell, no kid from Alabama—let alone Tarsus, Alabama (population 7,022)—had ever gone. I still couldn't believe I got in.

Getting accepted was tough, but the biggest hurdle was winning over The Preacher. I mean, my dad. I first called him "Preacher" when I was five since Momma and everyone else did. At the time, I half expected him to send me to bed early or take away my television privileges, but he smiled real big and halfway nodded, so the name stuck. I tried calling Momma "Anna" around the same time, but that didn't go over so well.

Anyway, the very day I got my Columbia acceptance letter, Momma and I role-played my conversation with The Preacher so I could perfect my sales pitch. The two major hurdles we had to clear were the price of the program and the fact that it began the very week of our church's Vacation

Bible School. The Preacher thought I was going to be the Vacation Bible School Director this year because, well, I sort of said that I would. But that was before I even knew about the Columbia program.

Sitting at my place at the kitchen table, Momma lowered her voice to play me and I played my dad, even scratching my balls for effect since he's one of the last great ball scratchers. We continued for a solid hour and put together a winning platform.

To be clear, we didn't do this all the time—just for big events, like in third grade when I had a shot at a free German Shepherd puppy and when I recently requested an extension on my eleven o'clock curfew for a school dance. I never got the puppy but I was victorious on the curfew, if you count a one-time thirty-minute curfew extension a victory.

But over dinner that evening, The Preacher cut me off before I even got going good. He said, "Jake, you agreed to lead Vacation Bible School this summer, right? You can't be at church and Columbia at the same time."

Momma jumped right in. "But it's a huge opportunity for him," she said. "Columbia's—"

"There's no more important work than the Lord's work," The Preacher said, then turned to me. "And how much would this cost, anyway?"

I shuffled my feet. "Five thousand dollars."

The Preacher glanced at me then did a double take. "Son, we don't have that kind of money."

I casually leaned in just as Momma had when we rehearsed this exact scenario earlier. "But I have a few thousand saved—"

"You are not touching your college fund," he said with a dismissive wave. "You're going to need it next year."

"But this is for classes at a college," I said, holding The Preacher's gaze. "One of the best colleges in the world."

"I said 'no' and that's final. Plus, there's another youth service in July and you're preaching."

2

My chest tightened at the thought of preaching again—my last sermon had been an epic failure and quite possibly the most humiliating experience of my life. "The Columbia program ends a few days before that, but, Dad, I really don't want to—"

"Jake, you've got to get back in the saddle and preach again." The Preacher looked down at his plate and continued eating.

I kept at him over the ensuing days since my offer to attend was only good for a couple of weeks, but each time the conversation got shorter and the I-said-no-and-that's-final got louder. Despite his resistance, I couldn't let it go; my love for journalism was just too deep, having begun not long after I learned to read. In elementary school, I wrote and bound a series of adventure stories about Papaw's old birddog, and penned new verses for my favorite gospel songs. But when my essay on a student field trip to the local "Jerusalem in Miniature" made the church newsletter, I was hooked on journalism and signed up for the *Tarsus Junior High Journal* the first day of seventh grade.

Plus, this was more than just a chance to study at one of the top journalism schools in the world, it was the chance to *not* be a Preacher's Kid—or PK for short—for a few precious weeks and for the first time in my life. As a PK, I was held to what I called the "Jesus Standard" by everyone in town on absolutely everything I did. Anytime I came up short, they went running to The Preacher. I wouldn't wish it on anybody.

A few weeks later, on the very evening that my Columbia acceptance was to expire, I began to panic and decided to go for broke. With no real plan in mind, I tiptoed down the hallway just before dinner and peeked through the partially opened door of The Preacher's study, walls lined with bookcases jam-packed with Biblical texts. It was like he never had a life outside the church, which was pretty accurate since Papaw had been a preacher too, as had my Great Papaw on Mamaw's side. Of course, they were both Pentecostal, meaning they put a lot of emphasis on the supernatural aspects of Christianity like speaking in tongues (the ability to speak in a language you've never studied). As a One-Way Bible minister, The Preacher was more focused on theology and less on theatrics. In fact, his knowledge of the Bible was absolutely staggering.

As I expected, The Preacher was sitting at his big oak desk, peering through his reading glasses at a miniature model of the proposed church complex. He ran his finger along the thick molding just below the roofline.

"Oh, um, is that the latest?" I asked as I stepped into the room.

He jerked his finger away from the model and looked up. "Sure is! Including the balcony, the sanctuary will sit eight hundred."

"Wow! I bet that's even bigger than First Methodist!"

He glowed with pride. "It'll be the largest sanctuary between Montgomery and Mobile."

"That's great, Preacher." I meant it too—my poor dad had spent years trying to get this new sanctuary off the ground and it looked like it was finally going to happen.

I stroked the razor sharp part in my hair, thick and black just like his. That's about the only feature we share other than our height: at six-foot-two inches, I'm actually an inch taller, but have the Clarke side of the family's blue eyes, fair skin and cleft that rides up the base of my chin like a baby's booty—my nickname in grade school was "Bootette" (it wasn't particularly clever, just annoying). People often complimented my "good looks," but The Preacher was the showstopper in the family with his dark skin, lumberjack build, and rugged features. Some said he looked like a movie star. He was sort of a fortyish Mel Gibson without all the baggage.

He took off his reading glasses and moved the model aside. "What's up?"

"Oh, um, Preacher, I want—I *need* to talk about Columbia."

The look on his face made it clear he had nothing left to say on the matter. "I'm not discussing this again, Jake."

We just stared at each other. I'd already told him a million times that this Columbia program was just what I needed as the new editor of the *Tarsus High School Tattler*. It would teach me all the ins and outs of running a newspaper and could even come in handy for the church's website and monthly newsletter. Plus, being immersed in journalism 24/7 would help me figure out if that was indeed the path I wanted to take in my life. But every time, he always countered with "there's no more important work than the Lord's work" or "choosing God's way and not our own is tough, but separation from God is even worse." Deep down, I knew that this Columbia program was a thousand times more important than Vacation Bible School, but how could I argue with his godly line of reasoning?

Suddenly, I realized there was another angle—one that might just get through to him.

"Preacher, please hear me out—the day I submitted that Columbia application, I got down on my knees and prayed God would let me get in if He wanted me to go. So it was really, like, a sign when I was accepted. I was putting out the fleece—like Gideon."

One-Way Bible people often ask God for signs like this. We call it "putting out the fleece" in reference to the Old Testament story of Gideon, who asked God to make a piece of wool on his doorstep dry and the ground around it wet if he should lead Israel to battle against the Midianites. It was just one way we incorporated our faith into our daily lives, and it wasn't that wacky when you thought about it—wasn't everyone going through life looking for signs to guide them?

Momma stuck her grayish auburn head through the doorway. She was about the same age Grandmother Clarke had been when her hair began falling out, so Momma didn't color or even tease her hair like most women her age since there was too much at risk, I guess. "Private party?" she asked.

"Your son thinks God's sending him to Columbia. I see your sister's fingerprints all over this. She just wants to get him up to New York City so she can fill his head with her liberal garbage." The Preacher looked at me like it was time to 'fess up.

I held my breath, hoping not to give anything away, but my dad practically had a degree in sizing people up. Aunt Phoebe *had* been the one who told me about the Columbia program, a fact Momma and I agreed The Preacher didn't need to know. I swallowed hard.

Momma walked in and grabbed the back of one of the two brown leather chairs facing The Preacher's desk. "She's actually changed a lot in the last few years," she said. "Gone back to being a good Episcopalian."

"What exactly does *that* mean anymore, Anna? They're marrying gays now, you know. What's next—farm animals?"

"Hey," she said, digging her fingers into the back of the chair. "I was raised Episcopal."

This was all pretty weird—my parents *never* got testy with each other, but I was the one area where my father's spiritual realm and my mother's domestic realm overlapped. I sensed The Preacher didn't care for her gourmet dishes like the Swedish meatballs or seven-layer salad, just like I suspected Momma didn't agree with everything The Preacher said from the pulpit. Each had their sovereign territory, which the other never challenged, or if so, not in front of me.

By now, my dad looked more hurt than angry. This was about more than Vacation Bible School, and we all knew it. To be fair, he had mostly encouraged my journalistic pursuits up until that point, saying that the writing and people skills I developed would come in handy no matter what path I took. Of course, it wasn't lost on me that writing and people skills are two of the most basic requirements for a preacher.

"I thought you wanted to be a preacher like me and Papaw," he said. "The church is in your blood, son. I mean, why else would you bother learning Ancient Greek?"

All One-Way Bible ministers study Ancient Greek, the language of the New Testament, at seminary. A few years back, I became obsessed with the language and got The Preacher to tutor me using his old textbooks. Momma was thrilled knowing that it would help me on the SAT since loads of English words have Ancient Greek roots. To be perfectly honest, I studied Ancient Greek so I could personally interpret the more troubling New Testament passages like the ones on sexual immorality, not because I wanted to go into the ministry. But to hear my dad talk, it would be a complete disaster if our family's long line of preachers ended on his watch. If I'd been born a girl, I'm sure my father would've insisted on trying again and again until he had a male heir who could fill the pulpit since women aren't allowed to be preachers—or deacons for that matter—at One-Way Bible churches.

Sure, I'd thought about becoming a preacher when I was younger—what son doesn't consider following in his father's footsteps? But being a preacher meant spending your entire life under a microscope, getting sized up on whether you were living up to the Jesus Standard. It also meant writing a weekly sermon, which was nothing more than an editorial. I love journalism but was recently forced to write my first editorial, just after being elected editor of the *Tarsus High School Tattler*. When I sat down to write it, my mind just went blank. In the end, I based my editorial on one of The Preacher's recent sermons and he helped me put it in my voice. But the fact was that I preferred news. News was truth, and it was time The Preacher heard mine, we'd dodged this issue long enough. "Preacher, I—I want to be a journalist."

"What? Journalism's dead, son. The Tarsus paper went out of business years ago and you saw that story a few months back about all those people getting laid off at *TIME Magazine*. I tell you there's no future in journalism."

"News isn't going away, Preacher," Momma said. "It's just all going online, isn't that right, Jake?"

"Yes, ma'am," I said and grabbed the back of the other brown leather chair.

Momma and I gazed down at the Preacher in solidarity, but he didn't miss a beat.

"And did you read about those three teenagers who were kidnapped in Harlem last week?" he asked. "They'll probably never be seen nor heard from again. You don't want to become some statistic now, do you?"

"No, sir, but, um, Columbia's in Morningside Heights, not Harlem."

The Preacher put on his glasses and turned back to the model. "Τὸ πεπρωμένον φυγεῖν ἀδύνατον." Translation: "It is impossible to escape from what is destined."

A big part of learning Ancient Greek is memorizing sayings from Plato, Aristotle, and Homer. It's completely dorky but my dad and I spout them to each other for fun, but that particular quote (from Sophocles' play *Oedipus Rex*) at that particular moment was like a punch to the stomach. Since junior high, I'd busted my butt learning every aspect of journalism, from writing leads to conducting effective interviews. This program could really jump-start my journalistic career and my dad just wanted me to accept what *he* thought was destined? Was I just supposed to follow orders?

Heat rose in my chest so fast that my face stung and for the first time in ages, I raised my voice at The Preacher. "All my friends have a say in what they're doing this summer, but, once again, I can do anything I want as long as it's exactly what you tell me to!"

The Preacher raised a finger at me. "Watch your mouth, young man."

My jaw was trembling, but I wasn't scared, I was pissed. "Dad, it's an important summer. Don't you remember the summer before your senior year?"

The Preacher looked past me, reflecting on something. "Yes, I went to a Pentecostal Youth Camp. It was…" He sank back in his chair and stared up at the ceiling.

Momma and I glanced at each other then back at The Preacher, who was just looking off into space.

I took a deep breath and calmed myself. "'It was...'" I prompted.

The Preacher sighed, but I couldn't tell if he was sad or just tired. "It was probably the reason I went into the ministry," he said. "At least, that's when I seriously started considering it." He clucked his tongue. "Let me think about it."

"Dad, I have to notify Columbia by midnight tonight! If I don't go, I'll be defying God. That really scares me."

The Preacher looked me dead in the face, but I just stared right back. Implying that he was keeping me from doing the Lord's will was a big accusation in this house, but I was determined to stand my ground for once.

"And what about the five thousand dollar tuition?" he asked.

I shoved my hands in my pocket. "Well, Aunt Phoebe offered—"

"I'll pay for it," Momma said.

I turned to her. "What? How?"

"My Honorarium Fund, of course."

Dad received honorariums when he preached special weeknight revival services at One-Way Bible churches outside our town. Papaw always gave his honorariums to Mamaw, so The Preacher did the same with Momma. I had no idea how much a kitchen renovation cost, but she had begun looking at appliances and countertops, so she had to be close to having enough saved up. Giving me this money would set her back a few years at least, since The Preacher only got about $100 per revival.

"But Momma, that's for your new kitchen—"

"I can spend it any way I like," she said, hands on hips. "Henry, I want him to have this opportunity. I'm not going to stand in his way."

"But Jake has already committed to leading Vacation

Bible School this summer," The Preacher said. "Everyone is depending on him."

She scrunched up her face like she was at her wits' end. "Henry, please!"

Momma rarely confronted The Preacher like that, and I wondered what would happen next.

A stillness fell over the room as my dad stared down at his desk and pinched his nose. Had we gotten through to him? He certainly seemed to be weighing the options. Finally, he looked up at me. "I don't like this. I don't like it at all. But if this is truly where you think God is leading you, then who am I to stand in His way? You can go to New York on two—"

I was overwhelmed—Momma had just delayed her kitchen renovation by years so I could spend six weeks in New York. Even in the face of this incredible sacrifice, her eyes sparkled. "Momma, I'll pay you back one day I promise."

She pulled me close.

"Hear me out!" The Preacher said. "You can go to New York on two conditions. One. We'll put out the fleece again to see if God wants you to be a preacher or a journalist."

Could it really be that simple? Certainly, I wanted to do the Lord's will above everything else. I had been taught to do that my whole life. The Preacher's favorite line struck me again: Choosing God's way and not our own is hard, but separation from God is even worse. "Okay. What sign will we ask for?"

The Preacher thought for a moment. "Columbia must give out awards at the end of this program."

"Yes, sir. Several."

"Let's pray you win one of these awards if you're meant to be a journalist. Otherwise, God wants you to be a minister."

"Okay—you're The Preacher," I said. I'd just have to work like crazy to be sure I won.

"*Two.* You'll pursue the path God reveals to you with all your heart, mind, and spirit."

"Of course."

"That would mean quitting the school paper your senior year if God points you toward the ministry."

I froze. Was he serious? I had only just been elected, and the entire staff was now depending on me. "But I made a commitment to be editor—"

He cocked his head at me. "Just like you made a commitment to lead Vacation Bible School."

Momma frowned and shook her head.

Was I really willing to risk my high school editorship—and my entire journalism career—for a six-week journalism program? But it wasn't just any journalism program—it was *the* journalism program, given by the very school that awards the Pulitzer Prizes (the highest journalism awards in the nation). There was no telling what I might learn and the connections I might make. Plus I could see what it was like to not be a PK for once and spend time with Aunt Phoebe, who had a habit of spoiling me rotten.

"Okay," I said, not having much of a choice.

The Preacher held out his hands for Momma and me to take. The scar on his wrist where he'd fallen on a broken Dr. Pepper bottle as a kid always reminded me of a large translucent spider. His hand swallowed mine whole. People say I have beautiful hands—piano playing hands—but that sounded so fragile and, well, girl-like. I wished I had hands that could palm a basketball or dribble one for that matter.

We bowed our heads in prayer.

"Our Heavenly Father," The Preacher began, "we come to you this day seeking your guidance for Jake's life."

That all happened weeks ago, and I'd been filled with such anticipation ever since that I thought I would burst. Phoebe had overnighted me several New York City guides and, within days, I had dog-eared more pages in them than not. New York was suddenly all I could talk about—I bet everyone in my life was sick of hearing about it except maybe Momma.

But while sitting on the tarmac, waiting for our gate to open up, I was suddenly struck once again by the fact that I had wagered my entire future to get here, including the editorship of *The Tattler*. I shook my head, trying to erase the memory of my pact with God, but it wouldn't go away: everything depended on my bringing home a piece of Lucite embossed with the Columbia Crown. Absolutely everything.

CHAPTER 2

We waited so long on the tarmac for our gate to free up that I started fantasizing about taking the emergency exit since I couldn't wait to set foot in New York! When the fasten seatbelt sign finally chimed off, I shot up into the aisle and got halfway to the exit before most people were even up good. My mind raced through the sights I'd see—Times Square, The Empire State Building, Rockefeller Center, Ground Zero—but what actually greeted me when I stepped off the plane was a grungy terminal with garbage cans spilling over. The air was heavy and musty-smelling.

As The Preacher had suggested, I placed my wallet in my front pocket, then hiked my backpack onto my shoulders and made my way to the central passage. I walked with a sense of purpose so as not to attract pickpockets, but after several yards without a single sign for baggage claim, I stopped short and turned around. A burly man wearing a black leather vest and shades slammed into me. "Watch where ya going, kid!"

"Oh, sorry, sir. Can you tell me where baggage—" but the man was gone. I turned to an older red-haired woman in a white linen suit as she passed. "Sorry to bother you, ma'am, but could you tell me where…"

After attempting to stop a nun who seemed equally lost, I went up to a businessman in suit and tie. "Baggage claim?"

The man continued walking but pointed behind me.

"Thanks, sir!" I called out.

I hurried along a wide hallway then took two sets of escalators down to baggage claim. As soon as I stepped off the final escalator, I spotted a woman yakking on a cell phone, her trim waist peeking from beneath her lime green blouse despite her forty-plus years. Although I hadn't seen her in over two years, she looked exactly as I remembered.

"Aunt Phoebe!" I shouted then waved.

She turned and shot out her arms, nearly dropping her phone. "Jake!"

While I favored Momma, even she admitted that I looked more like Aunt Phoebe. Her black hair was curlier than mine, but our ocean blue eyes and dimpled chins matched to a T.

"It's my Jake! I can't believe you're finally here!" She gave me a big hug, engulfing me in her vanilla-scented perfume.

Her scent brought back the great times we'd had those two Christmases in Atlanta before my grandparents died: camping out for the Lasershow Spectacular at Stone Mountain, riding the longest escalator in the Southeast at Atlanta's Peachtree Center MARTA subway station, and eating two chocolate sundaes *each* at the rotating Sundial restaurant atop the Westin Peachtree Plaza, the tallest hotel in North America.

"Let's drop the 'Aunt' while you're in New York, okay?" she said in her bright Atlanta accent, pretty much intact even after thirty years in New York.

I chuckled. "Okay."

Knowing Phoebe, she'd try passing me off as her little brother. I loved her to death, but she was obsessed with her looks and especially her body—according to legend, she only weighed herself nude and probably spat beforehand.

"Here he is, Anna," she said into her cell phone. She handed me the phone then rummaged through her orange leather purse with oversized handles and a brass padlock.

"Hey, Momma! I made it!" My heart swelled up a little; although I was psyched to be in New York, I'd never been away from my parents for more than a week. I was only a thousand miles from Tarsus, but it felt a lot farther—like I was on the other side of the planet.

Momma ticked off a slew of reminders as if she was

reading from a list (and she probably was): phone home every day, our cell phone "must answer" policy remained in effect, eat my vegetables, get plenty of sleep, and don't get some shirttail of a girl pregnant.

"Momma, we've been over this a thousand times," I said, exhaling dramatically for Aunt Phoebe's benefit. "I got it." I'd never gotten into any real trouble my entire life, but Momma still treated me like a twelve-year-old with latent criminal tendencies. Usually, I'd just let it roll off my back but it was kind of embarrassing with Aunt Phoebe watching.

"I know but I'm your Momma and this is my job. I love you, honey."

"I love you too, Momma," I said. "Say 'hi' to The Preacher."

I hung up and handed the phone back to Phoebe. She put it away then looked me up and down as she applied a dark red lipstick. "Just look at you—these New York girls are going to eat you right up, especially with that Southern drawl." She pulled up the back vent of my blazer. "And where did you get that bubble butt?"

A prickly heat swept out to my ears, and my face felt like it had gone beet red.

Strangers turned and smirked, but Phoebe didn't seem to notice. She just clapped her hands and said, "Next stop: Columbia!"

We barreled down the freeway toward Manhattan in Phoebe's silver convertible—opened to the evening sky— with the cool air whipping through our hair. I'd experienced open-air driving before, but it was always from the back of a pickup. A few drivers checked us out as we passed and one older lady smiled at me. I'd never felt so cool in my entire life, like I was a celebrity or something.

"Okay, Jake," Phoebe called out. "Let's see how well you studied those guidebooks I sent you. What's the building there with the wedged top?"

A glistening white skyscraper with a slanted roof towered above the surrounding buildings, making them look like adobe huts. "The Citicorp Center!" I shouted as we crossed the Triborough Bridge and followed the signs for Manhattan. "You know the roof was angled like that to house solar panels, but they never put them on."

"Really?"

"Yes, ma'am."

She pointed at the skyline. "Okay, and the one with the lighted crown and tire?"

"Tire?"

"*Spire*! That big antenna thing on top!"

In the overgrown skyline, I wasn't sure which building she was talking about, but then I spotted a lighted skyscraper decked out with crowns on top of crowns like some temple dedicated to an ancient sun god. It was unmistakable, even at dusk. "The Chrysler Building!"

"You really did your homework, Jake!" Phoebe shouted.

We took a long, steep curve off the bridge and onto a six-lane highway with only a beat-up guardrail to separate us from the northbound traffic.

"Welcome to Manhattan!" Phoebe said.

"We're in Manhattan?" I checked out the beat-up guardrail that stood in for a median—something the Alabama Highway Department would never allow—and how narrow the lanes were compared to the ones back home. Honestly, Manhattan was a bit of a letdown so far, or at least the highway was.

Phoebe laughed. "Yes. Spanish Harlem."

My heart skipped a beat. "Harlem? Isn't that where those teens were kidnapped? Shouldn't we put the top up?"

"Nah! This whole island is like Disneyland. Well, there are a few pockets that are still a little rough, I guess."

"Which pockets?"

"Let's see. As long as you stay below 96th Street, you have nothing to worry about."

"But Columbia's at 116th Street."

"Well, except around Columbia. That's fine."

I combed the side streets to see if there were any strange-looking characters. "But we're north of 96th now with the top down."

She brushed off my worry with a wave. "Oh, this neighborhood's fine. I'm just saying rule of thumb—you're totally safe below 96th Street and around Columbia. Just don't go north of Columbia without someone who knows the area."

We took an exit that landed us right in the middle of Spanish Harlem and continued west. The tall buildings wedged next to each other on every block looked like downtown Tarsus on steroids. Cars filled the streets, and they were three times as wide as our Main Street. Amazingly, the shortest buildings were five stories high. Most of them had rickety external fire escapes and window air-conditioning units—Brother Roberts, the Chairman of the Deacons at our church, could make a fortune installing central air for these folks.

The streets were teeming with all sorts of people. Even though it was getting dark, Phoebe still didn't raise the convertible top, but at least at our lower speed, we no longer had to shout.

"So is your dorm right on campus?" Phoebe asked.

"Yes. Sounds like most everyone from the program is on the same floor."

"That's nice. And classes start tomorrow?"

"There was a technology boot camp over the weekend, but The Preacher didn't want me missing church this morning. The camp mostly covered newspaper layout and design; I'm pretty good at that so…"

I didn't mention that the camp cost an extra $500!

She rolled her eyes at the mention of my dad, but didn't say anything against The Preacher. It had to be killing her. While my dad's main purpose as a preacher was to enforce social norms, Phoebe didn't seem to give them a second thought. She added her "personal touch" to just about everything and loved nothing more than getting The Preacher's goat.

It's hard to believe it now, but there was a time Aunt Phoebe wasn't a part of my life or anyone else's in the family. I still don't know why she went AWOL, as Grandfather Clarke used to put it. I'm told she was at my parents' wedding, but I only met her six years ago, in 2001—I remember because it was right after the 9/11 terrorist attacks. She showed up unannounced for Christmas dinner at my grandparents' big Tudor house in Atlanta before we'd even sat down good. No one asked where she'd been the last decade or what made her show up that day, but I guess it didn't really matter as long as she was back: even Grandfather Clarke had trouble holding back tears. Since then, she'd given me generous college fund checks for Christmas. Well, at first they were for Christmas but after Grandmother Clarke died a couple years later, Aunt Phoebe began flying down to our home in Tarsus for Christmas. She also began putting my checks in Kwanzaa cards, a holiday The Preacher dismissed as pagan.

Like clockwork, she'd be the last person at the breakfast table on December 26, the first day of Kwanzaa, sporting a black, red, and green robe. She'd bow slightly saying, "Joyous Kwanzaa" as she offered me the card with one eye on The Preacher, sitting at the head of the table looking like he was about to have a stroke. Of course she probably never celebrated Kwanzaa herself, but she just couldn't pass up an opportunity to "enlighten" me and stick it to The Preacher.

Making our way through Harlem, we eventually pulled up to a red light beside a decaying Gothic church, surrounded by a ten-foot-tall chain link fence. I'd never seen a fence around a church, and it made me wonder who they were trying to keep out. It was now completely dark and with so few people on the street, I was beginning to get the creeps.

"Could you spare a dollar, miss?" someone said from right beside me.

Startled, I turned and yelped. The piercing blue eyes of a scraggly man with dreadlocks was just inches away.

He stepped back. "I'm just trying to get something to eat."

My heart was pounding in my throat.

Phoebe took a dollar from her fancy padlock purse, reached in front of me, and handed the money to the man as if he were her neighbor.

"God bless you," he said, then took the money with his blackened fingers and limped away.

The light changed and Phoebe sped off. "New York is full of homeless people. The winter's especially rough for them."

"Where do they sleep?" I asked, catching my breath.

"Public benches, sidewalks, in the parks. There are lots of shelters around the city but not enough."

"How do they become homeless?"

"Oh, I don't know. Maybe they lost their jobs and can no longer pay the rent. Many struggle with addiction. Some are your age or even younger—they either ran away from home or got kicked out. Each one has his own story, like all of us."

I tried to imagine what homelessness would be like. If I fell on hard times, I'd just call my parents or one of my friends. I couldn't imagine getting to a place where I had no one to turn to. I should've just given the man some money instead of squealing like a baby. Besides, I was feeling pretty flush—before I left home, Momma handed me a big roll of cash, which would delay her kitchen renovation further. She had given up so much for me to attend Columbia, and I would *not* let her down: I would do whatever it took to bring home an award and prove that I was indeed worthy of her sacrifice. In the process, I'd show The Preacher once and for all that my future was in the press box and not the pulpit.

Phoebe turned north onto Broadway, where the sidewalks were packed with people of all ages, like it was Saturday afternoon instead of Sunday evening.

"Columbia's just up ahead," Phoebe said.

I had to remind myself to breathe as we pulled before Columbia University's main entrance at 116th Street. The pair of black iron gates, trimmed in what looked like real gold, opened onto the street. Somehow, they seemed wider than in the pictures in my admissions package. I couldn't believe that I had earned the right to walk through those gates. I suddenly wanted to yell, "Halleluiah!"

Then I noticed two partially robed stone giants glaring down at me; the female clutched an open text and the male rested a globe against his chiseled torso. They bore witness to every student that had ever walked through those gates, and they seemed to be sizing me up. My stomach suddenly felt queasy. Did I really belong here? Maybe admissions had made a mistake.

"Well, what're you waiting for? An escort?" Phoebe said with a laugh.

"How will I ever explain all this to my friends back home?"

"You're a journalist, remember? You'll find a way. But first *you* need to see it for yourself."

I gave her the biggest hug I'd ever given anyone in my life. "I'm going to make you so proud of me."

"Jake, I'm already proud of you, and I know you'll do great."

I kissed her goodbye, jumped out of the car, and grabbed my luggage from the back seat.

"Dinner Saturday—bring an overnight bag!" she shouted, and sped off as I waved goodbye.

I put my luggage down and just stood there as students darted around me. I never thought this moment would actually happen. Just past the gates, a wide tree-lined walkway, lit by old-fashioned lampposts, led into campus. I finally picked up my bags and double-timed it through the entrance, feeling on top of the world. Of course, the only way to go from there was down.

CHAPTER 3

As I lugged my suitcase down a narrow corridor in Carman Hall, I dodged a few phone zombies (kids who wander like the undead as they text on their cell phones) while a familiar hip-hop song with a catchy beat played from a distant room. I was obsessing about my new roommate. This was Columbia so maybe he'd be a Trump or the son of a Nobel Laureate or something. I'd never lived with anyone but my parents, and here I was about to share a room with a total stranger. Would we get along? What would he think of me?

Six weeks at Columbia wasn't going to make me "Ivy League," but I was psyched to study at one of the world's most prestigious universities. When Phoebe first mentioned the program, I'd actually never heard of Columbia. Sure, I'd heard of some of the other "Ivies" like Harvard, Princeton and Yale, but Brown? Nope. Dartmouth? Vaguely. It may sound like I'd been living under a rock, but the aspirational colleges back home were Auburn University and the University of Alabama. Most Tarsus High School graduates actually began their undergraduate education at a local two-year junior college, then transferred to a four-year institution if their grades were good enough.

Of course, after I got into the Columbia Summer Program, I learned everything I could about the place from their admissions brochure and the Internet. In addition to being the home to the Pulitzer Prizes, Columbia was the birthplace of FM radio and the first American school to grant the MD degree. Columbia was also steeped in history, originally founded as Kings College by King George II of

England in 1754 and renamed Columbia after the Revolutionary War.

I was basically ready to lead campus tours.

The door to room 720 was wide open but no one appeared to be inside. The room was furnished with identical twin beds, two dressers and two desks. It reminded me of a semi-private hospital room with its fluorescent ceiling lights, linoleum floors, and metal blinds. The only thing missing was the divider curtain. I dropped my suitcase and blazer on the bed that didn't look like it had been slept in and my backpack on the empty desk, both near the door.

A handsome, dark-skinned kid with a scraggly beard stepped out of the bathroom wearing jeans, a purple polo shirt, and a black turban. His eyes were large and welcoming like a Disney cartoon character, and he was drinking a light blue liquid from a clear plastic tumbler. "Greetings!" he said with a big grin. "I am Rajinderpal Singh but please call me Raj. I am from New Delhi. You are Jacob, right?" RETURNS TO DELHI?

"Oh, um, yes but everyone calls me Jake. I'm from Alabama." I stuck out my hand for some stupid reason. I guess I was nervous. He stared at it for a second, then finally shook it while I tried looking at anything other than his turban, but my eyes just couldn't help themselves. I was also a little confused: the only Indians I knew ran the Comfort Inn on the Tarsus Bypass, and they didn't wear turbans. Neither did Gandhi, come to think of it. Then it hit me—this kid must be Muslim. I'd never seen a real live Muslim before and wondered if he'd ever been to Mecca. Only Muslims are allowed to enter Mecca, which makes me want to go there that much more. As a Christian, the only place off limits for me is the women's bathroom, and what guy hasn't been in a women's bathroom?

Raj pointed at my suitcase. "Got a banjo in there?"

I had no idea what he was talking about.

"I come from Alabama with a banjo on my knee!" Raj sang in a bad Southern accent, then slapped his knee.

22

His words might've stung coming from someone else, but I was amazed and kind of proud that he knew that old song about my home state. And when you added in his thick accent and the fact that he looked like he was about to wet himself laughing, it was totally cool.

I decided to play along.

"No. Just my snake-charming flute. Gertrude didn't make it through security."

"Gertrude?"

"My pet cobra."

Raj laughed even louder. "Touché! Funny guy!" He held up his tumbler. "Want one?"

"What is it?"

"A Blue Lion. I made it up myself. It is vodka, curacao, and Sprite."

Raj's question was like a beam of sunlight breaking through a dark cloudy sky. As a PK, people are always on their best behavior around me, but Raj had no idea that my father was a preacher. Back home, a few of my classmates drank and smoked in the bowling alley parking lot on weekends, but since I was a PK, no one ever offered me a single cigarette let alone a beer. I'd never take them up on it, but I'd like to be treated like everyone else. Instead, when my friends swear in front of me, they actually apologize. I always felt like I was on the outside looking in and wondered if I'd ever feel like I belonged in any circle.

"That's alright," I said, unpacking my backpack. "I'm good."

"More for me!" Raj checked out my tie through his dresser mirror while grooming his beard, then dabbed a woodsy-smelling cologne on his neck. He plunked the bottle down next to a silver-framed picture of a kind-faced, white-bearded man with an outstretched palm and a sunburst that peeked from behind his yellow turban. Muhammad maybe?

I placed a framed photo of my parents on my desk, then plucked my Bible from my backpack. I considered tucking it inside my desk drawer but that sort of felt like I was hiding it. Wasn't I proud of being a Christian? I put it on the corner of my desk, the same place it went at home. ९०००.

"I am going out shortly. I met hot babe at cafeteria. Do not wait up." Raj winked then pulled a black leather belt from his dresser and began putting it on.

The way Raj dropped his articles would've driven Momma nuts. She got her masters in English from Emory University and started me on the list of "101 Great Books for College-Bound Readers" in junior high. When I was younger, she always threatened to wash my mouth out with soap if I said "ain't" and she still stops me mid-sentence if I hijack a word like "grill" to mean "smile" or use an invented word like "e-tact" when referring to someone's email tactfulness.

I sat my laptop down on the desk beside a booklet titled *Columbia Summer in Journalism Student Directory*. Curious, I opened it; the introductory page noted that over half of the students were from outside the U.S., hailing from countries like Japan, Argentina, and Greece. Flipping through the directory, I only spotted one other student from the South and he was from Palm Beach, Florida, which was probably one of the richest cities in the country. Seeing my photo somehow made my being here seem less like an admissions oversight. I glowed over my short bio, which included the photograph Tracy, my best friend and assistant editor of the *Tarsus High School Tattler*, took of me; she had insisted that I clench my jaw and flair my nostrils. I looked like a linebacker, but nothing could be further from the truth. I couldn't throw or catch a football worth crap.

I pulled a bottle of water from my backpack and took a big chug.

"What's up!" someone said from behind me.

I flinched, causing the water to go down the wrong pipe. I struggled to suppress a coughing fit and catch my breath, but the water had gurgled out my nose.

"Oh, hey, Sam," Raj said, suddenly all business. "Jake

arrived after all so you will have to ask him about tonight. I have to go." Raj left with his shoulder bag.

Collecting myself, I wiped my nose, turned around, and froze.

A blond kid, wearing nothing but skimpy orange briefs with a thick purple waistband, stood just outside the bathroom door. His body belonged on the cover of a fitness magazine, and I could suddenly smell his grapefruit-scented cologne clear across the room.

Sam stepped forward and offered his hand. "Nice to meet you, brah. I'm Sam Horowitz from Holmby Hills."

I gazed at his forehead, afraid to look any further south; when I grasped Sam's hand, an unwelcome surge of desire ripped through me, and it took me a few seconds to regain my ability to speak. "Where's that?" I asked, eventually.

"Los Angeles. I'm in the next room—we share the bathroom?"

I finally had no choice but to meet his deep-set blue eyes. He had a square jaw and tanned skin that was a little pockmarked. Put a cowboy hat on him and he'd look like the real deal, not some actor playing the part.

I quickly released his hand. My heart was pounding, but I attempted to compose myself. "I'm Jake Powell from Tarsus, Alabama."

Sam hooked his thumb in the waistband of his briefs. "Hey y'all!" He smiled and flashed the whitest teeth I'd ever seen. While holding my gaze, he picked up the bottle of water. "You mind?"

I shrugged like I couldn't care less, but I was thrilled that he seemed to want to hang out.

He plopped right down on my bed, pulled his legs up Indian-style, and took a long slow drink. "Alexandros!" he shouted. "Alex, come here, dude!" The way Sam looked me up and down reminded me of how Janet Walters had looked at me before we went behind the bowling alley a few months back so she could teach me how to French kiss. She seemed very into it while my tongue was down her throat, but back at school, she called me "the lizard" and blabbed to everyone that I'd kept my hands in my pockets the entire time. How was I supposed to know to use my hands when I kissed? No one ever mentioned that!

An olive-complexioned teenager with thick black hair and overly groomed eyebrows—what Tracy and I call "guybrows"—peeked through the bathroom doorway, yakking on his cell phone in a language I couldn't quite identify.

"This is Jake Powell from Alabama. Jake, this is Alexandros Mikos from Athens."

I shook his hand and suddenly realized that he must've been speaking Greek. I was surprised I didn't pick up on it right away. "Γνῶθι σεαυτόν," I said.

Alexandros squinted at me while still halfway listening on his cell phone.

I knew my accent had to stink. "Know thyself?" I said. "Socrates' famous line? Well, they think it was Socrates."

He cupped his phone and repeated the Greek phrase back to me with a choppy accent that reminded me of Dracula. "The omega is like the 'AW' in 'awe' and the omicron, well, you would do better to learn Modern Greek." He disappeared back into the bathroom, continuing his phone conversation.

I *knew* my accent stank.

"So anyways, Raj is sleeping out tonight and said Alexandros could use his bed if it's okay with you. I've sort of, well, I've got a date," Sam said.

I wasn't exactly following him. "So, you're asking her over to play video games or something?"

A corner of his mouth turned upward, like he was amused. "You're joking, right?"

"About what?"

He laughed. "Dude, it's a guy and he's not coming over to play video games."

I felt my face go flush. I didn't see that coming. "A guy? OH!"

That's why he gave me the Janet Walter's once-over, but he didn't act gay in the stereotypical way that you see on television sometimes. Of course, I knew that people in certain parts of the country sometimes chose to live a gay lifestyle, but since Sam could totally pass for straight, I was surprised he was so open about it. Was he that out in Los Angeles? I was well aware that I had feelings that swung that way as well, but there's a big difference between having gay thoughts and being gay. I would never act on them outside of my fantasies, but then, I wouldn't judge anyone for living the gay lifestyle either. Like Jesus said, "He that is without sin among you, let him first cast a stone."

But what Sam was asking me to do was kind of a big deal for me. I took a vow of celibacy in eighth grade and would feel like a traitor if I were a "sexual enabler" for anyone. Lord knows we didn't even get into enabling a *gay* hookup—we didn't have to. A gay anything was strictly off limits back home. Last year, a bill came before the Alabama legislature to ban public libraries from buying books and plays written by gay authors—including Tennessee Williams and Truman Capote—no matter whether they had any actual gay content or not. Not wanting to come across like some hick from the South, I had to think fast. "Oh, um, Sam I'm sorry, but not tonight. I haven't even unpacked."

I turned around and started digging through my backpack for nothing in particular.

He stood and walked toward me. "It's just this once. We sort of already had it all worked out." He sounded desperate.

"But I just got here and need to get situated. Classes start tomorrow, you know," I said, still rummaging through my backpack.

He reached around me, closer than necessary, and placed the bottle of water next to my Bible. I suddenly felt like I was floating and could hardly catch my breath.

"C'mon, man. I'll return the favor," he said. The hair on his tan forearm was bleached white from all that California

27

sun. Maybe he'd spent the last few weeks lifeguarding or surfing. Wasn't Los Angeles just one big beach? I wondered if he wore trunks or Speedos. Probably Speedos judging by his briefs.

Then Sam suddenly froze, pointing a finger at my Bible embossed JACOB HENRY POWELL, JR., ONE-WAY BIBLE CHURCH.

"You're...you're, like, a member of the One-Way Bible Church?"

The tone of his voice had suddenly shifted from desperate to damning. I had no idea why, but if he could be open about who he was, I didn't see why I couldn't as well.

"Oh, um, yes. My dad's our preacher," I said, accidentally giving myself away as a PK. I guess my brain wasn't fully in gear with his standing so close. "Are you One-Way Bible too?"

His face pinched up at me like he'd just bitten down on a sour pickle.

"Well, we don't have that many congregations out west," I rambled on. "I know there's one in Boise. There might be one near you. It'd be easy for me to find out. Want me to?"

He took a step back. "That'd be great," he deadpanned. "Can I bring my boyfriend too?"

Did he really have a boyfriend? If so, why would he be going out on a date? Why did I care? My head was flooded with so many of my own questions that I didn't have the bandwidth to focus on his.

He looked at me eye to eye. "If I had a boyfriend, could I bring him along? Could we, like, hold hands in church?"

So he *didn't* have a boyfriend. I was strangely relieved, but then realized he was actually waiting for an answer.

"Well, um, everyone's welcome." Even as I said that, I knew it wasn't exactly true and felt myself crashing to earth. Everyone *was* welcome, but gay people would find it hard to sit through some of the Preacher's sermons, especially the ones where he talks about gays going to hell. Of course, that might turn them to Jesus who could heal them from homosexuality if they truly wanted to be. There are countless examples of ways that God intervenes in the lives of people who are truly dedicated to him. Just last year, my dad preached about this deacon from a One-Way Bible Church in Dothan who was healed from cancer of the liver, brain, and bones after praying for God's healing hand. The Preacher said that we'd see a lot more healing like that if we had more faith in God. If God could do that, he could certainly heal people from homosexual feelings. That's what I was betting on for myself; I had certainly prayed for this healing many times, but either my faith wasn't yet strong enough or the timing wasn't right—God does things in His time and not when we think He should.

Sam shook his head like I was beyond hope. He hooked his thumb in the waistband of his briefs again.

My heartbeat quickened once more and the room suddenly got warm. Why did he hook his thumb in his briefs like that? I wished he'd stop it and at the same time hoped he wasn't going to avoid me just because I was One-Way Bible.

He turned to leave through the bathroom. The guy had one of the best-defined backs I'd ever seen, like a wrestling superstar. A small birthmark in the shape of a sickle rested just below his right shoulder blade and a circular tattoo at the base of his spine peeked out from beneath his briefs.

He suddenly stopped and turned around. I raised my eyes quickly but we both knew he'd caught me checking out his backside. How'd he know I was looking?

Sam winked at me like we suddenly shared a secret. I'd never had a guy wink at me before. I froze and suddenly realized that my mouth was wide open.

"See you in class tomorrow, Jacob Henry Powell," he said, then saluted me.

My tongue was completely tied, I had no idea what to say. I guess I could've just repeated his words back to him, but by the time I realized that, he was already gone.

When I closed the bathroom door, the weirdness I'd felt for Sam completely vanished, as if the physical barrier somehow killed it. In fact, it was almost like those feelings hadn't happened in the first place. What I felt was probably just excitement about being in New York and making new friends. I was just reading too much into the whole thing. There was certainly no reason to get upset because he caught me checking out his tattoo. People check out tattoos all the time. He probably walked around half-naked just so he could show the blasted thing off. Big deal. It didn't mean anything.

Or did it?

I grabbed my old tweed suitcase, placed it on my bed, and popped open its two brass latches with a *ping, ping*. The last time I'd unpacked it was the night I brought home an All-Alabama High School Newspaper award from Birmingham, back in April. I won because of an article I wrote on teen suicide, which had somehow captured the imagination of the judges. That night, I had gotten home real late and was hoping for a quick kiss goodnight, but Momma kept going on so about my acrylic All-Alabama plaque, it was almost like winning it all over again.

Except for one tiny detail.

That plaque wasn't the only thing I brought home from Birmingham, just the only thing I could show my parents.

Momma had just about convinced herself and me both that I was now ready to run the *Montgomery Advertiser* when The Preacher jumped in. He said he wasn't surprised at all by my win since journalism and the ministry both require great communication skills. In fact, Preacher Ronald Cartwright, the One-Way Bible minister my father respected most, started out as a writer for the *Meridian Star*. The Preacher then pulled out a stack of index cards with the words "Ἀγάπη—God's Unconditional Love For Us" printed on the top card in his ragged cursive script. It was the sermon I was to preach the following morning at our youth service, which occurred every fifth Sunday—the last Sunday of any month with five Sundays.

I had preached Fifth Sundays since I was fourteen and had become somewhat of a mini-celebrity in Davis County. Just last year, The Preacher overheard someone at the Super Wal-Mart talking about that boy preacher at One-Way Bible and how he sure takes after his daddy. It was a compliment to The Preacher, too, since he always wrote my sermons. People probably thought I wrote them, and I felt a little guilty about that, but sermons, like editorials, are filled with opinions and usually a little controversy. I'm just not a controversial person and was totally cool with that.

We all finally kissed goodnight around midnight. I tucked the index cards inside my navy blue blazer hanging in my closet. Then, I kept peeking down the hallway, waiting for the light underneath my parents' bedroom door to go off. When it finally did, such a surge of energy shot through me, I thought I'd explode.

I inched my bedroom door closed, locked it, then tiptoed over to the unpacked suitcase on my bed. Opening it, I was careful to catch each brass latch as it flew up so it wouldn't ping.

Even with my door locked, I still glanced over my shoulder before prying open the inside cardboard base. It came right off, and from this secret hiding place I pulled out *Exercise*, a men's fitness magazine I'd bought in the hotel gift shop while I was at The All-Alabama Conference. A bare-chested young man with broad shoulders and ripped abs was on the cover dressed in skimpy gym shorts and holding a shiny metal dumbbell. He was the most beautiful creature I'd ever seen.

I couldn't get my pants off fast enough.

But five minutes later, I wanted to fling that magazine all the way back to Birmingham. The guy on the cover didn't even look that hot anymore. What was this raging monster inside of me that feasted on such nasty thoughts? That was Slip-up #219. That's what I called it when I did this sort of thing, but only if I thought of a guy. Of course, I always seemed to think of a guy. When I thought of a girl, it was a lot more work and I inevitably threw in some hot guy to speed things along.

The first time I slipped up like that was four years ago, and I actually fasted afterwards to repent. Since that time, fasting had become sort of a ritual after these slipups—not every time but often enough—because it helped with the guilt and made me think twice before I slipped up again.

I hid the magazine in my bookcase behind an Ancient Greek reference book, cut off my light, and lay there on my bed with my eyes closed, waiting for the guilty feelings to pass.

But they didn't. God and I both knew where that magazine was. To truly repent—and have His blessing during my sermon tomorrow—I had to get it out of the house.

I grabbed the magazine and tiptoed through the kitchen, out the garage door, and around the back of the house to the garbage cans, grateful for the full moon. The air was cool and the only sound was the *hoo* from a distant owl. I looked up at my parents' window, quietly opened the lid of one of the cans, and took *Exercise*, which I had tucked into the elastic waist of my pajama pants in case I miraculously ran into someone on the way to the garbage cans at one in the morning, and shoved it to the bottom of a bag beneath the eggshells and coffee grounds.

By the time I got back inside, the burr of anxiety that had been lodged in my stomach for years was digging in deep. I washed my filthy hands in the kitchen sink, carefully closed my bedroom door, then threw myself face down on my bed.

Why had I brought that blasted magazine home? If I had not yielded to temptation, I would've been reveling in my All-Alabama victory instead of hating myself.

I rolled over and picked up the devotional I kept on my nightstand. I'd already read the devotional for Saturday (I do my devotions in the morning), so I decided to get a jump on Sunday's. The scripture reading was at the top of the page and written by the Apostle Paul:

> To keep me from becoming conceited because of
> these surpassingly great revelations, there was given
> me a thorn in my flesh, a messenger of Satan, to
> torment me. (2 Corinthians 12:7)

I looked up from the devotional. "Thorn in my flesh," I repeated aloud.

Kneeling by my bed, I folded my hands and prayed. "Jesus, please take away this thorn in my flesh, these unclean desires. Heal me from this abomination. Take my life before I act on these feelings. I choose to be straight. I choose to be straight."

I had prayed many versions of that prayer, each time switching up my words and gestures slightly in the hope that God would finally find my prayer offering satisfactory and heal me. Sometimes I'd pray standing with my hands held high above my head. Other times I'd fall flat on the floor with my face buried in the musty fibers of my brown carpet. Once I even chatted with God as if we were just friends hanging out. I had prayed my butt off over the years, and the gist of my prayer was always the same: if I couldn't be healed, I didn't want to live. The way I saw it, the Bible damns homosexuals to hell, so better to have an abbreviated-but-pure life and an eternity in heaven than a long life with even just one homosexual act and an eternity in hell.

I got into bed and turned off my light, wishing the next day wasn't Fifth Sunday. I'd never slipped up the night before a sermon. Slipping up distanced me from God. Of course, I had prayed and He had certainly forgiven me, but the distance was still there.

For a while, I gazed up at my cottage cheese ceiling, illuminated by the blue glow of my digital clock, but I wasn't at all tired. I switched on my bedside lamp, took the index cards from my blazer, and got back into bed. I read the sermon a couple of times but my mind kept wandering back to that guy's washboard abs. Nothing got me going like a nice

six-pack. Well, actually, a lot of things did—a little facial
scruff, a perfect field of chest hair, or even a hawkish nose. It
was pretty random, and as I had gotten older the list had only
gotten longer.

I placed the index cards on my nightstand and threw off
the covers. I paused outside my parents' door. Reassured by
The Preacher's rhythmic snoring, I tiptoed down the hall and
out the kitchen door to the garbage cans.

I removed the garbage can lid and rummaged through the
bag, looking for that magazine. My hands—like the
magazine—were covered with coffee grounds and a streak of
yellow slime. I re-tied the bag but just as I picked up the metal
lid, I saw a snake about a yard from my left foot.

The lid dropped with a crash.

The lights in my parents' bedroom came on. I dashed
behind the thick holly bush next to the garbage cans as The
Preacher threw open the window. I held my breath the best I
could as my heart pounded at my throat.

"What in the world?" he said to no one in particular.

"Probably just a raccoon," I heard Momma's sleepy
voice saying.

"I'll go put the lid back on. Otherwise, we'll have a big
mess to clean up tomorrow."

My mind raced. Did I leave my door open? Would my
parents check on me? Should I climb in through my window?
Wait! Where was that snake?!

I looked over at the garbage cans. The snake hadn't
budged a bit, and it was the exact same thickness from end to
end; looking closer, I saw it was just an old rope! I'd put
myself in this fix for no good reason and absolutely deserved
to get caught.

"You'll do no such thing," Momma said. "What if it's a
bobcat? We'll take care of it in the morning. Come back to
bed."

When they switched off the lights, I let out a sigh. *Thank-
you-Jesus.*

CHAPTER 4

I bolted straight up in bed, completely freaked out by a recurring nightmare of me at the pulpit, going all fire-and-brimstone on our congregation then suddenly realizing I was standing there stark naked.

Something was hissing. I looked around in the shadowy space before everything came rushing back: Columbia dorm, Indian roommate, gay neighbor.

Class!

It was just after eight—I'd set the radio alarm for seven but obviously failed to tune to an actual station. I slammed off the alarm, silencing the hissing static, then threw the covers off and jumped up seeing Raj's bed was empty. I had crashed just after eleven, but sirens screaming throughout the night woke me constantly. New York is truly the city that never sleeps and, evidently, that was strictly enforced.

CRUNCH! BANG! BOOM!

The noise came from outside. I yanked open the blinds, and looked out onto 114th Street. Two orange-vested men were collecting the oversized black garbage bags lining the street and flinging them into the back of a green garbage truck. A compacting panel slid down over the garbage, creating all the commotion.

Classes started at eight-thirty, which left me just nineteen minutes to have my morning devotion, shower, dress, and get to the journalism building, which I had located on my way to the dorm the prior evening.

I grabbed the devotional from my nightstand, read the day's

Bible verse but skipped the commentary, and prayed in the shower to save time. I threw on my most Ivy League-looking shirt and khakis, and put on my lucky horseshoe-patterned socks, the ones I was wearing when I won the All-Alabama. I grabbed my backpack and ran out, taking the first door I saw on the ground floor of Carman Hall. Instead of a quiet campus with majestic Greek temples of higher learning, I found a congested city street clogged with traffic, horns blaring. For a moment, I thought I'd stumbled upon a wormhole, then looked up at the street sign: 114th and Broadway.

I'd exited out the wrong side! I turned to run back into Carman Hall just as the metal door clicked shut, locked from the inside. I looked down at my watch. It was 8:26 a.m. If I could just find those gates where Phoebe dropped me off, I'd have my bearings.

"Which way to the Columbia gates?" I asked a spiky-haired student who pointed behind himself.

I ran two blocks, cut through the gates and down College Walk, the central cobble-stoned artery of campus. Taking a quick right at Low Library, I doubled back to the entrance of the Journalism Building, which was only a hundred yards from Carman Hall unless you took the scenic route, like me.

A tall, good-looking brunette wearing a white camisole and khaki shorts was chatting on her cell phone in front of the building. She was showing a lot of skin, and it might've come across as trashy on anyone else, but she somehow made it look sophisticated. I sensed that she was watching me from behind her oversized tortoise shell sunglasses as I took the stairs, two at a time.

I went flying into the lobby, my stomping feet echoing off the high ceiling and marble walls. A group of students and Columbia staff all turned around and stared from the registration table.

The first thing I noticed was that everyone else was in jeans, and the other guys wore short-sleeve shirts, while I'd opted for a long-sleeve button-down. I smiled at the tall, lanky kid watching me from the end of the line. His curly, copper-colored hair was like a thick shag carpet. "I thought I was late," I said to him as if he expected an explanation.

"No, class starts at nine," he said. "They announced it yesterday at boot camp."

I wondered what else I'd missed at boot camp.

A full ten minutes passed before I finally got my registration package. I smiled real big at the young woman who was checking everyone in. "Oh, um, miss, where do we go now?" I asked while removing the backing from my nametag and aligning it perfectly between two of the horizontal stripes of my brown and white plaid shirt.

"Room 205. Up the stairs," she said, and signaled the next person in line to step forward.

"Thanks, miss."

On my way to class, I looked through the registration package, which included a welcome letter, syllabus, article submission procedures, campus map, and several additional pages.

Room 205 had five raised, semi-circular rows of dark wood tables and smelled like fresh paint. A stack of the *New York Times* was by the door. Following the lead of a girl who walked in just before me, I took one and looked up at the classroom.

Nearly all forty students had already taken their seats and were talking to each other—and not just in English—as if they were old friends. Most of them probably had met at the technology boot camp. I suddenly felt even more behind.

All the center seats were taken, as were the window seats on the far right overlooking the landscaped grounds. I spotted Sam in the second row, poured into a blue T-shirt with WILDCAT WRESTLING emblazoned across the front in orange letters. Wow. I turned away quick, not wanting him to catch me gawking a second time.

Alexandros sat behind Sam and, in the very back, a guy was slumped over his computer, typing. I suddenly panicked, wondering if we were supposed to bring our laptops. I looked around, relieved that he was the only one who had his out.

A dark hand waved at me from Sam's row. It was Raj,

wearing the same clothes from last night and drinking from a paper coffee cup.

I waved back, suddenly feeling popular with at least one person.

Raj gave me a "thumbs up" then pointed to the empty seat next to him. I stepped up to the second row then slid behind Sam, busy reading the *New York Times*. I took the opportunity to check out Sam's closely cropped hair and was amazed at how huge his shoulders looked from this angle. My mind immediately strayed into unholy territory.

I took the spot next to Raj, which left an empty seat between Sam and me.

Raj elbowed me. "Late night?"

I shook my head no, then smirked at his shirt. "You know, that outfit looks awfully familiar."

He laughed.

Sam stuffed the newspaper into his messenger bag and pulled out a leather-bound notebook, which looked all Hollywood compared to my standard-issue spiral bound number. He turned to an empty page.

With no professor in sight, I flipped through the newspaper and tried to concentrate on an article with the headline "Arrest Made in Bombing at Texas Abortion Clinic," but images of Sam in his underwear kept popping into my head. I needed to focus on winning one of those awards, not get mixed up in anything stupid while I was up here. But I just couldn't help myself. I glanced over at him. "Cool shirt," I said, and then held my breath.

His eyes lit right up. "What's up, brah?"

His simple acknowledgement gave me this tingling sensation all over, and I was relieved that he didn't seem to hold a grudge over my being One-Way Bible. "Not much. You a big wrestler?"

"What?" he asked and sort of laughed. "Oh, my shirt! No, but I dated a guy who—well we sort of dated. Anyways, he gave me this shirt."

I tried to imagine what it would be like for some guy to just up and give me a wrestling T-shirt, especially if it was a guy I was *dating*. My mind couldn't even fathom it.

Sam pointed to a black and red patch on my backpack. The patch had the words "Owner's Manual" written below a Holy Bible. "I have to admit, that's clever," he said.

"Thanks! That's from my Bible Drill days."

"Bible Drill?"

"You never heard of Bible Drill?"

He shook his head.

"It's mostly for younger kids. It's like a spelling bee but instead of calling out words, they call out Bible verses. The first person to find the verse scores a point."

"Sounds like a riot, brah," he said sarcastically

I chuckled. "Yeah, it's something to do, I guess."

A heavyset man around fifty years old with gray hair and dressed in a rumpled blue oxford entered. He placed an empty red milk crate beside a large podium.

The girl I'd seen outside talking on her cell phone entered just behind him. Unlike the other students, Cell Phone Girl wasn't wearing a nametag. She finished up her conversation in front of all of us and looked around the room, searching for a seat.

Raj sat taller and leaned over to me. "Check out the hot babe."

I glanced over but didn't want to gawk like Raj. Besides, I could tell she was entering our row just by watching his widening grin.

Sure enough, a tan leather purse plopped down next to my elbow.

The chair between Sam and me screeched back.

I willed myself not to look up and mention that I'd seen her earlier, which was a tall order—I had that Southern congenital disorder that forced me to acknowledge every familiar face that crossed my path.

Someone tapped me on the shoulder.

I jumped then stared up into her big brown eyes.

"Excuse me but I was sitting here," she said, as if that was the most obvious thing in the world.

"Oh, sorry." I stood, took my backpack, and stepped out of her way.

She checked out my khakis, then took my original seat, removed the tortoiseshell sunglasses from her head and placed them in a brown leather case she had grabbed out of her bag.

I looked down at my new chair to find a black ink stain on the blue padded seat. Only then did I realize that I'd been duped. It was a first-rate job, but I'd get her back.

I tested the ink-stained seat with my fingers to see if it was dry while Raj shot her a flirty grin.

I took my seat between Deceitful Cell Phone Girl and Sam. Being so close to Sam made my body tingle even more than before, like I was a tuning fork that resonated at his frequency. I took in his grapefruit-scented cologne. Most guys I knew didn't wear cologne but those who did limited their selection to one of the classics, like Aramis or Polo. Sam's cologne had a sweetness to it that was somehow still masculine and, well, sexy. I noticed a whopping Chinese character resembling the number "4" was tattooed on his inner right forearm. How did I miss this second tattoo of his yesterday? If I got one, The Preacher would lecture me over "defacing the Lord's temple" and Momma would say something like, "It's your body—if you want to graffiti it all up then be my guest." But I didn't think tattoos were such a big deal, and the ones Sam chose seemed kind of interesting. Especially on Sam.

Wait, what was I doing? I had to keep my mind on class and out of the gutter. I'd always been taught that homosexuality comes from Satan. While Satan was powerful, even the mention of Jesus' name caused him to flee. In that moment, I claimed Jesus' power over Satan and my predicament by silently saying to myself, *Satan, get thee behind me in the name of Jesus, Amen.*

The professor cleared his throat and began. "Welcome to Columbia University! I hope registration wasn't too painful."

Cell Phone Girl raised her hand. "I thought this *was* registration."

"Orientation. Registration's downstairs. You can go after class."

"Oh," she whined. I wondered what language that was. Maybe Portuguese.

"My name is Professor Greenberg," the Professor said, moving right along. "We had applications from every state and twenty-six foreign countries. With a few exceptions, you are all new editors of your respective high school newspaper, and over the next six weeks, this program will help you create a better paper. We will complete three distinct modules on editorial, design, and production along with two lectures on ethics. I will be your primary professor, but Professors Kelly Ellis and Michael Cates will also—"

The brunette's cell phone rang. She quickly dug through her purse, silenced the phone, but still checked the caller ID, which read "Joshua." (I didn't mean to peek, but truly all eyes were on her, including Professor Greenberg's.)

She tucked a long strand of her thick brown hair behind an ear, then stood and looked down at him. "So sorry, but I really need to take this."

The professor glared at her. "People, please silence your cell phones prior to class. Interruptions of this kind will not be tolerated."

She sat back down and put her phone in her lap.

He waited while several students scrambled to retrieve their phones and silence them. He then cleared his throat and continued. "These are hard times for newspapers and that's not going to change. Print is becoming a less crucial part of the media mix since the business model is broken and no one knows what it'll look like even two years from now. Online will probably be driving print by then but it's all uncharted territory. How many of you have some sort of journalist presence online, whether it's your newspaper, a personal website, or some sort of blog?"

Over half the class raised their hands, including Sam,

making me feel so out of it, but my parents limited my web use to news, academic, and Christian sites; everything else was strictly forbidden. We planned to get *The Tattler* online next year but had a lot of fundraising to do first.

For the next two hours, Professor Greenberg covered several topics, including a detailed discussion on how new media had changed news delivery forever. He said that we can no longer just *tell* the news with a knockout article, we had to *show* it through more photos, video clips, and web-based slide shows. He called this "packaging" our story and assigned further reading on the topic for that evening.

While all this was going on, Cell Phone Girl was pecking away at her phone under the table while seemingly hanging on Professor Greenberg's every word.

"News is as important as ever," Professor Greenberg said. "So we'll concentrate on newsgathering, including how to evaluate the quality of information from our sources. As journalists, we must have a finely honed ability to identify bias to be sure we're maintaining the standard of independence our readers expect."

Professor Greenberg removed a large stack of papers from the podium and began passing them out. "Okay, this is your first assignment. For tomorrow, bring one New York news story idea. It can be anything from hard news on New York City politics or current events or it can be soft news such as a review of an art exhibit or a movie, but it must focus on New York. I'll divide you into groups of three where you'll decide on the news story you'll complete. Be sure it's something that you can finish by tomorrow; don't come in here with the idea you're going to interview some Broadway star unless you know you can get the interview. Also, check the syllabus in your registration packet—it includes your daily reading assignments and login information for the Associated Press News Center, which you can use for story ideas. It also provides instructions for submitting your work electronically and accessing the online blackboard, so don't lose it."

We all looked over the syllabus. Most days, classes ran

from nine until four-thirty with an hour for lunch and a couple of short breaks, but we also had field assignments at least two afternoons each week.

Cell Phone Girl rolled her eyes and said to me, "Why can't we write about somewhere interesting, like Paris or Rome? Jesus!"

"Maybe New York will grow on you," I said.

"Grow on me? I've lived here seventeen freakin' years."

I laughed. "That's impressive. You think I'll last six weeks?"

She looked me up and down and chuckled. "Doubtful. I'm Julie Aaron, by the way."

"Jake Powell from Tarsus, Alabama."

Raj flashed his Casanova grin. "My name is Rajinderpal Singh, but you can call me Raj. I am from New Delhi and am pleased to make your acquaintance."

Sam leaned over. "I'm Sam Horowitz from L.A."

"Where in L.A.?" Julie asked

"Western Los Angeles."

"Hollywood? Beverly Hills? Bel Air?" she asked with the sweep of a hand.

"Near there. Holmby Hills?"

She nodded then pointed to his tattoo. "I'm digging your ink. I have a friend with a similar one, but it's, well, let's just say it's not on his arm." She winked at him.

Sam flashed his perfect white teeth.

Professor Greenberg cleared his throat, signaling for us to quiet down. "Okay, I'm sure I don't have to remind you all about the four awards that Columbia will hand out at the end of the program. Past winners of these awards have gone on to attend the most prestigious journalism programs in the world—it's an excellent way to distinguish yourself. The full rules are contained on the final page of the handout."

I raised my hand. "How will the winners be determined?" I always hated to be the first one to ask a question, but this was important.

"A panel from three of the country's most prestigious newspapers will evaluate your final projects. It's great exposure for you all.

"Can we read some of the winning projects from prior years?" I asked. By reading the prior winning entries, I'd get a better sense of what the judges were looking for. No sense stumbling around in the dark.

The Professor seemed especially impressed by this question. "Sure, check the archives in Butler Library. Okay, that's it. If you brought an issue of your student paper for my review, please hand it to me as you leave."

I dug through my backpack for the three issues of the *Tarsus High School Tattler* that I'd brought. Only the final issue had been published with me as editor, but each included at least one of my articles. I paused at the issue I had written on teen suicide, which was my winning entry for the All-Alabama. But I had already submitted that article as part of my Columbia application while the final issue had me at the top of the masthead. It also had a color photo on the front page and included my only editorial, "The Christian Work Ethic," based on one of The Preacher's sermons. He'd bragged on that editorial big-time, which made me feel real good.

Sam pulled out his newspaper, the *University High School Wildcat*, a full twenty-two-inch-long broadsheet. By comparison, *The Tattler* looked like a Piggly Wiggly circular. Suddenly, I wondered if I was completely out of my league. Here I was, surrounded by all these talented students from the farthest reaches of the planet. This was world-class, and somehow, I was a part of it.

Julie didn't pull out any paper at all. She just grabbed her purse, stood, and started to walk out.

"Excuse me, Julie, but don't forget to turn in your newspaper," I called after her.

She scrunched her eyebrows together. "I don't work for that Mickey Mouse paper."

"How did you get into program if you are not editor?"

44

Raj asked as he stood, holding a tabloid-sized newspaper written in an Indian script with a colorful masthead—maybe a little too colorful.

Julie examined one of her perfectly manicured fingernails. "Connections. I'm going to be a fashion photographer."

"So why not go to some art school like Parsons?" Sam asked.

Julie's eyes narrowed. "Parsons? I made that mistake last year. They only do black and white, thirty-five millimeter photography. Columbia's got the best digital equipment and lighting packages money can buy."

Raj gazed into Julie's eyes. "Why do we not grab coffee?"

"Thanks, but I already have plans," Julie said then walked out.

Sam elbowed me and pointed at my socks. "Are those your lucky socks or something, bro?" he asked, referring to the horseshoes on them.

"I guess," I said with a chuckle as we both stood and made our way to the line forming in front of the professor.

Sam looked down at my newspaper. "Like, how far is Tarsus from Bay Minette?" he asked. "I've been blogging about that Scotty Joe Weaver murder trial."

Scotty Joe Weaver was this eighteen-year-old kid who was basically decapitated then set on fire three years ago just because he was gay. Just last week, his murderer was sentenced to life in prison without parole. It was all over the local news in Alabama, but I was surprised Sam had heard about it all the way out in California.

"Yeah, that was awful. Tarsus is about an hour north of Bay Minette, like you're going towards Montgomery."

After we dropped off our papers, Sam turned to me and asked, "I'm gonna grab a cappuccino. Wanna join me?"

I wanted to join him more than anything, but Sam—looking so hot in that wrestling T-shirt—could be a huge source of temptation for me. In First Timothy, the Apostle Paul tells us to flee temptations and pursue righteousness. I don't drink coffee anyway.

"Thanks, but I think I'll get a jump on our assignment."

Sam smiled at me curiously, like he knew more about what I was thinking than I did. If that was true, I hoped he was the only one who could tell.

CHAPTER 5

I sprinted down College Walk towards the Columbia gates while humming that cheesy "New York, New York" song, double-time. But that's how I felt—if I could make it here, I could make it anywhere. Translation: if I brought home one of those Columbia journalism awards, I could have a career in journalism. Otherwise, I'd spend my life in the pulpit.

Just outside the gates, I stopped and pulled out an Associated Press printout from my backpack with the headline "NYC Firedog Receives Governor's Award for Rescuing Boy." It was about a dog that saved a young kid trapped in a burning building on the Upper West Side, just south of Columbia.

The story intrigued me and had a perfect New York angle. Everyone in class would pick up on its broad appeal, and whoever got there first could arrange an exclusive.

I had to act fast.

The fire station where that dog lived was only about two miles south, and the subway I would take was just outside the Columbia gates. I spotted the entrance: concrete stairs led down into a gaping hole surrounded on three sides by green prison bars about waist-high. I wondered why New York City didn't rate escalators like Atlanta's subway stations.

I flung my backpack over my shoulders and headed for the subway entrance. I'd been away from home for less than twenty-four hours and already I was beginning to find my way around. I took the stairs, leaving the nice breeze of the June day for the heat of the crowded and un-air-conditioned subway platform. The place smelled like a peculiar blend of perfume, sweat, earth, and urine. It seemed fitting that the station had bathroom-tiled walls.

The concrete platform was about half the width of the ones in Atlanta, forcing people to stand right up to the edge, so I did the same. It was only a four-foot drop to the trackbed, but the electricity running through that third rail could cook you good. Out of the corner of my eye, I saw one of the rails move. When I looked closer, my heart sprang into my throat: two huge rats were having a field day with a donut that someone had discarded on the track.

A single drop of sweat slid down the small of my back.

There was no display showing when the next train was coming—like there was in Atlanta—so I just looked down the tunnel hoping to spot the next train. I smiled at a few people on the packed platform, but one by one they all turned away quick. Back home, we call that being friendly, but I guess New Yorkers are suspicious of everything, including a smile.

I removed my backpack and wiped the sweat from my forehead. That subway platform in June would've felt like the hottest summer day in Alabama if only there'd been a breeze. Finally, I heard the most god-awful screeching sound of metal against metal—a train was barreling into the station from the opposite direction I had been looking. I stepped back and held my hands over my ears as it came to a halt, but no one else even flinched.

A pair of subway car doors opened right in front of me, but the car was packed to the gills. I stepped back as people pushed their way out of the train, then stayed put so the women and children could board first. But all the other guys pushed their way in like there was a free puppy for the first hundred passengers or something. I guess that heat could make anyone forget their manners. The final woman to board acknowledged my kindness with a nod then shouted into the crowded train, "Can you please move in!" When no one budged, she shoved her way on.

48

I squeezed in behind her as the cool air conditioning enveloped me, but had trouble inching past the doorway. In the aisle, two young women were in each other's face. I couldn't make out exactly what was going on, but I could sure hear what they were saying.

"You better don't!"

"No she didn't!"

"Don't make me put my baby down!"

The doors closed on my backpack with a crunch, then sprung open automatically.

"Please do not block the doors—there is another train directly behind this one," the conductor announced through the train's public address system.

Everyone stared at me as if to say, "He's talking to you, bud." Even the two squabbling women stopped and turned my way, seeming to agree on this one point.

"Would you people let this kid on!" the woman who boarded just before me announced. Miraculously, people made room for me so I squeezed in, and the train sped off.

The trained crawled along while I tried to find something to hold on to in order to steady myself, but the only thing available was the fluorescent light housing above the door so that's what I grabbed.

A few minutes later, the train emerged into a sunlit urban landscape dotted with massive housing projects, grocery stores with Spanish names emblazoned on painted metal signs, and cars dating back to the first Bush Administration. I turned to the nice woman who had helped me on. "Excuse me, but where are we?"

"Harlem," she said.

Harlem? Where those kids got kidnapped?! I was going the wrong way!

The moment the doors opened at the next stop, I ran out onto the raised platform of the 125th Street Station. I didn't stop running until I'd made it down the stairs and out the turnstiles to an information kiosk where an attendant sat inside reading a magazine.

I was sweating and breathing hard. "Excuse me, sir, but how do I get to 77th Street?"

"Downtown," the attendant said without looking up.

"Excuse me?"

"Downtown," he said a little louder.

"I mean, um, which train do I take?"

He looked up with a huff and pointed to a sign on the other side of the turnstiles reading "DOWNTOWN."

"Oh. Thank you," I said, "How do I get back in? I already paid."

The attendant continued reading his magazine. I took out my wallet and paid again.

I checked the address on the Associated Press page once more, not believing that a fire station could be sandwiched amongst all the parking garages, rental car outlets, and apartment houses on 77th Street. I walked a few blocks east and saw a fire truck pulling into a building mid-block.

I stuck out my hand to a curly-headed fireman as he stepped off the truck. "I'm Jake Powell, a student at Columbia University." Dropping the Columbia name was like a badge of honor that made me feel more confident. Plus I was afraid my Southern accent would mark me as a tourist.

He looked at me suspiciously as we shook hands, like he was afraid I'd introduce myself as his long-lost son or something, but I guess seventeen-year-olds don't just pop by the firehouse every day.

"I'm Dominick," he said finally.

"Good to meet you. I'm taking a summer journalism course, and our first assignment is to cover a local news story. I read about Red Dog online—what he did has all the makings of a great feature article. May I meet him?"

At that, he let his guard down. "Her! That dog gets more attention than the Mayor." The fireman clapped his hands together and shouted, "Red Dog!"

A cry came from the back. It wasn't Red Dog, but

another fireman in a navy cap, lying shirtless on a bench, straining to lift a fully loaded barbell. A second guy with reddish hair stood behind the bench, spotting him.

Just then, an oversized German Shepherd bounded around a corner and up to Mr. Dominick, who tossed her a treat from his jacket. "Jake, meet Red Dog."

Red Dog's ears stood straight up as she looked into my eyes and offered a paw. I knelt and shook it, then laughed when she licked my face. "Well, I can see why the governor took to her—she's a big flirt."

The fireman snickered. "Don't let her winning personality fool you—she's a trained killer."

Red Dog's tail was wagging like it had a motor attached to it.

"Oh sure, she might lick me to death." I said, then scratched behind Red Dog's ears, her back leg just a thumping.

He chuckled. "You know your dogs, kid."

"This is exactly the type of story people warm up to. It's just for a class assignment, but I might be able to use it for my paper back home. Did she really rescue a little boy from a burning building?"

"Sure did. Just last month."

"What happened?"

"It was a three-alarm fire about eight blocks south of here. The moment we arrived, Red Dog went barreling inside and up the stairs and began barking her head off until we got to her. We found her covered in soot and crouched down next to an eight-year-old boy who was trapped inside. He almost didn't make it."

"But he's okay now?"

"Yeah. He spent a couple of weeks in the hospital."

"Would it be possible for me to speak with him?"

"Afraid not. His parents don't want his name disclosed."

"Well, I'm glad he's okay. Could I bring a couple of classmates down tomorrow to interview you and Red Dog? I'm not sure what time. Probably before noon."

"That should work. I'll make sure Red Dog is here, even if I'm out on a run."

"Thanks, sir. Do you think I could get the exclusive?"

He looked at me like he didn't know what I was asking. "The exclusive? Oh! Kid, it's not like people are lining up to interview her."

"I mean, just for tomorrow and just for, you know, my class at Columbia?"

He chuckled again. "You got it."

I'd landed my first story for Columbia, and got an exclusive to boot! I just about jumped in the air but shook his hand instead. "Thank you!"

Red Dog gave me a friendly bark.

"See you tomorrow, girl!"

As I turned to leave, I stole one final look at the redheaded fireman with the wide grin and sparkling eyes. He seemed like a nice guy—maybe I'd get to meet him tomorrow.

CHAPTER 6

I sat back at my dorm room desk, smiling at the completed Red Dog pitch on my laptop. Was it the most captivating journalistic piece ever pitched? Probably not, but journalists had to believe that every assignment held that kind of potential—you just had to find the story. It was annoying that I couldn't interview the kid, but Red Dog was the focus of the story anyway, and the recent medal from the Governor was a great hook.

Although the class assignment had been to pitch a potential news story verbally, I created an actual news brief. Maybe writing the news brief was a little over-the-top, but getting lost in a news story transported me to a place that's about three feet from heaven, where I can forget all my troubles. Plus, immersing myself in the program was the best preparation for that final project. If I could just win one of those awards, The Preacher would have to let me pursue journalism. Otherwise, it would be back to the pulpit, a place I'd certainly go if that was where God led me. But it was hard to imagine enjoying the role of spiritual leader for an entire congregation, who would look to me for answers during the twists and turns of life—I had enough trouble trying to figure out the answers for myself.

I suddenly realized that I had some free time, and hanging out alone in my dorm room seemed pretty lame. On a whim, I stuck my head out into the hallway but didn't see a single person. They were probably all running around town, having fun. It never occurred to me that skipping boot camp would put me so far behind on the social front.

Well, I could have a little adventure all by myself, right? After all, I was at the center of the universe, so there was plenty of stuff to do—I just needed to figure out where to start.

I launched the web browser on my laptop and searched "New York events activities." I clicked on the first link, a site called *Time Out New York*. I clicked through pieces on New York theater, food, and shopping. I scanned past "Film" and stopped at a link titled "Gay and Lesbian."

That seemed out of place on such a mainstream site.

I'd never visited a gay site before and told myself not to go there, but it was like the time I heard about that two-headed cow at the State Fair. I couldn't explain why I had to see it, I just did. And I dragged Tracy along too.

I disabled my web browser history so my activity wouldn't be recorded. (An ounce of prevention is worth a pound of cure, as Grandmother Clarke used to say.)

I entered a virtual world filled with gay theaters, art exhibitions, bars, restaurants, and gyms. One page featured last year's Gay Pride with all kinds of risqué photos: shirtless Adonises dancing on floats, "drag queens" in ball gowns, and topless women on motorcycles. Sure, I liked looking at guys, but couldn't imagine dancing with one and didn't understand why a guy would dress up like a girl to attract a guy who wasn't into girls? I just didn't relate and was about to move on to the site's City Guide when I noticed a sidebar titled, "What?! Gay Bashings in New York?" It noted that the number of gay hate crimes in New York City was down from the prior year, but that the severity of the attacks had increased. So New York wasn't the safe haven I'd imagined. Sam had better be careful.

I continued in the "Gay and Lesbian" section and got caught up in an article about a Broadway show I'd never heard of called *Avenue* Q; one of the main characters was gay and it had won several Tony Awards, including best musical. Apparently, the breakout song for the show was "The Internet is for Porn."

The room suddenly felt warm.

Why hadn't I thought of that earlier? Of course, I could never visit an even remotely questionable site at home, since I could accidentally download a computer virus that might somehow find its way onto the church network and then be traced back to me; no amount of fancy footwork could explain *that* away. But Columbia's network must have the latest anti-virus software.

I locked the doors to the bathroom and dorm room, then pulled up an Internet image search page on my web browser. My pulse quickened as I entered "gay porn." The farthest I'd ventured down this path before was when I brought home that fitness magazine, but that wasn't actual porn, even if it left little to the imagination. This was a lot more serious. Jesus said that if you think something evil, you're just as guilty as someone who's done it. If I looked at gay porn, I'd be no different than Sam. And what was next? Sequin gowns? I stared at the enter key. I wanted to hit it more than anything, but on top of all the other potential consequences, I also worried that Columbia's systems folks might be monitoring my web activity. Would they report me? Could I get sent home? That's truly the only thing that kept me from doing the search. I deleted the entry and typed "gym body" instead.

Rows of thumbnail images appeared. I clicked on the image of a blond, broad-shouldered guy and waited while it loaded from top to bottom. I immediately recognized him as a teen actor from an old TV show. The guy was powerfully built with abs like interlocking bricks and shoulders that would barely fit through a doorway. His eyes were narrowed menacingly but there was a playfulness about his mouth, like he was holding a water balloon behind his back or something. I paged down to check out his obliques, then my eyes landed on the following text:

Adam Strong (1970 - 1993)
Please Join the Fight Against HIV/AIDS

This guy, who also had blue eyes and fair skin, died of AIDS when he was just a little older than me. Take a few years and his gym membership away, and we could almost pass as brothers.

Of all the hot photos I could've checked out, what caused me to click on this one? Was this a warning from God? Would this be my path?

God's answer to the gay agenda is AIDS!

I'd heard The Preacher say those words from the pulpit my entire life—even before I knew what they meant. He claimed that homosexual feelings were a conscious choice, like you just wake up one day and start fantasizing about gay sex just for kicks. Well, he's wrong about that—those feelings snuck up on you, or at least they snuck up on me. I had no idea what was going on at the time, but looking back, I could connect the dots.

The first dot was the dizziness and shortness of breath I felt whenever I was around my neighbor Wade Hanson, high school football star. That was right after we moved to Tarsus, so I must've been about eight years old.

I experienced a similar dizziness, accompanied by a gooey warmth, when I stumbled upon a Bowflex commercial the following summer.

In fifth grade, I was watching TV at a neighbor's house when professional wrestling came on. Seeing two athletes pin each other was even better than a Bowflex commercial, so I started tuning in at home when my parents weren't around. Dot three.

I didn't give any of this much thought until the sixth grade, when I decided that all guys must have these sorts of feelings but just didn't talk about them. My parents had recently come clean about Santa, and I figured this was somehow similar—a truth that was generally known but not discussed.

I held onto this "Santa theory" for a while, but in seventh grade, a switch went off; not in me, but in a lot of guys in class—they started going girl crazy. That was when I began to question my Santa theory, and the next dot appeared.

It happened in gym class during a tornado warning.

"Okay, boys, on the court—we're playing basketball!" shouted Coach Douglas, fiddling with the whistle dangling from his neck.

The moldy rankness and "drip, drip, drip" from the dreaded showers filled the locker room where thirty of us changed into black gym shorts and white T-shirts with "Tarsus Junior High Tigers" emblazed in gold letters. John Taylor, the handsome and muscular black basketball star of our class, stripped down to his tight white underwear and pulled a Tarsus Junior High gym shirt out of his backpack.

I propped my right shoe on the varnished oak bench, retied it, then did something I'd never done before—I took a good long look at John as he changed. A greedy thirst took hold of me as I lapped up his toned back and arms. My shorts were suddenly snug.

Someone elbowed me from behind.

My mouth was wide open so I shut it quickly and turned around.

It was Kenny Ballard, a soft-spoken blond kid who'd been the butt of every gay joke since I could remember. He shook his head as if to say, "Don't do that."

I couldn't tell if he was ridiculing me for sizing up John or simply trying to protect me from being discovered for the freak that I was by the other guys in class.

Had I been that obvious? A wave of fear crashed inside me and my face suddenly burned.

I avoided eye contact by looking at the plaque hanging above Kenny's head, which read "Our Values: Spirit, Teamwork, Respect."

Kenny followed my eyes to the sign, then smiled broadly at me as if he now had a new best friend. "Let's go work on our values," he said.

He suddenly disgusted me.

I checked out his tie-dyed gym shirt, then glared at him. I wanted to punch him in the face. If he said anything, it would be his word against mine. Was I to become like Kenny, the kind of kid who tie-dyed his clothes, used words like "cute" and "fabulous," and was basically friendless? I didn't look or act like Kenny so how could we be alike?

I told myself I was making a big deal over nothing as the scrambled eggs from breakfast gurgled up my throat. I swallowed hard and hit the court, but a few days later, dreamed that John and I were racing our BMX bikes down an old logging trail behind the school. He jumped off his bike at Persimmon Creek, stripped naked, and jumped in with a splash. I followed suit, feeling especially free with nothing between the cool, murky waters and my private parts. I surfaced with a kick, and found myself face-to-face with the business end of a snaggletooth crocodile.

We tore out of that creek, ran back up the shore and then collapsed on the ground, laughing. John rose up on one arm and brushed my face with his hand, water dripping from his chin. And just before his lips touched mine, I woke up.

I tried willing myself back into that dream, but just ended up finishing myself off. Afterwards, a big slab of shame pressed down on me so hard I could hardly breathe. I got down on my knees and prayed aloud as earnestly as I could. "God forgive me for those thoughts. Take these impure desires from me in Jesus' name. Amen."

I plunked my head down on my bed, telling myself that God had forgiven me, but I needed to show Him that I was *truly* sorry. But how? When people were distraught in Bible times, they'd tear their clothes to show their grief, but I was wearing my best pajamas—Momma would have had my hide, and there was no good explanation I could give for doing such a thing.

Then it hit me. King David *fasted* after he committed adultery with Bathsheba. What better way to show the Lord how sorry I was? I'd fast during school lunch tomorrow then

God and I would be square. The food in the cafeteria was crappy anyway. I bet even The Preacher had never fasted.

And just like that, the heaviness that struck me after Slip-up #1 began to shrink, and eventually settled inside me like a burr. Some days it was bigger than others, depending on how long I could hold out between slip-ups. Once I went nearly two weeks. Still, that greedy thirst always managed to win out in the end, and I've slipped-up 235 more times since. I didn't set out to count these slip-ups, but I guess it's sort of like speeding tickets: you can't help but keep track of how many you've gotten (zero for me so far). It certainly didn't make me feel any better—it only reminded me of how bad my willpower was and how far I'd strayed.

Sitting there in my Columbia dorm, I wondered, would this be my life? Pretending to be straight but checking out hot guys online when no one was watching?

The photo of Adam Strong, AIDS victim, stared at me from my laptop. That could be me in a few years if I kept going down this path.

I killed the web browser, slammed my laptop shut, then picked up my Bible and began turning the pages wildly, looking for any underlined passages that might give me comfort. I always underlined verses, especially those that contained promises of hope for moments like this.

The first underlined passage I came to was in Romans 1, written by the Apostle Paul:

26 Because of this, God gave them over to shameful lusts. Even their women exchanged natural relations for unnatural ones.
27 In the same way the men also abandoned natural relations with women and were inflamed with lust for one another. Men committed indecent acts with other men, and received in themselves the due penalty for their perversion.

This passage was no help at all. In fact, it was as if God himself were calling me out. This was my spiritual death sentence, the keystone of what our One-Way Bible literature calls "The Big Eight"—the eight Bible passages that condemn gays to hell.

I reopened my laptop and pulled up the original Ancient Greek version of the text like I had a thousand times before.

26 Δια τουτο παρεδωκεν αυτους ο θεος εις παθη ατιμιας αι τε γαρ θηλειαι αυτων μετηλλαξαν την φυσικην χρησιν εις την παρα φυσιν

27 Ομοιως τε και οι αρρενες αφεντες την φυσικην χρησιν της θηλειας εξεκαυθησαν εν τη ορεξει αυτων εις αλληλους αρσενες εν αρσεσιν την ασχημοσυνην κατεργαζομενοι και την αντιμισθιαν ην εδει της πλανης αυτων εν εαυτοις απολαμβανοντες

I turned back to my New International Version Bible and, at that moment, finally accepted that the translation was dead-on accurate; my years of studying Ancient Greek to explain away these troubling verses against homosexuality had been a big waste of time. The Preacher often used one verse to help explain another, but even my desperate search for a Biblical loophole had come up empty. There was simply no getting around it: acting on these homosexual desires would one day land me in hell.

Suddenly, it felt like the Apostle Paul had a shotgun pointed between my eyes and was squeezing down on the trigger. Instinctively, my fingers flipped the pages faster and faster—as if fleeing from a hitman—until I ripped one a couple of inches from the top. My hand shot to my mouth with the realization that I had inadvertently defiled the Word of God. I stared at the tear in horror, as if I expected it to bleed.

I rummaged through my desk and came up with my

transparent tape. I repaired the damage with the precision of a surgeon then looked down at the text. Mark 11:24 was underlined and printed in red ink, indicating the words of Jesus:

24 Therefore I tell you, whatever you ask for in prayer, believe that you have received it, and it will be yours.

Anger rose up inside me like a geyser. How could Jesus make that claim? I'd been begging God to heal me for years, trying every possible technique I could think of. I guess if you're the Son of God, you can just pray for anything you want, and the next thing you know you're changing water into wine, raising people from the dead, and skipping across the Sea of Galilee without so much as your ankles getting wet. Well, that's just so obviously not my reality.

I knelt by my bed, dug my fists into the mattress, and whispered so angrily that spit shot out my mouth. "God, for four years I've fasted, I've prayed, and I've read my Bible daily. Even so, all I can manage is a mustard seed of faith, but with that faith and my entire heart and soul I have begged you to take this thorn from me. God, why do you keep ignoring me? Why do I feel like I'm in this alone? I need your divine intervention because I can't beat this thing by myself—I've tried and tried and tried, but I just can't. God, for the last time I'm begging you to be real! Be Real To Me! In the name of Jesus, HEAL ME FROM THIS ABOMINATION OR GET OUT OF MY LIFE!"

What happened next was beyond anything I could have ever dreamed. Waves of joy surged from my heart to my fingertips, removing any trace of the worry and hurt that had completely consumed me moments earlier. This wasn't some vague feeling of peace but an overwhelming sense of God's love pulsating throughout my entire body. In that moment, I realized that God hadn't been ignoring me at all but had been with me all along. I was so excited that I wanted to shout.

Then it all passed as quickly as it had come.

I felt so loved and special and grateful that God had singled me out to receive whatever it was that just happened. I didn't even know what to call it, but it was like I'd stumbled onto some divine portal that gave me a direct line to heaven and God had finally found my prayer offering satisfactory. Did this mean—could this mean—that I had been healed? Had my anger somehow strengthened my faith sufficiently for God to heal me from homosexuality the way he had healed that deacon in Dothan from cancer? My questions seemed laced with doubt, which was no way to claim the healing power of Jesus. No, I had to truly believe that God had healed me for it to be so, the same way that Luke Skywalker in *Star Wars* had to trust the force for him to defeat the Empire, or Dorothy in *The Wizard of Oz* had to wish with all her heart to return to Kansas for it to happen. Maybe God hadn't been ignoring me over the years but was simply building my faith so that I could earn this healing. He probably would've healed me the first time I'd asked, if my faith had been strong enough. I just had to claim this victory and it would be so—I had to believe with all my heart that my thorn was no more.

I jumped to my feet and raised my hands to heaven. "Thank you Jesus! I knew you'd heal me! I knew you'd heal me!"

I grabbed my cell phone and called home. "Momma! Is The Preacher there too? There's something I want to tell you both!"

"Preacher, it's Jake!" she shouted. I could hear the smile in her voice.

"He's coming. So, how's your first day of class going?"

"Really great. I'm finishing up my first assign—"

The Preacher picked up. "Hey, son!"

"Preacher, you're not going to believe this, but I had this amazing experience where the Holy Spirit washed over me in huge waves of joy. It was so amazing! I wanted to shout out!"

The Preacher was silent. It was so unlike him not to just chime right in on a spiritual matter.

I thought the phone had gone dead but then Momma cleared her throat. "That's really great, honey," she said hesitantly.

"I wish Papaw were still around so I could tell him," I said.

"He'd be thrilled," The Preacher said warmly. "Did you speak in tongues?"

"What? No. I didn't say anything, but I felt God's presence like he was standing right beside me."

"That's often how it begins. It sounds like you were about to speak in tongues. Just go with it next time."

"Really?" I was amazed. Speaking in tongues was the ability to talk in a language you've never studied, even though you might not understand what you were saying. Understanding was a separate supernatural gift of the Holy Spirit called the Gift of Interpretation. Other gifts included the Gift of Healing and the Gift of Miracles. We didn't talk about those things much at One-Way Bible, but they're right there in First Corinthians. I guess we just focused more on theology than things like the gifts of the spirit.

I remembered back to the powerful sermons Papaw used to preach at First Monroeville Pentecostal Church. One of his favorite lines was, "Show me a Christian who don't speak in tongues and I'll show you a man who ain't Christian."

The Preacher said, "It feels like it's coming from deep down inside, doesn't it?"

"Yes! And there's this great sense of peace."

"What brought this on?" Momma asked.

That brought me right back down to earth. I shuffled my feet. "Oh, um, I don't know. I was just praying and the next thing I knew it happened."

Keys rustled in the door.

I stood up as Raj walked in with his book bag and flung it on his bed.

What a lucky break—I so didn't want to talk about what

I was doing before God healed me. "My roommate's back so I'd better go—I'll call you tomorrow."

"This is great, Jake," Momma said. "We love you."

I cupped the phone and turned away from Raj. "I love you too," I whispered, then put the phone away, still overjoyed from my experience, no matter what brought it on.

"Hey, Raj!" I said enthusiastically.

His nose was buried in the armpit of his polo shirt, the one he'd been wearing since last night. He jerked his head around and looked over with those big eyes of his. "Just the guy I wanted to see. So, I have hot date tonight with this girl I met at the Hungarian Pastry Shop."

I was hoping that we'd all go out for dinner and was a little disappointed. "Oh, that girl from last night?" I sat down at my desk.

"What? No, that was Jenny. This is Sarah. I mean Suzie. Suzie? Yes, Suzie!" Raj removed his shirt and began unbuckling his belt. "Anyway, I was thinking you could sleep in Sam's bed since he has overnight date too and won't need it."

"Raj, c'mon man. You guys are gonna get caught." Curfew was eleven during weekdays and one in the morning on weekends. We were all issued white security cards that we had to scan when we entered and left the dorm. Students who broke curfew could be sent home. I brought a signed permission slip from Momma that allowed me to spend weekends with Phoebe but even then I had to call the front desk every night I was away.

Raj stripped down to a pair of white, drawstring underwear. His chest was completely hairless, which was surprising given how full his beard was. I took a good hard look at his body to see if my homosexual tendencies were now gone. Sure enough, I didn't feel any desires toward him at all, but then, I hadn't thought of Raj that way before either. The real test would be Sam.

"It is no problem," he said. "I will scan in for the night at eight, then sneak out back entrance for date with Sarah."

I shook my head. "Suzie!"

"Right. At eleven, Sandman comes on."

"Who's that?"

"The night security guard. We call him Sandman because he sleeps at post. I will call you when Suzie and I are outside. We just need you to go down and let us in secret entrance—it opens right onto Broadway but locks from inside."

"I know the door. I call it the wormhole because…never mind."

"Good, so make sure Sandman is sleeping first." He took out his cell phone. "What is your cell number?"

"If the security guard is asleep, why not just waltz through the front door?"

"After eleven, door is double-locked so guard must buzz you in. Cell number?"

I'd heard enough. "Raj, I'm not going to be some sexual enabler for you two. Get Alexandros to do it?"

He thought for a moment. "Well, what if Alexandros slept in my bed?"

"Whatever—just keep me out of it. Okay, ████?"

Raj grabbed his shaving kit from his top dresser drawer. "Okay, I will speak to Alexandros," he said, sounding somewhat perturbed.

I picked up my Bible and read the passage from Mark again. Maybe God had allowed me to rip the page so I would read that verse. The Lord truly did work in mysterious ways.

CHAPTER 7

On the way to class the following morning, Raj and I took the wormhole from Carman Hall so he could grab a coffee from a street vendor. After all his elaborate planning, Suzie had invited her roommate along for the evening and it apparently went downhill from there.

We waited in line outside a tiny stainless steel kiosk parked on the sidewalk where an Indian man sold tea, coffee and pastries. Sweat poured from beneath his turban, but he smiled real big and knew most people by sight.

"So, um, have you ever been to Mecca?" I asked Raj as the vendor handed me my glazed donut and orange juice.

He took a swig of his coffee, then cocked his head at me as we headed toward class. "Mecca? No. Why do you ask?"

He couldn't seem more indifferent. Maybe he wasn't that religious after all. Was that portrait of Muhammad on his dresser just for show? "No reason," I said.

At the classroom entrance, Raj and I scooped up copies of the *New York Times*. The lead article read "Washington Refuses Use of Qur'an for Islamic Congressman's Swearing In."

When I glanced up, I saw Julie, who was rummaging through a white leather bag with huge flapped pockets on the front. She looked like a model in her clingy turquoise blouse with a plunging neckline, and her thick, long dark hair shimmered from the sunlight streaming through the windows.

A tiny switch went off inside me—I suddenly wanted to kiss her. Yes, I really wanted to kiss her! Still, I needed to be cautious here since I'd certainly had moments in the past when I thought I'd been healed only for these urges to come roaring back. But I'd never had such a spiritual experience as I'd had yesterday, which maybe explained why the burr that had haunted me for years felt more distant than ever.

Several students had moved around to take new seats, but Julie and Sam had stayed put. In fact, Sam was staring right at me, but he quickly looked away when I caught sight of him.

I followed Raj up two steps, then took my place between Julie and Sam. For a moment, I was nervous that being next to Sam might set off that tuning fork sensation again, but I decided to not even focus on that. I had to believe, Luke Skywalker style. I said a quick prayer of thanks as Professor Greenberg entered the room.

"Good morning," he said, oblivious of the coffee stain on his white button down. "I hope you're comfortable because the seats you're in today are now your assigned seats for the duration of the program. Today I'll start with an overview on journalistic writing and reporting."

Professor Greenberg opened his notes and went over stuff like attention-grabbing headlines and the who-what-when-where-and-how of good leads. He also discussed the inverted pyramid, which dictated that the most important information in an article be placed first to save the reader time and to allow editors to cut the story from the bottom to fit the available space if need be. He then discussed tips for being a good reporter such as immediately identifying yourself and the paper you work for, making small talk initially rather than launching right into your questions, asking your toughest questions with confidence, and covering all sides of the story.

For nearly two hours, he went over the basics, but none of it was really new to me since I'd been working on newspapers since junior high. I was raring to get to our group assignment, especially since I had the Red Dog exclusive. He finally put his notes away just before eleven o'clock and began walking around the room. "I hope everyone brought good story ideas. As I divide you into groups, pitch your ideas to each other and decide on the story your group will complete, who will write it, and who will be the photographer. Email your final article and photo to me no later than six o'clock tonight."

A few students snickered, clearly thinking he was joking.

"I'm serious, folks. This is how the real journalism world works, so you might as well get used to it. Journalists are on tight deadlines every day, and no editor is going to hold the press because you're not feeling well or have a bad case of writer's block. Camera equipment checkout is down the hall."

The professor walked around the classroom dividing us into groups of three by pointing and counting off. "Okay, one, two, three. You're Group One. One, two, three. Group Two. One, two, three. Group Three."

This placed me in a group with Sam and Julie. What luck—I got to spend the whole day with her! On the other hand, being around Sam sort of felt like playing with fire. I mean, what if those awful urges came roaring back?

I'd have to be vigilant to be sure my mind didn't stray.

I handed a copy of my news brief to both of them, feeling quite pleased with myself. "I've got a great idea for a story. There's this dog from one of New York's firehouses who saved a kid's life and just received a medal of honor from the governor."

"I'm allergic to fur," Julie interrupted without looking at the news brief. "What kind of dog?"

"It's in the brief—a big ol' German Shepherd."

"Sorry. I'd rather stick pins in my eyes." She looked past me at Sam. "What's your idea?"

My heart sank. How allergic was she? Would her eyes just water or would her throat completely close up, cutting off her air supply? It hardly seemed like a question I could ask, of course.

Sam shrugged at me then smiled, seeming to get a kick out of how Julie was assuming control. He leaned in to us and said, "Just yesterday, a New York judge ruled that a law banning same-sex marriage in New York is, like, unconstitutional. I reached out to one of the gay couples who brought the lawsuit and they've agreed to speak with us."

The last thing I needed after being rid of my thorn was to be surrounded by a bunch of gay people—there was no sense in tempting fate. "But the dog story has much broader appeal, don't you think?" I asked. "I've scheduled an appointment for us at eleven. Julie, can't you just take a Benadryl?"

"That stuff puts me to sleep. Listen, if you two want to do the story on your own…"

I couldn't believe this. If she was going to play the allergy card, I didn't see that we had much of a choice. "Okay," I said.

"It's Gay Pride Week so the timing of our story is, like, perfect!" Sam said while he and Julie rose to their feet; I just sat there feeling deflated.

"Great shirt," Julie said, pointing to the huge eagle embroidered on the back of Sam's black and white checked shirt. "Josie would so love that!"

"Josie?" Sam asked.

"Actually, he hates it when I call him that. His name's Joshua, the guy I was telling you about yesterday? With the tattoo? He's actually the Mayor's son. Maybe I should fix you two up?" Julie reached down for her backpack and purse. "Jake, you coming?"

I swallowed my pride and rose to my feet. "Sure. Want me to carry your backpack?"

"Thanks." She flung it at me, then took Sam's arm like he was escorting her to the prom or something. "So Joshua's at the Cape now, but he's back next week."

"Sounds cool," Sam said to Julie while I followed a couple of paces behind.

As soon as we stepped out of the subway car, Julie ran ahead so she could make a phone call since there was no cell reception in the underground subway station. Sam and I, weighted down with backpacks and camera equipment, pushed our way through a stampeding herd of New Yorkers in the sweltering bowels of the station. I had the worst case of swamp ass ever and wanted nothing more than a shower and a change of clothes.

Sam was all smiles, giving me the blow by blow of his Saturday evening escapades in this particular neighborhood, explaining that Chelsea had lots of great gay bars.

"But you're underage," I said.

He grinned. "Not according to my drivers license."

We found Julie chatting on her cell phone at the top of the subway stairs. She cupped her phone and turned to Sam, "Josie can do next Friday, does that work for you?"

"Awesome," he said.

"Great! One week from this Friday, Josh. You two can compare tattoos." Julie giggled then hung up. She spun me around so she could stuff the phone in her backpack. That was the most attention she'd given me all day.

Most of the guys along 8th Avenue had short hair and gym bodies, which was kind of intriguing. A couple of them smiled at me as they passed—just like people do back home— so I smiled right back. I guessed that some New York neighborhoods were friendlier than others; I just had to get the lay of the land.

"People seem a lot friendlier downtown," I said to Julie.

"*Real* friendly," she said, pointing at two teenage guys kissing outside of Heaven Bar.

My jaw just about fell right off. Their hands were all over each other and they didn't seem to care that people were watching. I could never make out with a girl in public like that. I'm just too private a person. me too.

Julie and Sam laughed—clearly at me and *not* the two guys making out. I realized I was blushing but only because I'd never seen two guys making out before, at least not in person.

"Laugh if you want. Back home, those kids are liable to end up in a ditch someplace."

"Oh please!" Julie said.

"I'm just saying…"

"He's totally right," Sam said, shaking his head. "Jake and I were just talking about that yesterday."

I was sort of touched that he stuck up for me like that.

Sam led us to an industrial building on West 19th Street. Inside, he consulted his smartphone then punched a code into a telephone-like keypad, causing lights around a bubble contraption to come to life.

"Who is it?" said a man's staticky voice from the security console.

"Sam Horowitz from Columbia," Sam said.

After a moment, a buzzer went off. Julie walked around me, pushed open a big black door with a wire mesh glass window, and looked back at me. "I guess you've never seen one of these before," she said.

"Sure I have—at the state prison," I said.

She chuckled then headed up the stairs.

"Where's the elevator?" I shouted after her.

"It's a walkup!" she yelled down.

Sam and I tried to keep up with her despite all the stuff we were lugging. As I climbed those stairs, I realized that I was in a gay neighborhood and about to visit my first gay household. Was there a reason this was happening just after the mountaintop experience I'd had with God yesterday? Was this coincidence or was God testing me somehow? An uneasiness settled deep inside me, like that burr was not entirely gone yet after all. I needed to keep my guard up so as not to fall back into my old ways.

Sam and I were out of breath by the time we caught up with Julie on the fifth floor.

Sam rang the doorbell of apartment 5F while we stood there gasping. I wondered what we'd find on the other side of that door. As the son of a preacher, I'd visited many nonbelievers' homes with my dad and was an old pro at ignoring the occasional *Playboy* magazine on a coffee table or the six-pack of beer on a kitchen counter. I just hoped I could do the same if I saw two guys making out again.

A man with dark hair just graying around the temples and flour on the front of his charcoal T-shirt answered. "You must be Sam. Come in! I'm Gary."

"Thanks for seeing us on such short notice." Sam shook the man's hand as he and Julie marched in, but I trailed behind.

The apartment smelled of freshly baked cookies. A few family photographs hung on the entryway's exposed brick walls, and a rug made of a heavy twine covered the oak floors. This wasn't at all what I imagined. I had expected a place that was, well, more gay with crystal chandeliers, antique French furniture, and a doorbell that sounded like Big Ben—their actual doorbell sounded more like Mamaw's alarm clock.

A bald man wearing a red polo shirt and jeans joined us. He was toting a light-skinned kid with tight black ringlets and almond-shaped eyes. The kid was very cute, dressed in a purple polo shirt with cargo shorts.

"Hello!" the bald guy said, setting the kid down. "I'm Raúl."

I squatted to get a closer look at the little kid who was now clinging to the leg of Gary's jeans. "And who do we have here?"

"Can you tell the gentleman your name?" Gary asked.

The child hid behind Gary's leg.

Gary snickered. "We're a little shy today. This is Max."

With a sudden burst of confidence, Max peeked out, holding up three fingers. "I'm three!"

"My, you're nearly grown!" I said.

That was about all the socializing Max could handle. He ran over to Raúl who picked him up and led us into the living room, which had identical tan sofas opposite each other. A plate of chocolate chip cookies sat on a toy chest that doubled as a coffee table. Max played on the floor with a yellow Tonka bulldozer, identical to the one I had as a kid. Despite my unease, something about that toy bulldozer made the entire situation feel a little more normal.

Gary and Raúl sat on one sofa facing Sam, Julie, and me on the other. I looked around the room trying to find a good icebreaker. As a journalist, it's important to put the people you interview at ease by showing your interest in them as a person. It was not any different than when we did our door-to-door outreach at church; we didn't start off by asking if someone had accepted Jesus as their Lord and Savior—we worked up to that. As humans, we simply needed to connect with one another before we opened up, and you absolutely had to be authentic about it. "I like your matching sofas," I offered.

"Thanks," Gary said. "It took us forever to agree on a color. We finally settled on 'harvest.'"

"Yeah, we were afraid 'chamomile' would show too much dirt," Raúl said.

Sam smirked at me like that was the worst icebreaker ever. He then took out a pen and pad and looked up at Gary. "Congratulations again on winning the lawsuit against the City. That's amazing! So the judge sided with you and the other couples but, like, what does that mean exactly?"

Gary brushed the flour from his T-shirt. "The judge recognized our case as a civil rights issue, which was huge. The court ruled that gays are not being treated equally under the law since they can't marry. Basically, we deserve the same security and protection that straight couples receive when they marry.

"So what are they doing to make that happen?" Sam asked.

"Well, the City could start issuing marriage licenses to gay couples."

"No way!" Sam said. "When?"

"The judge ordered a thirty day stay pending appeal by the State Attorney General. He'll definitely appeal, so the ruling could be in limbo for years."

"That's so freakin' lame," Julie said. *like Josue*

Raúl said, pointing to Julie and Sam, "Gary and I have been together for fifteen years, but if you two married today, you'd have more rights than we do."

I wondered why he pointed at Sam rather than me. When Sam was trying to land this interview, he must've told them he was gay, too, to get them to agree to it.

"What do you think of President Bush's move to 'protect the institution of marriage'?" Sam asked.

Raúl looked at Gary. "We just want the same rights as straight couples, not just for ourselves, but also for Max."

My cell phone rang—the caller ID read "Dad-Mobile." Crap. We have a "must answer" policy in the Powell house: one of the conditions for getting and keeping my cell phone was that I always had to answer my parents' calls unless I was driving (when my phone was to be off). Typically, when I knew I was going to be unavailable like this, I texted my parents to let them know, but this time I'd totally forgotten.

Julie glared at me. "Jake! We're trying to do an interview here?"

Of all people, Julie had some nerve making a ruckus over a phone call. "I apologize but it's...I'll just be a second."

I stepped into the foyer and answered the phone. "Hello, Preacher." I looked at my watch. It was already two forty-five—a little over three hours left before the deadline for submitting the article.

"How's school?" he asked. "You running things up there yet?"

I snickered. "Not yet. Listen, Dad, we're doing an interview so—"

"Already? They sure don't mess around at Columbia. Who're you interviewing?"

If I told him the truth, The Preacher might've called up the president of Columbia to complain. I had to get him off the phone. "You're breaking up, Preacher."

"WHO ARE YOU INTERVIEWING?"

74

I didn't know what to say. I'm an awful liar.

"Jake!" Julie shouted. *WHAT A BITCH! NY.*

"Preacher, if you can hear me, I'll call you later," I said, feeling horrible for basically hanging up on my dad.

Back in the living room, I caught the end of something Julie was saying, "—since his father's some fundamentalist preacher."

I couldn't believe they were talking about me. Sam must've told her I was a PK. It wasn't a big secret or anything, but I had wanted to keep it under wraps so people wouldn't judge me or start apologizing around me for swearing. I had hoped to step away from all that while I was up here.

Sam cleared his throat, obviously to indicate that I'd returned. Julie quieted down. *IS THAT POSSIBLE?*

Gary turned to me as I sat down. "So, Jake, what do you think about all this?"

Time to pick on the PK. I'd had a lifetime of these situations and learned early on not to take sides. When people realized I'm not some big holy roller, they lost interest quick. "It's not my battle," I said.

"You must have an opinion, though," Gary said.

Truth was, I didn't know what to think. It seemed great that Gary and Raúl had adopted little Max who seemed happy as a clam. I was sure The Preacher would have something to say about it, though. "Sir, we're here to cover *your* story, not mine, you know."

"Well, what denomination are you?" Gary asked. *NOT BIZ. your*

This guy just wouldn't leave well enough alone. I took a deep breath. "One-Way Bible." *AN*

"We were both raised Catholic," Raúl said, perhaps to make me feel less like an outsider. "We're more spiritual than religious now. Jake, there were gay characters in the Bible, you know, right? In fact, there's at least one record of a gay marriage."

I crinkled my forehead. There was no way that could be true. "Where?"

75

[handwritten: —OT STORIES.]

"It's in First or Second Samuel," he said, standing up and heading to the bookcase on the far side of the room. "David was married to a man." *[handwritten: OT STORIES.]*

Julie clapped her hands together, thrilled by this. "David as in David and Goliath?"

"Exactly! Right after he killed Goliath, David returned to King Saul to give him the news. But while David was talking with the King, his son entered and, well, it was love at first sight."

Raúl sat back down and flipped through the Bible.

I shook my head, prepared to squash this crazy interpretation of scripture, but at least they took an interest in the Bible, even if their theology was kind of wacky. "Jonathan and David were just friends," I said. "*Best* friends,"

Raúl was still flipping through his Bible. "Jonathan! Yes, that's his name. But, Jake, they were much more than friends. King Saul recognized their relationship as a marriage." *[handwritten: HOW DO]*

This guy was on crack. *[handwritten: U KNOW ?]*

I could tell Sam was getting impatient, and I was, too. We'd come to do a story, not debate the Bible. I was about ready to go over and give Raúl a Biblical assist when he stopped flipping and nodded. Handing me the Bible, he pointed to First Samuel 18:1-4, underlined in pink. I read aloud.

And it came to pass, when he had made an end of speaking unto Saul, that the soul of Jonathan was knit with the soul of David, and Jonathan loved him as his own soul. And Saul took him that day, and would let him go no more home to his father's house. Then Jonathan and David made a covenant, because he loved him as his own soul. And Jonathan stripped himself of the robe that was upon him, and gave it to David, and his apparel, even to his sword, and to his bow, and to his girdle.

[handwritten: NO MENTION OF MARRIAGE!]

The passage didn't seem any different than what I'd remembered from my own Bible, but I'd never heard anyone come to Raúl's conclusion. I handed the Bible back to Raúl. "They were just friends—people made grand gestures like that in Bible times. David married a woman, Michal. Can we get back to—"

"How do you know all this stuff?" Julie asked me.

I shrugged, but sat a little taller.

Raúl shook his head. "He married her *after* Jonathan's death. King Saul stated that David's union with Michal would make David his son-in-law for a second time." Raúl read the underlined portion in his Bible beginning with verse 20.

And Michal, Saul's daughter, loved David: and they told Saul, and the thing pleased him…wherefore Saul said to David, thou shalt this day be my son-in-law a second time.

I thought for a moment, suddenly aware that Julie was looking at me. So was everyone else, including Max. "That was the second daughter the King had offered to David. That's what he's referring to."

Raúl smiled. "Perhaps. But when Jonathan died, read what David said." Raúl offered me his Bible, but I pulled mine from my backpack. His Bible felt kind of rigged.

"Which verse?"

"Second Samuel 1:26"

I opened my Bible to the passage and read aloud.

I grieve for you, Jonathan my brother; you were very dear to me. Your love for me was wonderful, more wonderful than that of women.

"Whoa!" Julie said, "He sounds like a big 'mo to me!"

Sam took the Bible from Raúl, running his fingers under the passage, apparently to make sure he'd heard correctly. "That's crazy! I'm totally posting this on my blog!"

I slumped down and read the last verse again, silently. How had I never noticed this? Even in the New Testament, men and women were never friends—women were always considered inferior, which is why Jesus' equal treatment of women was so radical for his time. I don't know Hebrew, the language of the Old Testament, but the Ancient Greeks acknowledged three types of love. There is certainly no way David could've been speaking of φιλία (friendship) between a man and a woman in 500 B.C. He was referring to ἔρως (sexual love) or αγάπη (unconditional or ~~spousal~~ love) with Jonathan. Either way...

I absentmindedly grabbed a chocolate chip cookie from the plate on the coffee table. It looked soft and chewy, just like Momma's, and I needed something to help bring me back to reality.

"You've taken this out of context," I said, finally. "We know from Leviticus that homosexuality was strictly forbidden in Bible times. It's an intriguing theory, but David is probably turning over in his grave right now."

"We'll just have to agree to disagree," Raúl said, smiling.

"So back to our discussion," Sam said, checking his Rolex. "What do you think about the term 'marriage' when referring to same-sex unions?" PARTNERSHIP

"Raúl and I completely disagree," Gary said. "I believe anything less than the word 'marriage' makes our union second class to the union of a man and a woman. If Raúl is in critical condition in some hospital, the last thing I need is to explain the complexities of a civil union to the hospital staff. I'd just want to walk in, see my ~~husband~~ BoyfriEND, and do everything I can to make sure he gets better, just like any straight couple."

Raúl patted Gary's hand.

Sam continued with his questions while I sat there not knowing what to think. It was only my second full day in New York and everything was already happening so fast. Here I was in my first gay apartment—in what was quite possibly the gayest neighborhood in the ~~world~~ US—being lectured by a lapsed Catholic on how David and Jonathan were actually in a gay marriage. As if that wasn't enough, he proceeded to profess his love for the man sitting next to him while their three-year-old son crawled around pushing a Tonka truck. What was next?

The room suddenly got quiet, and I realized that my mind had been wandering.

"That's all my questions," Sam said. "Jake, Julie, do you have any more?"

I shook my head.

Julie took a digital camera out of the equipment bag at her feet, "Max is just so cute! Do you mind if I take a photo of the three of you?"

"Sure," Gary said.

Max jumped up on the sofa between Raúl and Gary. He clearly worshipped them.

Julie stood and adjusted Max's collar. "Sam, Jake— would you mind grabbing the lights?"

Sam shook his head. "Julie, we're behind schedule. Can't we, like, use available light?"

Julie motioned around the room in disbelief. "Are you serious?"

Sam just sat there.

She sighed and pointed at a floor lamp. "Look at the horrible shadows that lamp is casting—we'll miss how Max's purple shirt brings out his green eyes. Plus the lights will make their faces pop against that dark wall."

"But, like, we've still gotta write the article and we only have—"

"Didn't you read about story packaging? Copy isn't everything."

I just wanted to get the hell out of there. "C'mon, y'all. Let's just do this." I opened the big gray plastic suitcase filled with three studio lights and tripods cleverly packed in foam cutouts. I'd lugged that heavy case all the way from Columbia (Julie had charmed the freshman attendant at the equipment checkout into letting us use the kit).

Julie snapped a few shots. "I'll just need the 300 and one barndoor."

Sam and I stared blankly at each other.

"The small light, a tripod, and that black metal gizmo."

If she only needed the one small light, why did she make us lug the entire kit?

Raúl kissed Gary smack dab on the lips.

I closed my eyes long enough to pray silently, *God-thank-you-for-healing-me-from-homosexuality.*

DOES PUT U OFF
& I AM

CHAPTER 8

Back in my dorm room, I sat at my desk with Julie looking over my shoulder at her photos of Max, Raúl, and Gary on my laptop. It was getting pretty close to our six o'clock deadline so we quickly agreed on the best one. "I'll just crop this tighter," I said.

Julie leaned in further, sizing up the photo. "And take out that wet spot on Max's shirt."

She seemed completely serious.

"You can't tamper with news photographs," I said.

She rolled her eyes. "It's just a wet spot. How is that news?"

Turning and looking her square in the face, I said, "We can adjust contrast and saturation but anything more is simply unethical." POT / KETTLE!

"~~Jesus~~!" she said. "I can't believe you sometimes."

Although it hadn't been my intention, getting her riled up like that was kind of exciting. If we hadn't been on deadline, I might've stirred the pot a little more.

Meanwhile, Sam typed on his laptop from Raj's desk. His computer looked a lot like mine but ran some open source operating system called Linux. I'd never heard of it.

"Okay, brah, I'm emailing the article to you now."

I kept hitting my email refresh button until Sam's message appeared. His article noted that Gary, Raúl, and Max were a family to emulate and applauded the State Attorney General for living up to his mandate of ensuring the liberty of every citizen rather than enforcing some ~~outdated~~ moral code—a clear reference to the Bible. Although the byline would be Sam's since he wrote it, the article was a reflection on the entire team, and I certainly didn't want my name associated with anything that went out of its way to attack the Bible. Plus, it needed heavy editing and when you got right down to it, the piece read like an editorial rather than a news article. I decided to speak up.

"Sam, you mind if I make a few suggestions?" I asked.

"Go ahead," he said, sitting back, arms crossed.

"This lead's a tad long and the article could be a little more balanced—there's opinion embedded everywhere. And I don't love the headline 'Gay Civil Rights Hit the Empire State.'"

"Yeah, that sounds kind of dorky," Julie said, sneering.

Sam's eyes narrowed. Perhaps he wasn't accustomed to feedback.

I thought for a moment. "What about 'Liberty and Justice for All?' With a question mark?"

Julie nodded. "I really like that."

Sam looked away and exhaled slowly. "Yeah, for sure," he said. I didn't know if he meant it, though.

I tightened the lead and tried to soften Sam's editorial views infused throughout the article. He had gone into such a rant over the "blatant violation of constitutional rights" gays had suffered and even compared it to the fight for interracial marriage, which apparently was once banned in many states until the 1960s. Sam sure knew how to stir things up.

I printed copies of the revised article for us all to review a few minutes before the six o'clock deadline.

"Jake, this is much better," Julie said. "We should add your name to the byline."

"Sure, that's cool," Sam said, and he actually seemed to mean it.

"Oh, um, that's okay. It's really Sam's work, plus the assignment was for *one* person to write the article." Although I was thrilled that Sam and Julie were impressed by my contribution, I didn't want my name on a gay article—it might end up on the Internet someplace and then it'd only be a matter of time before someone forwarded it to The Preacher. That would bring my summer in New York to an abrupt halt to say the least.

I attached the photo and article and emailed it to Professor Greenberg.

"That's it!" I said, relieved that we'd made the deadline.

"Awesome!" Sam said. "Just in time, too—I've got a date so I'm outta here."

Julie stood and grabbed her purse. "Well, don't get married before you meet Josie."

"Oh, it's nothing like that," Sam said, and then winked at her.

Julie smirked and waved a finger at him. "Tsk, tsk."

Sam slapped my back. "Good work, brah. That article wouldn't have been as strong without your help."

"Oh, it was nothing. I barely did anything." As soon as the words were out of my mouth, I wondered why I downplayed my work. Was I just being modest, or was I trying to distance myself from the article? Maybe it was a little bit of both.

I picked up Julie's backpack. "I'll head out with you—I'm off to the library."

Julie and I strolled down College Walk toward the Columbia gates. We passed students hanging out on the grass and others clustered on the steps of Low Library, a dome-topped pantheon (πάνθειον, temple of all gods). We'd never been alone together and, without Sam around, I couldn't think of one thing to say. She hadn't said anything either since we left the dorm, probably because she couldn't wait to get away from me and onto whatever fancy plans she had for the evening. This was my chance to make a great impression, and I was blowing it.

"I think this is the most beautiful campus I've ever seen," I said to break the silence.

"Really? You should see it during the holidays. These trees are all filled with sparkling lights. It's magical, especially after a fresh snow."

Right then and there, I knew that Columbia was where I wanted to go to college, but the university had one of the lowest acceptance rates in the ~~world~~. Maybe if I won one of those awards at the end of the program, Columbia admissions would sit up and take notice. Of course, if I *didn't* win one of those awards it wouldn't even matter: I'd be off to the seminary.

"You know this is where they filmed that movie *Ghostbusters*?" Julie asked, gesturing over at a brick path flanked by plush green hedges.

"I once saw the trailer online. It looks hilarious."

Her mouth fell open. "You've never seen *Ghostbusters*? ~~Jesus~~!"

"You know, The Preacher would wash your mouth out good for taking the Lord's name in vain like that," I said half-jokingly.

"The Preacher?" Julie asked.

"Don't act all ignorant. I heard y'all talking about me back there at Raúl and Gary's."

"Oops," Julie said, covering her mouth. "But you really call your father 'The Preacher?' What does he call you?"

"The Stud."

"Really?"

Was she that gullible? "No! He calls me Jake."

She punched my shoulder.

I laughed and suddenly wanted to hold her hand, give her a piggyback ride, or another one of the many romantic things I'd seen men and women do in movies and firsthand. Instead, I decided to open up a little, and I hoped she'd do the same.

"Seriously, everyone calls my dad 'The Preacher,'" I explained. "It's a sign of respect. I come from a long line of Preachers. I'm one too, actually. I mean, not all the time like my dad, but I preach Fifth Sundays."

"What's Fifth Sunday?"

"You've never heard of Fifth Sunday? It's the last Sunday of any month with five Sundays—there's one coming up next month. That's when we have our youth services."

"You sound like one of those born agains," she said, almost like that was a bad thing.

Having a serious conversation about religion was the last thing I expected, but I somehow liked her more for it. Or maybe it was just the fact that we were now talking about real stuff rather than old movies.

"Aren't you?" I asked. I couldn't think of a single person back home who wouldn't claim to be a born again—even if they weren't regular churchgoers.

"I'm Jewish. Hello?"

Julie's last name was Aaron—the name of Moses' brother and Israel's first high priest—but it hadn't crossed my mind that she was Jewish. Julie could actually have Moses' DNA! Secretly, I'd always wanted to be Jewish, partially because every major Biblical hero like Jesus, Moses, and Noah were, but mostly because the Book of Exodus refers to them as "God's chosen people," like they had His seal of approval or something. Who wouldn't want that? "Wow! You're the first Jewish person I've ever met!"

She laughed. "You think I'm the first Jewish person you've met? What about Sam Horowitz or Professor Greenberg?"

"They're Jewish?" My mind started wandering about Sam. What Biblical character might he be related to? Maybe Samson, who had super-human strength that ebbed and flowed with the length of his hair. Sam was certainly built like an ox and had great hair.

"Well, yeah. Neither is very observant. I mean, Sam has a tattoo and it's not like Professor Greenberg wears a yarmulke."

"What's a yarmulke?"

"You really scare me sometimes."

I chuckled, awkwardly. Back home in Tarsus, you could pretty much assume that everyone was One-Way Bible, Baptist, or Methodist. Clearly, that wasn't the case in New York. "But how can you tell?"

Julie rolled her eyes, but then slowed her pace and turned to me with a raised eyebrow. "So are you, like, a virgin?"

My face suddenly felt hot and prickly, but I didn't know how to respond. Back home, no one would ever ask such a question. At least no one you just met. Flustered, I simply asked, "Are you?"

She grinned then studied my hair like she was imagining me with highlights or something. "So, why are you going to the library?"

I gazed back at the limestone edifice of Butler Library, which had the names of Aristotle, Homer, Dante, and other great writers carved just below the roofline. "To see what sort of projects won awards in this program over the last several years."

"Why would you do that?"

I so didn't want to get into this since I knew she'd never understand, but to try and change the subject would've just piqued her interest. "I, um, *need* to win, so I want to see what's won in the past."

"You mean you *want* to win," she said.

Truly, I would've preferred talking about my virginity. "Never mind..."

She grabbed my arm. "No, I want to know. Why do you *need* to win?"

I let out a deep sigh. "If I don't, my dad will make me give up journalism."

"What?" she asked, tilting her head.

"It was the only way he'd let me come," I whispered, embarrassed that she might now see me as a child, completely controlled by my parents. "If I win an award, I can pursue journalism. If I don't, I have to become a preacher."

"That's awful!" She just stood there with as genuine a look of concern as I'd ever seen.

I placed my hand in the small of her back so she'd continue walking. We exited through the gates and stopped at the subway entrance. Julie reached over and messed up my hair a little. "Much better," she said with a grin.

Was she flirting with me? I flung her backpack at her the way she'd flung it at me that morning. She was a good catch.

"See you tomorrow, preacher boy."

"Hey, who you calling a boy?"

She raised an eyebrow, walked backwards a few paces, then turned and hopped down the subway stairs. Was it even in the realm of possibilities that Julie was into me? I stared after her then realized I'd forgotten to breathe. Don't go there.

See you tomorrow, preacher boy. Pushy NY

I clung to her final words, but I hardly deserved that title. Sure, I'd delivered some knockout Fifth Sunday sermons over the years, but my last one had been a complete disaster. I should've known that I'd bomb after Slip-up #219 with that "fitness" magazine. It hadn't helped that, just before I took the pulpit, The Preacher had gone on a tear, punctuated by his disdain for homosexuals, as if he knew about my actions from the prior evening and was issuing a warning. "God's patience is running out!" he had said. "If the church continues to sit back, this country will fall and another will rise up to take its place. And then we'll say, 'Jesus, why didn't you give us a sign?' Well, he's given us plenty of signs. God's answer to the gay agenda is AIDS, and 9/11 was His judgment for throwing Christ out of the public squares of America and our schools."

The Preacher's tirade generated a healthy round of "Amens" by several deacons in the packed sanctuary.

By the time my dad called on me to preach, I wanted to crawl under the pew and hide, but instead, I jumped to my feet like I was the ultimate authority on living your life for Christ and couldn't wait to get to the front of the church to tell everyone about it.

My foot caught as I stumbled up the stairs to the pulpit. I didn't fall or anything, but all at once, I was set off kilter. As I reached for the index cards in the inside pocket of my suit jacket, my hands shook and my lungs felt like they were filling with a swarm of angry bees, cutting off my air supply.

All eyes were fixed on me like needles in a pincushion. I knew lots of people were rooting for me, like my former babysitter, Mrs. Roberts, who was nodding at me as if to say, "Jake, you can do this."

But not everyone was rooting for me; Miss Ruby Smith with her teased white hair and steel blue eyes magnified by her thick, gold-framed eyeglasses was holding her mouth like she was sucking on a lemon drop, sizing me up. I could tell I was coming up short and she loved it.

The first line of the sermon was right there on the top card, written in The Preacher's ragged script: "Our best is as filthy rags in Jesus' sight." The sermon was about how Jesus' love for each of us was unconditional. But how could I say that when I didn't believe it myself? I'd read all eight Bible verses against homosexuality and knew that if I went by the literal interpretation of the Bible, my soul was in eternal jeopardy.

I was fundamentally screwed.

I mustered my courage but "Our best is..." was as far as I got.

I-can-do-all-things-through-Christ-who-strengthens-me.

I stared out at the crowd as the room began to spin. If these people really knew my secret, they'd throw me out of the church. What right did I have to be up here? I'm not worthy. I indulged in pornography. Gay pornography.

I could feel my lips kinda moving but my throat was clogged; nothing more would come out. By the time the crowd began to murmur, it was all over.

I shook my head at The Preacher.

As he stood and approached the pulpit, the murmuring grew louder.

"I'm sorry," I mouthed, then walked off the stage and past Momma at the piano who reached out for me.

I just kept walking and didn't stop until I was all the way home.

Standing there at the Columbia gates in the middle of summer, a shiver coursed through me from reliving that awful day. Although two months had passed, the wound was fresh as ever. I once again pondered Julie's words. *Preacher boy.*

No, I think not.

CHAPTER 9

A couple of days later, Professor Greenberg handed back our first assignment at the beginning of class.

"Overall, the articles were good but remember to take meticulous notes, don't make assumptions, and—" he plopped our paper with the headline "Liberty and Justice for All?" in front of Sam and looked directly at him, "—cover every side of the story." *NOT JUST THE LIBERAL ONE.*

The paper was marked "B-" with the note "Unbalanced. Cover every side of the story."

Julie shook her head at Sam. "We told you that article wasn't balanced."

"Actually, that was Jake. You were too obsessed with the wet spot on Max's shirt, remember?" He looked away in a huff.

Julie rolled her eyes at Sam for my benefit, seeming suddenly to favor me.

I showed her the note beneath her photograph: "Very well composed and lighted."

"Well, it is," she said, then continued texting on her cell phone beneath the table, careful that Greenberg wasn't watching.

I turned back around, elbowed Sam, then whispered, "C'mon, man. It's not like this was the final project. We'll do better next time."

He nodded but kept looking forward with his jaw clenched.

I couldn't tell if he was upset for not doing better or because he felt he had let us down. "Truly, I'm amazed you were able to pull the interview and article together in such a short time, especially considering you just got to New York. Thanks for taking the lead on this one, Sam."

A ghost of a smile crept onto his face. "Thanks, Jake."

The professor held up an article for all to see. "Thomas, Troy, and Tina, I'll return this shortly," he said, motioning behind me. "There was one article that really stood out, with the headline 'Money For Nothing,' about a Bronx check cashing operation that was just busted by New York bank regulators. I've posted it to the online blackboard. Study it. The article demonstrates great coverage of breaking news."

All eyes turned to Thomas, Troy, and Tina, fist bumping each other.

"Okay, today we'll focus on editorials, one of the few opportunities a journalist has to express his own opinion. As you surely noted in last night's reading, editorials are emotional by definition and should motivate or at least entertain your reader. They should also address a current issue and be backed by facts."

The professor went on to discuss editorials in great length and even said that you're not editor material if you can't write an editorial.

That stung a bit since editorials just weren't my thing. But if you ask me, there's a lot more involved in being a good editor than just writing editorials. Like supervising section editors, editing stories, and recruiting talented staff, not to mention the entire business side.

Professor Greenberg wrapped up by saying, "Now, pitch your individual ideas for an editorial to the team I assigned you to yesterday. Remember, it must incorporate a current news event, and be sure to rotate roles on each of your assignments. Your editorials are due by six p.m. *today*."

Sam, Julie, and I huddled together. I had an idea.

"I just read about a diner that's being shut down after sixty years," I said. "The Empire Diner."

Julie's jaw dropped. "In Chelsea? No!"

I nodded. "Yep. The landlord wants to build a high-rise condo slap dab on the spot where that diner's parked."

Sam wasn't impressed. "A diner? C'mon—we need something edgy. There must be a thousand diners in New York. Does anyone care?"

"This isn't just any diner," Julie said. "It's legendary. Okay, maybe it's not the Plaza Hotel, but it's been featured in a million movies and television shows. My dad and I used to eat there all the time."

I pulled a computer printout from my backpack and handed it to Sam. "Plus, in three of the past five years, this program gave out awards for articles involving eating establishments."

Sam scanned the list. "Wow, Jake, you really did your homework. I'm impressed. Okay, broh, I'm in."

On the way to the diner, my mind was in overdrive. As I already mentioned, I'd only written one editorial before and relied heavily on The Preacher's input. While The Preacher and Sam got a kick going off on how they thought things should be, I preferred reporting on the way things were. News rocks. It's neat and clean and there's nothing more satisfying than covering every aspect of a news story so that there are absolutely no outstanding questions. Like the answers in the back of a math textbook, you just checked the facts with news to verify your work was airtight. If someone took offense at the article, you just pointed to the facts.

By comparison, editorials don't have anything remotely resembling an answer key—you just stick your neck out and no amount of fact checking can keep the world from going all Marie Antoinette on you. If it were up to me, newspapers wouldn't even have editorials—they'd just present every detail so readers could form their own opinions. After all, it's a *news*paper, right? Fortunately, The Preacher took great interest in editorials and really helped me out the last time, and I knew he'd do the same today. I just didn't want Julie and Sam knowing I was an editorial lightweight, so I'd have to first gather all the facts about the diner then sneak in a quick call to The Preacher. He could always be counted on for an opinion—that was for sure.

Julie had insisted we bring the camera equipment, although no self-respecting editor would include a photograph in an editorial. Sam didn't argue and I didn't care as long as we made our six o'clock deadline. I was just glad everyone seemed to be getting along.

Sam lugged the camera equipment this time while I toted Julie's and my backpacks towards an old-fashioned stainless steel and glass dining car restaurant. I got the door for Julie, who strolled right in, yakking on her cell phone to the mayor's son like she owned the place.

We all hung out by the door while Julie continued her conversation. "Josh, I've got connections at Zegna and Ralph Lauren. I was thinking of a big fashion spread for your dad. Something to let the public see our mayor in a different way."

A heavyset waitress marched from behind the counter. She had almost no chin—her face simply melted right into the folds of her stubby neck. She glared at Julie and pointed to a NO CELL PHONES! sign taped to the glass door.

Julie held up one finger at her to indicate "just a minute" then turned her back. "Josh, think regal yet understated."

"Excuse me," the waitress said to Julie, impatiently.

Julie cupped the phone. "Sorry, just one more sec—I'm on the phone with the Mayor's son."

"I don't care if you're on the phone with the Pope. This is a cell phone-free diner."

Julie's eyes narrowed. "Josh, I'll have to call you back." She closed her phone and said coldly. "We're here to see Mr. Hagler. The *owner?*"

Julie was about as subtle as a tornado.

"My name's Debbie. Debbie *Hagler*. And you're..."

I extended my hand. "Hi, ma'am. I'm Jake Powell and these are my, um, colleagues Julie and Sam from Columbia

University. We contacted Mr. Hagler about writing an article on your lovely diner here."

Her attitude softened instantly. "Well, sure, hon. My husband is expecting you. Have a seat. He's a little hard of hearing, so speak up." She motioned to a booth at the window, then as if an afterthought, glared at Julie.

NOT A² Mrs. Hagler came back with Mr. Hagler, an energetic white-haired man with a potbelly. He wore his white short-sleeve shirt tucked into his gray polyester pants. I stood politely to greet him and shook his hand.

"I'm grateful to you kids for your interest in the diner," Mr. Hagler said. "Debbie, please get these students whatever they want—on the house."

I waved my hand. "Oh, we couldn't possibly accept—"

"May I see a menu?" Julie asked.

"But we insist on paying, especially considering what y'all are going through," I said.

Sam nodded. "Yeah, we insist."

Journalists aren't allowed to accept gifts or special treatment of any kind since it could be misconstrued as a bribe.

Mrs. Hagler removed a pad and pen from her apron pocket. "What'll it be?"

After a great amount of deliberation on Julie's part, we all ordered cheesecake, which Mrs. Hagler brought while Mr. Hagler explained the situation they were in.

"Let's see," I said, jotting notes down on my pad. "Forty-nine-year lease…adverse possession."

"So, like, she gave you no notice at all?" Sam asked.

"Nope. The landlord said we had thirty days to get the diner off her property. That's a load of crap if you ask me."

"But you think she's probably within her legal rights since the lease is up?" I asked.

"Son, I don't care if the law is on her side. My grandfather put this diner here sixty years ago—it's not going down on my watch. I'll fight to the bitter end."

"Do you have any other recourse?" I asked.

"I tried the New York City Landmark Commission, but they weren't much help. It's not like George Washington slept here. But this particular area wasn't even zoned for a high rise until earlier this year. How did she get the permits, I ask you? I bet somebody at City Hall got paid off."

I checked the time on the neon clock above the cash register—we only had thirty minutes before our interview with the landlady at three-thirty. She'd been extremely wary when I phoned and only agreed to go on record after I mentioned our connection to the mayor. (I never said it was a strong connection.)

"Well, I think that covers it," I said. "Do you mind if we speak with some of your customers?"

"Go right ahead," Mr. Hagler said with a wave of his hand.

Julie removed the digital camera from our camera bag. "And we also need a photo of you and Debbie."

Mr. Hagler shouted toward the kitchen, "Debbie, they want our photo. Debbie! C'mon and get your picture taken."

"One sec!" Mrs. Hagler wandered out of the kitchen, removed her apron, then hit a key on the cash register causing the drawer to open with a ding. She retrieved a lipstick tube and applied it with the help of the mirrored wall behind the counter.

After we paid the bill, I rushed outside before the rest of the group, telling Sam I needed to make a quick phone call. I thought my dad would never pick up, but he finally did, and I wasted little time getting to the point. "Preacher, I need your help on this editorial I've got to write."

"I can't right now, son. I'm meeting with the architect, and he's charging about a hundred dollars a minute."

"Well, it's about this restaurant. The landlord's kicking out the family that's run it for sixty years because she wants to—"

"Let's talk tonight after church? Around nine?"

"But it's due at six."

"Just ask yourself what Jesus would do, and you'll have your answer," he said, then went on with more assurances that weren't all that helpful.

My heart sank. I bit down on my lip and stared out into space as I waited to say goodbye.

"Jake!" Julie shouted from the diner entrance. "Are you coming?"

I held up a finger to Julie. "Right. Thanks, Preacher."

Back at my dorm room desk, I was propped on my elbow, staring at the blinking cursor on my computer screen while Sam and Julie, both behind me, debated the fate of the diner. We had gotten both sides of the story—the landlord's lawyer was actually present during her interview—and a few great quotes, including this one from a diner regular: "Just what this city needs—another faceless condo. Who needs pancakes or sunlight for that matter?"

It would've made a great news article, but the assignment was to write an editorial and I'd drawn the short straw. What if Professor Green~~berg~~ disagreed with my conclusion, once I figured out what it was? With my luck, he'd be a personal friend of the landlady if I sided with the Haglers, and vice versa. What if he knew of some legal precedent I failed to cite? I haven't passed the bar so who was I to say whether the diner should stay or go? Let the reader decide! It was a complete waste of time. I didn't know what to write and, in fact, hadn't written a single word.

"I hate that they have to close," Julie said. "But the landlady said the lease ran out years ago. By law, she only had to give them thirty days notice."

"You're kidding, right?" Sam said. "Thirty days isn't enough time for them to find a new location for their diner, much less move it. They *so* deserve better after sixty years. Jake, how's our editorial coming along?"

"Um, well, I've got a great headline. What do you think of 'The Fall of an Empire?'"

"That works," Julie said, stabbing away at her phone.

Sam walked over, seeing that that was all I had—the headline.

"Jake, what've you been doing, brah? This thing is due in forty-five minutes."

I ran my fingers along the rigid part in my hair. I didn't know what to write. The law said they had to leave, but that didn't pass the what-would-Jesus-do test. I had turned that question over in my head so much I didn't know whether I was coming or going. "I know but if there's a clear-cut solution, I sure don't see it. What do you think, Julie?"

She let out a big sigh. "Jake, just write the damn editorial so we can get out of here."

My mind was still blank, so I just started talking. "Well, it doesn't seem very Christian of the landlady, but it's the law. I mean, it'd be awful nice if she'd let them stay. That's what Jesus would do."

Julie looked at me like I was nuts. "That's what *Jesus* would do?"

"Yes, maybe if they prayed about it or something," I said, my voice trailing off, realizing how lame I sounded.

"That's your entire assessment?" Sam asked. "Like, they should just hold hands and pray about it? Really?"

I looked away, and my eyes landed on the portrait of my parents. "Guys, I've only written one editorial in my life and got a lot of help from my dad. If y'all will write this thing, I'll write the next *two* news stories to make up for it." I turned to Sam with pleading eyes. "Editorials just aren't my thing."

"But, dude, Professor Greenberg said we had to trade off on the writing," Sam said.

"I took the photo," Julie said, like that mattered. Who includes a photo with an editorial? No one. Everyone knows that.

"Our time is running out," I said. "Sam, can't you write it? You seem to have a strong opinion. You just said the Haglers deserve better."

Sam threw up his hands, "Okay, okay. I'll write it."

"Thanks, Sam! I really appreciate it. I'll make this up to you, I promise."

Sam sat down at my computer and started typing away. I knew I really would have to make it up to him. I don't know why, but I needed him to respect me in a way that I didn't need from Julie. Both Sam and Julie mattered to me, but in different ways. I just wasn't exactly sure why.

After Julie and Sam left, I just sat alone in my room while my stomach churned and a red neon sign in my head flashed LOSER! I couldn't stop thinking about my failure. Granted, my headline was killer and I had tightened Sam's writing, but I should've just plunged right in and written that editorial *myself*, as if it were any other article. What was wrong with me? Was I afraid of taking a stand? Maybe I just didn't know what I stood for. How pathetic.

Making matters worse, I'd only been gone from home for four days, but I longed for my big comfy bed and a decent glass of iced tea. Most of all, I really missed my parents. It may sound lame, but knowing that I had five weeks plus before I saw them again suddenly seemed unbearable. Maybe it was because I was an only child or maybe I was just scared: scared that I wouldn't fit in; scared of the consequences of not winning an award; but mostly, scared that those old nagging desires of mine weren't completely gone.

Trying to pull myself together, I checked my email to see if there was any news from home. I had several messages from friends, but focused on the one from Tracy; I really hated being away from her at such a critical time—her parents were talking divorce.

Everything in her email was in code, probably just in case her mom and dad were monitoring her account. She said that things were really quiet around the house, so the "news must be out." She was afraid they might "buy a second home," which I'm sure meant she feared her parents might actually get a divorce. Poor Tracy. I'll never forget the day she told me the news about her parents, right after my first meeting as editor of *The Tattler.*

She was driving me home after school in the pouring rain. Earlier that day, we'd had a huge argument in front of the entire *Tattler* staff over whether to run Kenny Ballard's All-State baton-twirling championship win on the front page. Kenny's win was certainly a big deal, but I had nixed the article: if I put a guy wearing a leotard on the front page of the paper—not to mention the first issue with me as editor—it would raise more than a few eyebrows with the biggest ones being The Preacher's. People would ask why I'd do such a thing and say, "Where there's smoke there's fire." I couldn't afford to get caught up in that whole program but had sacrificed my journalistic integrity in the process and Tracy knew it.

Even though we disagreed from time to time, Tracy and I had a mutual understanding that nothing would come between our friendship. Of course, that didn't stop her from giving me the silent treatment.

Neither of us spoke on the entire drive to my house until we pulled onto my street. She stopped the car half a block from my driveway and stared ahead as her hands trembled on the steering wheel.

I felt horrible for wimping out on the Kenny Ballard article and deserved everything Tracy was about to throw my way. I crossed my arms and took a deep breath, preparing myself for one of her big hissy fits.

"My father's having an affair," she finally said, then burst into tears.

"What? Tracy, there's no way Mr. Scruggs would do that," I said, but I could see in her eyes it was true, and she proceeded to tell me every detail.

"Do you want me to tell The Preacher?" I asked. "He'd know how to help."

"God no!" she said, turning to me. "Jake, promise you won't tell anyone!"

"I promise!"

I couldn't blame her—if the situation were reversed and I suspected one of my parents was having an affair, I don't think I'd tell anyone. Not even Tracy. Once the genie was out of the bottle, he wasn't going back in, as Grandmother Clarke used to say.

"Tracy, want to come in for some cookies or maybe some ice cream?"

"No, I'd better get home."

That all happened just last month. I hammered off a quick email to her but decided not to mention Sam and Professor Greenberg until later since I wanted to focus solely on her. I wasn't sure if I could ever bring up Julie since that felt like a betrayal. (Although Tracy and I were just friends, the way she looked at me sometimes made me think she wanted more.)

But even on the off chance that Julie was into me, I wasn't sure I could ever go out with her since she wasn't Christian. Our church literature advocated a Christian-only dating policy since that's the only way to be sure you'd marry one. But if I really liked Julie, would I let that stop me from dating her while I was in New York? Perhaps I could find a way to bring up the subject of Jesus, although she'd probably just laugh at me. I'd have to try. Besides, none of us could save anyone—only Jesus could do that. All I could do was put it out there and hope the Spirit moved her to accept Jesus as her Lord and Savior.

After going through the rest of my email, I took the photo of my parents from my desk. It was an outtake from the most recent photo session for the annual church directory. The Preacher was grinning ear to ear as he gazed upon Momma, who had her head thrown back in a fit of laughter. I realized how much I'd taken them for granted all these years. Being away from them for a few days made me aware of how much I needed them. They always wanted to know about my day and were quick to say how proud they were of me and how much they loved me. I felt the same about them. I only had one more year left at home before college and decided at that moment that I would cherish every single day. I didn't want to be one of those people who only grasped how great their parents were after they were gone.

There was no sense calling them since they wouldn't be home from church until around nine. I was kind of lonely so I dialed Phoebe and was surprised to find her home.

"Aunt Phoebe—I mean, Phoebe!" I said. "Just calling to confirm dinner Saturday."

"Yes, eight o'clock," she said.

That seemed awfully late for dinner. I'd have to grab a snack beforehand.

"Remember to bring your overnight bag," she said. "I'm throwing a dinner party for you and my dinner parties always run late."

No one had ever thrown me a dinner party before. "You'd do that? For me?"

"Of course! Who's better than you? Got a new friend you'd like to bring?" she asked, mischievously.

I suddenly perked up. "I could ask my friend Julie."

"Great! Tell her it's a hip-hop theme."

"Hip-hop?" I asked, but she had already hung up or we lost the connection. I wondered what Phoebe could possibly know about hip-hop.

CHAPTER 10

I checked the street number to be sure the towering apartment building on 72nd Street was indeed Phoebe's. This part of the Upper West Side was just a few subway stops downtown from Columbia and not far from the firehouse I'd visited earlier in the week, but it was a much fancier world. Each building had an awning that ran to the curb and a doorman standing at attention like he was waiting for the President to arrive or something. The doorman at Phoebe's building wore an emerald green uniform and would've fit right in at the gates of Oz.

I stuck out my hand. "Excuse me, sir. My name's Jake Powell, and I'm here to see Phoebe Clarke. She's my aunt."

The man hesitated but shook my hand. "Oh yes, Mrs. Clarke said you can go right up."

"Thank you, sir. I—I didn't catch your name?"

"My name is Chee."

"Nice to meet you, Mr. Chee."

I made my way through a huge limestone lobby with beige everything: dark beige rugs, striped beige chairs, and light beige drapes. It's like the whole place had been caramelized.

It seemed kind of over-the-top for Phoebe to throw a dinner party for me, especially since I wouldn't know anyone there, but that's just Phoebe. She is, without a doubt, the coolest adult I know.

As I stepped off the elevator into the hallway, I could just make out a distant beat that grew louder as I approached apartment 16H. The music was definitely coming from Phoebe's apartment and of the hip-hop variety—you'd have thought a bunch of teenagers lived there rather than a single forty-plus-year-old. I loved it.

I rang the bronze doorbell labeled "Clarke" but didn't hear a bell go off. No one came to the door, so I knocked. Still no one answered. I rang the doorbell again and rapped on the door a little harder, hoping I wasn't disturbing the neighbors. Finally, a brawny, fair skinned man with hair spiked into a blond fin, flung it open. Around his neck, a huge chunky gold necklace with a dangling "NYC" charm sparkled in the hallway light.

"I'm Jake Powell, Phoebe's nephew?" I said, holding my hand out.

He shook my hand. "I'm Bruno," he said, baring a mouthful of crooked teeth. "Come on in. I'll put your backpack in your room. Can I get you a drink?"

"No, thank you." I entered a long foyer lined with huge modern paintings that all looked really expensive. But Phoebe could afford it—she had her own advertising firm.

Other than the artwork and the loudish hip-hop music playing from the recessed wall speakers, everything else would've fit Momma's taste to a T. The dark wood floor was covered with a purplish Oriental rug, and two green wingback chairs flanked a mahogany table. Phoebe wasn't afraid of a little color.

"The other guests are in there," Bruno said over the loud music. He nodded for me to go through a far left door while he disappeared with my bag.

I walked to the end of the foyer but stopped short of the living room just as some bass-heavy rap song came on. I chuckled when I saw the crowd: except for one guy in Malcolm X glasses, the four adults standing around Phoebe—including one priest—all wore chunky gold necklaces with dangling charms in various shapes, including dollar signs, baseball bats, and hearts. Phoebe wore light purple shades, and her necklace had a New York Yankees charm dangling from it that was nearly the size of a dessert plate. They all had glasses of red wine.

Feeling overdressed and amazed that Phoebe was actually throwing a hip-hop party, I removed my tie, tucked it in my suit jacket then slipped into the living room. No one even noticed me—everyone was watching Phoebe offer a chunky gold heart necklace to the man with the Malcolm X glasses. She shouted over the music, "Oh come on, Patrick. Be a sport!"

"I am *not* wearing that thing," Patrick shouted back. "Looks like it came off some clearance rack. Like you."

Everyone chuckled, including Phoebe, while Patrick sipped from his wine glass.

"But I chose this hip-hop theme specifically for you after you threw such a fit at my last party," she said.

"Which one was that?"

"When Claire challenged you to a hog-calling contest."

"Oh, right! That was loads of fun. The only thing missing was the pig."

"Depends on who you ask," Phoebe said.

Everyone burst out laughing except Patrick, but even he finally snickered and said, "Good one."

Phoebe turned to toss the necklace onto a shiny red coffee table but spotted me. "Jake—you made it!"

She put the necklace on me and gave me a big hug.

"Where's Julie?" she asked, then picked up her wine glass from the coffee table.

I had invited Julie to Aunt Phoebe's dinner party, but her weekend was already booked. "She couldn't come."

"Well, I'm just glad you're here." She patted my shoulder and turned to the room. "Jake already has a love interest at Columbia."

Aunt Phoebe's words made it sound like I was one popular guy. Truth was, Julie hadn't accepted my invitation for that evening, and I couldn't be sure if it was because she was booked or just didn't want to go out with me. And I was still going back and forth on whether it was okay to date a non-Christian during my limited time in New York.

Phoebe gestured toward the priest and a beautiful olive-skinned woman with eyes that were almost as dark as her black hair. "Jake, this is Father Claude Brown and his wife, Miriam."

Father Claude shook my hand. He was tall and thin with shoulder-length gray hair and a silver goatee. I'd never seen a priest with a goatee before—not even an Episcopal one. He looked like a fading rock star.

Miriam wore distressed jeans and an iridescent green blouse. She offered her hand. "It's so great to finally meet you, Jake."

I shook her hand. "Good to meet you, Mrs. Miriam."

"Please, call me Miriam. Phoebe was so excited when you were accepted into the Summer Program."

"Miriam teaches ethics at Columbia, and Claude is my priest at St. Bartholomew's," Phoebe said.

Up until that moment, Phoebe had never done or said anything to make me think she ever went to church—I only knew that she did because Momma mentioned it on occasion. I imagined Phoebe as a closet churchgoer, Bible tucked deep inside her bag as she hopped from church to church, always arriving late and sitting alone in the back pew. The fact that she invited her priest and his wife over for dinner made me think that Phoebe might actually be pretty involved in her church. But that still didn't explain why she never brought it up.

"We'd love to have you in church tomorrow," Father Claude said.

"Sure. I brought my Bible." I was curious to see what type of churchgoer Phoebe was. Although The Preacher and I had talked about my going to the One-Way Bible Church in Brooklyn while I was in New York, it's not like I promised to go every Sunday.

"Great!" he said. "I hope you'll make St. Bartholomew your home church while you're in New York City."

"Thank you," I said, knowing that would never fly with The Preacher, but one Sunday wasn't going to kill me.

Patrick took a remote control from a small server and shut the music off. "Phoebe, this music is giving me a headache. Don't you have something classical? I'd even settle for Wagner at this point."

Phoebe rolled her eyes playfully and said, "And that guy over there sucking all the fun out of the room is Patrick Rosenberg. He's in fashion, but you can probably tell that by his glasses."

Patrick stuck out his tongue at Phoebe then shook my hand.

"Nice to meet you, Mr. Patrick."

"Mr. Patrick? Please! It's just Patrick. Congratulations on getting into Columbia for the summer, Jake."

"Thank you, Patrick." It seemed weird to call adults by their first names, but as the ancient saying goes, "When in Rome, do as the Romans do."

Phoebe beamed at a middle-aged woman with bushy red hair, standing to Patrick's left. "And this is Patrick's lovely wife, Leah, and their son, Christopher, is over there on the sofa."

Bruno walked in with a bottle of wine.

"Bruno, let's go ahead and sit for dinner," Phoebe said. "We're only going to be seven."

After a few minutes, Phoebe herded us all into the adjoining dining room. The table was filled with twinkly candles that cast an eerie glow on the modern paintings on the walls. Were we about to have a séance? Maybe The Preacher was right about Phoebe—he'd once referred to her as "that witch" after she'd sent him a trophy in the shape of a horse's rear end via overnight courier (it's a long story). But he immediately took it back even though Momma wasn't around.

There was a bowl of soup and place cards at every seat with Phoebe at the head and Father Claude at the other end flanked by Leah and Patrick, who were negotiating with their son. "You can play your Nintendo after dinner," Patrick said. "Now behave yourself or I'll take it away completely."

I used to have the same exact discussions with Momma over my old GameBoy.

Phoebe patted the place to her right. "Jake, you're here next to me."

I sat and scooted my chair in, then smiled at Miriam who sat right across from me.

"Jake, would you bless this humble *soupe glacée à l'avocat?*" Phoebe asked. "I made it myself."

I didn't know Phoebe cooked, and I could tell by Patrick's bugged out eyes that I wasn't the only one.

"I took a class at the Culinary Institute," Phoebe said proudly. "It's quite simple really—just a three step process."

Father Claude took Leah's hand, then she offered her left hand to me. Everyone followed suit.

I bowed my head. "Jesus, we thank you for this food and all the blessings you have bestowed on us. Thank you for Phoebe and her wonderful hospitality. For we pray in the name above every name, Jesus Christ. Amen."

"*Besm Allah Alrahman Alrahem,*" Miriam said, or something like that. It was probably Latin. Episcopalians can be awfully formal.

Phoebe picked up her soupspoon.

I could hear Momma's voice saying, "Dip away from you." I pulled the spoon brimming with a gray-green mixture to my mouth and blew, careful to keep the dangling heart on my necklace from walloping it. I wondered why Miriam was smiling at me until I put the spoon in my mouth—the soup was cold and bland. *Yuck.* If Momma were here, she'd jazz it right up with some garlic powder and a little heat.

Bruno poured red wine for the guests but I stuck with water. His shoulder muscles and arms bulged beneath his tight purple T-shirt. He had to have seriously worked out to get that big. I wondered who he was and if he had a girlfriend.

"So, Jake, tell us about this program at Columbia," Patrick said.

"It's very prestigious," Miriam said.

As a PK, I was quite comfortable at dinner parties, but Tracy called this "performing bear" time: well-meaning adults threw the lone kid at the dinner table questions the size of a beach ball, which the kid balanced on his nose while clapping before tossing it back. Tracy said it made the adults feel benevolent, and afterwards the kid could go into hibernation while the grown-ups talked. Tracy was a riot—I sure did miss her.

"It's a six-week program for forty high school newspaper editors from around the world. We're studying writing, reporting, copyediting, online publishing, and the whole business side too. The program just started last Monday, and we've already been on two field assignments where we interviewed New Yorkers making the news."

"Like who?" Leah asked, leaning in.

Although the Gary and Raúl story had received more coverage, I didn't want to dwell on anything gay. I fully believed that God had healed me, but as I've said before, I had to remain vigilant. "Like the owners of the Empire Diner in Chelsea. You know it's closing? Or it may close. Anyway, it's really intense, but I'm learning a lot and *love* my classmates. I'm honestly surprised I got in."

"Well, I'm more surprised your father let you come," Phoebe said.

I could now see the humor in what I went through to get The Preacher's okay; I decided to phrase my reply in a way that Phoebe might appreciate, using my best deadpan delivery. "It wasn't easy. He sees New York as sort of a Sodom and Gomorrah with a few Islamic terrorists thrown in."

"Islamic terrorists?" Miriam said. "Could someone please explain why the American media didn't call the Christian who bombed that Texas abortion clinic a Christian terrorist?"

She hadn't directed the question at me, but it was such a slow pitch I decided to go another round. "Well, blowing up an abortion clinic is hardly Christian, ma'am."

"So, you're suggesting that blowing up the World Trade Center is an act that is in keeping with the tenets of Islam?" Miriam asked, abruptly. "How so?"

All eyes turned toward me like compasses pointed north.

Suddenly, my face felt hot and tingly. I'd read and said "Islamic Terrorist" countless times and hadn't considered what it insinuated. "I've never heard it put quite like that," I said. "I didn't mean…"

"You've stumbled upon one of Miriam's pet peeves, I'm afraid," Father Claude said, smiling. "She has a few."

Miriam sat up straight and grabbed her wine glass. "Words are important, so we should take note of what we're saying. Jake, I know you didn't coin the term 'Islamic terrorist.' Even if I weren't Muslim, I would still take offense at how the news media flatters the terrorists and demeans Islam every time they use it. I've written letters to the major news outlets, encouraging them to just say 'terrorist,' but I've gotten nowhere."

So Miriam was Muslim, just like Raj. I hadn't seen that coming. "Well, you've convinced me," I said in an attempt to patch things up. "We'll never use that term under my watch at *The Tattler*. That's my school paper."

"Then I'm finally making some progress," she said with a playful nod.

We all smiled, but that whole exchange put a kibosh on the conversation. The only sound for the next several moments was spoon to porcelain as we all finished our soup.

Phoebe picked up a basket containing the longest loaf of bread I'd ever seen, tore off a piece, and passed it to me. "Baguette?"

I tore off a chunk and took a bite. I wasn't too crazy about the bread—it was as bland as the soup. What we all needed was some cornbread.

Feeling bad about my earlier gaffe, I decided to try again with Miriam. "So, um, Miriam, have you ever been to Mecca?"

"I always hope that I'll go next year, but I never get the chance."

I tried to lighten the mood. "Hey, do you think you could sneak Father Claude in, too?"

"Yeah, honey," Father Claude joined in playfully. "Could you get me in?"

"Sure. All you have to do is convert."

Father Claude swayed his head back and forth, as if he were entertaining the idea, then finally said, "They may not like that back at the office."

Everyone chuckled.

"I'm sure the Big, Big Boss wouldn't mind though," Miriam quipped.

The closest I'd ever seen to an interfaith marriage was a Catholic marrying a Presbyterian, but they were both still Christian. Miriam and Father Claude's relationship intrigued me. "All joking aside, how did you two reconcile your faiths? I mean, if you don't mind my asking."

Miriam and Father Claude locked eyes.

"Claude has his path to heaven and I have mine. That's enough for us," Miriam said.

"What? That's it?" The words just flew out of my mouth, but I was surprised by the simplicity of her explanation. If a One-Way Bible preacher married outside the faith, he'd have to leave the ministry. I suspected there was more to this story than they were letting on.

"We didn't get there overnight," Father Claude said.

"It took a couple years actually," Miriam added.

Father Claude nodded. "There were the regular concerns—would our families accept this, how we'd raise our children if we had them, how we'd celebrate the holidays— but what troubled me most was whether I'd see Miriam in heaven."

"And vice versa," Miriam said. "We didn't want to enter

the marriage unless we both felt comfortable that our separate paths led to God."

"We searched our hearts and realized that we do," Father Claude said.

If I married a non-Christian, I'd be a nervous wreck, afraid that she'd die before accepting Christ and end up burning in hell for eternity. I'm sure Julie and Sam would laugh at that, but Jesus clearly says in the Gospel of John, "No man comes to the Father but by Me." Perhaps Claude hoped deep down to eventually bring Miriam to Christ.

"Our next problem was that the Qur'an forbids women marrying outside Islam," Miriam said.

"How did you come to terms with that?" I asked her, more curious than ever.

"Allah is neither Jewish nor Christian nor Muslim. Claude and I have different paths, but we worship the same God, even if we call Him by different names."

I probably should've shut up at that point, but I turned to Father Claude. "How did you get past that verse in John where Jesus clearly says—"

"'No man comes to the Father but by Me?'" Father Claude asked.

"Exactly."

He looked at me more seriously than he'd done up to that point. "You have to understand the context of that passage. It was written fifty years after Christ's death and just after the Jewish temple had been destroyed. It was a period when Christian Jews were being expelled from Jewish society. I believe John was pretty upset when he wrote those words, and that the reality is much more inclusive."

I'd never heard a minister treat the Bible so casually, but Father Claude was Episcopalian, which is about as far as you can get from fundamentalist in my hometown. "So you just don't pay that verse any attention?"

"That's right," he said. "The Bible was written by men after all." BUT QUOTING GOD'S, CHRIST'S WORDS.

"My dad always says, 'If one word of the Bible is wrong, it's all wrong.' What do you think of that?"

Father Claude started to speak but took a swig of wine instead. "I'm sure your father is a great man," he said, finally. "But I wouldn't let my faith stand or fall based on whether the Bible was one hundred percent accurate."

Father Claude's view sounded a bit wishy-washy to me, but he and Miriam both seemed okay with it. And who was I to judge? Besides, it wasn't my battle. "Well, I guess it's true that love conquers all," I said.

Phoebe raised her glass. "To love!"

That was something we all could agree on. We clinked glasses.

While I was helping clean up after dinner, my parents called. I was surprised they were up so late, although the clocks were one-hour earlier in Alabama since it was a different time zone. "Yes, ma'am, it was a real lively dinner," I said, then walked to the back of the apartment to get out of Phoebe's earshot. I spotted my backpack in the second bedroom and went inside.

"Did she serve alcohol?" The Preacher asked.

I ran my fingertips along the part in my hair. "Well, yes, sir, she served wine." Alcohol of any kind is strictly forbidden in our church, even though Jesus' first miracle was turning water into wine. This miracle wasn't a big secret or anything, but we didn't talk about it much. WINE AT LAST SUPPER.

I sat on the edge of the bed and removed my Bible and shaving kit from my backpack. "Dad, I promised Phoebe's preacher I'd go to his church tomorrow, but I'll make it to Brother Watson's church next Sunday." I wished I could take back my promise to Father Claude since going to a One-Way service could be the slice of home I was craving and would be a great excuse to explore Brooklyn. I'd been to exactly two Episcopal services before and nodded off both times. The hymns had no real beat to them and, compared to

CHURCH!

The Preacher, the sermons were delivered in a hushed monotone.

"Any pretty girls in New York?" The Preacher asked out of nowhere.

That question had always annoyed me, but I now welcomed it. "Yes, sir. I sit next to one who's from right here in New York City. Her name's Julie."

"You gonna ask her out?"

I was surprised The Preacher didn't ask if she was Christian. "Well…yeah, why not?"

Phoebe knocked and walked in. I mouthed to her "Momma and Dad."

She nodded and waved.

"Oh, here she is now," I said. "She says 'hi.'"

"Preacher, we'd better get to bed," Momma said. "You've gotta get to church early in the morning. Jake, please give Phoebe our love."

"Okay, I love y'all—I'll call you tomorrow," I said, then put the phone down.

Phoebe handed me a key. "Here's your very own key to Chez Phoebe. Just think of this place as your weekend vacation home away from school."

"For real? That's so great of you, Phoebe!" I wanted to hug her.

"But next weekend we're invited to the Hamptons!" she said with a big grin, like the Queen of England had sent us a handwritten invitation for dinner or something.

"Who are they?"

She tried to suppress a laugh. "Long Island. The beach!"

I loved the beach but realized that next weekend might bring a boatload of homework or maybe even a date with Julie. I just couldn't plan that far ahead right now. "Sounds like fun—can I get back to you? This program is sort of intense."

"Of course," she said, as if she doubted that everything I was up to was school-related. "Now let's get you unpacked. I'll make some space for you in the closet."

Phoebe opened the closet door and pushed aside some of the hanging clothes.

Although I'd never been in her apartment before, I felt right at home in that bedroom—the highboy had been my grandparents' and was the cousin to my dresser back home. My grandparents' photo sat front and center on the built-in desk.

I took off my suit jacket and tried to squeeze it into the tiny space Phoebe made for me in the closet. Unfortunately, it was jam-packed with colorful blouses, handbags, designer high-heeled shoes, and several of Grandmother Clarke's hats. I hoped Phoebe never needed them—her hair certainly seemed to be holding up pretty well.

"Thanks for throwing the dinner party for me," I said. "It was awfully nice."

She leaned back against the desk and crossed her arms. "Are you kidding? It was completely selfish: I wanted to show off my handsome, smart, and engaging nephew, and you were a complete hit. Everyone loved you!"

I removed a folded white shirt and tie from my overnight bag and picked up an empty hanger. "Oh, I think I came across as a bit of a hick with that 'Islamic terrorist' comment."

"Don't give it another thought—that livened things right up. I'm just sorry Julie couldn't join."

My thoughts suddenly turned back to Julie. She was probably on a date with some prep school type. While my head recognized that she was so out of my league, there was no convincing my heart of that. I wouldn't see her until Monday and that seemed like an eternity away. "Yeah, me too. Maybe I'll ask her out next week. What's a good romantic place? Well, romantic but not crazy romantic."

"Like cool-romantic? Try Sushi Samba."

I closed the closet door and crinkled my nose. "Sushi?"

"If you really want to impress her—it'll be my treat!" she said.

"Oh, that's alright. I've got plenty of money. Honest."

"Jake, I'd be thrilled to pick up the tab."

"That's okay," I said. She'd already done so much for me as it was. "Phoebe, thanks for telling me about this program at Columbia. I never thought I'd have the opportunity to spend six weeks in New York, much less study at the most prestigious journalism program in the world. It wouldn't have happened without you."

She grinned. "Six weeks? I could easily see you living here—that's why I wanted you to come while you're still young. After church tomorrow, I've arranged a tour of the entire city."

"Cool! All the way down to Ground Zero?"

"Oh, um, if you want to," she said, like that hadn't been on the itinerary. "I think you're going to love St. Bart's tomorrow. Claude is preaching and he is hilarious in the pulpit."

"I didn't realize you were such a big churchgoer," I said. "I think that's great. What brought you to the Lord?"

She halfway chuckled. "We don't even talk like that in my church, but I know what you're asking. I used to despise religion. I thought it was for the weak-minded, an escape that wasn't any better than booze or drugs or fast love. I mean, do any of them get you any closer to the truth?"

"So what changed your mind about church?" I asked.

Her eyes suddenly turned glassy, like she was looking inside herself. "I don't know. I guess I just softened with age. And I eventually realized that it's better than booze and drugs and fast love."

"I see," I said, but I really didn't.

Phoebe looked at her watch. "Goodness, it's late. Do you have everything you need? Got a toothbrush? Would you like some water?"

"I'm all good."

As I hugged her goodnight, I wondered what Phoebe could be hiding. What brought her to church? Could it have something to do with her suddenly turning up at my grandparents for the holidays a few years back? Whatever it was, she wasn't talking, which made me that much more curious. Fortunately, I had five more weeks to figure it out.

CHAPTER 11

Back at the dorm on Monday morning, I was standing before the bathroom mirror with my hair unparted and messy, the way Julie seemed to like it. I had decided to ask her out again, if not today then tomorrow, and was practicing my pitch.

"Julie, would you be my guest for..."

"Hey, I was thinking about maybe heading downtown..."

"Ever had sushi? I figured maybe it was time I—"

Someone knocked. "Jake, are you almost finished in there?" Raj called through our bathroom door.

How embarrassing—I hoped he hadn't heard me. "Sure, come on in," I said, standing back so the door wouldn't smack me.

A shirtless Raj entered with his toothbrush and toothpaste.

"Good morning," I said, checking out his white, drawstring underwear.

"What did you do to your hair?" he asked.

"Oh, um, I'm trying something new," I said, then scurried out of the bathroom.

When Raj and I walked into class, I spotted Julie turned around chatting with Alexandros, dangling her arm on the back of my chair. She playfully smacked his knee and laughed, as if he'd said something slightly off-color. Alexandros smiled and leaned in.

I was confused. Was she into him? Hadn't Julie and I shared a real moment the other night at the subway steps? Or was she just playing with me? Was I that stupid? Or maybe it was all in my head—it's not like she took me up on my offer

117

to have dinner at Phoebe's. Those thoughts knocked all the air out of my plan to ask her out.

I followed Raj into our row but, even after we arrived, Julie didn't move her arm. I felt invisible as I stood there, waiting for her to move, until she finally shifted long enough for me to take my chair between her and Sam.

Sam slapped my shoulder. "Morning, brah!"

He held my gaze for just a second too long. It seemed innocent enough but there was something intoxicating and dangerous about it, too, like a Ouija board.

I looked away and played it cool. "Morning, sir. How was your date Saturday night?"

Maybe that was a little too cool: I wasn't that curious about Sam's date, but I was an ace at filling awkward moments with stupid questions.

"I thought it went awesome, but I've texted him twice and haven't heard back."

"That sucks," I said to the poor guy.

His eyes moved upward, toward my hair. "I like your new look, man. That took some work. Julie, check out Jake's hair."

I wanted to die. Now Julie would think I styled my hair for her benefit. I mean, I did but I didn't want *her* to know that.

"What's that?" she asked. "Oh, hey, Jake. Not bad for a first effort. I like."

My face must've gone ten shades of red. I suddenly realized I was covering my privates. I guess somewhere deep down, I felt naked.

A short woman with frizzy blond hair walked in and placed her books on the podium. She looked maybe twenty-five but her thick eyeglasses reminded me of the pair Miss Ruby Smith wore back home. Unlike Miss Ruby, I could actually imagine this woman smiling.

"I'm Professor Kelly Ellis, and today I'll provide an overview of ethics in journalism. Professor Greenberg is still marking your editorials and will return them later this week."

I was bummed since I viewed my failure to write that editorial as epic, and now it would be hanging over my head for at least another day.   _Not todays lib news._

Professor Ellis delved into ethics, emphasizing the importance of accuracy, truthfulness, unbiased reporting, and objectivity. She differentiated between public figures and private persons and explained how reporters in many countries, including the U.S., have much more protection against civil suits when reporting on public figures, but that this varies from country to country. Minimizing harm was a big theme, and especially for those who were inexperienced in speaking with reporters.

It was all very interesting, but after about an hour, I began to zone out. Julie was flipping through a Saks Fifth Avenue handbag catalogue and even Sam was doodling in the margin of his leather notebook.

"Who can tell me about Jayson Blair?" Professor Ellis asked out of the blue.

Every student raised his hand except Julie, who was fixated on handbags.

The professor scanned the room, then consulted her seating chart and called out, "Julie Aaron."

"Here," Julie said absentmindedly.

"Well, Miss Aaron, would you please answer the question?" she asked, tucking a frizzy strand of blond hair behind an ear.

The students in the front row peered back at Julie like buzzards anticipating the final breath of a fallen deer.

Professor Ellis glared at Julie through her thick, gold-rimmed glasses.

Without thinking, I whispered, "Plagiarizer." My Southern gentility simply overpowered my moral compass right there in the middle of an ethics lecture.

The professor suddenly stared right at me. Uh-oh. Had she caught me?

Julie looked up but didn't bother closing the catalogue. "Please repeat the question."

"Can you tell me about Jayson Blair?"

"Of course. In May 2003, Jayson Thomas Blair resigned from the *New York Times* in disgrace. The paper discovered he had plagiarized articles from other newspapers, fabricated quotes, and even entire interviews. He was twenty-seven."

Maybe Julie knew more about journalism than she was letting on.

"Correct. *The Times* launched a full investigation, discovering problems with over half of Mr. Blair's articles. They later printed an unprecedented front page apology that attempted to set the record straight."

Julie closed the catalogue and whispered back, "Photographic memory. It's a curse."

I chuckled and resolved once again to ask her out. For a few precious moments, I got caught up in the excitement of what a date with Julie would be like. I'd insist on picking her up at her building, splurging for a cab, and arranging for a nice corner table at a candlelit restaurant.

When I came back to reality, I realized that I'd missed Professor Ellis's last comments so I peeked over on Sam's paper to copy from his notes. He instinctively moved his left forearm so I could see. I was sort of touched by that.

"What *Washington Post* reporter received the Pulitzer Prize in 1981 only to have it taken away?" Professor Ellis asked. "Jacob Powell?"

My head swung around like it was spring-loaded.

Professor Ellis was looking right at me, having apparently singled me out.

I stared at the wall behind her attempting to summon the answer.

"I'll give you a hint. The name of the article was 'Jimmy's World.' It was in your reading assignment for last night," she said, putting a hand on her hip.

Last night's reading assignment was nearly a hundred pages long and about the last thing I wanted to do after such a great day with Phoebe and Miriam; we'd blown off the regular New York tourist attractions in favor of a modern furniture exhibition at Sotheby's, a seventy-five-foot-tall ancient Egyptian obelisk in Central Park, and drinks at the Carlyle Hotel. Miriam and I did finally hit Ground Zero but Phoebe opted out due to some business meeting she had in midtown. All this to say that I did read the first half of our assignment but only skimmed the rest. I was pretty sure the story revolved around drugs, but I couldn't remember if the reporter took the drugs or was writing about them.

Think! Think! Think! My heart was flopping around like a fish out of water. I finally said, "I'm sorry, professor, but I can't quite recall."

She then consulted her seating chart and called out, "Carlos Ramirez."

"Janet Cooke," Carlos said from behind me. "The story was about an eight-year-old heroin addict, but there was no such kid. Miss Cooke made him up."

That's right! The whole blasted story suddenly came rushing back to me. ᴸᵗᴮ ᴾᴬᴾᴱᴿ

"That put the *Washington Post* in hot water," the Professor said. "The paper ordered an entire investigation into the matter. The executive editor later apologized to the mayor and police chief of Washington, DC, for the incident. In both instances, the *Washington Post* and the *New York Times* took these ethical breaches very seriously. Why was that?"

I raised my hand so high I was practically airborne, but the professor called on Alex who said, "Because the credibility of the paper came into question—it is the biggest asset any paper has." ᴺᵒᵀ ᴬⁿʸ ᴹᵒᴿᴱ

"That is correct."

And quite possibly the easiest question ever.

As the class continued, the professor dove further into her lecture on ethics then assigned an essay for the next day. She instructed us to read the Op-Ed pages of the major U.S. papers including the *Washington Post*, the *New York Times*, and the *Wall Street Journal*.

"So learn from the mistakes of those who came before you. We're entrusted with significant power as journalists, but a great deal of responsibility comes along with it. Okay, that's all the time we have today."

As everyone began packing up, Alexandros leaned forward and whispered something in Julie's ear; they started giggling again. What did she see in him? I guess he was handsome if you were into guybrowy types. His father was some big shipping magnate—maybe Julie just went for rich guys, and I had to be the poorest kid in class.

As Sam left, he saluted me then tossed his messenger bag over his shoulder. There was something about him that still seemed to pull at me. Why was that? Maybe God hadn't exactly healed me last week but instead reset my sexual impulses so that I could choose between boys and girls. Was I now standing at a sort of sexual crossroads? Why was this all so confusing? It seemed that the older I got, the less I had things figured out. I murmured to myself, "Ἓν οἶδα ὅτι οὐδὲν οἶδα." One thing I know is that I know nothing.

Julie chuckled. "Socrates!" she said.

I must've said it louder than I thought. "You know Ancient Greek?" I asked.

"Some. From my classics courses."

She was full of surprises. If I was at a sexual crossroads, it was time for me to make a choice, and I was definitely choosing Julie over Sam. Maybe my knowledge of Ancient Greek bumped me up in her eyes a little. I took a deep breath—it was now or never. "Hey, I'm going to go check out this sushi place downtown. Sushi Samba?"

"I love Sushi Samba!" she said.

I sat a little taller. "Wanna join me? I could sure use some help with those chopsticks."

"I was going to hit Saks," she said somewhat dismissively.

I decided to go for broke. "Well, we could do both?"

"No, that's okay," she said. "I can go to Saks another time."

I jumped to my feet. "It's a straight shot on the 1 train, heading downtown," I said, grabbing her backpack.

"What kind of sushi do you like?" she asked.

"Well, I've never actually had sushi."

Yuck! "You're in for a treat!" she said with an evil grin. *RAW FISH UGH!*

Julie and I were hanging out at a table on the open roof garden of Sushi Samba, enjoying the cool night air and the view of Greenwich Village. Except for a handful of white brick apartment buildings and the yellow taxis moseying down Seventh Avenue, "the Village" is right out of *Oliver Twist* with its brick row houses huddled together on such a maze of narrow streets that even Julie admitted she sometimes had to ask directions to get around. She pointed at the distant peak of the Empire State Building, lit in red, white, and blue with Independence Day just around the corner. Looking at it was like a reality check—I was really in New York, eating sushi at this unbelievably posh restaurant with the most gorgeous and amazing girl I'd ever met. In that moment, I totally had that sensation of "being in the center of the universe."

A Japanese waiter plopped down a white platter filled with slices of <u>fish flesh</u> from every segment of the color wheel. Okay, perhaps the blues were underrepresented but every other hue was present and accounted for. Some of the orange, red, and even purple fish slices were kicking back on little rice beds while others were stuffed into little tiny rice wheels with green treads.

Julie had ordered the sushi using words like "Mekajiki" and "Tairagai." It all looked like shark bait to me, but *each one* of those tiny pieces of fish costs more than an entire McDonald's Value Meal supersized. I'd have to eat tuna fish sandwiches the rest of the week just to get back on budget.

The waiter produced a white ceramic bottle and poured a black liquid into two little dishes. It looked like it came from a squid's backside.

A big lump of disgust rose up my throat. "What's that?" I asked, trying to remain calm.

123

"That's just soy sauce," Julie said.

I hoped she wasn't pulling my leg.

With her chopsticks, Julie mixed some green paste into the alleged soy sauce. I felt the color drain right out of my face as she grabbed a disc of rice with her chopsticks, and swirled it in the mixture. It was filled with chunks of green and brown and had little red flecks of what looked like sesame seeds. Except sesame seeds weren't red.

She held the disc to my lips. "It's an eel cucumber roll. Just try it. The eel is cooked—nothing's raw."

"Promise?"

"Well, everything except the cucumber and the flying fish roe."

"Those little specs are fish eggs?" I asked, somewhat horrified.

"Yes and they're quite yummy."

My lips trembled as I inched forward and bit down on the roll from Julie's chopsticks.

"No, you have to take the whole thing." Julie jammed the roll into my mouth and giggled.

I scrunched my eyes and chewed with a frown that slowly righted itself. The soft and flaky eel contrasted nicely with the crunchy cucumber, and the overall effect was sweet and salty with a sting of horseradish. "Wow, that's really good, but something's missing." I flagged down a waiter. "Sir, can we get some tartar sauce?"

He looked completely baffled.

Julie chuckled. "The Japanese don't eat tartar sauce!"

At that, the waiter frowned, then scurried away.

"Now, let's try something a little more exotic." Julie picked up a slimy yellow blob, dragged it through the soy sauce, and held it to my lips. She was smiling way too big—like Dr. Frankenstein before he threw the switch.

"What's that?"

"Just try it," she said, gazing at me with her hypnotic brown eyes.

Somehow, being with Julie was as thrilling as any ride at the State Fair, even though it didn't require seatbelts. I couldn't believe she was feeding me the way I'd seen romantic couples do in the movies. Did that mean something? Was she feeling something for me too? The possibility made me feel more adventuresome, but if she wanted me to eat whatever it was at the end of those chopsticks, she'd have to earn it. Plus, a little resistance would probably make it that much more thrilling for her. "But, what is it?" I asked.

"Oh, it's just sea urchin. Listen, if you don't want—"

"No, I want the full experience." I closed my eyes and opened wide.

Julie stuffed the sushi in my mouth then held her head back and hollered. "Ewww!"

The taste was sweet but earthy with a slimy texture. I wouldn't go running out for more, but it wasn't bad.

"Do you know what you just ate?" she asked, snickering.

"Sea urchin," I said, still chewing.

Julie laughed so hard she was pounding the table with her palm. "Yes, but that was the *sex organ* of the sea urchin! They're hermaphrodites."

"Give me those chopsticks!" I said playfully, then studied the platter.

She looked at me like I was in way over my head, but I'd used chopsticks plenty of times at the China Town restaurant on the Tarsus Bypass. I wasn't exactly a pro, but I wasn't going to launch the sushi across the restaurant, either.

I maneuvered the chopsticks around a piece of sushi brimming with what looked like fifty tiny orange eyeballs or maybe they were eggs too. I made a buzzing sound while moving it in circles toward Julie's mouth as if it were a big bumblebee. She was crying with laughter but suddenly lunged for the sushi.

She chewed a couple of times, giggled, then covered her mouth.

I laughed my butt off at her and thought she might spit

her food clear across the table. She finally managed to swallow, then took a swig of water.

The connection I felt with Julie in that moment caused any lingering insecurities I had about her to simply vanish. I put the chopsticks down and leaned in on my elbows. "Wanna come to my aunt's house for supper Thursday night?" My words came out effortlessly, almost like someone else had spoken them.

"You have an aunt in New York?" she asked.

I suddenly felt cool as hell. "Yes! Momma's older sister. She's a hoot!"

Julie plucked up a piece of red sushi with her chopsticks, and swirled it idly around in the soy sauce. "I can't, but maybe you'll be my date Friday night? I'm setting Sam up with my friend Joshua. It's actually supposed to be a double date but I don't have a date yet myself. They're going to look so hot together. ~~And~~ Don't you think Sam is hot?"

Why was she bringing up Sam? He was the last person I wanted to think about—I wanted to focus on Julie and me. I halfway opened my mouth for her to feed me, but she stuck the sushi in her own. Disappointed, I picked up my chopsticks and stabbed for another one of the red numbers.

"Sam's hot, don't you think?" she repeated.

"I haven't really thought about it," I said. Or at least I'd been trying not to.

"You mean, you can't tell a hot guy from an ugly one?" she asked skeptically.

This was completely ruining the moment. I'd left Sam back at the sexual crossroads when I asked Julie out, but she wasn't going to let this go. "Well, yes, I guess if I ever stopped to think about it."

She put her chopsticks down and tapped her chin. "Okay, let's say you had to choose between Sam and ~~Raj~~, which would you pick? I mean, if you were gay."

I knew Julie was just trying to be provocative, but she was making me uncomfortable. Like a reformed smoker who steered clear of the smoking lounge, I didn't want to get into a discussion about hot guys. "Julie, you're sick. Why do you want to fix Sam up so much anyway?"

She leaned in, as if we were plotting a great caper together. "If they hit it off, Josie will owe me for sure, so maybe he'll convince his father to sit for one of my fashion shoots. I'm sure I could get portraits of the Mayor in *Harper's Bazaar*, which would totally get me discovered."

"Well, I might be able to join you. It's just that my aunt asked me to go to this place called the Hamptons this weekend. Ever heard of it?"

Julie smiled, then stroked my hand. "Which would you rather do?" she whispered.

I looked deep into her big brown eyes and allowed the excitement of the moment to cover me. How was it possible that I had captured the attention of this gorgeous, smart, funny, and superbly opinionated girl? In that moment, I somehow knew that Julie and I were destined to be together, which made me the luckiest guy on the planet. Maybe one reason God allowed me to come to New York was to meet her. Maybe that was the main reason. Of course, there was still the issue of our different faiths, but what I felt for her seemed powerful enough to overcome anything.

I flipped my palm over and held her hand. "I'd rather be with you on Friday. You've got a date."

CHAPTER 12

By the time Friday rolled around, Julie and I had had three more dates, if you counted our lunches together—just the two of us—a date. It certainly felt like we were dating. I found myself thinking about her all the time and playing back our conversations in my head when we were apart. Tonight was the night she was setting Sam up with Joshua, and that was definitely a date.

In class that day, our Layout and Design instructor, Professor Cates, handed back our marked-up editorials while we all loaded the day's assignment on our laptop. He was a dead ringer for Albert Einstein with his crazy white hair and matching mustache.

I was excited to finally get Professor Greenberg's feedback on our Empire Diner editorial, but was shocked that we'd gotten a "B-" with the note: "I'm docking you for not rotating roles. Horowitz can't write everything!"

Julie shrugged it off, but Sam shook his head at me, and I felt awful for wimping out on the writing. If I couldn't even complete a regular assignment, how did I expect to win an award?

Professor Cates launched into "best practices" for newspaper layout, such as letting news dictate design, giving each page a focal point, using fonts and borders to keep unrelated stories distinct, and varying the headline type to avoid "tombstoning" and "butting heads." His passion for design was only outweighed by his love of technology, and I think he intentionally set off a class-wide debate on whether the newspaper layout software worked better on Macs or PCs.

"You guys should get a Mac—everything's easier on a Mac," Julie said to Sam and me, then rolled her eyes.

Something stirred inside me when she rolled her eyes like that. I suddenly realized that I'd never met anyone more adorable in my entire life, and that made me want to kiss her right then and there, but I didn't, of course.

Professor Cates gestured for the class to quiet down and then promised he'd cover website design when he was back next week. "I think that's it for week two," he said, scanning a scrap sheet of paper on the podium. "Oh, one more thing: Professor Greenberg asked that I remind you to bring in *another* editorial idea for Monday and the one paragraph pitch on your final project concept."

The class let out a collective moan, but Julie had no trouble moving on from the day's lecture.

"So, Joshua and I will meet you guys at the theater just before seven?" she said to Sam and me.

"Awesome," Sam said. "Thanks for setting me up— that's so cool. He sounds like a lot of fun."

"Oh, he's dying to meet you!" Julie said.

"I'll get the tickets," I said.

SLASHER was plastered all over the theater marquee at Broadway and 84th Street. Sam and I were hanging outside with the tickets. I'd planned to wear my favorite blue Oxford shirt and khakis but Sam had insisted I wear one of his black polos—untucked—and a pair of his low waist jeans. If I bent over too far, my butt would've fallen right out.

As we waited, Sam couldn't seem to get comfortable; he clasped his hands, then put them in his pocket, then crossed his arms. As he scratched the back of his head, I peeked at the tattoo on his forearm then realized he'd caught me. I looked away but could feel him still staring at me. "So, um, tell me about your '4' tattoo," I said.

He held out his arm like he wanted me to hold it, but I didn't. "You're looking at it upside down, brah. It's *li liang*— the Chinese character for *strength*."

I studied Sam's forearm as if I were going to be tested on it later. Root-like veins twisted down to his black leather cuff and that mysterious tattoo was centered perfectly in the thick of it.

"I'm working on a larger design that'll cover my entire forearm."

"And your parents were cool about it?" I asked.

"It took my mom, like, a week to notice," Sam said.

I nodded and turned away but his gaze felt like a laser beam on my cheek. It had been nearly two weeks since I met Sam and although I'd gotten to know him somewhat, I still couldn't guess what he was really thinking. He never did or said anything to me that made me think he was doing it in a "gay" way, but there were moments when he came close. Like the time he put his hand on my back and kept it there as he told a funny story about his friend who was "sexually bipolar" (the guy constantly flip-flopped from tramp to celibate). That made me wonder about him and about myself. I'd certainly become more and more relaxed around Sam, and like Julie said, he was sexy. Just because I recognized that didn't necessarily mean that I was back at some sexual crossroads. Julie made it sound like it was okay for guys to notice other guys. Women complimented each other's looks all the time, but that didn't mean they were lesbians.

Sam started fidgeting again. He was clearly stressed and I was too: back home, taking a date to a movie rarely involved watching the show—it was just a convenient place to make out. What if Julie wanted to make out during the show? Janet Walters certainly hadn't given me high marks during my first attempt at making out, as everyone at Tarsus High can attest to. What if Julie thought my kissing stank too? Would she go blabbing to everyone at Columbia?

"Relax—this is supposed to be fun, remember?" I said, as much for my benefit as Sam's.

"I know," he said, then gestured at his tight, black T-shirt. "I wish I'd worn a different shirt."

"You look great," I said, trying to calm the guy down. "That cuff and those patent leather sneakers make you look like a super hero."

"More like a big gay cliché."

I laughed.

"So how many dates have you and Julie gone out on, brah?" Sam asked. "We've all noticed you sneaking away together at lunchtime."

It was exciting to think that people had noticed and were talking about us. Suddenly, I felt like a total stud. "And we thought we were being so clever," I said with a wink.

"Not so much."

I knew the answer, of course, but to play it cool, acted like I needed to do the math. "Let's see, this is our fifth date if you count the lunches."

"Have you kissed her yet?"

"Oh, man, I don't kiss and tell—out of respect for the girl." I said it like I was an old pro, but, of course, Janet Walters was the only girl I'd ever really kissed.

"Time to make your move, brah, if you haven't already."

I knew he was right, but this discussion wasn't exactly helping my nerves.

As a man wearing a white tank top passed, Sam checked him out. The guy was all arms and shoulders, and I wondered if that was Sam's type. I'd heard him talk about four different guys since I arrived in New York, and I wondered if they were all arms and shoulders as well. But from the way he looked at me sometimes, I wondered if I was Sam's type. Maybe he had multiple types. Wait, why was I thinking about Sam's type?

"So anyways, Jake, if it works out tonight that Joshua and I hit it off, do you think Alexandros could crash with you?"

I let out a groan. Sam was the most open person about sex I'd ever met, but I was a total virgin, still trying to master the art of the French kiss; sex was the last thing I felt comfortable talking about.

"I promise to return the favor," he said with a smirk.

Was that smirk some sort of challenge? Did he think that I'd never make a move with Julie? Or was that smirk his way of treating me like one of the guys? His request *was* the sort of favor guy friends ask of each other, although it normally involved a *girl*. Was I ready to abandon my vow of chastity by becoming a sexual enabler or going so far as to have sex with Julie myself? Certainly, the thought of leaving my virginity in New York was kind of thrilling because it would somehow connect me with the City for the rest of my life. People went to New York for stuff like that all the time.

I decided to hedge my bets about tonight. "Sam, you're pretty cool, but I wish you weren't such a tramp."

He grinned, making his square jaw even more pronounced. He was hot—to use Julie's term—and could probably have any gay guy he wanted, and he seemed to want them all.

I checked my watch. "Where are they? The movie starts in eight minutes."

"Who knows with Julie?" he said. "I'd better go save seats."

I handed him a ticket, then we did that awkward thing where you both move to the same side, then the other, then back, in step. As we continued this shuffle, face-to-face, my head was filled with his grapefruit cologne, and all that back and forth made me kind of dizzy.

I finally stood still, and as he passed, we both turned and smiled as blood rushed to my face—I guess I was just embarrassed from the awkwardness of it all, but Sam didn't seem to notice.

I gazed toward downtown hoping to spot Julie, but Broadway seemed awfully quiet for a Friday night. Dark clouds were heading in from the west, and it smelled like rain. I was glad I brought my umbrella.

I quickly texted my parents that I wouldn't be reachable until nine-thirty New York time, in compliance with our "must answer" policy. I just hoped they assumed I was at dinner rather than seeing an R movie. While I was at it, I sent a quick text to Tracy: "Sup? Seeing Slasher 2nite!"

Just then, someone covered my eyes from behind and said, "Guess who?"

I smiled. "Hmmm. Let's see. Big hands. Questionable breath. Professor Greenberg?"

Julie chuckled and playfully slapped my back.

"I like him already," a deep, inviting voice said.

I turned and faced a tan guy with green eyes and brown hair, wearing white jeans and a snug, black shirt. He stood a little taller than Julie and definitely knew his way around the gym.

Julie looked stunning in her khaki jeans and a blue, scoop-necked blouse. "Hey, get your own man, pawtna. Joshua, this is my classmate Jake."

"Classmate" stung a little—weren't we kind of dating?

I smiled and shook Joshua's hand. "Sam's inside saving seats. Y'all go on in. I'll get the popcorn."

My phone vibrated. Tracy's text read: "Going bowling 2nite. You behave! ;-)"

Inside, I nearly broke the bank, buying four bottles of water and two tubs of popcorn, stacking one on top of the other. I had to stick my umbrella in my back pocket, and by the time I got into the theater, previews had started. It took me a while to find my posse in the dark, crowded theater. Joshua and Sam were chatting away, completely oblivious to the fact that everyone was trying to watch the previews. Clearly, things were off to a good start for them.

I handed Sam a big tub of popcorn and two bottles of water.

"Thanks, brah," he said, barely looking at me.

Julie motioned over at them and gave me a thumbs up. She took a water and the other tub while I settled in.

There was something nice and peaceful about the moment, even though we were about to see a movie billed as "the bloodiest film of all time." I'd been in town for less than two weeks but was already making some good friends, going on my first real date, and even hanging out with the son of the Mayor of New York. That's ridiculous! And it had nothing to do with the fact that my father was a big preacher. A huge surge of enthusiasm pulsed through me with the realization that I was hanging with the cool kids for the first time in my life.

I woofed down a handful of popcorn as the movie began with creepy music and an insane asylum illuminated by a sudden burst of lightning. Certainly the opening wasn't very original.

Julie seemed totally into the movie without any indication of wanting to make out.

Although the show was bloody and suspenseful, I spent much of it ticking back and forth obsessively between two thoughts like an out-of-control metronome.

The first obsessive thought was over Sam's request to use my room. If I let him, I'd not only be a sexual enabler, I'd be condoning his lifestyle. But that seemed so judgmental, which was something I'd quit being a long time ago. The fact was that I could stay in my crappy bare-bones dorm room or have Phoebe's entire apartment to myself. I wondered if I should ask her permission first, but she did say that I should treat it as my "vacation home." If I stayed at her apartment tonight, I'd just phone her up tomorrow and let her know since it was a last minute thing.

My second obsessive thought was over Julie. She still hadn't given any indication of wanting to make out, but then no one was making out in the theater as far as I could tell. I began to question whether this was even a date, but she did ask that I be her date tonight, right? If it was a date though, why did she call me her "classmate" earlier? Sushi Samba had been a date for sure—she fed me with chopsticks, I picked up the check, and we even held hands—and we'd had lunch together three times since, as I kept reminding myself. Maybe she wanted Joshua's stamp of approval before we moved along in our relationship. Come to think of it, she probably put Sam up to dressing me so I'd be more presentable to Joshua.

Julie let out a shout then self-consciously laughed at herself right away. That brought me back to the moment. Honestly, she was more entertaining than the show.

Sam and Joshua were leaning in real close, too close if you asked me, considering it was their first date. Maybe they *were* a match—I didn't know the first thing about gay dating.

But I found courage in their boldness—if these two guys could get close in the movies, then I could too. I took a deep breath and placed my arm around Julie.

She smiled at me and nuzzled in.

Yes!

I got so caught up in how great it was to be sitting there like any guy with his arm around a girl that I hardly paid any attention to the movie.

When the film finally came to its predictable ending and the not-quite-latched door of the insane asylum flung open with a clang—setting the wheels in motion for the inevitable *Slasher 2*—Julie screamed then laughed herself silly.

As the lights of the theater came up, Julie and Joshua tore off to the bathroom, but I wondered if they weren't just ducking away to compare notes on the date. I was dying to do exactly that with Sam. Even though I didn't exactly understand his gay lifestyle, I wanted to be there for him as a friend one hundred percent.

When I asked how it was going with Joshua, Sam looked disappointed. "He only, like, talks about himself. I don't think he's into me."

I could tell that Sam was already preparing himself for rejection. "From where I was sitting," I said, "you guys looked like you were getting along just dandy."

"We'll see."

My cell phone rang—the caller ID read "Dad-Mobile." It was nine-thirty on the dot. I started to answer but silenced it instead. Whatever "event" I was at could've just run over by a few minutes—I just hoped he wouldn't leave a message because then I'd have to call him back.

"Hey, maybe we should all go out for dessert," I said. "Julie and Joshua picked the movie so we could plan what we do next. What do you say?"

"Sounds fun, but I doubt Joshua will be into it."

"Then it'll just be the three of us," I said. Even if Joshua didn't appreciate Sam, I wanted him to know that Julie and I did. And speaking on behalf of Julie was exhilarating; it made me feel like she and I were an item even though we hadn't even kissed yet.

Sam smiled. "That's cool."

Joshua and Julie were giggling when they joined us near the exit. "Hey, you guys," Julie said, "Joshua has to take off to meet some friends."

Sam pouted at me as if to say, "Told ya!"

Then Joshua turned to Sam. "Wanna join me?"

Sam's face lit right up. "Sure!"

I was glad Sam wasn't being dumped, but at the same time, I was hurt that Sam had blown off my dessert invitation. It felt like that moment in *Bambi* when the young deer couldn't find his mother and you just knew she was dead. In the same way, I had this budding sense of dread that Sam would be hanging out with Joshua so much he wouldn't have time for me. I'd been abandoned by enough female friends in new relationships to know that Sam and I would spend a lot less time together if he and Joshua hit it off. I realized how selfish that line of thinking was and immediately reprimanded myself for it. Besides, seeing less of Sam might help me put my sexual crossroads in the rearview mirror once and for all. Every time I thought I finally had this thorn whipped, Sam would appear and it was like drawing a "Go to Jail" card in a game of Monopoly except it was a "Go to Hell" card and it was for real.

As Joshua kissed Julie goodbye, I leaned over and whispered to Sam, "Alexandros can sleep over tonight."

Sam smiled and slapped my back. "Thanks, Jake!"

I gave Joshua my best handshake to let him know that I wasn't raised in a barn and, as he and Sam ran out into the pouring rain, Julie asked, "What did Sam give you that big thank you for?"

I grinned, suddenly feeling like one of the boys. "Just a guy thing. How about dessert? There's this great place just around the corner—"

"But it's raining!"

I held out my umbrella, walked outside and popped it open in one fell swoop. It was truly a Hollywood-worthy performance, and one I could never repeat if my life depended on it. Holding the glass door open, I shouted back at her in my best New York accent, "Oh! So we'll get a little wet."

Julie laughed and hopped outside under my umbrella. We both darted down the block in the pouring rain toward the dessert shop.

Aunt Phoebe had suggested Café Lalo as a great after-movie spot and, boy, did she pick a winner. When we arrived, there were a few people waiting for a table ahead of us, but the hostess seemed to take a liking to Julie the moment she asked about something called a Chocolate Indulgence. She marched Julie and me past a fifteen-foot-long glass case filled with about a hundred different pies, cakes, and tarts, and then showed us to a window table.

Since Julie already knew what she wanted, I just ordered a slice of New York-style cheesecake myself, figuring that had to be on the menu.

I was still thinking about whether Sam would even notice me anymore if he and Joshua started dating. It suddenly seemed like a foregone conclusion that he wouldn't, and I wasn't very happy about that. On some level, I enjoyed all the attention he gave me, especially how he looked me up and down from time to time. There was something intoxicating about being appreciated like that, even when the person doing the appreciating was a guy.

I was dying to know what Julie thought about Joshua and Sam, but wondered how I could bring that up without seeming too eager.

I shouldn't have worried.

"So what did Sam think of Joshua?" Julie asked the moment we got settled.

Not wanting to betray Sam's confidence, I just shrugged and said, "I guess he thought Joshua was alright. Sam can be so secretive about these things, you know?"

She seemed to buy that. "Well, Joshua thinks Sam is totally hot," she said, leaning in with a grin. "I so see them together."

My insides suddenly burned like I was jealous or something. It was totally irrational, and I brushed it away as best I could. "I guess we all agree that Sam is a hot guy. You're a regular matchmaker, Julie."

"Not really," she said. "But I have a good feeling about this."

Over dessert, Julie went on to tell me that she and Joshua met in kindergarten and had run in the same circles ever since. Still, they weren't best friends or anything and, in fact, Joshua was a bit of an enigma to her, even after all these years. "I'm not sure he'll even *talk* to his father about my final project," she concluded.

"You're really proposing a fashion shoot of the Mayor as your final project?" I asked.

"Yes," she said. "We'll see if Josie comes through."

"You know there's a big difference between a photo essay and a fashion shoot. You need to tell a story, and there's no retouching—"

Julie dismissed my concern with a flick of her hand. "If I get this into *Harper's*, none of that other crap really matters, does it?"

I chuckled, admiring the way she ignored the rules and blazed her own trail. I wished I could do that sometimes.

"He really liked you, by the way."

"Who?"

"Joshua."

That made me feel even guiltier for my jealousy, but I didn't want to let on. "I hope so—I feel half-naked walking around in these hip-huggers Sam made me wear. They should come with a warning label: low clearance."

Julie nearly spewed tea all over me. She grabbed a napkin and covered her mouth.

"You put him up to dressing me, didn't you?" I asked.

Julie gasped like she was shocked I could even think such a thing. "What? You think I'd do that?"

I looked at her cockeyed. "C'mon, 'fess up."

"Well, maybe I dropped a hint."

"Yeah, I'm sure you were real subtle."

She laughed. "What about you—what's your final project?" she asked.

"I'm thinking about doing an investigative report on the Empire Diner. Something doesn't smell quite right about that zoning situation."

"Maybe Joshua would help you locate the city official who gave the landlord those special building permits," she said.

I liked Joshua more and more by the second. "Wow! Do you think he would?"

"Hard to say, but his dad would certainly know the best person for you to contact," she said, suppressing a yawn and checking her watch. "I should get home. My parents will be calling from La Jolla around eleven."

"La Jolla? Where's that?"

"Outside of San Diego—they go every summer."

"For the *entire* summer?"

"Yes."

I couldn't imagine my parent's taking a vacation without me, nor could I imagine them letting me have the run of the house for even one evening, much less an entire summer. "Why don't you go with them?"

"I used to. It's a beautiful place but after a week of sunbathing and 'important parties,' I just want to kill myself. Plus my stepmom's a complete tyrant. I got out of going last year by taking that Parson's photography course, and that's really why I'm at Columbia now. Everyone's happier this way. Trust me."

It almost sounded like Julie's family viewed her as some kind of burden, or at least her stepmother did. I wondered why she never mentioned her mother. "So, are your parents divorced?"

Julie shook her head. "My mom died when I was eight."

I instinctively reached for her hand. "Oh Julie, I'm so sorry. What happened?"

She shrugged. "One minute we were on the floor playing with my dolls and the next she was collapsed against the wall. She wouldn't wake up."

"Gosh, was it a heart attack or something?"

"Aneurism. Thoracic aortic."

"Julie, that is so completely awful. I—"

She pulled her hand away. "Don't. It's okay."

"I'm—I'm just—"

"I know. Everyone is."

As a PK, I've seen tons of sickness and death, and learned early on that sympathy makes some people uncomfortable. I guess Julie was one of those people.

She took a long, deep breath and tossed her napkin down on the table. "Let's get out of here."

I didn't want the evening to end, but it sounded like she needed to get home.

I grabbed the bill before Julie could. I just needed to say goodbye then swing by the dorm to pick up Phoebe's key and sign out for the night. Curfew wasn't until one in the morning on Fridays so I had plenty of time.

"Jake, you got the movie," she said. "I wanted to get this."

"I've really had a great time," I said, waving her off like

it was nothing, but between the other night at Sushi Samba and picking up the movie tickets and refreshments for everyone tonight, I was going broke fast.

She looked up at me with her big brown eyes. "I was sort of hoping you'd see me home."

Why hadn't I, a supposed Southern gentleman, thought of that? Especially after what she'd just shared? Could I be more clueless? "It would be my pleasure, Miss Aaron," I said, trying to lighten the moment with my thickest Southern drawl.

A bus stop was right outside the café, but Julie insisted on taking a taxi due to the rain—her treat. We hopped into a big yellow Ford.

"550 Park," she said to the dark, bearded driver.

For the first time since the movie, Julie and I sat in silence. She was probably pondering whether to invite me upstairs, and I was pondering whether I'd accept should she choose to do so. Our church literature specifically advocated *never* taking a date home if your parents weren't there, since that could lead to overwhelming temptation. But after our fifth date, shouldn't we at least kiss? It wasn't our fault that our parents weren't in town and wouldn't be for the entire summer. Were we to just never do anything? Sam would probably want to compare notes on our respective dates and Raj would certainly ask if we'd made out. Of course, I wouldn't kiss and tell but Julie probably would. With that thought, my pulse began to race, and I willed my hand over to hers.

She took it! *Score!* We smiled at each other, and I lit up like Times Square.

By the time I had worked up my courage to lean over and kiss her, the cab pulled up to this Versailles-looking apartment building on Park Avenue. I'd never seen anything quite like it—Phoebe's brick building was nice but this one was all beige-colored stone. Maybe even marble.

Julie insisted on paying. I jumped out with my flimsy umbrella and covered us both as best I could while we scurried through the pouring rain to her entrance.

"It's really coming down!" she said. "Why don't you come up until it stops?"

"Sure," I said, thrilled with the idea.

We were both laughing as we entered her huge lobby with ceilings twenty feet high.

I followed her past the night doorman, who was reading *The Post*. "Hello, Jimmy," she said to him. "No need helping me and my cousin out of the rain. You're obviously so busy here."

Jimmy turned the page without looking up. "You sure have lots of cousins, Miss Aaron."

"Very funny, Jimmy," she said, whisking past him.

Julie and I jumped into an oak-paneled elevator with little brass lamps mounted to the walls—I bet even Phoebe would've been impressed. Julie fished through her designer bag and pulled out her keys, inserted one into a lock next to "PH" on the control panel and turned the key.

I took a deep breath. This was big. I'd never gone home with a girl when her parents weren't there, much less a rich girl who lived in a Park Avenue penthouse. I was in completely uncharted territory, but Julie didn't seem nervous at all. She threw her glistening wet hair back over her shoulders, causing a single bead of water to shoot down her cleavage. I felt my face go red and was glad she couldn't read my thoughts.

As the elevator made its smooth climb to the top, I rubbed the back of my neck and ran through Janet Walters' three-step approach to French kissing in my head.

When the elevator doors opened, Julie stepped out into darkness, her heels clink-clink-clinking on the floor. Something started beeping and a light above a wall keypad sprang to life. Even in the dim light, I sensed the space was huge by the way those beeps resonated off the walls and the large picture windows in the distance.

She punched a code into the keypad and hit a bank of light switches. As the lights came up, I realized we were standing in a marble hallway with twelve-foot ceilings and sparkling marble floors that could've been right out of the soap opera Mamaw used to watch. Phoebe's home looked like a doublewide by comparison.

I followed Julie into a huge living room filled with modern sofas, chairs, and rugs all in beige, which I was beginning to realize was New York's signature color.

I was so impressed by the surroundings, I could only think to say, "This sure is a nice place you've got here."

"Thanks. My stepmother and I managed to redesign this room last year without killing each other. That was during my interior design period. Pre-fashion photography. I chose most of the colors. She insisted on that coffee table there." Julie pointed at an oversized coppertop coffee table surrounded by a host of sofas and chairs. "Isn't it awful? Feel free to put your feet on it."

I laughed as I walked over to the big windows. From this height and time of night, the trees in Central Park looked like clumps of broccoli.

"I'm having a glass of champagne—want some?"

"Got any Sprite?"

"If you must," she said, taking a couple of glasses from a shelf.

I sat down on one of the two sofas and started pumping my leg nervously. I heard a low tick-tick-tick. It came from an expensive-looking black metal clock on the side table with engraved Roman numerals surrounding glass-enclosed hands. I couldn't resist picking it up, and it was heavier than it looked. I looked at the time: ten forty-five.

I'd have to leave by twelve-thirty to make curfew. If only I'd brought Phoebe's key, I could've just called the front desk at Carman Hall then headed right to her apartment. I wanted to kick myself.

Julie punched a few keys on another wall pad; slow music came up.

She walked over with two champagne glasses and placed

them on the coffee table in front of me, then sat close by, smiling at nothing in particular. It could've been the lighting or the way she loosened up at home, but Julie was more gorgeous than ever—her eyes actually seemed to glow. Everything about the moment seemed perfect.

My heart began to race as I raised my glass to hers. "To new adventures."

She looked deep into my eyes and clinked my glass. "To new adventures."

Only then did I stop pumping my leg.

We both took a sip and then sat quietly, staring at the room.

Awkward.

Finally, I pointed to one of the sofas. "So what color would you call that fabric there?"

"That? It's called café cream."

"And these walls?" I said, gesturing around.

"Antique parchment."

"And that side chair?"

"That's my favorite, it's—"

I chuckled.

"What?"

I snuffed out my smile. "Sorry. What color is it?"

"Honeycomb. What's so funny?"

"Oh, I'm just making a list of all the ways you New Yorkers can say 'beige.'"

Julie smiled then chugged half her champagne. I'd seen guys in the bowling alley parking lot do that to their beers, but never a girl. But then I'd never met a girl like Julie before. She was so confident, so sure of herself. Not even the smartest, most sophisticated girls back home were in the same league as her. Not even Tracy. I mean, how could they be, living in Tarsus when Julie was in a Park Avenue penthouse? Her confidence and sophistication was as intoxicating as her beauty. Maybe more so. Rude & aggressive JY

She looked at my lips and then into my eyes. My heart

started racing again and my hands suddenly felt clammy. I took a deep breath and thought back to the three-step approach Janet Walters had taught me.

One: Begin with a slow approach. I sat our glasses down on the coffee table, looked into Julie's eyes and leaned in. She met me half way. I closed my eyes as our mouths met. Janet Walters' lipstick had tasted like vanilla but Julie's reminded me of a crayon I'd eaten in pre-school. But why was I thinking of Janet Walters' lipstick? I needed to focus.

Two: Be gentle. Her lips were soft and playful. I was careful not to press too hard and kept my tongue in check— that would come later. I pulled away for a moment but kept my mouth close to hers.

I peeked at Julie: seeing her eyes closed and lips pursed, Julie looked like she was standing in front of a birthday cake, making a wish, but then she moved in just like Janet said.

We kissed a moment longer before Julie pulled away and opened her eyes. "You okay?" she asked.

"Absolutely!" I said, then lunged in for another round just to prove to her it was true. Maybe I overdid it a tad because she placed a hand on my chest like she was now trying to slow me down.

Tick-tick-tick.

I peered over Julie's shoulder at the clock on the table, which said it was almost eleven. Getting home would require a bus, a walk, and a subway. I'd need to allow thirty to forty-five minutes, which meant I'd need to leave by twelve-fifteen to make our one o'clock curfew. That gave Julie and me an hour and twenty-two minutes. Would we keep doing this for an hour and twenty-two minutes?

Julie cupped my head in her hands. Why didn't I think of that? She moaned softly then leaned further in.

I decided to kick this into overdrive. I leaned in and parroted back Julie's moans, but mine sounded kind of silly to me.

Tick-tick-tick. We'd only been making out a few minutes

and had well over an hour to go. I started thinking that maybe I should leave at midnight since the buses might not run that often late at night. If I missed curfew, Columbia could send me home. Well, they probably wouldn't but you never knew.

Wait, what was the third step Janet taught me? With all those thoughts rushing through my head, I couldn't remember. Focus, Jake! Maybe I just needed a quick jump-start. I conjured up Sam, only in underwear, sitting cross-legged on my bed. Suddenly, that gooey warm feeling came flooding in as I imagined holding him tight, kissing him, then putting my—

Hands! That was the third step. But I didn't know what to do with my hands. If this were Sam, I would...wait, what am I doing? This is so messed up!

A wave of shame covered me like a lead quilt.

My toes curled and I suddenly felt nauseous, like I'd just swallowed spoiled milk. It was the taste of disgust, and it wasn't because of Julie—I was disgusted with myself and suddenly wanted to hightail it out of there and never look back.

"Do whatever you want. Whatever makes you feel right," she whispered.

She clearly wasn't picking up on what was happening inside my head: the only thing that was going to make me feel right was to explain that I wasn't feeling it at all, but what explanation could I give? That I just wasn't into hot, intelligent, rich girls? It was a little late to say I only dated Christians, but I needed to give her some reason so she wouldn't go around blabbing that I hadn't used my hands the way Janet Walters had done. Knowing Julie, she'd come right out and say it—Jake doesn't like making out with girls.

Tick-tick-tick.

While still kissing me, Julie slipped her hand down the front of my shirt then started unbuttoning it in a tender but greedy way, moaning all along.

My throat seized up with a sudden realization: I was gay all right—I hated hunting, I hated college football, and I hated making out with girls. How many more data points did I need? There was just no pretending otherwise. God hadn't healed me that day; I was probably just having some sort of nervous breakdown. I suddenly had to get the hell out of there.

I giggled and backed away from Julie's probing hand, trying to pass my withdrawal off as ticklishness. "Julie, I've gotta check in at the dorm before midnight or they could send me home on the next bus."

"Isn't curfew at one o'clock on weekends?"

"No, I—I think it's midnight," I lied.

"Sam told me it's at one."

"It's midnight—I'm pretty sure," I lied again.

I wanted to just up and run but had to play it cool so Julie wouldn't suspect anything. I leaned in and pecked her on the lips, then stood and smiled down at her while buttoning up my shirt.

She looked into her champagne glass. I collected mine and walked it over to the bar. "Talk tomorrow?" I asked.

"Sure," she said.

I stood there, wondering if I should just tell her the truth, but once that genie's out of the bottle... "Julie, I—I—"

She looked up at me and forced a smile.

"It's not just the curfew. I think you hung the moon, and, well, I feel I should go before things get, you know, too carried away."

She nodded.

I felt awful—I was now leading her on even more.

We just looked at each other for a few seconds, until I finally turned away. "Okay, I'm going to go then."

She nodded but didn't stand.

I walked into the entryway and laid down on the elevator button.

Click. Click. Click.

Her footsteps were getting louder and louder—she was coming up behind me. I held my breath, willing myself not to turn around.

147

She stopped right behind me.

A chill coursed through me, like Julie was staring daggers right at me.

The elevator doors opened with a ding. I jumped in and tried not to look up but couldn't help myself. Julie stood, arms crossed, looking confused and disappointed. She wasn't staring daggers at all.

But tomorrow she'd be pissed as hell.

CHAPTER 13

I swung by my dorm room around eleven-thirty to grab Phoebe's keys. Neither Raj nor Alexandros were there so I switched on the light and slammed the door. I paced back and forth as that burr grew, digging deeper and deeper into my gut, just like old times. I'd wasted the last four years begging God to take away this homosexual desire that raged inside of me. "Heal me Jesus! Take this thorn from me!" It was like talking to a brick wall. Jesus clearly had no intention of healing me! Why did it take me so long to figure that out? *Idiot! Idiot! Idiot!*

Just hours ago, I was stupid enough to think that Julie and I could spend our lives together, but now I wondered if she would ever even speak to me again. She'd looked so hurt when I left. She deserved better; I never should've even asked her out. I mean, there I was, fantasizing about Sam before our first make-out session even got going good. She's off-the-charts gorgeous, and I'm fantasizing about a guy?

But even now, just thinking about Sam...

The Bible on my desk seemed to mock me, as if inviting me to read once again what a hopeless sinner I was, destined for eternal damnation.

And from Raj's dresser, the once-gentle eyes of his yellow-turbaned Muhammad picture now seemed to glare at me, as if he was in on this too.

How could God fool me like this? What more did He want? Would it finally appease Him if I opened a vein and offered myself as a human sacrifice? Furious, I snatched up my Bible, wanting to rip it in two. "Lies. All lies!" I hissed, then threw it into the garbage can next to my desk. A pang of guilt welled up inside me like I had betrayed an old friend. Some friend! I hated myself even more for fishing the so-called Word of God out of the trash almost as quickly as I'd tossed it in, but I slammed it inside my desk drawer, out of sight. Good riddance!

Papaw once preached that God allowed our burdens to be there for a reason, and it was futile to pray for Him to take them away. He said we could try going *over*, *under*, *and around them* but we'd never get beyond them until we went *through* them. At the time, I thought his words showed a surprising shortfall of faith, but now I realized that he clearly knew what he was talking about. Maybe the Jesus I had created in my head was too much like Santa Claus: eager to give me whatever I threw on my wish list.

It was simply time to accept that I was in this *alone*. It was time I went *through* this.

I sat down at my desk and pulled up the *Time Out New York* site on my computer. I clicked on the "Gay and Lesbian" link. Photos of guys in tight T-shirts—and a few with no shirts at all—filled the screen. I still felt guilty for these desires, the same way I once felt guilty for eating steak after learning it was really cow. But that guilt didn't stop me from eating the steak, and this guilt would no longer stop me from kissing a boy. I was gay, and I was carnivore. Big deal. That was simply who I was.

I scanned the list of bars, but they were all for ages twenty-one and over. Unlike Sam and Raj, I'd never bothered with a fake ID—I never thought I'd need one. Then I saw a listing for Heaven Bar with the tagline "New York's only gay teen party place." That was the bar I saw those hot gay teenagers walk out of in Chelsea a while back.

Sam's jeans I had on were fine, but I needed to lose the polo since not one guy in the photos was wearing one. I plundered through my dresser finding a tight white T-shirt I'd over-dried a few days earlier and put it on.

I woke up Sandman downstairs, signed out for the weekend, then headed to the subway. It seemed like everyone was gawking at me, probably because people in the Columbia neighborhood don't go parading around in tight T-shirts. Except people like Sam.

The train unexpectedly ran express south of 96th Street, and I was standing across from Heaven Bar in no time with my heart drumming in my ears. The courage that had filled me back at the dorm had all but evaporated, and I was wracking my brain for a good reason to cross the street and go inside. What if I was opening a door that might not close again? But I had to do this. It was now or never. If I saw anyone I knew, I could always say I was meeting Sam.

The sign outside the bar was very clear: ID REQUIRED—NO PATRONS OVER 20 ALLOWED.

A tall, well-built security guard sat on a stool to the left of the door. My heart thumped as I presented him my Alabama driver's license with this awful shot of me in braces. He looked from the license to me and then handed it back. And just like that, I entered my first bar ever, and it was a gay bar to boot.

Club music blared from large speakers scattered throughout, and everything was white: white floors, white low-back bar stools, and a white bar that glowed from within. I expected the place to be completely packed, but it was only about half filled, mostly with guys lined up alongside the walls, leaving a clear path to the bar.

As I headed to get a drink, I felt eyes track me as if I were on a parade route. I sat in front of the soda dispenser, next to a blond beefy guy in a buttoned shirt and khakis. He looked like a math geek with his wire-rimmed glasses, but there was something sexy about him. Mostly, he seemed safe and somewhat approachable.

I waved at the bartender like I'd seen on television. "Coca-Cola, please."

I felt the supposed math geek eyeing me but no matter how hard I willed it, my head wouldn't turn towards him.

The very moment the bartender sat my drink down, a voice behind me shouted over the music, "One Red Bull, please." A tan guy stepped between the blond and me, looking my way with a big smile. "Well, hello," he purred at me like that baton-twirling Kenny Ballard but without the Southern accent, then flashed me a 1,000-watt smile.

He was handsome and all, but his sleeveless T-shirt emblazoned with the latest female pop sensation was a complete turnoff. He sure wasn't anything like Sam or the geeky blond for that matter. "Hi," I said, then turned back around and took a swig of my drink.

"Man, isn't this place tragic?" he asked.

I nodded at him and smiled then took another sip. Of course, I couldn't ignore him, but I didn't want to encourage him either.

After a few minutes, the bartender sat his drink down.

"The only reason I even come here is because it's so close to my apartment," he said.

I half-nodded, willing him to leave now that he had his drink, since I wanted to talk to the blond. But after a few moments, the blond finished up his drink and left—I could've kicked myself for not making a move when I had the chance.

Of course, the sleeveless T-shirt guy took the empty seat and leaned over towards me. "Mind if I join you? My friends over there are driving me nuts."

I could tell that the only way to head this off was for me to leave, but that was fine—it was a huge breakthrough that I walked in here in the first place. I had survived this first "gay world" experience and God had not struck me down. It was time to get a good night's sleep and think about all of this some more tomorrow.

"Sure, but I've gotta go, unfortunately," I said, then finished up my drink.

"I'm Ryan, by the way," he said as I paid with a few bills.

As I turned to face the door, I saw Sam. *The* Sam. Blond

hair, square jaw, *li liang* tattoo. He was standing near the entrance with Joshua and three other guys. Joshua turned to walk my way.

Holy shit!

I ducked back down.

Had I walked right past them? Did they see me? Why would oh-so-cool Sam go to a teen joint when he had a fake ID? Then it hit me—the Mayor's son could never use a fake ID in New York City! *Shit!* Was this God's way of getting me back for trashing that Bible?

I swung around, eyeball to eyeball with Ryan, then swallowed hard. "Hi, I'm, um, Raj," I shouted.

"Well, hello, Raj." He smirked at me, probably because he knew good and well my name wasn't Raj. From the look on his face, he probably didn't care either.

We shook hands as someone saddled up behind me.

"Hey, Ryan!" Joshua shouted over my shoulder. "Did you forget about our drinks?"

"Sorry about that," Ryan answered in a tone that meant "Can't you see I'm busy!"

"Three Red Bulls, please," Joshua shouted to the bartender.

I suddenly froze like I'd just fallen face-first into a pit of rattlesnakes and didn't dare move. With my back to Joshua, I closed my eyes and managed to sway, pretending to take in the music, trying to calm myself down.

They probably spotted me the moment I walked in and now planned to out me right there in front of everyone. They'd laugh about this for years to come, that Alabama boy they outed, the one who wasn't too swift. The big, lying closet case. Sam was probably calling Julie right now.

Ἀνερρίφθω κύβος. The die has been cast.

I braced myself for a tap on the shoulder, but Joshua just picked up the drinks and left.

"Wanna go somewhere?" Ryan asked. "Maybe back to my place."

Was he really inviting me home? I was in a gay bar for only ten minutes and this random guy was already trying to get me to go to bed with him. Was that the way it worked or was this guy just unusually promiscuous?

I scanned the bar and saw a sign indicating the bathrooms were downstairs. "Um, no, I—where's the restroom?"

"A naughty boy, are we?" Ryan took my hand and dragged me toward the back stairway, clearly misinterpreting my question. In spite of my panic, a hot flare of desire shot off inside me, weakening my resolve. No guy had every taken my hand before, and here this guy was taking it in such a greedy, carnal way.

At the back stairs, Ryan put his hand on my shoulder, turned me around and kissed me hard. All the times I had fantasized about kissing a guy, I never considered the sensation of whisker against whisker. I swear, my knees truly went weak. A sexual thirst welled up inside me like a hot spring, causing my brain to disengage and my body to take over. I pulled Ryan closer and ran my hands over his muscular back, drinking him in. I wanted to rip his shirt right off, but then Ryan reached down and squeezed my crotch, which instinctively made me seize up and pull away.

He looked at me slyly. "Too fast for you?"

"Yeah, a lot too fast," I said, catching my breath and collecting myself. Of course, there was part of me that wanted to do the same thing back to Ryan, but I couldn't with Sam and Joshua fifty feet away.

I broke away from Ryan. "I gotta go," I shouted over the music.

"Great, I'll come with you," he said.

But that wasn't part of my plan. I dropped Ryan's hand and headed stealthily for the door while observing Sam and Joshua with every step. Even if Sam and Joshua thought they saw me, I could deny it as long as we didn't actually speak. There are an awful lot of tall, blue-eyed, cleft-chinned seventeen year olds running around New York City in white T-shirts and jeans.

"I'm leaving too—let's share a cab," Ryan shouted, then jetted ahead of me.

"I thought you lived right here," I said.

But he ignored me and just held tight to my hand and kept walking. He nudged a couple of guys on the shoulder as we passed and clanked knuckles with another like he was the mayor or something. Would he do the same with Joshua?

I wasn't waiting around to find out.

I tore away from Ryan and bolted for the door. It was enough to get the attention of everyone in the place.

"Jake!" Sam called out. "Wait up!"

Out on the street, I ran up the sidewalk like a scalded dog, darting around clumps of people. I turned onto a residential street and kept running until, after a few blocks, I ducked around a corner and down a short staircase.

A moment later, Sam ran by.

I stood real still in the shadows. When I finally felt it was safe, I exhaled then drew a deep breath.

What had I done? Julie could only suspect I was a big sissy, but Sam and Josh now *knew* it!

I buried my face in my arms as the inside corners of my eyes burned. I willed myself not to cry. I couldn't even remember the last time I'd cried, but there was no stopping it; I cried my butt off right there on those steps. Years of grief streamed down my cheeks, and realizing the source of my tears made me cry even harder.

"You okay?" I heard someone say.

I looked up seeing a beautiful woman in a white evening gown.

I wiped at the tears.

"Oh, honey, look at you—you're a mess. What's wrong? You can tell Sandy." She handed me a tissue from her purse.

At that moment, it seemed like the kindest thing anyone had ever done for me. To think that I could actually talk to someone about this instead of keeping it all sealed up inside. I looked up to thank her but realized that she was no woman. It was something about his eyes or the shape of his face—I didn't stick around to figure it out.

I bolted out of there and ran north, towards Phoebe's. Sam had probably already phoned Julie and they could already be badmouthing me. Julie would say something like, "That explains why he was more interested in the color of my sofas than anything else in the room. Including me."

They'd laugh their freakin' asses off.

Julie would start calling me "Jacquelyn" or "Powella" or something even more humiliating, if she spoke to me at all. By noon tomorrow, the entire class would know even though it was a Saturday. And sooner or later, word would somehow find its way to Tarsus and my entire life would be ruined. There would be no putting this back in the bottle.

It was a good two miles to Phoebe's, but I ran/walked the whole way and was sopping wet with sweat by the time I got to her place.

Phoebe's apartment was still, and I half expected her to shout out, "Who's there?" I marched back to the bed and plopped face down with my mind in "what if" mode.

What if I:

…hadn't gone home with Julie?

…trashed that Bible?

…walked into Heaven?

…kissed Ryan?

…ran out like a lunatic?

What if I'd never come to New York?

All of this was punctuated by a muted beep every so often. It almost sounded like…my cell phone.

I rolled over and dug the phone out of my jeans pocket. One voicemail. *Word travels fast!* I absolutely did not want to check it, but my curiosity got the best of me. I hit my voice mail speed dial.

"Jake," my dad began, "I have great news! Brother Watson

wants you to preach one week from Sunday. I'm just tickled, son! Call me tonight when you get home. I'll be up late writing your sermon."

My life was already a flaming pile of you-know-what and the world kept heaping more on. I threw my phone down on the bed, covered my eyes, and allowed myself to really imagine telling my parents about this thing. Sure, we'd talked about homosexuality before, but only conceptually, involving strangers from far away places. Like when Rosie O'Donnell came out on national television a few years back and started advocating for gay adoption. But what if I moved this discussion to Tarsus? To our very home?

I pictured us, sitting around the kitchen table. I'd begin by saying that I had something I wanted to tell them and then start sobbing or something. They'd hold my hands and probably assume I got some girl pregnant, which is about the worst thing they could ever imagine.

"Honey, what is it?" Momma would beg. "We're family—you can tell us anything! We love you and nothing can change that."

The Preacher would have on his I-can-do-all-things-through-Christ-who-strengthens-me mask. The one he wore to deliver Mamaw's and then—five month's later—Papaw's eulogy. Both times, that mask washed right off once he got back to the house and started sobbing over their deaths, but he'd wear it when he said, "Son, now you go ahead and tell us. We're with you come hell or high water and nothing can ever change that."

I'd believe him, muster my strength and—no, I would insist we prayed first. Yes, we'd hold hands and say a prayer of great hope, love, and acceptance. But however I did it, I would eventually have to utter the words that would change my life forever. "Momma, Dad, I'm gay."

It would be the last thing they'd expect to hear. At first, they would think I was kidding, but then they'd see the awful truth in my eyes. They'd suddenly understand why my best friend was a girl, why I sucked at sports, and why I couldn't give a rat's ass about the annual Auburn-Alabama football game unlike every other normal guy in town.

The Preacher would look like he got hit by an eighteen-wheeler, and that mask of his would shatter into a million pieces. He'd walk out of the kitchen and sink so low he might not ever recover. When he finally realized that having a gay son would kill his ministry, he might even put a bullet through his own head.

Momma's expression would turn dark and her voice would crack. "Not this! Anything but this!"

What a day to look forward to. I snapped out of that scenario and looked at my grandparents' highboy, then their photo on the desk. Thank God they didn't have to be dragged through all this, since they were already dead.

Death used to terrify me but now it seemed comforting, even intoxicating. The older I got, the worse life seemed. I longed for the days when the worst thing that could happen to me was a spanking or the loss of television privileges. My problems now seemed endless and mine to deal with alone: this homosexuality was like a cancer that would slowly eat away at every aspect of my life from my relationships with my family and friends to the inability to marry, settle down and have children. And one day, I'd eventually get AIDS. I just knew it.

I never asked to be in this world, especially not with this crappy gay hand I got dealt.

I could just take the emergency exit.

Phoebe had to have a rope around here some place or I could jump out one of her sixteenth-floor windows—that would definitely do it. I just needed to ask God's forgiveness after I set the wheels in motion since there was a lot of debate in our church over whether God actually forgives us of sins we didn't repent for. Just like it only took one sin to get Adam and Eve kicked out of the Garden of Eden, it only took one unforgiven sin to land you in hell. And you couldn't repent of a sin before you committed it—that's premeditation. No, I definitely needed to ask forgiveness *after* I'd set the wheels in motion and couldn't be sure I'd have the time or the wherewithal to get in a prayer after jumping out a window. Anyway, I didn't want anything bloody—I'd seen enough shot animals that suffered as they died during my few hunting trips. I just wanted to go to sleep and not wake up.

Like Papaw.

Maybe he didn't die from a broken heart after all—he could've taken matters into his own hands too. How would he have done it?

I felt an incredible calm as I headed down the hall to Phoebe's bedroom, around her large canopy bed, and into her bathroom off to one side. When I opened her medicine cabinet, the first thing I saw was a tiny bottle with a nipple top, like a miniature baby bottle. The lilac label read "Women's Rogaine Hair Regrowth Treatment, Unscented."

My eyes went wide. Phoebe had inherited Grandmother's thinning hair curse! Why, why, why did life have to be so sucky? At every turn there was just more bad news.

I put the Rogaine back and rummaged through several bottles of pills, including the same thyroid medication Momma takes. I doubted her thyroid medication would do the trick but there was every headache remedy in there you could imagine. I wasn't familiar with the other pharmaceuticals: Paxil, Lipitor, Soma. Then I saw a bottle labeled Upnosicm. Root word: Ύπνοσ. Sleep. The label read "take one pill before bedtime." Yes!

I grabbed the sleeping pills then went to the kitchen for a big glass of water, but spotted a bottle of vodka next to the ice in the freezer. Even better! I filled my glass with vodka and took a swallow. The liquid burned like hell going down, so I cut it with some Diet Coke from the fridge.

Suddenly, I realized that I'd have to write a suicide note if I was going through with this. I took another swallow as the hairs on my forearms stood on end.

Killing myself would be bad enough, but I couldn't have my parents wondering the rest of their lives if this was over something they'd done. My death would be a hard blow for them but they'd eventually get over it. It would certainly be easier on them than having to endure the daily shame over my being gay. Now that the genie was out of the bottle, it was only a matter of time before my parents would find out. I'd learned that from experience time and again.

Back in the bedroom, I sat at Phoebe's desk and took a good long look at my grandparents' photo; if I went through with this, I'd see them shortly, Mamaw and Papaw too. I stared at a blank notepad while a pen trembled in my hand. I would be doing everyone a big freakin' favor and probably saving The Preacher's life—and certainly his career—in the process, but was this really what I wanted? Did I really want Phoebe to walk in on Sunday and find my rotting corpse swarming with flies, and then having to call my parents and give them the news?

No, I didn't want to destroy the lives of the very people I held most dear, but living with this misery one more second seemed absolutely unbearable.

I felt totally trapped.

How was it that I'd managed to hold things together for seventeen years in Tarsus but couldn't survive two weeks up North without wanting to kill myself? I'd simply had enough of New York. And the thought of being back home was absolutely intoxicating, certainly more so than my crappy drink—I kept waiting for it to kick in. Wasn't vodka supposed to dull the pain? I threw back another gulp, and then crawled into bed and stared at that bottle of sleeping pills. The room was perfectly quiet except for an occasional horn and the drumming of my heart.

I'd spent the last four years—a quarter of my life—trying to conquer these desires. Was there any Biblical stone I'd left unturned? Was there some divine solution I had somehow missed? My mind started racing and every path it took brought me back to the same question: if every word of the Bible was true, why hadn't God healed me from homosexuality when I had asked Him to in *Jesus' name*? I just couldn't get my head around that question. What could possibly explain it? The Apostle Paul made it perfectly clear that homosexuality was an abomination, so certainly it was God's will to heal me from homosexuality. So why hadn't He?

I drowned out all those nagging thoughts by closing my eyes and saying three glorious words, "I don't care."

Those words were like magic, better than any abracadabra or alakazam. And with them, I finally found some peace.

A tingly vertigo swept over me as the vodka finally kicked in. I began to drift off, but suddenly, a new thought hit me: maybe Paul's stance against homosexuality was his opinion and not God's truth.

I tried snuffing that thought out by focusing on my mantra: I don't care.

But that thought wouldn't go away, like my mind wasn't giving up on trying to figure this out even though I had. Maybe the Apostle Paul didn't know what he was talking about!

I. DON'T. CARE.

I told myself to go to sleep and I would just hop the next flight back home tomorrow and figure the rest of it out when I got there.

But I couldn't think of one thing Jesus had ever said against homosexuals.

I DON'T CARE! I DON'T CARE! I DON'T CARE!

I grabbed my drink to guzzle it down, but stumbled to the kitchen and dumped it instead.

CHAPTER 14

Back home, Tracy and I hurried down Tarsus High School's main hallway, lined with dull grey steel lockers, while Principal Law's voice boomed through the school's public address system, covering every corner of the building. "I repeat, this is a tornado warning. Walk, do not run, to your designated area, and *do not* go outside under any circumstances. Again, this is not a drill."

"Let's get to the cafeteria," Tracy said, grabbing my hand and pulling me behind her before I could argue.

We pushed our way around a few phone zombies and students whose clamoring and locker door slamming bounced off the brown tiled walls and floor. When she shoved on the steel bar of the exit door, the wind sent it slamming open, causing a few girls to scream, then bolt up the hallway for safety.

Tracy dropped my hand and dashed down the breezeway towards the yellow cinderblock cafeteria with its high-pitched roof.

"Tracy!" I hurried after her.

She darted into the cafeteria, grabbed the steel bar of the door with both hands and pulled back on it.

"Wait for me!" I yelled, high-tailing it towards her and waving real big.

Something like the sound of a broken piano chord boomed all around me.

I felt my body tense up. I turned around just as the entire breezeway roof above me went airborne, then disappeared into a green swirl of sky.

Something plowed into my shoulder. I instinctively shielded my face. "Aaah!!" I yelled.

"Jake! Wake up!" someone shouted. It sounded like Phoebe but she was back in New York.

My eyes shot open.

Phoebe sat on the corner of my bed, shaking me. She was ghost-white and looked older than I remembered. "Jake, it's time to get back to school. You promised."

There was a bottle of Mylanta next to the bedside clock. It was seven forty-five in the morning.

She stood and opened the blinds. "Someone needs a shave."

Suddenly, everything came rushing back.

The Julie disaster date.

Sam at Heaven Bar.

The bottle of sleeping pills.

On Sunday, I forced myself to call Phoebe to say that I'd spent the weekend at her apartment because I was sick, even though I wasn't (at least not physically). Despite my reassurances, she came right home from the Hamptons. I think she was afraid I'd die on her watch or something.

I told her it must be a stomach bug, and she immediately looped Momma in and started me on a diet of Jell-O, saltines, and chicken soup. That was a welcome change from the Diet Coke and cereal bars I'd eked by on. Every time she came in my room, I held my breath, afraid she'd say something about the dent I put in her bottle of vodka, but she hadn't so far.

My limbs had gotten heavy, like my bones were morphing into rebar and my flesh, concrete. Even eating was a huge effort. I'd missed the Monday deadline for my final project pitch, but it took every ounce of energy I had each evening just to call Carman Hall security—as required by school policy—to let them know I was still alive. After I called Sunday night, they turned right around and phoned my parents who then called me back for another update even though we'd already spoken twice that day.

What a freakin' mess.

But I could no more find the energy to bang out a one-paragraph pitch for my final project—let alone go to class—than scale the Empire State Building barefoot.

It was now Wednesday, the day I'd promised Phoebe I'd go back to school.

"I'll make you some breakfast," Phoebe said. "How about a protein shake or maybe a ~~bagel and lox?~~ *slice of SALMON*

I turned her way, shielding my eyes from the sunlight.

~~"Huh?"~~

"Smoked salmon."

I rolled over on my back. "Sounds like a poor substitute for a sausage biscuit."

She chuckled. "Someone's getting their sense of humor back."

"Phoebe, I just need one more day and I'll be over this bug."

She sat back down and shook her head. "I made a doctor's appointment for you today at one o'clock. We should've gone Monday."

I looked away. "Gosh, Phoebe—that's not necessary, honest."

"I've got to pop into the office for a couple of hours, but I'll swing by and pick you up around noon. You know the number if you need anything. What about breakfast?"

"I'll make some cereal when I get up."

Phoebe gazed into my eyes as if trying to read my thoughts. I stared back casually, like I hadn't wanted to kill myself days earlier and wasn't now planning to drop out of the Summer Program. She finally kissed my forehead then stood to leave.

"Just one request—could you shut the blinds, please?" I asked.

She pulled the blinds, then left.

As I thought back to my brush with suicide, my body turned to ice; I shuddered at what almost happened.

Life seemed a little more tolerable than it had on Friday

but not by much. I still wanted to go home and forget about everything that had happened since coming to New York. But would The Preacher let me forget about the pact I'd made with God? Strictly speaking, I'd be coming home empty handed, which would land me in the freakin' pulpit for the rest of my life. That was the only thing that had kept me from returning home after the events last Friday. Still, being in the pulpit for the rest of my life seemed like a small price to pay for not having to go back to Columbia and endure the ensuing humiliation with my classmates over being a big homo.

I grabbed my cell phone from the nightstand and called the wisest person I knew. "Hey, Momma."

"Jake! How you feeling, honey?"

"Not too swift."

"Are you drinking plenty of fluids and gargling with warm salty water?"

If only it were that simple. "It's really not a throat thing."

"Then what is it?"

"I think I'm just a little down."

"Down? About what?"

I wished I could share the whole bloomin' chain of events that led me to this bed, but that would absolutely kill her. Still, I had to come clean a little since it was my only chance of getting the hell out of New York now while my reputation was still somewhat intact. "It's just that—I feel like I keep trying to be something I'm not."

"What are you talking about?" she asked with genuine surprise. "You're an award-winning journalist. Your dad and I couldn't love you more or be more prouder."

I knew she meant every word, but if she ever discovered the whole truth, she'd feel differently. No doubt about that. "Momma, have you ever felt like an imposter? I mean, like a total fraud? I'm just curious."

She sighed. "Jake, I'm a preacher's wife, so I do sometimes keep up appearances, if that's what you're asking."

"Like when?"

"Well, at the grocery checkout, I look over my shoulder for fear someone might see the lamb chops and start blabbing that everyone should eat as well as The Preacher. It doesn't matter that they were on sale. And if I attended every wedding, birthday party, and funeral I was invited to, I'd never have any down time so I sometimes say I'm not feeling well when that's not exactly the case. You know what I'm talking about—being a PK is tough too."

"You can say that again."

"So I do feel like an imposter at times but, Jake, you're not. You're going to be a great journalist—no one ever said it'd be easy, but you can do it."

I put the phone down so she couldn't hear and sobbed to myself for a moment.

"Jake? You there?"

I put the phone back to my ear. "Yes, ma'am," I said. "I guess I just don't know who I am anymore."

"Well, whoever you are, you're still my son," she said.

"No matter what?" I asked, perking up.

"No matter what."

I wiped my eyes on the sleeve of the robe Phoebe had let me borrow. "Can I just come home?"

"Absolutely not," she said more sternly than I expected. She wasn't going to let me off so easily. "I know Columbia must be demanding, but Powells are not quitters. You can do this, Jake. Just put one foot in front of the next and stop looking at everything all at once. You'll be fine."

"I knew you'd say that."

"You're going to do great. Trust me. I've been your mother for seventeen years. I know you."

But of course she really didn't know me—not the whole me. "I love you," I said.

"I love you too, honey."

I hung up and cried myself to sleep. I didn't wake up until Phoebe knocked on my door at lunchtime. "Jake, we've gotta go. Have you even dressed or eaten anything?"

"No, ma'am."

She handed me a small shopping bag. "I got you a razor. I'm gonna warm you up some soup. Here, get dressed. We've gotta be at the doctor in an hour."

"Phoebe, I really don't need to go to the doctor."

She sat down on the bed, switched on a bedside lamp, and placed the back of her hand against my forehead. "You don't feel feverish."

The doorbell rang.

"Who could that be?" Phoebe sighed then marched out of the room.

I didn't care who it was. I was happy to be alone, but then I heard a voice that sounded like Julie's, but it couldn't be. "Yes, sparkling water with a lime if you have it."

Julie had left me two call-me texts since Monday (I always texted back that I was sick but in good hands). Sam had texted nine times and called twice but only left one message, saying to hurry back—Raj had turned my dorm room into a veritable love den.

I held my breath and leaned towards the door, trying to make out the voice.

"I'll just give him a quick update on class," Julie called out, her voice becoming more distinct.

Adrenaline ripped through me. There was no place to hide, so I turned off the lamp and closed my eyes shut.

The door creaked open. "Jake?" Julie whispered.

I kept my breaths slow and shallow to mimic sleep, but my heart was pounding at about a hundred beats a *second*.

"Nice try," she said, "but no one sleeps with their knees up like that. Amateur."

My lungs burned, demanding more air to keep up with my out-of-control pulse. I willed my chest to rise and fall calmly to keep up appearances, but I was slowly suffocating.

"Okay, if you're really sleeping, I'll just hang out until you wake up. I brought my *Cosmo*," she said, then fanned the pages of a magazine right in my ear.

I gasped for air.

She clutched her chest, acting all surprised. "Oh, you're awake? How you feeling, party boy?"

I coughed. "What? Just a bad cold I think."

"Mmm-hmm," she said, arms crossed.

"Phoebe's taking me to the doctor. We're just about to leave."

"Mmm-hmm."

"My appointment's at one so…"

"Mmm-hmm."

"I appreciate your concern, but I'm in good hands."

"I'm sure you're getting the best medical care money can buy," she said sarcastically. "Are we going to talk about this?"

I looked over her shoulder, willing Phoebe to appear and whisk me away to the doctor. "Talk about what?"

"Friday night."

"What about Friday night?" I suddenly felt nauseous. Where was Phoebe?

"Let's see," she said. "I heard someone went to an after-party after our date. A place called Heaven Bar. Ever heard of it?"

"Oh that! I was—I was just researching a potential news story."

She cackled. "Sam told me you'd say that!"

So they *had* talked—I was doomed.

Julie sat on my bed and peered down at me. "You okay?"

"Just dandy," I said, looking away.

"You know, I think you're a bigger drama queen than Josie."

"I'm not gay!" I snapped. "I told you I was researching a story. It's called being a journalist."

"It's called being gay. What straight guy," she said with a wave of her hand, "could say no to this?"

I couldn't help but chuckle and she smiled real big.

"Let me think for a minute," I said, then turned away and quickly did the tally on the pros and cons of coming clean, starting with a con.

Julie would definitely tell Sam who would tell Alexandros who would tell Raj. Then, the whole class would find out.

But none of them would care—they certainly all seemed to like Sam and didn't treat him any differently for being gay.

But back home, people would care, deeply. What if word got out there? It would be a huge scandal. The son of a One-Way Bible preacher can't be gay. Not for long, at least. I'd either be sent to one of those camps to change me, or The Preacher would have to leave the church. It would ruin our lives.

But how could the news possibly jump all the way from Manhattan to Tarsus in the next four weeks?

Phoebe! She could somehow find out and tell Momma.

But she wouldn't tell if I asked her not to, and I couldn't imagine she cared if I was gay or not. She probably already suspected it. Maybe that's one reason she suggested New York in the first place. Am I that obvious?

If I continued to deny this, Julie would just see me as a big liar, lose all respect for me, and I'd continue to suffer alone and lose her friendship.

But if I came clean, I'd have someone to help me see the way forward, and it might actually salvage our friendship.

I rose up on an elbow and rubbed my forehead.

She eyed me expectantly, practically daring me not to come out.

This was it. I was about to let the genie out of the bottle. I took a deep breath. "Okay. I'm gay," I said, then collapsed back onto the bed.

"Duh!"

"But…but don't you hate me?"

"Of course I do," she said playfully. "But I'm sick of Sam bossing me around. He's made me write the last two articles, and one of them involved a wastewater treatment plant in Queens. Can you imagine me at a wastewater treatment plant? Well, I was, thanks to Sam. We need you back before we kill each other."

"Honestly, I'm not surprised. You both are so bullheaded."

She laughed, and then leaned over and hugged me.

I felt so unworthy of her friendship. It was all too much—I began sobbing just as Phoebe knocked.

"What's all this?" she asked, seeing me crying.

I straightened up and cleared my throat. "Phoebe, could you give us just a second?" I asked, embarrassed that she'd caught me in such a state.

She handed Julie her sparkling water and looked at her watch. "Okay. One more minute, but we've got to get you to the doctor."

Phoebe stepped outside.

I pinched my nose. "The doctor. That'll be *another* disaster."

"Look on the bright side—things can't get any worse," Julie said.

"I wouldn't be so sure."

Julie took my hand. "Jake, life can be sucky sometimes. When my mother died, I thought my life was over, too, even though I was just a kid. But I eventually learned to take one day at a time, and today all you have to do is march in there and tell Phoebe that you're gay. It's either that or the doctor."

"I can't," I whined. "That'd be letting the genie out of the bottle and once—"

"Jake, trust me, the genie is already out of the bottle. Oh my god, Sam said he knew the day he met you, which of course I'll never forgive him for. I didn't see it at all."

I looked away. "Sam probably thinks I'm the biggest loser ever."

"Actually, he said you'd be a great addition to the tribe."

"The tribe?" I asked, not knowing what she meant.

She rolled her eyes. "The gay tribe. Jake, tell Phoebe. What's the worst that could happen?"

"She could tell my parents."

"But would she if you asked her not to?"

"I was just pondering that. No, she wouldn't. But she'll still look at me differently."

"Well, of course she will. You can't go around worrying about that."

I shook my head at her. "Easy for you to say."

"What?! Jake, I'm the little girl who found her mommy dead, remember? People have been looking at me differently ever since. They give me that 'pity face.' See—you're giving it to me right now."

She was right.

"What I'm trying to say is that if anyone gives you the pity face *for being gay*, I hope you'll just give it right back to them because they're a five-star dumbass. They're not worth your time. I only just met Phoebe but I've known women a lot like her my entire life. Believe me, they *all* have gay friends because gay men are drawn to fabulousness, and Phoebe is most definitely fabulous. And fabulous women are drawn to gay men. It's just the way it works."

Did that explain why I'd adored Phoebe for as long as I could remember? Is that why she's been so good to me all these years? Because she knew I was gay, at least on some level?

"Sure, it might take some people time to adjust to the real you, but they'll come around if they really love you. Just think how long it took you to come to terms with it yourself. I mean, you have, haven't you?"

"Yes. Maybe... Well, I guess. But I'm just so...ashamed."

"Ashamed of who you are? Please! That's something *you'll* have to get over. Jesus, *you're* a five-star dumbass."

The next thing I knew, we were laughing our butts off.

"Jake, you're only as sick as your deepest, darkest secrets."

"Huh," I said, letting that sink in. "That's pretty profound, Julie."

"Well, it's not like I made that up, but it's gotten me

through a lot. Don't keep this inside. Just look Phoebe straight in the eye and say the words. No beating around the bush."

I nodded, knowing that she was right. The time had come and I just hoped I could do it.

Julie kissed me on the forehead and gave a little wave goodbye, almost bumping into Phoebe as she left.

"Jake, you're still in those old PJs, honey? C'mon, we've got to get going."

I sat on the edge of the bed and gazed up at her. I'd been running away from myself for four years and that sure had to change. It was now or never, but as much as I willed my mouth to say the words, nothing was coming out.

Phoebe stood there, waiting for me to get a move on.

I shook my head. "Phoebe, I'm not sick. I'm just..."

She sat next to me on the bed and put her arm around me. "What is it, honey?" she asked.

I wondered if this was a big mistake. In theory, I was just adding "gay" to the long list of labels that describe me—All-Alabama editor, boy preacher, Bible Drill champion, Southerner, carnivore—but it felt a lot bigger than the others, like an entirely new skin.

Looking at the floor, I said, "Phoebe, it's just that...I'm gay. I thought it was like a thorn that would eventually work its way out, but it hasn't and it never will."

She threw her arms around me and held me tight. "Oh, honey, why didn't you tell me? How long have you known?"

I shrugged. "I've had these feelings for years. You don't just suddenly know—it sneaks up on you. Just last week I convinced myself I was straight. Remember, I had those dates with Julie? The first one was great but it sort of went downhill after that."

She let go and raised an eyebrow. "I've suspected this for a long time. I've got great gaydar. I tried to casually raise the subject with your mom but never got anywhere. But once you tell her—"

"I can't! It would kill her."

She held out her hands for me to take. "Well, let's start by telling God."

"God?" I asked through clenched teeth. "Don't you think I've talked to *Him* about this? He just left me to rot! In the Bible, Jesus said, 'Ask *anything* in My name and it will be given to you.' That's BS! Trust me, I've tried it about five thousand times."

"I see," Phoebe said quietly, allowing me to calm down.

I leaned in and said, "And you know what? I think the Apostle Paul could've been gay. I can totally see it."

"Maybe he was," she said. "Does it matter?"

"Does it matter?" I shot back. "DOES IT MATTER? What kind of question is that? Of course it matters! He said all those horrible things about gays going to hell. What if he was just covering for being gay himself? What if that was *his* thorn?"

"That could be, but may I make a suggestion?"

"I'm all ears," I said helplessly.

"Let's let the Apostle Paul rest in peace. He's been dead nearly two thousand years, you know?"

"Well, he's still messing with people, let me tell you."

"Jake, I know you can't see this now, but you're really an incredible young man. You're smart, handsome, gracious, loving, the total package. Quit worrying so much about what the Apostle Paul or anyone else might think about you and just embrace the wonder that is you. Live the best life you can *for you*. Otherwise, you'll wind up married to the *perfect* girl your momma picked out, working at the *perfect* job that your father chose, hanging out with crazy friends worthy of their own reality show, and wondering why you're so miserable. Do what's right for you, everyone else be damned. Including me."

"I'll try."

"I know you can't possibly believe this now, but one day, you'll be grateful that you're gay. You'll view it as a gift."

"How can I ever view this as a gift?" I scoffed.

"I don't know—I'm not gay. But I have lots of gay friends and they all seem to feel that way, but for different reasons. You'll see. And when you do, I want you to call me and tell me I was right. I want you to promise that, okay?"

"Okay, I promise. But don't hold your breath."

CHAPTER 15

I took a nice, long shower and headed back to campus.

As I trudged past the stone giants standing at the Columbia gates, the sun was mercifully setting. I say "mercifully" because I was wearing the only clothes I had at Phoebe's: the tight white T-shirt and jeans from Friday night.

I took a quick mental inventory of my current situation. I felt a whole lot lighter and a lot less alone after sharing my darkest secret with Phoebe and Julie, and I was especially glad Sam knew, but I was coming up real short on the academic front and was prepared to pull an all-nighter to catch up if I had to. I just needed to figure out what I'd missed and hoped that Raj or Sam would help me get back on track.

I made a big ruckus over opening the door to my dorm room just in case Raj and whatever girl he had over were in the throes of passion. But no one was home. I switched on the lights and, before I even got the door closed good, Sam walked through the bathroom door.

In that moment, I relived the absolute humiliation I felt when he spotted me at Heaven Bar and saw me for the hypocrite that I was. I crossed my arms, feeling naked and exposed. "Sam, I don't even know what to say."

He shook his head and pulled me in for a bear hug. For the first time in my life, I felt free to hug a guy other than my father so intensely.

"Like, welcome to the tribe, Jake."

My heart swelled up with those words and the realization that I would be okay. After years of wandering alone in the proverbial wilderness, that moment with Sam felt like I'd finally made it home. On some level, I knew that if it weren't for Sam, I never would've made it this far. Before Sam, my attraction to guys had been completely physical, but Sam awakened something much deeper inside of me, something beyond admiration or fondness or desire, perhaps something even beyond words.

"Thanks, Sam," I said. "I can't believe how much my life has changed since Friday. I hope it's not all a big mistake."

Sam let go and looked me in the eye. "How can it be a mistake, brah? It's who you are."

I nodded, wanting to kiss him more than anything.

He glanced over his shoulder through the bathroom door. "So, Jake," he whispered. "Like, don't freak but Alexandros and Raj know about Friday night. Joshua told them. I don't know what got into him, but he promised not to tell anyone else. They're totally cool with it, of course, but…"

Maybe that's what Julie meant earlier when she said the genie was already out of the bottle.

I heard someone enter the bathroom, then Joshua stepped out and put his arm around Sam. "Hey, Jake," he said. "Feeling better?"

The magic of the moment completely vanished, and only then did I realize that Joshua must've spent a lot of time at the dorm since Friday to have already blabbed to both Alexandros and Raj. I guess my public outing at Heaven was a meaningful and especially hilarious detail from their first date, so it would naturally become part of the narrative that bound Sam and Joshua together for life.

"Yes, thanks," I said as Joshua pulled Sam away.

"Maybe tomorrow you can let me know what I missed in class?" I asked Sam.

"Sure," he said, then disappeared through the bathroom door with Joshua.

I was so emotionally flatlined, I didn't have the energy to care whether Sam and Joshua were now an item nor that

Joshua had outed me to Raj and Alexandros. I guess it was only a matter of time before they found out anyway. I was kind of glad they knew since it meant I no longer had to pretend I was straight in our dorm room.

In a city where the Mayor's son was completely out, maybe I could open the door a little, at least while I was in New York. Of course, Tarsus would be another story, but that was a few weeks away. For now, I'd try to live in the moment. As long as I stayed within certain boundaries, God really couldn't touch me. Well, He *could* but He wouldn't because His days of messing with earthly affairs were clearly so over. If He really wanted to influence the natural order of things here, He would've prevented the Holocaust and 9/11. He certainly wasn't going to bend the laws of nature just to put Jake Powell in his place! I was no longer so arrogant as to think that way.

I had to start catching up on my classwork and began by writing an explanation to Professor Greenberg. Hunching over my laptop, I struggled to find words to justify my three-day absence to him. In my email, I explained that I'd been under the weather and included a one-paragraph pitch for my final project: an investigative report on the Empire Diner situation. I just wished it wasn't two days late.

I sent the email and scanned through my inbox, seeing that The Preacher had already sent me my sermon for Sunday entitled "The Joy of Christian Living" and noted that there would be at least a thousand people in the One-Way Bible Brooklyn sanctuary. How perfect was that? I decided not to even open the sermon—I had too much reading as it was for class, and I was up past eleven o'clock finishing it up before going to bed. I didn't even hear Raj come home.

The next morning, I woke up to Raj's scurrying out of the bathroom fully dressed except for his shoes. I figured this was as good a time as any to talk about my big "gay news," but I needed to ease into it.

177

"So, how did you make out having the whole dorm room to yourself?"

"It was okay," he said, taking a seat on his bed to put on his shoes.

I rose up on one elbow. "Meet any new girls while I was gone?"

He shrugged as he laced up his red and black sneakers.

I was waiting for him to ask me about my five-day absence but he seemed awfully focused on getting ready for class even though it didn't start for another hour. "Did I miss a lot in class?"

He stood and grabbed his backpack. "You can borrow my notes later," he said and dashed out.

When I walked into class, the room seemed to quiet and several kids looked my way. My face suddenly felt flush. Had the news traveled farther than Julie let on? I wasn't sure if I was imagining it all or not.

Julie motioned at me like she needed to discuss something pressing.

I pounced up the stairs, and went to take my seat.

"How'd it go with Phoebe?" she asked.

"Really good," I said. "I couldn't have done it without you. Honest."

"It was nothing," she said. "By the way, I'm throwing a big party on Saturday. May I ask that you not show up in that awful brown plaid shirt of yours?"

I laughed. "You'll never see it again," I said.

All of this flew right past Raj, who was engrossed in the *New York Times*. The lead headline was "Britain at Top Terror Alert After Air Terminal Is Struck."

Sam arrived and started catching me up on the three days I'd missed, but we didn't get very far before Professor Greenberg walked in with a stack of papers and began handing them out. "Okay, these are your articles from Tuesday," he said. "They were much better overall."

Professor Greenberg handed Julie a paper with the

headline "Wastewater Treatment Workers compete in 20th Annual Sludge Olympics" marked with a "B." It had both her and Sam's name on it but Julie had the byline. "Good work, Aaron. I must say I was impressed."

"Thanks," Julie said, actually seeming sincere.

I suddenly felt even more behind and regretted not going to the doctor yesterday since I could've at least gotten a doctor's excuse. I wanted to say "Good morning" or something to Professor Greenberg—mostly to make sure we were on okay terms—but he walked right past me without acknowledgement and continued handing out the papers before beginning his lecture.

"Professional newspapers generate over seventy percent of their revenue from ad sales, and this can be a great source of supplemental income for high school papers as well. It can also increase your readership. Ad sales take a great amount of time and effort, so most serious high school newspapers have an advertising director."

Professor Greenberg went on to describe how to organize an advertising sales team, identify potential advertisers, develop a sales strategy, put together a rate sheet, set up a bank account, and bill your clients. He even gave us a sample sales script and advertising contract. This was certainly an area of *The Tattler* that could use some attention—Tracy and I were basically the entire ad sales department and not all that great at it. Maybe Aunt Phoebe would help us out.

After wrapping up class, Professor Greenberg acknowledged me for the first time that day by saying, "Powell, I'd like to see you now. Please come with me."

I swallowed hard.

"Why does he want to see you, broh?" Sam asked me.

"Yeah, any idea?" Julie asked.

I shrugged while packing up, but somehow knew what this was all about—the very fleece The Preacher had insisted I use in seeking God's career guidance.

As I followed Professor Greenberg to his office, my

mind went into overdrive, creating all kinds of disaster scenarios, including being disqualified from even competing for one of the final awards. Then, I started wondering if maybe my parents had gotten into some awful car accident, but if that had been the case, wouldn't Greenberg have told me at the beginning of class? If you could think it, I was worrying about it, and by the time we arrived in Professor Greenberg's cramped, paper-cluttered office, my stomach was in knots.

I stepped over a pile of books and sat in the lone oak chair before his desk. Out of habit, I began a silent prayer. *Jesus, please let this not be about—*

But then I caught myself and stopped, remembering that I wasn't on speaking terms with God. He didn't give a crap anyway.

Professor Greenberg wasted no time. "Mr. Powell, I think you know why I called you in. This isn't fun for either of us so let's just get it over with." He looked me in the eye. "You're out of the program."

He might as well have punched me in the stomach. "But, Professor Greenberg I—"

He leaned forward in his chair. "You've missed three days of class, the deadline for stating your final project and—"

"Didn't you get my email? I was sick and —"

He held up a finger. "You've also ignored my directive to write even one editorial."

"But I'm best with features and news stories and I'm great with the business side too."

"I'd classify your articles as amusing at best. It sure isn't journalism. If you want to write books, study literature."

Did he really think of me like that? "I'll work harder. I'll write my own editorials. I won't miss another day!" I pleaded, my hands shaking.

"Mr. Powell, you're decent at feature stories, and the teen suicide piece you wrote for your school paper showed promise, but you don't seem to have a journalist's perspective.

Your subjects hedge your questions and you never press them because—I don't know—maybe you care too much about whether they like you or not. Maybe you're too nice to be a journalist. Stick with fiction." u ʀ ϼɑᴛ ϩɛʋᴑʟϩʋꜰ ᴸ

I knew he was right. I wanted to be adored by everyone; it was like I was always running for public office or something. I desperately needed my shot and decided to go for broke since my entire journalism career depended on my winning one of those awards.

I took a deep breath. "You're absolutely right, sir," I said.

"You can try to get part of your tuition refunded—"

"I'm—I'm just surprised you'd give up on one of your students without saying a word," I said as calmly as I could. "Now you're just hanging me out to dry. I totally see where you're coming from, but I'm asking for another chance, now that we see eye to eye. Give me another week and if you still feel this way, I'll go home. No questions asked."

"So you're ready to pitch me on your final project? It has to be an editorial for you to meet the minimum requirements for completing the program."

"I'm proposing an investigative report on The Empire Diner. I sent you a full description in my email. We already did that editorial on it, but I just know I could blow the—"

He looked me square in the face. "Yes, Horow**itz** wrote the editorial if I remember correctly."

"Well, that's right but—"

"Consider your pitch officially rejected. Choose an editorial. We've got editors from national papers judging for the first time this year, so I'd recommend an editorial with broader appeal."

"Like what?"

"I'm not going to sit here and tell you what to write. You'll either give me your topic now, or go see the bursar."

My mind was racing. I thought back to all the news articles I'd read from the AP website and also from the *New York Times*. I certainly wasn't going to write about abortion—

that wasn't my battle. There had been an article on "Don't Ask, Don't Tell" but I wasn't going there either. Terrorism? Maybe. Then, an idea hit me.

"What about Farhad Syed? You know, the guy who wants to be sworn into Congress with a Qur'an instead of a Bible? He's taking Senator Eleanor Wright's seat since she died. There was a special election—"

"I know who he is. What about him?"

"Well, um, that's national news."

"Yes, but you're not writing a *news* article. Where's the editorial angle?"

I didn't know exactly where I was going, but I plunged ahead and pretended I did. "It's really perfect! Should this guy be sworn in with a Qur'an? What wins out: our traditional Christian roots or this man's beliefs?"

He pursed his lips in thought. I couldn't begin to guess what he was thinking, but whatever he said would determine my entire future.

He finally nodded. "Okay, you've got another week, but if I sense Horowitz or anyone else is ghostwriting your editorial or if you're just spewing cute anecdotes, you're out. I want an *editorial* from *you*. Understand?"

I exhaled real big. "Thank you. I really appreciate—"

"I'm also assigning you an additional news article that you are to complete by yourself. I want you to cover Columbia's proposed expansion into Harlem. One thousand words. Bring it with you to class on Monday."

"Yes, sir."

"That's in addition to all the other homework you missed."

"Of course."

"And there won't be any more talk of refunds once you walk out that door. You've got one week to prove yourself."

With that I stood and shook his hand. "Thank you, sir. You won't be sorry."

As I walked out the door, I wondered how I'd fallen so

far so fast. I was now hanging onto my Columbia seat by my fingernails so how the hell did I ever expect to win an award, especially one in the editorial category?

CHAPTER 16

I wanted to jump right into my final project but spent the next two days working like a dog, catching up on homework and writing the extra news article Professor Greenberg assigned me. Still, I made time to call Mr. Farhad Syed's office in Detroit daily and got as far as Mrs. Kanza Abass, his press secretary; she was nice and all, but Senator-elect Syed was never available to speak.

It was early Saturday evening before I was fully caught up on homework, but then I had to begin my sermon preparations for the next morning. I had only just begun reading "The Joy of Christian Living"— the sermon Dad had written for me—when Sam waltzed in, looking so hot in a black T-shirt and a leather cuff. I didn't even notice what he carried in his hand.

"Hey, brah, I grabbed your mail for you," he said, handing me a card with a familiar tight cursive script, perfectly centered, with a deep slant.

"Oh, thanks Sam!" I tore into Momma's card and got a paper cut. "Crap!" I stuck my bleeding finger in my mouth and finished opening the envelope with my free hand.

Sam shook his head at the madras shorts I had on. "You are so not wearing that to Julie's."

Buried in schoolwork, I'd totally forgotten about the party. "Oh, I can't go, Sam. I haven't even started my final project, and I've got to study this stupid sermon for tomorrow."

"Dude, you need a break, plus you don't want to piss Julie off. C'mon, get dressed."

A fifty-dollar bill dropped out of the card. "Sweet!" Momma's note was, too, although I got a little blood on it.

Jake:

I hope you're feeling better. I just want to come up there and give you a big hug. Honey, all you can do is your best, right? Mostly, I just hope you're enjoying yourself.

Good luck on that sermon, Sunday. You'll be great! It's a big day for the preacher too, since the congregation will be voting on whether to move forward with the new church complex. Please pray for him.

Love,

Momma

I felt pretty confident that the congregation would vote to proceed with the new church complex, but my sermon was another matter entirely. On top of everything else, how could I find the time and energy to practice tomorrow's sermon on Christian joy? *Christian joy!* That's an oxymoron if I'd ever heard one, but I had to get cranking on the sermon preparation. I could already feel those bees in my gut getting ready to attack, and I didn't want to crack in front of tomorrow's audience of a thousand or more like I had last time.

"Seriously, you could use a break, man. And you told Julie you were going."

I certainly didn't want any more trust issues with Julie. I decided to just make an appearance at the party and sneak out early to practice the sermon. I'd even print out a copy to bring along with me and read on the subway downtown.

I clicked the print icon on my screen and glanced up at Sam. "Okay. I'll be ready in five minutes. I just need to change."

"I'll wait," he said, then plopped down on my bed and

put his hands behind his head like he was expecting a floorshow. "Why don't you wear that blue shirt of yours, brah? Blue makes your eyes look like sapphires."

Did it? Was Sam just making a casual observation or did this mean that he was somehow into me? But who was I kidding—I could never compete with the likes of Joshua.

Taking my clothes off in front of Sam was like taking my clothes off for the first time—and not in a good way. I pulled my shorts down then realized my shoes were still on, so I yanked my shorts off then took off my shoes. *Brilliant.*

"Nice," Sam said. "For some reason, I thought you'd be a boxer guy."

So Sam had thought about me in underwear before. I wondered if that meant anything. My face began to tingle. I turned so my back was to him. Hoping to take the focus off of me, I asked, "So, are you meeting Joshua beforehand?"

"No, we're meeting there. He'll, like, show up with his entourage at some point. He always does."

I pulled on my jeans then buttoned my shirt, starting from the bottom for some reason. When I turned around, Sam was standing so close I could feel his breath. Suddenly, I was tingling all over. I wanted to throw him back on the bed and give him the Janet Walters once-over but looked down, afraid my eyes would betray me. "Wow, we'd better get going," I said, while nervously rubbing my wrist.

Sam unbuttoned my top button then tapped my chin.

"How much, brah?" he asked.

"How much for what?" I asked, not knowing what he was referring to.

"How much did you pay for that perfect dimpled chin?"

I let out a little laugh, wondering if he was flirting with me, and not really knowing what to do about it if he was, since Sam was dating Joshua. I flushed the thought from my mind as I grabbed the sermon from my printer and tucked it in my pocket. "Okay, let's go, sir," I said.

Julie spared no expense turning the dining room of her apartment into a dance floor, complete with a lighted mirrored ball and fog machine. Most of my classmates were there along with kids I didn't recognize. Raj made up pitchers of Blue Lions, which were a big hit, and he was chatting up a gorgeous blonde who kept flicking her hair around like a show pony.

Two guys, each named Todd, threw back their drinks then Julie motioned them over to dance. Sam and Julie joined the Todds, who started making out on the dance floor.

That left me alone at the bar, sipping a Coca-Cola while the reality of tomorrow morning's sermon flitted around my head like a fly at a picnic. I should've just stayed home and practiced the blasted thing. After I blew that last sermon, The Preacher just slapped my back and said that everyone has had a bad day. He told me how he'd completely blown his speech as high school class speaker but didn't let that keep him from pursuing the ministry. He said there was a blessing for me in there someplace, but even he seemed to have trouble finding it.

Maybe I really did just have a bad day back in April, but blowing two sermons in a row would be a trend.

I pulled the sermon from my pocket. In it, The Preacher had written that as Christians, our joy doesn't have to be tied to our circumstances (I hoped I could say that line with a straight face). Fortunately, the sermon was only about ten pages long and lighter than most sermons The Preacher had written for me in the past. I'd just stay at the party a few more minutes then sneak out and practice it back at the dorm.

Sam saluted me from the dance floor while Julie kept motioning for me to join them. Even the Todds were egging me on. I just waved them aside. I wasn't really "out" at school and didn't feel comfortable dancing with Julie and three gay guys. No sense rushing it—I'd just ease into this gay thing, take it one step at a time.

I was thinking about that when Joshua appeared. "Hey,

Jake!" he said. He stepped aside and plucked one of three guys from the entourage standing behind him. "You remember Ryan?"

It was the kid I'd made out with at Heaven Bar.

My cheeks suddenly burned. Ryan was the last person I expected to see here. "Oh, um, hey Ryan," I said timidly.

"Hey, Raj," Ryan said, bunching up a corner of his mouth sarcastically.

I shook my head and sighed but couldn't help checking out his form-fitting aqua T-shirt. "I'm Jake, actually."

Joshua smiled knowingly and walked away, leaving Ryan and me alone. Ryan must've thought I was some kind of nut case after my big outing at Heaven, so I was surprised that he was still interested.

I tucked the sermon into my pocket. "Sorry, man. That was—that was a rough night for me."

He dismissed the remark with a wave. "Listen, no explanation needed. At least we got the chance to meet. Wanna drink?"

That was awfully nice of him, but I had to get to the sermon. Plus, I wasn't sure I wanted to get caught up with a guy like Ryan. He seemed to be pretty trampy, although he sure was handsome. "No, thanks. I've got to get up at the crack of dawn tomorrow."

"Oh, c'mon. One drink. Can't you stick around for ten more minutes?"

I reconsidered. I was sick of being the PK, living life on the outside. I wondered how it would feel to just join in for once and be a part of the group? I could simply take a couple of sips and then leave. Besides, it wasn't the first time I'd had alcohol.

"Sure!" I said.

Halfway through our second Blue Lion, Ryan asked me to dance.

The idea of dancing with a guy seemed strange, like eating raw fish. I still wasn't up for that in front of my classmates, not even after two Blue Lions. "Oh, I'm not a big dancer," I said.

He moved in like he wanted to kiss me, causing that gooeyness inside me to bubble up, but I stepped back and took another sip, not wanting my friends to see.

Ryan didn't seem too happy about that. He tipped back his drink and looked around the room, like he was ready to move on to someone else. I figured I had to say something.

"Ryan, I'd love to, but my friends, you know?"

He placed his hand on the small of my back and leaned in. "My parents are out of town this weekend," he whispered. "Want to go back to my place?"

I thought back to Heaven and our first kiss—whisker against whisker, his thick arms wrapped around me. A wave of heat flashed through me and at that moment I would've sold my soul to kiss a guy even half as hot as Ryan. Besides, I'd be back in Tarsus in a couple of weeks and might not get a chance like this again until college.

"Okay," I said, wondering if I could actually go through with it. I could still change my mind once we got downstairs.

Ryan smiled and quickly finished the rest of his drink.

I did the same.

He grabbed my hand to lead me through the crowd, but I pulled it back and walked a few steps behind him.

"Whatcha guys up to?" Sam asked, appearing out of nowhere.

"We're heading doubt, I mean, out." I said, correcting myself.

Ryan cackled. "You're wasted, man!"

"Am not," I said, rubbing my face, but I could hear myself slurring. I decided to speak slowly and really enunciate my words so it wouldn't show so much.

"I'm leaving too," Sam said almost impulsively. "Wanna share a cab uptown?"

I fished through my pocket and handed him my white Columbia security card. "I'm going out with Ryan. Yes, you can have the room, just scan me in, okay?" I winked then popped him on the shoulder, feeling like one of the guys. I thought I was being clever, but he didn't laugh.

At the elevators, Ryan pushed the call button, then smiled at me. He looked like an angel with his wispy brown hair and sparkling white teeth. Where were we going again? Oh, right: his place. Maybe I'd spring for a taxi.

We hopped onto the elevator and, as the doors shut, I looked up to see Sam standing there all alone, looking somewhere between confused and disappointed. Well, he wasn't the only one allowed to have some fun. I was one of the boys too. *such an idiot !*

Beep-beep-beep. Beep-beep-beep. Beep-beep-beep.

"Shut that off, man," I heard someone say.

My eyes opened. The morning light danced on the room's gray walls in time with the swaying blinds at the window. The cinnamon scent from the spent candle on the nightstand brought everything screaming back to me. It had finally happened—and I had known exactly what to do with my hands. What was it that Ryan had said? Oh yeah, he couldn't believe it was my first time. That made me feel like a freakin' rock star. I wished we had time to go another round but I had a sermon to preach. I couldn't wait to get that behind me. Afterwards, I needed to work on my final project, but maybe Ryan and I could get together for dinner.

Beep-beep-beep. Beep-beep-beep. Beep-beep-beep.

"Raj or Jake or whatever your name is, shut that off!"

I hit every button on the alarm clock until the thing stopped beeping. I had to go—it was just after seven, and I had to be at church well before the eleven o'clock service.

Travel time to Columbia was probably thirty minutes, then it would take at least an hour to get out to Brooklyn. I'd barely have time to shower and change, but I could read through the sermon on the subway. Heck, I could even practice preaching on the subway. I'd fit right in—people preached and sang and did all kinds of sideshows on the New York subway all the time.

My mouth was bone dry and my head felt like I was wearing a hat about ten sizes too small. It could only be one thing—a hangover—but nothing could spoil the moment of waking up next to a guy for the first time. I kissed him quick and whispered, "I've got to go, but maybe we could get together later?"

"Let me see how my day goes," he said sleepily without even opening his eyes.

I nodded then tossed off the covers and rolled out of bed. I turned my briefs right side out and about fell putting them on. "I'm such a ᴚᴵᴰᴱ!" I said, chuckling.

But Ryan was already on his way back to sleep. We hadn't even exchanged numbers. "Hey, let's do dinner tonight," I said.

Ryan scrunched his eyes tighter. "I've got a busy day, so can we keep it loose?"

For someone who couldn't keep his hands off me last night, he suddenly seemed pretty noncommittal, but he was probably hungover too.

As I buttoned my shirt, I noticed the paper cut on my right index finger. It was half an inch long and red from end to end. I thought back to my sex education class and remembered that you should assume anyone you sleep with is HIV-positive. HIV could be contracted through the skin, but only if there was an *open wound*. Trouble was, I didn't see a scab on the paper cut, which meant it *was* an open wound.

I turned on the bedside lamp and put my finger under it.

Ryan stirred. "Do you mind?"

"S-sorry—just one second," I said, running a finger over the paper cut. I'd completely forgotten about it. Even under the light, I didn't see a scab.

God's answer to the gay agenda is AIDS! The Preacher's voice rang in my ears.

My insides suddenly felt hollow, like my blood and flesh and hopes and dreams had all vanished.

"C'mon man," Ryan said. "I'm trying to get some sleep."

I switched off the light. "Ryan, can I ask...are you HIV-negative?"

He didn't say anything.

I knelt down on the bed and touched his shoulder. "Ryan, are you—"

"Yes!" he shouted without opening his eyes.

My heart hiccupped. "Yes you're negative or—"

"Yes, I'm negative. Can I please get some sleep now?"

He didn't sound that convincing. People lied about stuff like this all the time.

I pulled away and stepped into my jeans. "So, when was the last time you were tested?"

"I don't know. Maybe a year ago. Don't freak out, man. We barely did anything."

Barely anything?! We did a lot and would've done even more if I hadn't put on the brakes.

A wave of fear pummeled me so hard that I suddenly felt dizzy. I studied my finger, trying to remember all the rules about what's safe and what's not. But as Mrs. Gruen put it in sex education class: "The only thing that's completely safe is abstinence."

I finished getting dressed, nodded goodbye, and marched out the bedroom door.

There was only one person I wanted to see.

At 116th Street, I felt awful for phoning Raj to ask that he meet me at the wormhole, but I had no other choice since I'd given my security card to Sam and couldn't walk through the front door without it. Raj didn't seem too happy about coming down, but moments after I arrived, the door clanged open ever so slightly. I scurried inside.

Back in the dorm room, Alexandros was fast asleep in my bed. I grabbed my backpack, tiptoed into the bathroom, closed the door, and turned on the light. I removed the travel-sized bottle of hand sanitizer from my backpack and popped the top. If the cut stung from the sanitizer, then I would know it was an open wound.

God-please-don't-let-this-thing-sting-in-Jesus-name-Amen.

I squirted the fluid on my index finger and waited. I didn't feel a sting. I DIDN'T FEEL A STING!

I had to be sure though.

I rubbed my damp index finger and thumb together to simulate the activities of last night. Suddenly, my finger was on fire. Did my finger sting last night? There were huge gaps in my memory, I couldn't know for sure.

At that point, my heart was in full gallop. I had to see Sam. He was the only one who could help.

I knocked on the second bathroom door, leading to his room. I knew I was probably killing the moment for him and Joshua but this couldn't wait.

No one answered, so I tried the knob and walked right in.

The room was dark with a hint of Sam's grapefruit cologne. Hearing me enter, he rose up in his bed on one elbow. "Jake? Everything okay?"

"Thank God you're here." I held up my finger. "I thought I was being safe with that Ryan guy, but I forgot about this paper cut."

"I'm not following you, broh."

"It's an open wound. What if I got HIV from Ryan?"

Sam yawned. "Is he positive? Wait, infection through a paper cut? That would take, like, a miracle."

"You saw how that thing bled yesterday. I just tested it. It's red. Red is blood, right?" I walked over so he could get a good look at the cut. "See?"

"You need to chill, Jake. First of all, you can only get infected if your partner is positive," he said, like I was an idiot.

I'd studied all this in sex education class. My finger was red. Red meant blood. HIV infects people by entering the bloodstream through body secretions like Ryan's semen, and there was no way I *didn't* get some on my finger.

"Ryan hasn't been tested in over a year, and he's as big a tramp as you!"

Sam smirked. "Look, I wasn't the one who tricked out last night."

I let out a big sigh. "God, you're right."

"I'm so lame—I'm sorry, brah."

"No, I deserve it. I'm supposed to preach in a couple of hours, but I'm hungover and the thought of what I did with Ryan last night makes me want to puke." It really did. How could I stand up before that congregation and preach when I was a bigger fraud than ever?

Sam sat up and switched on his light. "Let me see that paper cut again."

I sat next to him with my finger under the lamp. "See, there's no scab."

"So?"

"So that makes it an *open wound*. How could I be so stupid?"

"Jake, you were just having fun. It's fine. Relax."

I stared at my finger, feeling hopeless and stupid. "I might as well face it."

He let out a long sigh. "Okay, there's something we can do. Just in case. But we have to act now. Sam tossed his comforter aside and jumped out of bed wearing light blue briefs.

Even in my frazzled state, I couldn't help but stare.

He stepped over to his laptop. "Go get ready. You'll feel better if you take a shower and put on some fresh clothes. I'll, like, need a few minutes to find an HIV testing center that's open on a Sunday morning."

"A what?"

"Just get ready," Sam ordered. "I'll take care of the rest."

CHAPTER 17

Within half an hour, Sam and I were in a taxi, high-tailing it downtown. He researched my situation on his smartphone's web browser while I closed my eyes and braced myself for the call I'd put off as long as I could. I hated that I'd have to lie to my dad, but what other choice did I have? I couldn't tell him that I was headed for an emergency HIV test.

"Hey, Preacher," I said in my raspiest voice.

"It's your big day, son! You ready?"

"Dad, I'm just not feeling well—I don't think I can preach." I was hoping by some miracle he'd buy that explanation and I wouldn't have to get behind the pulpit that morning, but I'd worn a suit and tie and brought my sermon just in case I did.

"Do you have a fever?" he asked.

"I haven't checked, but it sure feels like I do." The lie made me feel even worse. I forced a cough to help make my case.

"Jake, Brother Watson's depending on you. Are you feeling so sick that you can't do this?"

Even with the hangover, I wouldn't call myself sick, but I was in no shape—physically, emotionally, spiritually or morally—to deliver a sermon that morning.

"I can't help it, Preacher. He sure doesn't want what I've got, neither does his congregation."

"Son, all you got here is a bad case of nerves. Just hand this over to the Lord, and I'll be praying for you too. You'll do great. You're a fine preacher—it runs in the family." I could hear the smile in his voice. "Call me afterwards."

I felt more desperate than ever. "Dad, I can't. Please just trust me this one time. I'll never ask for anything else again. Ever. Okay? Okay, Dad? Dad?"

He'd already hung up.

The Preacher was a big believer in tough love. When I was five, he threw me in the deep end of the county pool to teach me to swim, and that's pretty much what he was doing now.

"Great going, brah. Okay, listen up." Sam pointed to the open web browser on his smartphone. "It says here that if you've been exposed to HIV, you can begin a post-exposure prophylaxis—"

"A what?"

"It's called PEP for short. It's a course of antiretroviral pills you take to reduce the chance of seroconversion. The CDC recommends you begin it within, like, two hours. How long has it been?"

I stared ahead as the numbers on the taximeter ticked higher and higher like the enormity of my sins. "My dad will kill me if I don't preach."

"How many hours, Jake?"

I looked at my watch. "About nine."

"Twenty-four hours is the cutoff but it says the sooner the better. You need to decide, brah—the church or the clinic?"

I shook my head, not knowing what to do.

Sam touched my shoulder reassuringly. "You're way overreacting to this, Jake. If it were that easy to get HIV, half the world would be positive. I mean, what are the chances you'd get HIV the very first time you hooked up? I'll go with you to either place but this could be, like, your one chance to get me into church."

I appreciated Sam so much, but I'd read countless stories in our church literature that demonstrated the higher standard that God held born-again Christians to. There was the One-Way man in Kentucky who told God he would become a preacher but only after his little girl grew up—the following week, she was struck by a school bus and killed. In Mississippi, a One-Way preacher confronted a woman in his congregation who was fornicating with a man in the neighboring town. She seemed contrite but apparently decided to see the man one more time—on the way, her car struck the side of a bridge and burst into flames. She had a closed-casket funeral.

Of course, there was no time to explain all that to Sam so I just said, "The clinic."

I trailed behind Sam into the brightly lit waiting area of the Gay Healthcare Center. The cheerful orange walls and yellow carpet couldn't hide the gloominess of the place. I shook my head in disbelief upon seeing all the presumably gay men of all races packed together—we could be waiting a while. Sam and I were the youngest by at least five years, and a few guys were my parents' age or more.

I'd never felt so out of place in my entire life, but after living so many years as a God-fearing PK, it was hard to accept that I was now a gay, promiscuous drunk. But that's exactly what I was.

A spiky-haired receptionist greeted us with a smile.

I leaned in, looked her straight in the eye, and said, "I'm a big tramp." Well, that's what it felt like, but my actual words were, "I'm here for an HIV test?"

"What time is your appointment?" she asked, turning to her computer monitor.

I peered down at the orange Formica counter. "Oh, I, um, don't have an appointment."

She grabbed a clipboard and handed it to me. "Walk-ins are seen on a first-come-first-serve basis. Please complete these forms and be sure to sign at the bottom. Do you have insurance?"

"Yes."

"Good. That would help defray our costs. There won't be anything out of pocket."

I dug through my wallet for my insurance card and handed it to her. "About how long do you think?"

She glanced at her monitor. "An hour, maybe more."

"But I have to be seen right away—I may have been exposed to the virus last night," I whispered urgently.

"I'm sorry but we're one of the few testing centers open on Sundays, so it's one of our busiest days." She handed me an old-fashioned ticket with the number "33" on it. "We'll call you by your number."

Once I filled out the forms, I decided to call Brother Watson and get that over with. He was nice about the whole thing and even said he'd pray for a speedy recovery, but I feared that this would not only be a strike against me, but also against The Preacher; Brother Watson might question whether Dad could possibly accept more responsibility within the church if he couldn't even control his own son. I just hoped The Preacher would find it in his heart to forgive me.

When I got back to the waiting room, Sam had gotten us both Coca-Colas. He started asking me all kinds of questions, like what was my favorite movie and who my best friend back home was. He honestly seemed curious, but I knew he was just trying to keep my mind off the current situation and I was happy for the distraction.

But after about an hour, I was getting antsy. Just sitting there waiting was driving me nuts, not to mention the air conditioning system was doing a crappy job for all the ruckus it was making.

I turned to Sam, "Eleven hours. It's been eleven hours since Ryan and I did it the first time."

"Relax. That's well within the twenty-four hour window, brah. Anyways, you'll test negative. Chill out."

I wanted to tear out of there and never look back. Maybe it would be better to not know.

I stared straight ahead at a two-foot long crack that snaked up the orange wall in front of me. I wondered what caused it and why no one had fixed it. A peculiar thought struck me—I had a beginning and an end, just like that crack. I was here today but who knew when my time on this earth would be up. If I was positive, my time here might be even shorter.

Sam elbowed me. "What're you thinking?"

"What I'd change about my life if I'm positive."

"And?"

I counted off on my fingers. "One. I wouldn't worry so much about what everyone else thought. Two. I'd be the best editor you've ever seen. And three, I'd always write my own editorials."

Sam nodded. "Dude, I hope you'll do those things even if you're negative."

"Thirty-three!" a black male nurse called out.

Sam stood with me and looked me in the eye. "Jake, we're gonna be laughing about this one day. Trust me, you'll be fine."

I hoped he was right.

In the examining room, Nurse Barr sanitized my right index finger then pricked it with a lancet. He drew my blood into a tiny vial then transferred it to the digital-thermometer-looking tester, which he placed in the stand.

While we waited for the results, Nurse Barr asked me all kinds of questions about my sexual history and whether I always practiced safe sex.

I told him all about my first sexual encounter, then showed him my paper cut. "I thought I was being safe last night, but I forgot about this."

He leaned forward and examined my finger. "It would be nearly impossible for you to contract the virus through that paper cut."

"But it's an open wound—that's all HIV needs to get in!" I said almost hysterically.

He let go of my hand. "The results are coming up."

We both stared at the test kit, only he was seeing what was happening—I was just looking at the back of the stand.

Somewhere deep inside, I knew I was positive and for good reason—I had spit in God's face when I went home with Ryan. No, I had given Him the finger. Yes, I had waved my middle finger at God and He struck me down. The fact that I contracted HIV in such a "nearly impossible" way just made it an even clearer sign. But a sign of what? That God didn't want me to act on these feelings even though he wouldn't heal me? That I should go through life alone and sexless? Surely He didn't want me to pretend to be straight. That would be a freakin' lie.

Nurse Barr looked up at me. "Good news. Jake, you tested non-reactive meaning the kit did not detect HIV in your system but—"

I flopped back in my chair. "Thank, God! THANK, GOD!"

"Jake," Nurse Barr said, "you have to understand that this test was like a history report. It reveals your HIV status from *three months ago*. You'll have to wait three more months to get a conclusive test for what happened last night."

I suddenly felt dizzy and nauseous.

"But like I said, you were not at serious risk of exposure to HIV based on what you've told me. Of course, any time you have a sexual encounter there's always the risk of exposure. But based on what you said happened, you were at the lowest level of risk possible."

That just wasn't good enough. Time was wasting away while he talked probabilities. Did I have to explain the whole twenty-four hour PEP window to this guy? I would take the PEP and go right back in the closet and never come out again, plain and simple. "I want to get on that post-exposure prophylaxis just in case."

"Jake, the prophylaxis has severe side effects and is only prescribed in extreme cases like rape or for medical workers who are exposed to contaminated blood or if someone had full-on unprotected sex with a high risk partner. No doctor would recommend it in your case because you are at the lowest level of risk possible. Are you hearing me, Jake? *The lowest level of risk possible.* You have nothing to worry about."

I sat back in my chair and closed my eyes, letting Nurse Barr's words sink in: *The lowest level of risk possible.*

"Would you like to speak to one of our counselors?"

It suddenly struck me that everything in life comes with some sort of risk, from driving a car to getting behind the pulpit. Still, this somehow felt different. But why? I thought about that for a few seconds before realizing that the difference was *guilt.* I felt no guilt for driving or preaching, but I did for drinking and sex. This was new territory that I had to figure out; it was critical that I did because—even with this AIDS scare—I'd take this authentic life over my old pretend life any day. Although I had behaved safely with Ryan in retrospect, maybe I'd just slow things down a little. Hopefully, this bit of wisdom was all I got from last night and, according to Nurse Barr, it probably was.

"Are you okay, Jake?"

I stood and shook Nurse Barr's hand. "Yes, I'm really fine. Thanks for all your help. I really appreciate it."

When I got back to the waiting area, I plopped down next to Sam.

"Any news, brah?"

I nodded. "Sort of. I tested negative but—"

"Duh!" he said, rolling his eyes and putting his phone away.

"Well, the nurse said it's too early to test whether I got HIV from last night, but he said it would be nearly impossible."

"That sounds pretty promising," Sam said with a smirk. "Can we, like, get out of here?"

I let out a sigh. "Yes, but first I need to call my dad and tell him I didn't preach. He's going to kill me."

"Just tell your parents the truth, brah."

I turned to him in disbelief. "Good Lord. You mean, that

I got drunk last night, fooled around with a guy, and came to the gay clinic to get an HIV test? There's not one thing in that sentence I could tell them."

He shook his head. "Maybe you should, like, give your parents a little more credit? They weren't born yesterday."

"Do your parents know that you're gay, Sam?" I asked.

"I haven't seen my dad in, like, forever, but my mom asked me point blank when I was fifteen. I told her 'yes.' End of story."

Sam and his mom sounded all chummy with each other, but that's just not the relationship I had with my parents. I looked down at my watch. 1:23 p.m., which was 12:23 p.m. Alabama time. My parents were probably just getting home from church about now. "Okay, I'm going to call them," I said.

I walked just beyond the receptionist to the hallway that led to the bathrooms and called The Preacher. I first asked about the vote on the church complex (it had passed overwhelmingly) before telling him that I'd skipped the sermon. As expected, he wasted no words telling me how disappointed he was. The only way out was to invent another lie—an even bigger one than the fever—so out of nowhere I said that I had gone to a hospital for blood poisoning. That was all it took. Suddenly, the sermon was small potatoes and Momma got on the phone too, both of them overcome by concern, which made me feel like the biggest heel ever. Before we hung up, my parents made me promise to keep them updated on the blood poison scare, which meant that I had to continue that ruse for a little longer.

I put my phone away, leaned back against the wall and closed my eyes, feeling completely untethered and wondering who the hell I was—promiscuous drunk Jake or Bible-obsessed Jake. Would I settle on a spot between them or flip-flop the rest of my life? Was I neither or was I both? I had no idea.

I walked back into the waiting room and found Sam

standing by the elevator with my suit jacket. He was clearly ready to get out of there, and I was too.

"Well?" he asked, handing me the jacket.

I put it on. "The conversation went okay. I'd just rather not talk about it."

"Jake, you've had quite a day—let's grab lunch," he said, placing a hand on my shoulder.

The moment his hand hit my shoulder, I started tingling all over. I just stood there paralyzed and guilt stricken: not for being turned on by a guy, but for being turned on by a guy who was seeing someone else.

"My treat," he continued. "What're you in the mood for?"

I thought about what I was truly in the mood for with Sam, then felt my face go flush. Only when he dropped his hand did my gift of speech return. "I've got to get to the library and work on my final project. The first drafts are due Tuesday, you know? Aren't you seeing Joshua this afternoon?"

Sam looked away. "No. That's so over."

Half of me was thrilled and the other half felt guilty for being thrilled. Of course, I didn't let on. "It's over? Are you okay?"

"I guess," he said, biting his lip.

I couldn't believe he had stuck by my side all day through my non-drama—as it turned out—when his own hurt was so real. "Want me to beat him up? Just say the word."

"No, it was my choice. It was, like, always about him. Plus, I've been, like, crushing on someone else."

Boy, Sam really worked fast. "Anyone I know?"

Sam looked deep into my eyes and took a deep breath.

Only then did I suspect who he was talking about.

His eyes wandered down to my lips, and the air between us suddenly seemed charged. Then, right there in the waiting room of the Gay Healthcare Center, Sam's mouth inched toward mine.

As our lips met, a surge ripped right through me. It all

happened so fast—one second we were talking about lunch and the next he was kissing me like he'd been waiting to do that his entire life. I wrapped my arms around him, and we held each other tight.

For a moment, I was self-conscious, knowing the other gay guys were watching. There were "oohs" and "ahs" and one "get a room," but I didn't care; I was in Sam's arms and amongst my own tribe. I felt safe. And in that moment, all my cares melted away.

CHAPTER 18

The next day, as Professor Greenberg lectured about repurposing news stories for different media, I just sat there smiling at nothing, reliving the moment that Sam confessed his feelings for me, and then that first kiss. I hadn't seen that coming. Sam had filled my thoughts ever since, and I wondered if I filled his in the same way.

"As a reminder, the first drafts of your final project are due tomorrow," Professor Greenberg said at the end of class, like we needed reminding.

We were only halfway through the six-week program and our final project drafts were already due. I was way behind on mine, but Sam, Julie, and Raj were so caught up that they had planned an extravagant early dinner in midtown

I still hadn't heard back from Senator-elect Syed nor his press secretary and needed to do more research on his background, the separation of church and state, and the Constitutional guidelines for swearing-in members of Congress. I'd never even considered that a sacred vow could be taken on anything other than a Bible, but they probably used a Qur'an in Kabul, right?

On my way to the library, I called The Preacher to see if there was any fallout after his conversation with Brother Watson yesterday. Of course, I wasn't going to specifically bring that up, but I knew *he* would if there was a problem.

"So, how's your finger, Jake?" The Preacher asked. "I forgot to ask if they put you on antibiotics for the blood poison."

I made a quick promise to myself that once I put this lie to bed, I'd never tell another. "No sir. I—I just have to, um, monitor it."

"How you feeling now?" he asked.

"A little drained, but I'm doing fine. I'm heading to the library to work on my final project. Preacher, what do you think about…"

"What was that, Jake?" he asked.

I realized that I didn't need to ask my dad what he thought about using a Qur'an to swear in a member of congress. I already knew. In fact, I knew what my dad's opinion was on pretty much everything. It was my opinions that needed sorting out. "Never mind," I said.

Although a portion of Columbia's nearly ten million books had been digitized and were now available online, the majority of the ones I needed were not. I inched along the dust-covered American History shelves of Butler Library, pulling a few books and feeling sorry for myself. Professor Greenberg was a real jerk for making me write an editorial when he knew good and well that I was better at news. My editorial topic had seemed pretty clear-cut when I spouted it off to him, but after the research I did yesterday, I wasn't so sure.

I'd heard my entire life that this country was founded on Christianity. In my heart, I believed that Jesus was right there in the Pennsylvania State House when the Constitution was signed. So, the easy answer was that Senator-elect Syed should be sworn in using a Bible no matter what faith he was. That was what The Preacher would say too.

But what about the separation of church and state?

Well, I read the Constitution from beginning to end yesterday and didn't find "separation of church and state" in it anywhere. I thought I'd missed it, so I read it again but still didn't see it. After some further research, I learned that Thomas Jefferson coined that phrase years after the

Constitution was written. He said it was covered in the First Amendment (part of the Bill of Rights), which came into effect four years after the Constitution. I'd read the First Amendment so many times, I now had it committed to memory:

> Congress shall make no law respecting an establishment of religion, or prohibiting the free exercise thereof; or abridging the freedom of speech, or of the press; or the right of the people peaceably to assemble, and to petition the government for a redress of grievances.

I didn't see that as a clear-cut separation of church and state, but Thomas Jefferson was right there when it was penned, so he knew the intentions of the text better than me. Of course, Thomas Jefferson might've had his own agenda, but I couldn't help but notice that there was no mention of God in the entire U.S. Constitution *except* in the closing:

> Done in convention by the unanimous consent of the states present the seventeenth day of September in the Year of our Lord one thousand seven hundred and eighty seven and of the independence of the United States of America the twelfth.

In the Year of our Lord. Clearly, that refers to Jesus, which proves that our founding fathers were indeed Christian, right? Actually, they were—as far as I could tell—but "in the Year of our Lord" was just what people said back then instead of "A.D." (which meant exactly that). It's just a unit of measure like Fahrenheit or Celsius. In fact, the year is stated in both A.D. and in the birth years of the country—the twelfth year of the Independence of the United States. I'd never even noticed that before.

More digging was required.

I heaved six history books—the maximum allowed—onto the semicircular checkout counter along with my Columbia ID. I chose books that would give me a clearer picture of the signers of the constitution, religion during Colonial times, and a few more general books, including *Famous Oaths Throughout History.*

With some difficulty, I lugged the books back to my dorm room. It was just before five, so I phoned Senator-elect Syed's office again and left another message for his press secretary. I'd managed to get her direct number after calling so many times.

Back at my desk, I watched a few online interviews with Senator-elect Syed, and then pored through those books and Columbia's online resources to help me form a solid opinion on Senator-elect Syed's situation. I learned that religious oppression was as big a catalyst for the American Revolution as English rule, even though I'd been taught that we went to war solely over "taxation without representation." Ironically, even after English rule was long gone in America, religious oppression continued, but in a different form—nine out of the thirteen colonies declared official state churches, granted them power, and gave them financial support. In some colonies, any denomination other than the official one (either Anglican or Congregationalist) was basically out of luck. Muslims and Jews must've really had it bad in those times. very few about

In 1801, a Baptist group from Connecticut wrote then a heartfelt letter to Thomas Jefferson, the newly inaugurated president, asking that he clarify religious freedom in the United States since "our constitution of government is not specific." That's when Jefferson wrote his famous separation of church and state line.

What motivated Mr. Jefferson to do that? Was he anti-religion? He didn't belong to any established church, but he did construct his own version of the Gospel by creating a single narrative about Jesus, which was taken directly from various books of the New Testament. It's very telling that he removed everything that was beyond scientific understanding, and what was left was simply the philosophy of Jesus without any reference to miracles or to His being the Son of God.

As interesting as all this was, spending all night uncovering random facts wouldn't give me a solid first draft by the morning, but before I got started on the writing, I needed to understand more about oaths.

I learned that oaths are "sacred promises," which meant they must reference God or something that "deserves veneration." Romans would actually swear on their own testicles! (The book didn't say what women swore on.) The Hippocratic Oath, taken by doctors to this day, originally referenced the god Apollo. In Victorian England, a famous English atheist was elected to parliament but the House denied him his seat—they said he was technically unable to swear the Oath of Allegiance since he didn't believe in God.

My head was spinning with all these facts, and I wasn't sure where they'd take me. But there was only one way for me to find out. In journalism, there are two types of writers—*planners* know what they want to write before drafting an article, and *plungers* just jump in and figure it out as they go along.

I was a plunger.

Hours passed, and I was so fried by the time Raj got home that I was happy for the interruption.

"How was dinner?" I asked from my desk.

"Okay." Raj loosened the back of his turban, and unwound the black cloth round and round, gathering its twenty-foot length in his fist. There was a wood comb underneath that he laid aside.

"Hey, when're you gonna teach me how to tie that thing?" I asked.

"Yes, we must get to that," he said, checking himself out in the dresser mirror. Raj unwound his thick hair and flung it over his shoulders; the coarse, ragged ends landed just above his waist.

Maybe it was my imagination, but he'd seemed distant ever since my fateful night at Heaven. I could explain away his never asking about my big gay news as not wanting to pry, but he hadn't asked me about *anything* since I'd returned from my five days at Phoebe's. The only time he spoke to me was when I asked him a direct question and only then if he couldn't get away with a nod or a shrug. I wasn't exactly pissed—I just wanted to understand. As Plato used to say, "Εὐνόει• ὁ γὰρ πᾶς τυχὼν πονεῖ." Be kind, for everyone you meet is fighting a hard battle.

"Is everything okay?" I asked. "I mean, you've been acting sort of different around me lately."

"Different?" he asked, plopping down on his bed and untying his tennis shoes.

"Well, we never walk to class together anymore," I said sincerely. "Why is that?"

He shrugged. "I don't know. I've been getting to class earlier so I could read *The Times*."

That was certainly a logical explanation. I started to let it go but something deep down wouldn't let me—there was more to it than that. "It's like you, I don't know, just tolerate me or something. Sometimes I think you just tolerate Sam too, so you can use his room for your dates."

"Sam is cool," he said measuredly, removing his final shoe. "But I do not like the way you look at me sometimes."

This was news to me. I jerked my head back, not knowing what he was talking about. "When?"

He gestured at the mirror with his shoe. "Just now. In the dresser mirror."

"Raj, I was watching you undo your turban! That's all. Besides, I've seen you check me out, too. It doesn't mean anything."

"I have never checked you out," he said emphatically.

"Oh please!" I waved my hand and turned back to my laptop, realizing that this conversation was going nowhere.

"Oh, so now I am gay, too?" he asked with a sneer. "It does seem to be an epidemic in this town, but I assure you I am not."

I tensed up. "An epidemic? Are you suggesting there's something wrong with being gay?"

We stared each other down.

He finally shook his head and climbed into bed. He laid there in silence while I stared at my computer screen, unable to focus. Finally he said, "Have you ever slept with a girl?"

"No."

"A-ha!" he said, sitting up. "So how can you know you are gay?"

"Have you ever slept with a guy?" I shot right back at him.

"Of course not," he said.

"You're one to judge, Raj." I pointed at the framed print on his dresser with my chin. "What would Muhammad say about all your drinking and whoring around?"

Raj looked at the picture then back at me. "You think that—"

"And you have absolutely no interest in going to Mecca! I mean, what kind of Muslim are you?"

Raj exploded in laughter. "I am not Muslim and that is not Muhammad—it is Guru Nanak, founder of Sikhism!"

I'd never heard of Guru Nanak or his faith. Was Raj making this up? "Is that a branch of Hinduism or something?"

He rolled his eyes. "You are pathetic." He laid back down and pulled up the covers.

I did feel sort of pathetic for never having heard of his religion. "No, I want to know."

"Then look it up online," he said, and then turned off his bedside lamp, indicating the conversation was over.

After about an hour, Raj started ranting in his sleep. I'm sure he was pouring out his darkest secrets. Unfortunately, I didn't understand his native tongue. It didn't matter: I was engrossed in my writing.

Although I tried to be quiet, Raj woke up around 3 a.m. as I printed out the first draft of my editorial.

"Go to bed, Jake!" he said. "You can not keep burning oil from both ends."

There was something touching about the way he said it—like he really cared. Perhaps our conversation earlier had brought us a little closer together.

I switched off my desk lamp and went to bed.

Professor Greenberg waited until the end of class Friday to return our marked-up final project drafts. I'd put everything into that editorial and felt pretty upbeat about it. That is, until he plopped mine in front of me with a shake of his head. "By the skin of your teeth, Mr. Powell," he said. "I really wouldn't call this an editorial."

Just beneath the headline, there was a handwritten "C" with the comment "A total cop out. Take a stand—what do *you* think?"

I'd never gotten a "C" in my entire life, and it felt like someone had just punched me in the gut. My immediate thought was that Professor Greenberg was just out to get me. As I flipped through the editorial, I found it bleeding from his red-penned commentaries: "Reads like a feature story," "Not convincing," and "You're joking, right?"

I had stated the issue clearly and concluded that the Supreme Court should weigh in since the Court was charged with interpreting the Constitution. That's not a cop out—it's a fact!

I turned the paper on its face, but I wanted to throw it across the room. This is exactly why I hated writing editorials. I want to be a journalist, not a judge.

A professionally bound presentation landed squarely on Julie's desk with a thud. We both jumped.

"Miss Aaron, I'm afraid you'll have to follow the rules," Greenberg said. "This sounds more like a fashion shoot than a photo essay."

Julie glared back at him. "But this is the Mayor we're talking about. How can you give me a 'D'?"

"I didn't *give* you a 'D,' Miss Aaron. You earned it."

After he handed back all drafts, Professor Greenberg

said, "Final projects are due one week from today, so I'm dismissing class early. Enjoy your weekend."

"Jesus!" Julie said once Greenberg stepped away.

I was upset about my grade and hearing Julie take Jesus' name in vain for the thousandth time felt like she'd thrown ice water in my face. "Julie, please quit saying that around me. It's offensive."

"Saying what?" she asked.

I shook my head, amazed that she was really that unaware. "Taking The Lord's name in vain."

"Oh please!" she said. "I don't mean anything by it. He's not my 'Lord.'"

"That's not the point! Why can't you say something else?"

She shrugged her shoulders. "Like what?" moses!

"I don't know," I said, looking around. "How about 'Holy Cow!' or 'Gosh!' or just go with some deity no one cares about like—like—Zeus! Yes, why not say 'Zeus!' instead? That way you won't offend—" Then it dawned on me that I'd had a revelation. "Wait, that's it!" And just like that, my opinion on Senator-elect Syed's situation went from half-baked to fully formed.

"That's what?" Julie asked, clearly confused.

I kissed her square on the lips, then jumped up and stuffed my notebook in my backpack. "That's the missing piece to my editorial!"

I threw my backpack over my shoulder and ran out.

Finding an empty classroom around the corner, I took out my phone and called the direct number I had for Senator-elect Syed's press secretary.

"Hello, Miss Kanza," I said. "This is Jake Powell from Columbia University."

"Sorry I haven't returned your calls," she said.

"That's okay, but I'm up against a deadline. Is Senator-elect Syed available?"

"He's actually in New York, but I'm afraid he's fully booked."

I had to find a way to see him and decided to go for broke. "Miss Kanza, did I mention that our articles are being judged by *The Wall Street Journal, The Times,* and *The Washington Post*? I'd just need fifteen minutes of his time."

"Well, he did just have a cancellation. Are you available to meet with him at five o'clock today?"

I had to cover my mouth for a second to keep from hollering. "Sure, I can make that work."

I met Senator-elect Syed at Soho House, a private club in Manhattan's Meatpacking District. He was a little older than The Preacher with sandy-colored hair and no turban. He invited me to join him in the club's library at a large, round table. Leather-bound books lined the light-colored wood shelves complete with one of those movable ladders on a track that allowed easy access to the upper shelves.

We'd been speaking for about five minutes when I gave him my best serious interview face. "So, you're saying that you want to be sworn-in on the Qur'an for diversity reasons?" I asked.

He leaned in. "Absolutely. People forget that there is no religious requirement to be a Congressman, and they also forget that there are five million American Muslims who are underrepresented in Congress. I'll be sworn in on Thomas Jefferson's Qur'an, by the way."

Jefferson's name kept popping up. I had always thought of him as an also-ran to George Washington, but clearly he wasn't. "He studied Islam?"

Senator-elect Syed threw his arms out wide. "He studied everything. It's on loan from the Library of Congress just for the occasion."

I went into what I call my "probing interview mode," looking him right in the eye. "Would you call the people who don't want you to use the Qur'an 'bigots'?"

"I don't want to start name-calling," he said, taking the highroad. "Rather than focusing on our individual religious beliefs, we should just focus on the document that binds us together—the U.S. Constitution."

"Would this have been such a big deal pre-9/11?" I asked.

He tilted his head from side to side. "Yes and no. Some would be opposed to it, but it wouldn't have gotten this kind of media attention. Jake, I'm glad you brought up 9/11. Since that day, there's been a sense of despair in the Muslim community. The terrorists may have been Muslim, but they weren't representative of the Muslim community at large. They were radicals. There have been radical religious groups ever since there's been religion, and no faith is exempt."

"Yeah, I'm embarrassed by that so-called Christian group, God Hates Fags," I said. Sam would be so proud of me for citing that example, but would Senator-elect Syed now think I was gay? I mean, I was, but I was still trying to get used to that. I suddenly felt exposed.

"Exactly! American Muslims have been disenfranchised since 9/11 even though they have nothing more in common with the terrorists than you do with this group called God Hates Fags."

"How will using the Qur'an help change this?"

"It's just one small way Muslims can once again feel less marginalized and reclaim their status as equal to all other American citizens."

I had all the information I needed to write a killer editorial, but I had a big ethical dilemma. I was pretty sure I knew of a better tact Senator-elect Syed could take in defending his wish to use a Qur'an, but revealing that to him would have been highly unusual and possibly unethical. In journalism, the needs of the reader come before all others, and we journalists had to avoid even the appearance of anything other than total editorial independence; no journalist wanted to be perceived as a government official's water boy.

On the other hand, revealing my position really didn't sacrifice my independence nor the hypothetical reader's interest, but it could help defuse the situation for Senator-elect Syed and help bring the two sides together a little.

Still, my position wasn't so unique that Senator-elect Syed or a member of his staff couldn't come up with it on their own. He probably already had but was more concerned with pleasing his constituency—and getting some press—than building a bridge. He's a politician after all.

I smiled and shook his hand. "Thank you for your time," I said.

I left Soho House with a huge smile on my face, excited to write the piece that would determine my entire future.

CHAPTER 19

"Ready?" Sam asked, sitting on my bed with his laptop.

I was at my desk. "Not quite. I wanna read this through one last time before I submit it." I'd read my final project at least a dozen times already, but I wanted to make sure it was perfect. I'd even gotten feedback from Phoebe, Miriam, and Father Claude. That might seem like overkill, but my entire career was riding on winning an Excellence in Journalism Award.

Sam looked at his watch. "You've got fifteen minutes, brøh."

As if on cue, my cell phone rang. I stood and answered it.

"Hey, Jake, what're you up to?" The Preacher asked, brightly.

"Oh, a friend and I are just, um, finishing up our projects. They're due in fifteen minutes so…"

Sam crossed his eyes and puckered his lips to mimic a guppy. I motioned him away so I could focus.

"Momma and I are coming up to your awards ceremony next Thursday," The Preacher said with great enthusiasm. "We want to be there when God reveals his will to you."

This came out of nowhere. Of course, all of our parents were invited to the ceremony, but I hadn't even discussed the possibility with mine since it seemed ridiculous for them to travel all this way just to attend. Suddenly, I realized that my Tarsus and New York worlds were about to collide in what would almost certainly be a complete train wreck. A wave of panic ripped through me. "What? You're coming to New York for the ceremony?" I said, repeating his words to help them sink in. I leaned back on my desk, shocked.

Sam clapped his hands together. "I can't wait to meet The Preacher, L-O-L," he whispered, sarcastically.

I shushed Sam. "That's great, Preacher," I managed to say warmly. "I can't wait to see y'all. Give my love to Momma."

"Aren't you too old to call your mother 'Momma'?" Sam asked the moment I hung up the phone.

Back home, most everyone referred to their Momma that way—no matter how old they were—but now that he mentioned it, "Momma" did sound kind of juvenile. But what I called my mother seemed like such a small matter compared to all the catastrophes I imagined happening while my parents were here, like Sam kissing me square on the lips if I won that award, Julie taking Jesus' name in vain, and someone offering The Preacher a Blue Lion. A second wave of panic hit me. "This is going to end badly," I said.

"Earth to Jake—we've got, like, twelve minutes before our projects are due. Want to read yours to me?

"Okay," I said, sitting back down at my desk. I printed off my final editorial, "Mr. Syed Goes to Washington," and read it aloud.

On the first go-round, I had focused on facts: the exact requirements of the Constitution regarding the swearing-in of a congressman, the role Christianity played in the founding of this country, how our courts have ruled on First Amendment issues through the years, and the process by which we interpreted the Constitution. I had made the case that the Supreme Court should decide whether the use of a Biblical text was even permissible, given the separation of church and state but, in the meantime, Senator-elect Syed should at least consider using the Bible for the sake of tradition and the orderly transfer of power. *No he does nt believe it*

After receiving a "C" for that last effort, I realized I needed to dig deeper. *but does the Koran*

Getting that interview with Senator-elect Syed was huge, but my big breakthrough came when Julie took the Lord's name in vain for the thousandth time. Of course, it didn't mean anything to her since she didn't believe in Jesus.

So why ask a non-Christian to take a sacred oath on the New Testament when it wouldn't mean anything to him? Upholding the U.S. Constitution was a huge responsibility, so I argued that Senator-elect Syed should be required to swear on something he held dear, whether it's the Qur'an, his firstborn child, or even his testicles.

Once I was finished with my final read-through, Sam took my editorial and flipped to the final page. "I still think you should say this is, like, another example of how religion is used to subjugate people. Then you could work in how gays and lesbians are totally harassed by religious groups who—"

"Sam, *stop!* I know how you feel about this, but that's not what this editorial is about."

"Couldn't you add a line that totally sticks it to the religious right?" he asked.

I let out a sigh. "I know these people you're talking about firsthand. In fact, you'd lump just about everyone I know into that bucket. They're real people like my dad, who's trying to do his best just like everyone else. But he's not perfect. If I add another hot topic like gay civil rights to this editorial, it could easily be dismissed as another piece of liberal garbage. I know what you'd do, but I want to build a bridge here."

Sam shook his head as if I was a hopeless cause.

"Plus, I don't define myself as *just* gay," I said. "It's like you're constantly testing my commitment to 'the cause.' I don't think you're ever gonna let up until I'm standing next to you on your gay soapbox twenty-four/seven. This time next year, I might be waving a rainbow flag in some Gay Pride parade, but I just need time to figure all this out, okay?" I actually couldn't imagine myself walking in a Gay Pride parade, let alone waving a rainbow flag, but a few weeks ago, I couldn't have imagined myself kissing a guy. I just needed to take this one day at a time.

Sam turned back to his computer in a huff. "Whatever. It's your editorial."

I took a deep breath. Sam was just trying to help, and

here I was going off on him. "Okay, here goes nothing," I said and clicked the send icon.

Sam closed his laptop and just sat there with his arms crossed. Looking anywhere but at me.

"Sorry I went off like that," I said after a few moments, then took a seat next to him on the bed. "I know I sounded kinda harsh just now but, well, it's just all new territory for me. I really appreciate your help. I hope you know that."

He let out a big sigh. "Jake, I'm not trying to test you. I'm, like, trying to protect you."

"Protect me from what?"

He took my hand and kissed it. "From that closet you just stepped out of. Dude, it's going to take everything you've got not to go right back in it after you get home. These people you think so much of, the ones who're just trying to do their best? I hope they're as awesome as you say. I hope they change their way of thinking and rally around you, but if they don't, are you, like, ready to go it alone, because that closet is going to be calling your name, brah. It's going to look like the freakin' Garden of Eden, but it's really a grave."

I looked away. Although coming out to my parents and friends back home was the next logical step, the idea was terrifying since I'd be the only out person in my entire hometown. "Well, I'm part of the religious right and my views have changed, haven't they?" I asked, thinking aloud. "I just have to try. I have to believe…"

"I care about you, Jake," he said. "It's like whatever happens to you, now happens to me. You know, that kind of caring."

That was the sweetest thing anyone had ever said to me. "I care about you too, Sam. The exact same way."

"I just don't want to call you up in a month and hear that you and, like, Betsy Mae are totally an item, and it would be best if I didn't call again."

Was he serious? I couldn't imagine life without Sam. Even though we'd be separated geographically after Columbia, we'd talk and text ten times a day or more. That much I knew. I leaned over and pecked him on the lips. "That would never happen. Besides, the only Betsy I know is an old bird dog."

Sam laughed then leaned in and kissed me long and hard.

But I wasn't feeling it. There was a nagging question that had been bugging me ever since the day of our first kiss, and it was time we discussed it. I pulled away and looked into his big blue eyes. "Sam, there's something I want to ask you. Promise you won't think I'm weird?"

"Too late."

I elbowed him, playfully. "Sam, have you ever thought about becoming a Christian? I mean, it's sort of strange for me dating a nonbeliever."

"What do you mean by 'nonbeliever'?"

"Someone who doesn't believe in Jesus."

"I believe in God. Isn't that enough?"

"I struggle with that," I said, looking off to the side in thought. "I just always saw myself with a Christian."

He pulled me in close for a hug. "Until a couple weeks ago, you totally saw yourself with a girl."

Sam was right. All kinds of changes were happening to me at the speed of light. "True enough. Tell me, though, how do Jewish people get to heaven?"

"Most Jews I know don't see heaven as, like, angels and trumpets and streets paved with gold. We try to live a good life and repent of our sins once a year. On Yom Kippur. It's our annual day of atonement. We fast and attend synagogue." Then as an afterthought he added, "Well, a lot of people do."

"Do you and your Mom go to synagogue on Yom Kippur?"

"Not in years," he said.

"Do you fast?"

Sam chuckled and gave me one of his are-you-crazy looks.

I put my head on his shoulder and took in his grapefruit cologne. My head fit perfectly in the crook of his neck.

He rubbed my back as our breathing synched. "Jake, we don't have to figure all this out today, do we?"

"I guess not," I whispered, wondering how he read my mind. I pulled his lips to mine.

He kissed me back hard as we laid back on the bed. We'd only gone so far in the twelve days since we'd first kissed, and I intended to keep it that way.

"Let's keep it above the waist." I said, taking off my shirt.

"Above the waist," he said, removing his, then looking me up and down. "You're stunning, brah."

Sam Horowitz thinks I'm stunning! My entire body flushed with joy, but I wondered if he needed glasses. "You know," I said, sitting on top of him. "I'm pretty sure I can pin you."

"You think so, huh?" he asked, and before I knew it, he'd flipped me on my back and held my wrists tight against the mattress.

"No fair!" I said, laughing.

He smiled, loosened his vice-like grip and kissed me softly.

I wrapped my arms around his broad shoulders, kissing him back, the worries that had consumed me moments earlier disappearing. During the whole time we made out, I didn't once think about that Janet Walters multi-step approach. And even though I felt tempted, he was true to his word: we kept it above the waist.

CHAPTER 20

The day of the honors ceremony—my personal Judgment Day—arrived way too quickly. Shortly, my life's course would be set, based on whether I won or lost an Excellence in Journalism award. But what was weighing on me even more was the fact that it was my last day with Sam. We had gotten so close that I now needed to be with him the same way I needed to eat or breathe. How could I survive being two thousand miles away from him? Were our feelings for each other strong enough to survive that kind of distance? Was he thinking the same thing or would he just move on to the next guy once he got back to L.A.? I didn't think so, but I wanted to make a plan. We somehow hadn't talked about it, probably because neither of us wanted to even think about our final day together, but that day had come. I had to believe that if he was committed to "us" the same way I was, we'd find a way to survive our senior year and go to the same college. That made my need to win an award today even more critical, since I'd be headed to a One-Way seminary if I didn't. And One-Way Bible seminaries weren't located anywhere near the top universities that Sam would certainly be applying to.

Along with all my fretting over the award and my sadness over leaving Sam was an overarching dread around my parents' arrival. On the one hand, I was excited to see them and so touched that they'd travel all this way to attend the ceremony, but that's the kind of parents they were. They were my biggest fans and I never doubted their love for me, not for a second.

But having my parents and my New York friends together in the same space introduced a strange dynamic; my parents would expect to find the old Jake who was straight and believed everything they believed, while my New York friends—especially Sam—probably thought I should come right out to them the moment they arrived. Of course, I would eventually have to come out to them, and I hoped their love was deep enough to carry them through. But there was enough to worry about today without going there.

Starting with Julie.

Even though I'd spoken to her about it twice, I was still worried that she might slip in front of The Preacher by taking The Lord's name in vain or commenting on how cute Sam and I looked together or calling me a 'mo. With her, anything was possible.

It felt like I'd known Julie for a lifetime, but in reality I'd only known her six weeks. Six weeks. How could so much change for me in such a short amount of time from coming out to losing my virginity to dating Sam? I had learned a lot at Columbia, but my biggest lessons mostly came from outside the classroom. Regardless of the outcome of the awards, I was returning to Tarsus a new and better person. I was incredibly grateful for that.

Just before the ceremony began, I met Phoebe at the Columbia gates. Dressed in our Sunday best, we walked alongside parents and students down college walk and up the stairs to Low Memorial Library, an enormous Greek temple of a building capped by the largest granite dome in North America. Inside the ten-story rotunda, sunlight poured through six massive semi-circular windows running along the base of the dome, which was lined with Greek statues. I'm sure even the greatest Ancient Greek architects would've been impressed if they could just get past the fact that their best designs had been ripped off.

Although there couldn't have been much more than a hundred people inside, the echos off the marble walls and limestone floor made it sound more like a thousand. The seating was arranged in a U around four rows of blue velvet-draped chairs reserved for students.

Phoebe pointed at three empty seats together for my parents and her. "Over there," she called out. We made a dash for the seats. Each had a glossy program emblazoned with the blue Columbia crown insignia. I picked one up and was so rattled by what I saw that I immediately collapsed in a seat:

Program and Collection of Student Works

"Oh my God!" I said, feeling naked and exposed. "Why didn't Professor Greenberg tell us our work was going to be printed?"

"Oh, how nice," Phoebe said, taking the seat next to me and flipping through her copy.

I shook my head. "Nice? NICE? The Preacher will have a cow when he reads my editorial!"

"Why?" Phoebe asked,

"Are you serious? You read my editorial—The Preacher is going to hate it. I might as well have written that we should remove 'In God We Trust' from our currency." I looked through the collection, hoping my editorial had somehow been left out, but there it was. I suddenly had the urge to tear out of there and never look back.

Phoebe patted my leg. "Oh relax, Jake. This might be the best thing. Of course, it might be kind of awkward at first—"

Was she kidding? "At first? You mean the first few decades?"

Phoebe laughed. "What was it that Julie called you that day in my apartment? A drama queen?"

"You—you were listening?"

Phoebe laughed. "Of course! Anyway, what I'm trying to say is he might not agree with your opinion here, but I bet he'll respect the fact that you've got one. Plus, it might just open up his mind a little. Lord knows he could use that."

I shook my head in despair. The Preacher almost never changed his mind once it was set, or if he did, it always came with some pretty big strings attached. Like the way he'd only let me come to New York if I staked my entire journalism career on a single award.

Phoebe cupped my hands tight. "Jake, this is an excellent editorial, and it's not just me—Claude and Miriam think it's excellent too."

"Thanks, Phoebe, but you're all a little biased," I said.

Phoebe squeezed my hands tighter and looked in my eyes. "Do you believe everything you wrote here, honey?"

I let out a deep breath, then nodded. "I sure do."

"Have you written anything shameful?" she asked, pursing her lips.

I shook my head. "No, but The Preacher won't care for it much."

"You don't always have to agree, do you? Good Lord, Richard and I used to..." Phoebe looked away.

I'd never heard her mention a Richard before. Did she have a long lost kid or something? "Who's Richard?"

Phoebe dropped my hands and smoothed out her black linen dress. "I'm just saying this could lead to a more honest relationship with your father. It's a first step toward coming out. I'm sure he's had his own stuff to deal with—he might be more understanding than you think."

Somehow I always thought my father's past was kind of like Jesus': pretty flawless. Sure, Jesus once acted out in the temple and basically ran away from his parents another time, but he always had a good explanation for his actions. I'd never even contemplated that my father might have veered off the straight and narrow, but maybe Phoebe knew something I didn't. "How so?" I asked.

"Ha! Don't think he doesn't have baggage. We all do." She paused for a moment then whispered to me, "Ask him about that scar on his wrist sometime."

"The one he got from the Dr. Pepper bottle?"

Phoebe looked away. "We all have our thorns."

Talking about my dad made me wonder if they were going to be late. "What's taking them so long? They left JFK nearly two hours ago."

"They wanted to drop their bags off at the hotel," Phoebe said, shaking her head. "I wish they were staying with me, but I guess Henry would never seriously entertain that option."

I spotted Sam seating his mom, Cathy, on the other side of the auditorium. She was rail thin and had long blond hair that danced about her shoulders. Cathy had taken us both to lunch earlier that day, and I think I made a good impression because she said I could come out and visit them in L.A. anytime.

I waved and finally got Sam's attention. He waved back and started making his way over.

"That's him," I said to Phoebe. "That's the guy I've been seeing."

Phoebe covered her mouth. "That's Sam? My word, Jake, you certainly know how to pick 'em. I approve."

I laughed. Sam was all dressed up in a charcoal suit that set off his broad shoulders and an aqua tie that I'd insisted he wear because it made his blue eyes pop. He absolutely took my breath away. I wondered how I could leave this guy behind, but what choice did I have? "He's really sweet too," I said.

The overhead lights flickered, indicating that the program was about to begin.

"There they are!" Phoebe said, pointing over my shoulder.

I turned to see my father waving at me. Momma blew me a kiss.

My heart lit right up as I ran over to greet them.

Momma gave me a big hug, which calmed my nerves and made me feel a little more confident. "Look at my handsome young man. You're all grown up, honey." She looked so proud. I wondered if she still would be if she knew my whole story.

The Preacher was grinning ear to ear. He hugged me too. "Looks like we made it just under the wire," he said.

As I walked them over to Phoebe, who was already chatting up Sam, I tried to relax but how could I? It's more than a little unnerving to introduce the guy you're seeing to your parents who think you're into girls. Fortunately, the moment was truncated with Phoebe and Momma getting all misty-eyed as they hugged.

I took a deep breath. "Mom and Dad, this is my classmate, Sam."

That was the first time I'd called my mother anything but Momma since I was five, and her flinch was imperceptible to anyone who wasn't looking for it. I cocked my head slightly to make sure she was cool with her new handle, but she didn't miss a beat as she offered her hand.

While Sam and Mom shook hands, The Preacher held back, like he was sizing Sam up. Could he tell that Sam was gay? Did he sense that Sam and I were more than classmates? As I've mentioned before, The Preacher practically has a degree in sizing people up.

"Hello, Preacher," Sam said, shaking my father's hand firmly. "I hope you don't mind if I call you 'Preacher.'"

Smooth move, Horowitz.

The Preacher lit right up. "Not at all. Good to meet you, Sam."

After the quick introduction, I dragged Sam out of there as fast as I could. We needed to take our seats since the ceremony was about to start, but I mostly wanted to curtail any more sizing up activity by The Preacher.

We spotted Julie in a gorgeous but simple black dress in the front row of the student section. She looked stunning with her hair up but still spilling down around her shoulders in that way that girls somehow manage. I would've felt bad that her parents didn't come, but she specifically told them not to.

She stroked my arm as we arrived. "I was just thinking about that agreement you made with your dad. You nervous?"

"As hell," I said.

"Dude, your editorial is awesome!" Sam said. "You are so taking home a trophy. "

I smiled. "I hope we all do."

"Oh, I'm feeling real confident," Julie said sarcastically.

The lights dimmed as music right out of a network news program played. Sam winked at me then took his seat in the second row. I scurried over to my chair in the third row. I opened the program to check out the order of events. The Excellence in Editorial Writing Award was the last category in the ceremony, so I'd have to wait till the end to learn my fate.

I turned around. The Preacher was already scribbling notes right on his program. I had no doubt that he was marking up my editorial. I could imagine The Preacher's running commentary on each point. "This country was founded on Christianity! Sounds like his allegiance is to Islam, not America!"

My stomach clenched up as I thought about the lecture I'd get after the ceremony. I hunched over with my hands jammed into my armpits as if I were trying to disappear or at least make myself as small as possible.

My mind was racing, trying to figure out a scenario where The Preacher might sum up my final project with a *you-really-got-me-thinking-here-Jake*, but I knew better: when it came to religion, he only saw the world in black or white, right or wrong, or to put it bluntly, One-Way or the highway. I just clung to Phoebe's words that The Preacher and I didn't always have to see eye to eye and that he'd come to respect the fact that I had an opinion. I wasn't sure whether I agreed with her assessment, but once again that old Greek saying came to mind: "Ἓν οἶδα ὅτι οὐδὲν οἶδα!" One thing I know is that I know nothing!

I thought back to that evening in Phoebe's apartment when I wanted to kill myself. That night was horrible, but it made me realize that I had as much a right to my opinion as everyone else, including my dad. This editorial perfectly reflected what I felt about Senator-elect Syed's situation. A good editorial should invite debate, and if The Preacher wanted to talk about it, that was great.

Everyone clapped as Professors Cates and Ellis walked on stage in powder blue commencement gowns and took a seat behind a large mahogany lectern and a side table that held four gleaming acrylic trophies. I hoped to take one of those trophies home, but even if I didn't, that editorial was like my firstborn child, and I didn't need an acrylic trophy to be proud of it. Of course, I did need one if I ever hoped to write for a newspaper again.

I clapped harder when Professor Greenberg took the stage, now glad that he had pushed me so hard. I'd never been more proud of anything I'd written in my entire life.

Greenberg raised the lectern microphone up a tad. "Welcome to the honors ceremony for the Columbia Summer in Journalism program. I'm Professor Murray Greenberg. I've had the distinct pleasure of teaching these fine students over the past six weeks. We're here today to honor the entire class for a job well done. Students, look around you, this is the same venue Columbia uses to award the Pulitzer Prizes each year. One day, someone from this very class may join the likes of Roger Ebert of *The Chicago Sun-Times*, Maureen Dowd of the *New York Times*, and Garry Trudeau, the creator of the *Doonesbury* cartoon, all of whom have received Pulitzers."

Those were some big names, and to think they had all once walked up on this very stage to receive their Pulitzers somehow made the moment even more exciting.

"We will first present certificates to each student and then special honors will be bestowed on the students whose final projects were considered best-in-category by our distinguished panel of judges. Students, as I call your name, please come forward to receive your certificate."

Professor Greenberg called the names of the students row by row, and as they rose and walked on stage, everyone clapped and yelled for them. By the time my row was called up, I was feeling a whole lot better. Okay, maybe I wasn't feeling ten feet tall, but I was almost back to six-foot-two.

As I stepped up on stage, I looked out at the audience, grateful for all the friends I'd made, Sam especially. I'd learned a lot about him over the last six weeks. Maybe homosexuality was never a thorn for him but having an absentee father must have been. Raising Sam alone must have been tough on his mother as well.

I looked over at Julie, who had her own stuff with her mother dying right in front of her at such a young age. How do you ever get over something like that? I wondered if maybe that's why she had no trouble ignoring the rules as she blazed her own trail. Perhaps she needed that to feel more in control. Maybe it was her way of protecting herself.

I scanned the sea of people as they applauded. We all had our thorns. My thorn was no better or worse than any of theirs. It suddenly seemed silly to compare one person's thorn to another's since the thorn that looks the smallest may just be dug in the deepest. And let's face it: if not for that thorn, I'd probably be a closed-minded, judgmental, holier-than-thou mess. Plus, I never would've fallen for Sam.

I looked up and prayed silently. *Thank you, God, for the thorn you chose just for me and the wisdom and joy I've gained from it. It has made me a better person.*

"Jacob Henry Powell," Professor Greenberg called out.

I tried to play it cool but when everyone started clapping, I got this shit-eating grin. Phoebe and Mom were standing and clapping louder than anyone. The Preacher finished his scribbling and joined in, but from his stern expression it was clear that he had a lot on his mind. He was probably trying to figure out whether he really knew this cleft-chinned kid on stage. But how could he? I was just beginning to know myself.

As I shook Professor Greenberg's hand and took my certificate, I studied his face, trying to get a sense of my standing in the competition, hoping for a wink, a smirk, a nod, anything that would hint that I was at least in the running. But he was all business, which I chalked up to his unwavering professionalism. Heck, it was a miracle that I was still in the program. What did I expect him to do? I was just glad he wasn't one of the judges.

The awards portion of the ceremony began with Professor Greenberg rattling off the names of the prestigious judges and the unique attributes required to receive each special award. The first two categories came and went with Atsuto taking the photo essay award, and Carlos Ramirez winning in feature writing.

The next category was news reporting, the one Sam was competing in. He played it down, but I knew he wanted to win badly. Professor Ellis was the presenter and concluded her remarks by saying, "With the proliferation of alternative media, news reporting has become a huge challenge. The reporter not only has to think on his feet, but also must battle throngs of other reporters going after the same story. It is my honor to present the Columbia Award for Excellence in News Reporting to Samuel Horowitz for his article, 'Same-Sex Marriage Gains Momentum in NY State Assembly.'"

"Yes!" I yelled before I could catch myself, and then joined the applause.

Sam shot me a smile then went up to the stage with a spring in his step.

Phoebe clapped enthusiastically while The Preacher shook his head. My father couldn't have been happy that I was hanging out with the guy who would write such "liberal garbage," even if he did win an award. Was The Preacher now wondering if Sam was gay himself? What other scenarios were playing out in The Preacher's head?

Professor Greenberg returned to the lectern to present the final award. "Careers can be made and broken on a journalist's ability to write editorials," he began.

Those words really hit home: within minutes, I would either have a journalism career ahead of me or I wouldn't. I'd sweated this for weeks and whatever the outcome, I was strangely relieved that at least it would finally be over. I was sick of all that not-knowing. But what if it didn't go my way? What if God's decision was for me to be a preacher? That editorial would be the last piece of journalism I ever wrote, and I would have to go home and suffer the public humiliation of stepping down as editor of *The Tattler*—that was the deal. Even worse, would a career in the church mean that I'd spend the rest of my life in the closet, hiding who I was from the people closest and dearest to me? And what would that mean for Sam and me? Would he put up with such a scenario?

But what if I did win? Did I feel any grief about never preaching again?

Not really.

Only then did I remember that the Sunday coming up was a Fifth Sunday. If I won, I wouldn't have to preach—that was the deal too—which made me want to win even more.

As Professor Greenberg remarked on the importance of editorials in practically every media outlet, I shifted back and forth in my chair, crossing and uncrossing my legs and arms, but I couldn't get comfortable. Then Sam looked back at me and held up a hand, fingers crossed—that calmed my spirits a little. I wasn't in this alone.

I took a deep breath, sat up straight, and gazed at the final acrylic trophy on stage as I awaited my verdict.

"This year, there was an editorial piece that was groundbreaking and covered a very challenging topic with clarity, insight, and a fresh perspective," Professor Greenberg said. "It is my honor to present the Award for Excellence in Editorial Writing to…"

Professor Greenberg turned the page. I tensed up like I was about to take a bullet.

"Thomas James Horn, for his piece 'American Civil Liberties: Rest in Peace.'"

And just like that, I received God's answer. It was over. At first, my mind was uncharacteristically silent, like my brain was refusing to hear what my ears were conveying. I guess I was in shock from the smack of God's answer coupled with the sudden lifting of all that not-knowing. Then it came—cold, gritty waves of despair pummeled me, not just from having to go into the ministry, but also from having to give up journalism—including my editorship at *The Tattler*—along with Sam and the way of life I'd discovered in New York. The reality of all that loss made me wish I'd never come to New York in the first place: I'd gained so much only to lose it all.

Suddenly aware that everyone was clapping for Thomas, I joined in. By that point he was already back in the audience hugging and high-fiving friends.

That's when I focused on how awful it was going to be to attend some One-Way Bible seminary, where I would have to forget about being gay. Probably the only colleges in the country that didn't have some sort of LGBT student clubs were the One-Way Bible colleges. I'm sure there were gay students there, but they'd certainly get kicked out of school if they came out. It would be four years of closeted hell on top of the additional year of closeted hell I was about to endure under The Preacher's roof. Why did I even bother coming out? It was just going to be that much more painful to go back in.

If there was a way out of this mess, I didn't see it. Unless Columbia gave out some surprise fifth award this year. Yes! Maybe there would be one more award!

Professor Greenberg dashed any hopes of that with his closing remarks and a final "thank you for coming."

As everyone around me stood to congratulate each other and pose for photos, I wanted to yell at them to sit back down, that it couldn't be over.

But of course it was over. In every way.

I sat there trying to figure out what to do. Winning an award had seemed like my destiny, but I was clearly mistaken. Still, becoming a minister for a denomination that believed I was an abomination was the absolute wrong path for me. I knew that as much as I knew that I was gay. But what could I do about it now? My destiny was set.

Julie tapped me on the shoulder. "Sorry you didn't win,"

she said as seriously as I'd ever heard her. "I know you *needed* to."

I stood and gave her a big hug, unable to speak. On top of everything else, this was our goodbye. "Thank you for being such an amazing friend," I said on the verge of tears.

She rubbed my back. "I was, wasn't I? It was a mini-breakthrough."

I was sure going to miss Julie and her peculiar brand of friendship. I'd never met anyone who seemed so wrapped up in herself but was actually nurturing in a sort of detached passionate way. She was the one who pulled me out of my deep depression after the disaster at Heaven and taught me how to laugh again. I held her tighter. "I'm going to miss you."

"Oh, gawd," she said. "Let's not do this. For the sake of my mascara."

When we let go, Raj was standing right there. "Your humble servant awaits," he said sarcastically to Julie.

Julie had recruited Raj to help her throw a dinner for the "class orphans"—the kids whose parents didn't attend the ceremony—and had been ordering him around ever since.

"Want to meet up with us after your dinner?" Julie asked me.

"Aww. Thanks, but Sam and I sort of have a date later. In fact, Raj, would you, um, mind sleeping in Alexandros's bed tonight? I think tonight could be a, um, special night for Sam and me."

Raj knitted his brow and said in his best Southern drawl, "I am not going to be some sexual enabler for that lifestyle of yours!" Then he winked. "Sure."

"Thanks, Raj. I couldn't imagine this summer without you. I really enjoyed sharing a room with the class bartender," I said and stuck out my hand.

He shook my hand hard. "Yes, you were definitely my worst customer, but you show great promise."

I laughed in spite of my gloom.

"I'll call this weekend to see how things go with your dad," Julie said to me.

And with that, she and Raj headed out.

I made a beeline toward Sam as Phoebe and my parents headed my way, but a sea of classmates had already engulfed him with hugs and high-fives and back slaps. I had no idea how I was going to break through, but he started coming my way, dragging his mom and his fans along.

"Congratulations, Sam!" I said, then slapped his back a couple of times like we were nothing more than classmates just in case my parents were watching.

"Thanks, but brah, I'm...I'm just so sorry *you* didn't win," he said.

"I told you Sam was going to win," I said to Cathy.

"You were right!" she said, just as Phoebe and my parents walked up. Once again, I felt that my two worlds were colliding, but I didn't have the energy to care.

After I introduced everyone, The Preacher patted my back and Mom gave me a big hug, the kind you might give someone who just received a terminal medical diagnosis. Or was I just imagining that?

When we let go of each other, Professor Greenberg was standing there, offering Sam his hand. "Congratulations, Mr. Horowitz, on your winning article."

Sam thanked him, then Professor Greenberg turned to me. "Jake, that was an excellent editorial. Any other year, you would've had an acrylic plaque yourself. You were a close second."

I was completely floored—that was the first compliment I'd ever received from Professor Greenberg, which made it feel that much more mind-blowing. "Really?" I said as a small hope deep down inside me re-kindled. "Professor, I'll always remember what you did for me. Thank you so much!"

Professor Greenberg chuckled. "You mean that good stiff kick in the pants I gave you? That woke you up, didn't it? Now that you've found your voice, promise me you'll go with it."

"Yes, sir."

"And put me on the mailing list for your school paper. I'll go right down to Mississippi if I see you slipping."

I couldn't bring myself to tell him that I had to quit the paper. But maybe I didn't. Maybe The Preacher would let me slide this one time, especially after Professor Greenberg's praise. That little flame of hope inside me burned a little brighter. "Alabama. I'm from Alabama."

"Wherever. Mr. Powell, it's clear you've got talent. If you keep at it, I have no doubt you'll make an excellent journalist."

"Thank you, sir," I said, sounding like a soldier who just received a commendation from his commanding officer.

As Professor Greenberg excused himself, Mom clapped her hands together and said. "Did you hear that, Jake? You made quite an impression. I'm so proud of you!"

"Your editorial was much better than the one they chose," Phoebe said. "I mean, that one was good too, but we should demand a recount."

"A recount? But there were only three judges," I said, as I waited for The Preacher to chime in. Maybe by some miracle he'd at least give my journalism career a hall pass for the next year so I wouldn't have to quit *The Tattler.*

"I guess we'll keep him," The Preacher said.

That was it. There was no indication of a reprieve or a do-over or any other act of mercy or kindness. But I knew that no matter what Professor Greenberg had said, there was only one way to interpret what just went down: I had not won an award, so I was headed for the pulpit. That was the deal. Fair and square. End of story. Hopes dashed. I was sure to hear about it from The Preacher at dinner, where I'd almost certainly also receive a lecture on how this country was founded on Christianity and punctuated with the words "I'm disappointed in you."

Phoebe turned to Sam and Cathy, "We have a six-thirty reservation at Café Luxembourg. Can you join us?"

Was she crazy? How many panic attacks would I have to

endure in one afternoon? *Please God, give Sam the good sense to say "no."*

"Thank you, Phoebe," Sam said. "But we just made plans with my roommate and his parents."

I hugged Cathy goodbye and whispered to Sam, "I'll text you after dinner."

If I survived dinner, that is.

CHAPTER 21

Phoebe got us a back corner table for four at Café Luxembourg, a dimly lit French restaurant with crisp white tablecloths, red leather booths and an older Lincoln Center crowd. It was so fussy I'm surprised they didn't have a harpist strumming away in the corner someplace.

A broccoli stalk of a man with narrow shoulders, puffy hair and a long green apron clapped his hands and grinned. "*Bonsoir*, Phoebe!" he sang in a thick French accent. "I didn't see you once last week!" He handed menus to each of us.

"Olivier, I've been two-timing you at that new restaurant next door."

He pursed his lips. "Well, I see you are back, madam." He looked from Phoebe to The Preacher, sitting across from each other, as he offered the wine list. "And who will be ordering the wine tonight?"

Phoebe held out her hand.

Mom shook her head at Phoebe and mouthed "no!" The Preacher would never sit at a table where someone was drinking. As I've mentioned before, alcohol was strictly forbidden in our church, so he never allowed himself to be around an open container for fear it might damage his reputation. Phoebe turned her outstretched hand to a wave. "Now, Olivier, you know I never drink during the week."

Olivier raised an eyebrow. "Someone once told me that Thursday is the new Friday. Very well, I will be back shortly to take your order."

"They sure aren't giving anything away here," The Preacher said, scanning the menu.

"This is my treat, Henry," Phoebe said, then turned and gave me a kiss on the cheek. "I just want to celebrate my brilliant nephew here."

Since the ceremony, The Preacher hadn't said much of anything but Phoebe and Mom were now making a big fuss over my "accomplishment." The reality was that I hadn't accomplished anything other than getting a one-way ticket to the seminary, and I couldn't keep the celebratory charade up any longer when there was nothing to celebrate.

"But I didn't win," I said. "I'm sorry I let you down, Mom."

"Jake, do you realize that you just completed one of the most prestigious summer prep courses in the US world?" Mom said. "Plus you heard what that professor said about you. We're all awfully proud."

I tried for a smile but my mind was preoccupied with what my dad would say next.

"It *was* a huge accomplishment just to get in," The Preacher said with a warm smile. "But to receive such praise from your professor is truly incredible. This experience will help prepare you for what's ahead. Are you ready to be the next Billy Graham?" he asked, referring to the legendary evangelist.

My heart sank even further, which I didn't think was possible. "Gosh, I don't know," I said, trying to hide my devastation. Although I knew this conversation was coming, that didn't make it any less painful.

The Preacher took that occasion—before we'd even ordered—to pull out the program, turn to my editorial, and hand it to me. It was littered with his scribbles, including a few Bible verse citations. "There are a few things I want to talk to you about with this here editorial, son. I see your name on it but, well, the Jake I know wouldn't write something like this. I'm sort of at a loss and hoping you can help me out."

"I'll do my best," I said. I meant it too. Mom caught my eye, and we both knew I was about to get an earful.

The Preacher let out a heavy sigh, like he was talking to a delinquent. "Jake, you know better than this. We are a *Christian* nation. American soldiers are giving their lives every day in Iraq and Afghanistan to ensure our freedom and the American way."

"Preacher, I don't take my freedom for granted—if that's what you're saying—but freedom of religion is a big part of the package too, right?"

He went straight into his Preaching Voice. "I believe in freedom of religion. Heck, I even believe in freedom *from* religion for the people who want that. But like I said, we are fundamentally a Christian nation and people need to respect that. I'm surprised and disappointed to see that you think otherwise."

Phoebe acted like she was only casually listening, but I knew she was ready to jump in if I needed her.

"Don't you think Senator-elect Syed is worshipping the same God we are?" I asked.

The Preacher shrugged. "Maybe. Maybe not. Jesus said, 'I am the way, the truth, and the light, no man comes to the Father but by Me.'"

There was that verse again. The Preacher just didn't get it—quoting Bible verses was fine, but I wanted to discuss what we actually thought. I wanted to hear from my father the man, not my father The Man of God. Only then could we hope to find some middle ground. Why was it that when it came to anything involving belief and God, my father, who otherwise stood solidly on his own two feet, suddenly resorted to quoting verses and cute turns of phrases and clever anecdotes? I was sick of all that and wanted the bare-knuckled truth. What did *he* really think? Where was our common ground?

"Maybe Jesus said that, maybe He didn't," I said. "There are lots of passages we ignore in the Bible."

The Preacher's mouth flew wide open and for good reason—I had just questioned whether something in the Bible was true, which I'd never dared do until just a few weeks ago when life pushed me to the utter brink. That was about the worst thing you could do in the fundamentalist Powell household—even worse than coming home drunk.

"Like what?" he asked, incredulously.

"Well, the Bible says women should cover their heads in church and not speak."

"Good point," Phoebe said. She might as well have been holding pom-poms and yelling, "Go Jake!"

The Preacher gave Mom his I-told-you-so look.

Mom looked away, hoping to avoid being pulled into this exchange.

"You have to understand the context of that passage," The Preacher said.

He could dismiss the Apostle Paul's hateful words against women as *context*, so why couldn't he do the same for people of other faiths or even closer to home, homosexuals? "Since when did you talk context, Preacher? I thought you were a fundamentalist?"

My dad raised an eyebrow disapprovingly. "I thought you were too. Or you were the last time I saw you."

"Oh, maybe we can talk about all this another time," Mom said lightheartedly.

Phoebe motioned for Olivier. "Yes, let's get to dinner."

Throughout our meal, Mom and Phoebe shared funny recollections of when they were growing up while The Preacher just sat in silence. His eyes looked hollow, like he was more disappointed than angry, and I didn't know what disappointed him more—what I'd said or the fact that I'd stood up to him. I kept almost as quiet as he did until our plates were cleared.

"How about dessert?" Phoebe asked, motioning for Olivier.

Like clockwork, The Preacher looked at Mom and scratched his ear. It took me years but I'd finally figured out this secret I'm-ready-to-go signal of theirs.

Mom looked disappointed but pasted on a smile for Phoebe. "Well, we probably should get going."

"But you haven't really been to New York until you've had a piece of New York cheesecake," Phoebe said.

"Thanks, Phoebe," Mom said. "But our flight tomorrow's at seven in the morning."

"Yes, I know," Phoebe said. "I'm already driving Jake to the airport and would be happy to pick you up too."

"I doubt all our luggage would fit in your convertible, Phoebe," The Preacher said. "We'll just take a taxi."

Phoebe looked away and shook her head like she was taking all of this personally, but The Preacher was probably right about the luggage.

"Phoebe and I will see you two at the airport tomorrow morning then," I said to move things along so I could get to Sam.

Mom and Phoebe hugged a damp-eyed goodbye, then The Preacher and Phoebe halfway hugged. It was the most either of them was willing to give. I took the opportunity to text Sam that dinner was wrapping up.

"I'll see y'all at the airport at six," I said as I hugged my parents goodbye.

The Preacher nudged my shoulder. "Maybe you'll find your comb while you're packing up."

I gave The Preacher a smile, knowing that he was halfway joking, but at least we were speaking.

As they left, I felt a strange sensation inside me, a tugging, like a stage curtain was coming down. Then, my eyes started tingling like I was about to cry or something. I was bummed to leave New York and especially Sam, but there was something else going on, too—I just didn't know what.

My phone vibrated. Sam's text read: Columbus Circle at 8:30?

That gave me a little more time before I'd have to go. I texted an "ok" back, then said to Phoebe, "How about that cheesecake?"

She lit right up and grabbed Olivier, who'd been hovering around. "Two slices of cheesecake, *s'il vous plaît.*"

As she took her seat, I checked out the top of her head. By the light of a wall lamp, I saw a slight thinning of hair on her crown. It wasn't a bald spot like a guy, but I could actually see the scalp peeking through. Was this Phoebe's thorn? Would it be Mom's too?

I bent down and hugged her, my eyes tearing up from this new discovery. I told myself how silly it was to get upset over something like this when there were so many more awful things going on in the world. But it wasn't just *this*. It was *this* on top of everything else that had happened that day, and the fact that I would be leaving New York in a matter of hours. I tried stuffing the sadness down inside me, but it rushed back up with a whimper. I covered my eyes.

"Are you okay, honey?" she asked.

"I'm going to miss you so much," I said, taking my seat. "I've gotten so used to your being just a few subway stops away. I wish it didn't all have to end."

She rubbed my hand. "I'm going to miss you, Jake. Your time here just flew by."

"Phoebe, I feel trapped. I don't want to live in the closet anymore, but I don't know how to come out to my parents either. Do you think I should wait until I leave home for college? That's a whole year away."

"I wish I could advise you, Jake. I've heard enough about One-Way Bible's view on homosexuality to know that they believe it's a choice and not an orientation. Maybe I could talk to your Mom and plant a seed? I'll be super discreet."

I'd never heard Mom say anything about gays, one way or the other, almost like they didn't exist. Or was the whole topic simply off limits? "No, please don't. I just—I just wish I were normal sometimes."

"What is normal, Jake? No one is normal—not even in your sweet little perfect town. If you ever need to come live with me, you're always welcome. You know that, don't you?"

"Thanks, Phoebe, but my home's in Alabama. I'm just a fish out of water up here." Of course, that didn't quite cover it. I missed fried chicken, homemade gravy, Southern hospitality, and the rolling hills of Alabama, but New York had grown on me. Maybe I just associated New York with Sam, but he was going home too. I could be happy living just about anywhere as long as Sam was there. But without him, even New York wouldn't be the same.

"What? You don't belong in Alabama, can't you see that yet?" Phoebe asked. "You've done so well here and you're only just getting started good. Don't give up on New York— it's sure been great to me."

"You make living here look so easy, Phoebe. What brought you to New York?"

"I came here mostly to get away from Daddy. He was military before becoming a professor and he ran his house like a battleship. After college, I moved back to Atlanta for an advertising job. I lived a few miles from home, so Daddy felt I was somehow back in his jurisdiction. He started bossing me around again and, well, you think I'm strong-willed now! Ha! You should've seen me back then!" Phoebe chuckled. "Of course, your mother was the youngest and always 'Daddy's little girl.'"

Mom was the least materialistic person I knew. She rarely got new clothes or jewelry and was, in fact, always pinching pennies. I couldn't imagine her being a spoiled little daddy's girl. "Really?"

"Are you kidding? It was nauseating! She claimed to be all about women's rights growing up, but she basically went from being The Professor's daughter to The Preacher's wife. She married Daddy all over again with your father, let me tell you. I, on the other hand, was the black sheep of the family. I did it all—booze, free love, you name it. Daddy laid down the law, so I just up and left Atlanta and never looked back. It was only after 9/11 that I made an effort to get back in touch."

Olivier arrived with our slices of cheesecake, and then vanished.

"I don't understand," I said. "Why did 9/11 make you get back in touch with the family?"

Phoebe crossed her arms. "I don't know."

"Were you in one of the towers?" I asked, taking a bite of cheesecake.

"No," she said, looking away.

Phoebe was retreating into herself for some reason. I'd seen her do this before but where? Wait! It was when Phoebe, Miriam, and I were walking to Ground Zero. Phoebe suddenly took a big detour then had a business meeting in midtown that came out of nowhere. The 9/11 attacks affected us all, but it wasn't like the average American couldn't bear to see the spot where the World Trade Center once stood. In fact, it was a mandatory stop on any trip to New York yet Phoebe couldn't bring herself to go. Why was that?

Then it hit me. I suddenly realized why, or I had a hunch. "Well, did you lose someone in the towers?"

Phoebe stared down at her cheesecake, and then mechanically picked up her fork. "Why would you think that?"

I suddenly went into my probing interview mode. "Is that why you brought Miriam along on our tour around New York that Sunday—so you wouldn't have to go to Ground Zero?"

She sat back, then looked away.

Whatever happened, it must've been real painful for her. Backing down, I grabbed my fork and took a stab at my cheesecake. "Phoebe, that's okay. Just if you ever want to…"

She looked at me even more seriously than when we talked about my being gay. "What I'm about to tell you is just between us. Understand?"

I leaned forward, feeling awfully special that Phoebe would confide in me. "Of course."

She paused for a moment, as if to summon up her will to

come out about whatever this was. "I lost the love of my life on 9/11," she said. "I don't know how else to say it."

The love of her life? I'd never even known Phoebe to be in a relationship, much less be in love. "I—I had no idea."

"When I was a junior at Rice, Richard and I met at the *very first* Baker 13," she said. "Ever heard of the Baker 13? It's now legendary."

I shook my head. "No, but you did mention a Richard earlier today."

"Yes. Well, the Baker 13 is a riot. On the thirteenth day of each month, students from the Baker dorm run around Rice wearing nothing more than shoes and shaving cream. I found out about their plan beforehand and devised a counterattack. When the Baker students came round shouting insults at our dorm, we pelted them with water balloons from the second floor. Shaving cream is no match for water balloons and the very first guy I nailed was this towering redhead I recognized from the basketball team. I'll never forget what he shouted to me. 'I'm going to get you, Phoebe Clarke!'" she said that last part in a gruff voice, then chuckled. "I was surprised he called me by name since we'd never met. About a week later, we ran into each other at Willy's Pub and went out a few times." She leaned in. "That is, until I told him Lester Sykes was going to pin me."

"Pin you?"

"Oh, it was this silly thing we did back then to show we were going together. My hope was that Richard would pin me first but it backfired. He had a complete conniption. I'd never seen such a temper." She smiled brightly at the memory.

"We didn't speak again until our twenty-fifth reunion in 2001. Even after all that time, my heart got all fluttery when I saw him across the room, but I was afraid he'd make a scene so I avoided him. Later that evening, Richard came over and smiled and gave me a bear hug. He was almost completely white-headed by then and his blue eyes were deeper set, but he was in great shape, and I don't mean for his age. I mean *great shape* period. Just seeing him again like that brought me back to when I was young and the world seemed full of possibilities. We started going out again but it was a long-distance relationship—he lived in Charlotte but came to New York for business all the time. His bank had offices in the North Tower."

Phoebe stared off into space for a moment, and then sighed. "Fast-forward to September of that year. Richard was scheduled to arrive on the twelfth. After the terrorist attacks, I tried calling so he'd know I was okay and to see if he was driving up since the airports were all closed. I kept getting that stupid 'all circuits busy' message and it wasn't until the following day that I got through and left him a voicemail."

She shifted in her chair, the light that was in her eyes moments before was now completely gone. "I didn't panic right away but then another day passed and still no word. I called the 800 number for his bank and the operator connected me to his assistant. Come to find out, Richard had gotten to New York a day early to get all his meetings out of the way. He'd reserved a suite at the Pierre Hotel, which is something we'd often talked about doing. I've always said the worst part of being a New Yorker is that you never get to experience New York hotels. He knew the Pierre was my favorite."

Phoebe screwed her eyes shut. "I'm sure he was going to surprise me. If we hadn't been dating, he wouldn't have come up a day early."

"Oh, Phoebe, you can't think like that. It's not your fault."

She dabbed her eyes. "I think you two would've hit it off. Anyway, I was the last person you'd find in church back then, but there was nowhere else to go. I marched across the street from my office and went into St. Bart's to pray and, well, I eventually joined the church. You know the rest of the story."

"That's when you came to Grandmother's for Christmas?"

"Yes."

"So Mom really doesn't know?"

Phoebe shook her head. "She knows part of it. After I came back to the family fold, Anna was all up in my business, as you kids say. She just had to know what happened, what brought me back to the family. She was convinced I was dying or something. You know how Anna can be."

"Twenty questions!" we said in unison, then chuckled.

"Your mom knows I lost a friend on 9/11 but she thinks he was gay."

I was surprised Mom and Phoebe talked about someone being gay since I'd never even heard Mom say the word. "Why does she think that?"

"Because that's what I said to shut her up. Richard and I had agreed to keep our relationship private. I didn't even go to his funeral. You're the only one who knows other than Claude and Miriam."

I wondered if this Richard was married, but I didn't ask—I just let her talk. I'm pretty sure I knew the answer anyway. I mean, why else did the relationship need to be kept private?

"Anyway, the last time I'd seen the family was at your mom's wedding. I started taking inventory of my life. Your mom had been reaching out to me for years and kept sending photos of this little miracle that is you," she said with a smile. "I saw myself in that silly little dimpled chin and those blue eyes of yours. I decided it was time to reconnect with the family. Daddy was getting old and tired by that point, but then I had Henry to deal with."

It was never fun when two people you love didn't get along, and Phoebe's history with my father was one of life's big mysteries. "Phoebe, why exactly don't you like The Preacher?"

"Now, why would you think that?"

"You go out of your way to get his goat. Like when you put my college fund checks in Kwanzaa cards."

"He doesn't like that?" She tried to hold a straight face for a moment but then burst out laughing.

I couldn't help but laugh along with her.

"Honestly, I always felt bad at Christmas because I suspected my checks were larger than what your parents gave you. I didn't know what to do and thought maybe I should give you smaller checks, but as I was shopping for your Christmas card one year, I saw a sign that Kwanzaa began on December twenty-sixth. I didn't know anything about Kwanzaa but after studying its seven principles, I realized it was a holiday I could warm up to. So I decided to give you the check for Kwanzaa. That way, I wasn't competing with your parents."

"Wow, that was really thoughtful."

"Of course, I had no idea Henry would take offense to Kwanzaa—that was just an added bonus." She snickered then patted my arm. "Oh, Jake, I guess I like Henry. We may not agree on everything, but I can't help but respect someone who's so passionate about what he does. I guess he just reminds me of Daddy too much—he was a know-it-all too."

She sat her fork down and leaned in. "Jake, you're at a crossroads at this very moment. You can take your mother's path or you can take mine. There's no in-between and there's no taking both. The life you're capable of living is right here in New York. You can be who and whatever you want or go home and be who they want—'they' meaning everyone but you."

Phoebe continued talking but my mind locked onto those last words of hers. I wondered if "they" included God. Hadn't He just given me a mandate to be a minister for the rest of my life? But why would he put this journalistic passion inside of me if he wanted me to be a minister? Wait! Didn't I just go through the same blame thing about being gay? If God had wanted me to like girls, he would've made me straight, right? Well, if he wanted me to pursue the ministry, he would've put that passion inside of me instead of my passion for journalism. I didn't need to put out the fleece. That fleece was my Gordian Knot. According to legend, the King of Gordium tied an impossible knot and decreed that whoever untied it would become ruler of Asia. Of course, Alexander the Great didn't bother—he just drew his sword, sliced the thing in two, and became king.

It was time I put that fleece away and quit caring if it was wet or dry. What was I really doing when I put out the fleece? I was washing my hands of any responsibility for my decision. God wasn't in those bargains I tried to make with Him. The only sign I needed was my passion for journalism, and I intended to pursue it. No one said it would be easy.

I slapped my palm on the table causing Phoebe to jump. "That was exactly what I needed to hear. Thank you, Phoebe."

"Which part?" she asked.

"The part about being who and whatever I want," I said. "For some reason, the hardest part was figuring out what I wanted, but I just did. I'm pursuing journalism."

She patted my hand and smiled.

I looked down at my watch—it was nearly eight-twenty. I didn't want to keep Sam waiting. "Phoebe, I'm meeting Sam…"

"Of course," she said with a wave of her hand. "Go— have fun! I'll pick you up at the Columbia gates at five tomorrow morning, right where I dropped you off on your first day."

I gave her a big hug. "Thanks, Phoebe."

I ran out the door and jumped in a taxi, which was five times the price of the subway, but about twice as fast. Maybe that was a little frivolous, but I didn't want to be late: Sam and I only had a few hours left together and every second counted.

"Columbus Circle, please," I said to the driver.

CHAPTER 22

The taxi dropped me off at a busy traffic circle filled with beautifully lit trees and fountains that encircled a monument to Christopher Columbus. Sam, looking as hot as ever, stood on the granite steps of the towering monument. When he caught site of me, he smiled and walked over. "How was dinner?" he asked as cars honked and brakes squealed.

"I survived," I said, being overly dramatic. "How was yours?"

"Cathy, like, got a little carried away with the vino," Sam said, and then flashed a smile. We were both just trying to stay strong for the other and make the most of our final hours together.

Without another word, we turned north up Broadway, choked with traffic. Sam tried to take my hand, but I pulled it away.

"Sam, I just don't feel comfortable holding hands on the street."

"Would you feel weird holding a girl's hand?" he said with a huff.

"Straight people don't get beat up for holding hands."

"Oh, so that's it—you're just afraid we'll get bashed," he said sarcastically. "Right!"

I didn't want to spoil even one minute of our final hours together by arguing, so I just said, "Sam, be patient with me, okay? I'll get there."

I positioned him under a streetlight. "Smile," I said framing him in my cell phone's tiny LCD screen.

He shook his head and laughed, signaling a truce.

When we got to 72nd Street, I had us turn left, explaining that there was something I wanted to show him. As we walked west toward the Hudson River, the shops were mostly closed so the sidewalks were much quieter. Making good on my promise, I pointed out Phoebe's building as we passed.

"That's where I came out to Julie, and then Phoebe," I said, not believing it all happened just three weeks ago. "I was hating life so much at that point and now here I am with you." I swiped at tears that suddenly sprang out of nowhere. "Gosh, I don't know why I'm getting all emotional. I'm just being weird."

Sam smiled. "Brah, what would be weird would be, like, if you never found the courage to be who you are. Or never opened your heart."

How did he always know the right thing to say?

Rather than heading back to the congestion of Broadway, I led him toward Riverside Drive, which bordered a wooded park at the end of 72nd Street. This was a much quieter and more romantic route back to Columbia.

There at the park entrance, we stopped at a lighted bronze statue of a handsome woman with her chin propped up on one fist, the figure deep in thought. I read the engraved stone at her feet:

Where, after all,
do universal human rights begin?
In small places, close to home.
Such are the places
where every man, woman and child
seeks equal justice,
equal opportunity,
equal dignity.

Eleanor Roosevelt
1958

I'd never noticed the statue before—even though it was only half a block from Phoebe's—and was amazed that Eleanor Roosevelt had made that statement nearly fifty years ago. "That's exactly how I feel," I said. "All I want is to be who I am."

"The first step is to, like, come out to your parents, you know?"

"Yeah. But right now, that's the most impossible thing I can imagine."

Sam stroked my shoulder. "I'm sure it is, but you have to find a way. Stand up for yourself, brah. No one else is going to do it for you."

I looked into his eyes, which were filled with absolute, unwavering conviction. How could I explain to him that even the gay civil rights language he'd used in his award-winning article held no power in my hometown, where the Bible trumps absolutely everything?

"Sam, I *will* stand up for myself, but if word got out that I was gay, my dad would be run out of the church."

He shrugged. "Well, I guess he'll have to choose between you and the church."

"I'd never ask him to choose. I couldn't. That church is his entire life."

He put both hands on my shoulders and looked at me dead on. "Who is then?"

"Who's what?"

He held my shoulders tighter. "Who's asking him to choose? If you're not, someone must be."

I shook my head. "I still don't get what you're saying."

"Brah, I'm saying that you didn't set these boundaries, your church did, and they'll never go away if you keep tiptoeing around them."

I had hoped for a lot more romance and a lot less politics this evening. Even so, I realized that this was *the* issue that Sam and I had to get past for us to have a shot at anything long-term. We didn't need to see eye-to-eye tonight, but we had to at least understand *and respect* where the other was coming from.

I pulled away and led him up Riverside Drive as the trees rustled in the cool breeze whipping off the Hudson River in the distance.

"Sam, do you know how many gay people there are in my town? None. Not a one."

"Jake, about ten percent of the population is gay."

"Don't you think I know that? But not in my town."

"Come on," he said skeptically. "There must be, like, one person."

"Nope. No one is openly gay, but there's this one male baton twirler in my class who I suspect is gay, and my favorite teacher is a confirmed bachelor with one of those Louis Vuitton briefcases."

Sam chuckled. "Maybe he just has killer taste. So, will you, like, at least tell your parents once you get home?"

I shrugged. "I'd like to tell them, but what if The Preacher wants me to try a camp for gays, like the one in Mobile? You know, in an attempt to make me straight."

"You're kidding, right? Those camps are a joke. *They* don't even claim to make people straight anymore. You'll be eighteen in a few months and legally an adult. He can't touch you after that."

"Sam, this is my dad we're talking about, not my enemy. He *always* has my best interest in mind, but he's not going to understand this."

"Well, then make it clear that he'll have to find a way to love all of you—not just the part he understands."

I nodded, but I didn't really want to talk about *me*, I wanted to talk about *Sam and me*. I wanted to tell him how deeply I felt for him and how only having a few more hours together was like only having a few more hours to live. I wanted to see where his head was and maybe even put a label on our relationship—anything tangible that I could hold onto when I was back home trying to figure out the way forward. "I wish I didn't have to leave tomorrow," I said. "I'm really going to miss you, Sam. You have no idea how much."

Sam's eyes glistened. "What if I come at Christmas?"

"The Preacher would obviously remember you as the gay marriage article guy," I said. "I mean, now that you're a household name and all."

Sam nudged me. "Jake, if I have to dress up like Santa and hang out at your mall with a bell and a bucket, I'll be there."

The evening was back on track.

Farther north, Riverside Drive was pretty quiet except for the occasional car and a few people walking their dogs. As much as I was enjoying our walk, I wanted to get Sam back to the dorm where we could really be alone, but there were two big hurdles we needed to clear before we got to that, and it was now or never. Although it was totally hokey, this is what went through my mind before I brought up the first hurdle: *On your mark...get set...go!*

"So, are we, like, boyfriends?" I asked as nonchalantly as possible.

Sam slowed his pace. "I don't know, dude. No one's asked me."

We stopped and faced each other. By that point, my heart was pounding in my ears. "Sam, will you be my boyfriend?"

He laughed. "That's so lame!"

I crossed my arms, realizing that Sam wasn't ready to commit, which was understandable. I mean, soon we'd be two thousand miles apart and wouldn't see each other for months. It was a silly idea, but that didn't make his rejection any less devastating.

Sam suddenly put his arm around my waist and scooped me into him. "Yes," he said. "As ridiculous as it is, my answer is totally yes. Let's be boyfriends."

A feeling of absolute weightlessness swept over me, and I wanted to kiss him long and hard. But I didn't. Because there was one more hurdle that everything was riding on, at least for me. "Under one condition," I said.

"And what is that, Mr. Powell?"

This second question was as hard to ask as the first so I plunged right in. "That you start going to Yom Kippur service every year."

He reared his head back and laughed.

I knew he'd react that way, but I didn't even crack a smile. I wanted him to know I meant it.

He straightened up when he realized this was no joke. "Wait, you're serious?"

I nodded. "I've done some research and Yom Kippur sounds sort of like your doorway to heaven the same way Jesus is mine. Do you want to know how I see it?"

Sam gave me this what-am-I-going-to-do-with-you look, and then said, "Actually, I do."

"I think that maybe God is like a computer—he's just so complex, we need an operating system to communicate with him, but any number of operating systems will work. They all do pretty much the same thing, and why wouldn't God honor His original 'operating system'—the Old Testament. After all, it's a covenant he made with *your* people."

"My people?!" Sam said with a chuckle. "O-M-G. Jake, you're not going to ask me to sacrifice a goat are you?"

I laughed. "No. The way I see it, fasting on Yom Kippur is your sacrifice. I just need to know that you're on a path to heaven. I mean, it's not *my* path and it seems a lot harder than Christianity, but it doesn't matter as long as we end up together."

"You lost me, man."

"Sam, I need to know that we'll be in heaven together one day. That's why I want you to honor Yom Kippur."

He broke into a big grin and hugged me. "Oh man, that's so sweet and totally wonky at the same time."

I squeezed back. "I know, but it's important to me. So will you promise to go to Yom Kippur service each year?"

He held me tighter. "No one has ever said they wanted to spend eternity with me or tried to get me to synagogue. Okay, but I'm not fasting."

I pulled back and looked him in the eye. "But that's part of the deal. That's your sacrifice. What if I fast with you?"

"It's harder than you think," he said. "The one time I tried it, I got the worst headache and didn't make it past noon."

I suddenly realized that we'd cleared both hurdles and were now just talking logistics. That could wait. "We don't have to figure this all out tonight, do we?"

"No." Sam smiled at me. "We just feel right together, Jacob Henry Powell."

"I know. I love how we complement each other."

"Me too," he said, his eyes, pools of bliss. "I never could've dreamed you up, but I think we're perfect together, like it was meant to be."

I leaned in until my lips were about an inch from his. "I don't know if I feel more happy or lucky."

And then we kissed right there on Riverside Drive in an absolutely shameless display of public affection, like any normal couple falling in love. As Sam squeezed me tight, my love for him spilled out from my heart and saturated my entire being—it could no longer be contained.

CHAPTER 23

The next afternoon, as our plane descended through the rain for our landing in Montgomery, The Preacher tapped my shoulder and handed me a comb across the aisle. "Do something with that hair," he said.

I started to part my hair but caught myself. "But this is my new look," I said.

He bunched up one side of his mouth. "Looks like you just rolled out of bed."

"Great! I've finally perfected it," I said, like a smartass. It just slipped out, but I knew right then that I could never tell him I was gay. For my dad, there was a right way and a wrong way for everything—even how you wore your hair. He couldn't step away from his precious social norms.

"Everyone buckled up?" Mom asked from the window seat beside me, like everything was hunky dory.

The Preacher nodded and put his comb away.

I cupped the black leather cuff peaking beneath my shirtsleeve, like it was a life preserver. If not for this cuff that Sam had given me that morning "to remind me that I had a boyfriend," my time in Manhattan would've seemed like a dream. Our last night together had been nothing short of awesome. Once we got back to the dorm, I told him to grab his laptop and pick out his favorite playlist. That gave me time to start lighting the votive candles I'd set around my dorm room earlier in the day.

Before I got halfway done, Sam waltzed in through the bathroom door carrying his laptop with soft music playing and wearing nothing but the very same pair of skimpy orange briefs with the purple waistband he'd been wearing the day we met. Coincidence? Probably not, judging by the look he gave me. He must've known how attracted I was to him that very first day, and I for sure didn't feel any less so now.

That familiar surge of desire ripped through me, but this time I didn't divert my eyes and I didn't lose my ability to speak. "You look hot," I said. It felt so good to be able to say it. And it felt beyond *amazing* to be able to reach out and pull him against me, to feel him—all of him—and to feel his hands all over me. We still didn't do everything—we didn't go "all the way"—but I will say that neither of us held back, and those final candles never got lit.

Afterwards, Sam introduced me to this great thing called spooning, where two people lay front to back and fit together like spoons. We slept that way the whole night. Well, not the whole night, because we kept waking each other up and... not holding back some more. The world had seemed like an absolutely perfect place for those few precious hours.

But now it was back to reality.

Surprisingly, The Preacher let me drive home in the rain but suggested Mom take the backseat, probably because it was the safest, statistically speaking. While Mom and I talked, he tapped his fingers on the center console in time with the gospel music playing on Hallelujah 103.5 FM, central Alabama's most popular radio station. In the distance, there was a single patch of blue sky, and I hoped it was over Tarsus.

Just before the Tarsus exit, we came across a large One-Way Bible billboard with a picture of my dad preaching. Even though he and I weren't exactly seeing eye to eye at the moment, I felt a jab of pride upon seeing that twelve-foot tall image of him with his Bible held high. He took our church from dying to flying in no time flat: the One-Way Bible Association had ranked One-Way Bible Tarsus as one of the Top 50 Fastest Growing Congregations in America for the past eight years.

"There's our Preacher," Mom said, patting him on the shoulder.

The Preacher smiled, the first smile he'd shown in a good twenty-four hours. "It sure is good to be home. Maybe there's more to do in New York City but it's sure hard to beat Tarsus. I'm glad you had that experience, though, Jake."

"Really?" I asked, grabbing the steering wheel a little tighter, bracing myself for the punch line.

"Sure 'nough. I bet it did you some good to live life away from the comforts of home for a few weeks. Looks like you got some good critical thinking skills under your belt too. Did you learn a lot?"

"Sure did," I said, taking the Tarsus exit.

"Sounds like that Greenberg fellow knew what he was talking about."

I smiled, realizing my jaw had been clenched. "Yes, sir, and he was a complete drill sergeant!" The hardness that had been lodged in my chest all day began to melt and in its place I felt that strange, curtain-coming-down sensation I'd gotten back at Café Luxembourg. But this time, it felt kind of comforting, like one of those moist towelettes they give you at the BBQ Shack. There was no sadness in it at all.

As I pulled up to the red light at the end of the ramp, The Preacher pulled out a church bulletin and handed it to me. The listing for the sermon read "Sermon: Back To Basics....Jacob H. Powell."

"You know this is Fifth Sunday coming up," he said.

It was like he couldn't wait to get me on the path to becoming a preacher. "Yes, sir."

"The sermon is called 'Back to Basics,'" The Preacher said. "It's about building our lives firmly on the bedrock principles of Christianity. I left the index cards on your nightstand."

I took a left. We passed the crop of fast food restaurants at the Tarsus Bypass, then the cemetery where the Preacher had taught me to drive. Further down the road, we came up to the four decaying antebellum homes at the intersection that divided Tarsus neatly into quadrants. The poorest lived south of Main near our church, and the wealthiest lived in our neighborhood, north of Main and mostly west of Oak, in brick homes on wooded pine lots. It was a total fluke that we lived where we did: the congregation had expected us to reside in the single story, white clapboard house next door to the church called the "pastorium." But Mom supposedly pitched such a fit about "not raising our son in a lean-to" that Grandmother and Grandfather Clarke covered the down payment on our house and The Preacher convinced the church to rent out the pastorium and let us put the proceeds toward the monthly payment.

As I pulled the car to the end of our driveway, I noticed that all the marigolds Mom and I had planted back in the spring were ragged and frayed. I never cared much about the yard, but the state of those flowers felt like the death knell of summer, even though it was the last weekend in July.

"I'll get the mail while my two strong men take in the luggage," Mom said.

"I'm starving," I said, stepping out into the balmy Alabama air.

"Guess what we're having?" Mom asked. "Your favorite—ham, butterbeans, and cornbread."

Cornbread! How I'd missed cornbread! Those New Yorkers can have all the baguettes they want. "Fantastic!"

The Preacher and I brought the luggage inside the house while Mom walked to the mailbox at the curb. I couldn't wait to get to my computer to see if Sam had sent me an email, but I'd no sooner got it booted up before I heard The Preacher shout from the kitchen, "Jake, come in here! What is this?" The Preacher shouted louder. "JAKE!"

"I'm coming!" I shouted back.

When I entered the kitchen, I sensed that something wasn't quite right. Mom was leaning against the counter looking concerned while The Preacher peered through his glasses at what looked like a bill. He handed it to me without saying a word.

HEALTH ONE INSURANCE

PATIENT: JACOB H. POWELL
PROVIDER: GAY HEALTHCARE CENTER
TEST: RAPID HIV ANTIBODY
YOUR COPAY: $0

What the heck? My face was suddenly hot, and I felt like I was in a free fall, as if the entire kitchen floor had given way. For a moment, I thought that if I concentrated really, really hard I could go back in time and snatch my insurance card out of that spiky-haired receptionist's fingers so this would never have happened.

Mom looked over at me with pleading eyes. "Jake…"

The Preacher took the bill and looked it over. "So…so *this* was your blood poison scare?"

"What kind of test was this?" Mom asked.

I wanted to run but there was nowhere to go. "It's not what you think," I said defensively.

The lie came out, easy as pie, like all the lies and half-truths I'd told over the years to hide my true self. I considered saying that this was for an official Columbia project and how half the class got HIV tests because that's the level of investigative reporting Columbia expected of us. They'd buy it, too, or at least convince themselves it was true, because it would be a heck of a lot easier than accepting any other explanation. But the lying route would lead me right back in the closet, which—as Sam had predicted—suddenly looked like the freakin' Garden of Eden. I realized that the only way out of this quagmire was to tell them everything.

"Actually, it *is* what you think," I said, looking away. "Don't worry. I—I tested negative."

That bit of news—that I'd broken my vow of celibacy—must've been devastating enough to my parents all on its own, but of course that was just the tip of the iceberg. I took a deep breath. "Mom, Dad, there's something I've wanted to talk to you about since I was thirteen."

Mom nodded as the color drained from her face, like she already knew where this was headed. I had to help her and The Preacher understand that this wasn't anything awful, it was simply who I was. Like Sam once said, they weren't born yesterday—I should give them more credit. I just needed to tell my story in a way that they could grasp.

"You remember me at thirteen, don't you?" I asked. "That's the year I got braces and Mom, you threw that big party at the church for The Preacher's fortieth birthday? That was the same year church attendance passed 250 and, Dad, you started letting your sideburns grow out like Elvis?"

The Preacher looked at me stone-faced, then suddenly swept his big right hand through the air. "Jake, what's all this have to do with the test?"

I fought back tears. "Dad, trust me, it all relates—I just want to be sure that you remember me from that year."

He let out an exasperated sigh. "Of course. That's the year you won the state Bible Drill championship."

"Exactly! And it was during that time that I started having these...feelings. It's not like they started in New York."

"What feelings?" The Preacher asked. "Feelings for what?"

By the look on Mom's face, she could've finished my story herself, but I had to slow things down for The Preacher.

"Feelings for...people, I guess. In general and specifically. I realized that I wasn't like other guys. I know God makes us all *unique* but this seemed kind of radical. I didn't know for sure. I mean, how could I? I eventually figured out that I was different from every other guy I knew. But I thought maybe I'd grow out of it."

Mom buried her face in her hands. "Oh my God. I prayed this wasn't true."

The Preacher looked from Mom to me. "I'm just not following you, Jake. What wasn't true?"

I was talking ninety to nothing but there was so much to say and I could only speak one word at a time. Only then did I remember Julie's advice to just come out with it, but I was too far in. "What I'm trying to say is that since the days I was wearing braces and winning Bible Drill championships, I was aware of this other part of me. I'm the same Jake today that I was back then: the Jake that you know and love. It's just that you didn't know about *all* of me because, well, there was a part of me that I was ashamed of so I kind of buried it, or I tried to. But I'm not ashamed anymore. I came to terms with it in New York. Somehow it took leaving home to face the truth."

"The truth about what?" The Preacher asked, clearly alarmed at what was about to follow.

"My sexual orientation," I said.

The Preacher stared in anticipation as if he was still waiting for my big news. This was so far outside his sphere of understanding that he just wasn't going to get it until I actually said the words.

I stood there, summoning the courage to speak the truth. "Mom, Dad, I'm gay," I said, finally.

"Jake, you're not gay," The Preacher said with a dismissive wave. "That's absolute nonsense. Who in New York convinced you of that?"

"No one. Dad, I *am* gay. It's the first real secret I kept from you. I tried to squash it, but I couldn't. I fasted and prayed and—"

"I've never said anything against gays because—" Mom began, then closed her eyes and took a deep breath. She finally continued, "Because I knew people would never choose to be *that way*."

The Preacher looked from Mom to me again, then shook his head as if to make sense of all he was hearing.

I ran my fingers through my hair, relieved to get this off my chest but hating that my burden was now theirs too. This was the ultimate disappointment for them, perhaps worse than if I had died. One part of me realized how silly that was, but the other part of me totally got it. "Preacher, I know it's going to take a while for you to understand this, but—"

"That Phoebe put these thoughts in your head!" he shouted, banging his palm on the counter like it was his pulpit.

I wrapped my arms tightly around myself like that could fend off the wave of rejection I felt coming my way. "Dad, didn't you hear me? This has been going on for *four years*."

He walked over and grabbed my shoulders. "You're just confused, son. We can pray about this. Yes, we'll pray about this, Jake."

I shook my head. "Dad, I fasted and I prayed for *years*. This is just the way I am. This is the way God made me. Who are we to question that? It's gotta be some kind of blessing. We may not see that now but we will. I just know it."

He let go of me and stared at the kitchen table, like he was assessing the damage, trying to find words to describe what he now felt. He didn't say anything for what seemed like hours—but it was probably about thirty seconds—while Mom did her best to muffle her sobs.

I stood rock still, having no idea myself what to do or say next.

And then, right when I thought some great miracle of togetherness would rally our spirits, The Preacher let out a long, painful sigh. It was the sound of the world he'd painstakingly constructed over the years being destroyed in an instant. His broad shoulders slumped. "I wish I were dead," he said. "I truly wish I were dead." After a moment, he walked back toward his study without saying another word.

When I looked over, Mom was holding onto the kitchen counter with her back to me.

I went over and put my arm around her. "Oh, Mom."

She twisted away from me. "I—I just need a little space, okay honey?" she said, and walked back toward the bedroom.

Ten minutes ago, life had seemed pretty much back to normal, but how could it ever be normal again? I knew they couldn't handle this. Why didn't I just lie about the HIV test?

I once thought that nothing could damage my parents' love

for me. I thought it was boundless and unconditional. They'd always stood by my side, even after I blew that sermon back in April. That afternoon, Mom had insisted that I help her plant marigolds by the driveway, but it was just an excuse to get me alone so she could give me a pep talk. As we planted those flowers, she went on and on about stuff like my All-Alabama win and how neither she nor The Preacher had ever won a county award, let alone state, and come to think of it, where did I get my smarts? She eventually looked me straight in the eye and said, "Don't give today's sermon a second thought, Jake. You heard The Preacher—everyone has an off day, just get back in that saddle and try again. That's all you can do."

Mom's love had covered me like a warm blanket that day, but today, she ran away.

A surge of adrenaline shot through me.

I ran out into the garage and grabbed the water can from a shelf and filled it from an outdoor spigot. There could still be hope for those flowers.

Grass dug into my bare knees as I knelt before the marigolds that Mom and I had planted. Maybe if I could just keep these flowers alive, it would keep her love for me alive too, no matter how irrational that sounded.

I yanked up the hateful weeds that were choking the delicate stems. I bathed the marigolds with water and deadheaded their once perfect golden blossoms, now like tiny jaundiced mop heads.

Not a single plant had a live flower. Not one. There was just brown leaves and rot.

I flung the water can onto the lawn with a thud and pulled up the plants faster and faster until all that was left was one big hole in the ground, and another one in my heart.

CHAPTER 24

The next morning, I woke up thinking about all the drama of the prior evening: the insurance bill, the big speech, the horror in my parents' eyes, and my conversation with Sam. I'd called him around midnight; he'd suggested that I just take it day by day and keep the conversation going. By the time we'd finished talking, there was a big part of me that was glad I'd come out to my parents.

It was nearly ten. The Preacher would already be out of the house, thank God.

I grabbed the sermon index cards from my nightstand. "Back to Basics" was printed on the top card in The Preacher's ragged cursive script. Rehearsing that sermon for tomorrow was the last thing I wanted to do, but I didn't want to blow this one like I blew the last one. Of course, The Preacher could very well disown me before tomorrow.

I closed my eyes and felt myself sinking down, down, down, through a bottomless pool of blackness. Of all the groups discriminated against in the past, why did I have to be in the loneliest one of all? At least Jews, blacks, and other ethnic minorities were *born* into families that offered support and wisdom passed down from generation to generation. I had no such luck—no legacy of wisdom to guide me through the minefield of discrimination I would surely face the rest of my life.

"Drama queen!" That's what Julie would say about my pity-me party.

Maybe I *was* being a drama queen. After all, women

have been discriminated against since Bible times if not before. Heck, they couldn't even speak in church back then: the Apostle Paul made that perfectly clear in First Corinthians. I chuckled at the thought of One-Way trying to enforce *that* particular Biblical law in the modern age. I could just see The Preacher trying to enlist some poor junior deacon to hush all the women as they entered the sanctuary, because Lord knows The Preacher knew better than to try enforcing it himself. We could sell tickets!

Then it hit me. "Wait—that's it!" I said to no one in particular, then jumped out of bed.

I ran into the kitchen, hoping to find Mom. A note on the refrigerator said she was at the grocery store. I'd have to ask permission later.

I hurried into the utility room and pulled a long cord hanging from the ceiling. The folding wood stairs to the attic swung down with a clang. I rummaged around the attic until I found nine separate boxes labeled HATS—the better part of the collection Grandmother Clarke assembled over her adult life. I don't think she ever wore the same one twice.

She would've gotten a real kick out of my plans for them.

After her grocery shopping, I tried talking with Mom. I sensed that she would be a lot more understanding than The Preacher, which was not to say that it would be easy, just easier than with my dad, who might never come around.

She was running around like a chicken with its head cut off, whipping up a huge dinner. She hadn't cooked like that since the day Mamaw told us she had pancreatic cancer and only three months to live. I didn't know if Mom cooked during times of crisis to keep her mind off her problems or to prop up all our spirits. It was probably a little bit of both.

When The Preacher got home that evening, he washed his hands in the kitchen sink, then took his place at the head of the table filled with sweet and sour ribs, barbeque chicken, cornbread, and baked beans, all piping hot from the oven, smelling up the house. But even those smells couldn't mask the tension in the air, causing us to act like three complete strangers.

"Mom, you went all out," I said. I wanted to add, "Who died?" I took my place next to The Preacher at the table.

"Smells real good, honey," The Preacher said, looking out the picture window overlooking our pine forest of a backyard.

Mom took her usual seat across from him, and then we all held hands then bowed our heads as The Preacher led us in prayer.

For a while, we just ate in silence as my parents gazed up at the kitchen lights, down at their plates, over at the dirty dishes next to the sink, and basically anywhere else but at me. It took me a while to realize they weren't looking at each other either. It's like my coming out had severed our ties, leaving each of us adrift. The path forward now seemed dark and treacherous.

I'd spoken to Sam, Julie, and Phoebe at different points during that afternoon, and they'd all said that I had to keep the conversation going with my parents. Phoebe had once again offered to talk to Mom, but I made her promise to hold off—I didn't want Mom thinking we were ganging up on her.

I wished there were some fast-forward button to get through the agonizing silence of our new existence, and a pill that would dissolve the perpetual knot in my stomach. But there was no such fast-forward button, nor was there any such pill: Mom, Dad, and I had to trudge down this path, and the sooner we got started, the faster it would be behind us. Trouble was, I didn't know what to say, but I couldn't stand the quiet a second longer. "All this silence is making me crazy," I said. "Do you want to talk some more about…what I told you last night?"

Honestly, I sort of hoped they'd say "no."

"You're just playing this stunt so I don't make you quit

the newspaper," The Preacher said, pushing some beans up on his fork. "Fine. Do what you want. You win." He jammed the fork in his mouth.

Was he kidding? "Dad, that's not what this is about. It's about my being…"

The Preacher's jaw started trembling. "I don't even know you—I want my son, Jake, back!" he shouted. He picked up his plate, then stood to leave.

I sat there like a soldier who'd just taken a bullet, telling myself that I was fine since I felt no pain, then realizing I didn't feel anything at all.

"Henry, sit down!" Mom said.

But he just stood there, the plate trembling in his hand. Finally, he collapsed into his chair and stared at the congealed salad.

I turned to Dad. "I know you must hate what I told you last night. It took me four years to get my head around it myself. I'm mortified by how you found out, but I'm glad I no longer have this secret from you."

Mom was red-faced, her eyes now locked on me. "Why didn't you tell us about this, this, this…"

"Thorn. That's what I called it. How could I tell you when I knew it would break your heart? I turned to God, thinking he would heal me."

"Heal you?" she said incredulously. She was stepping into The Preacher's sovereign territory—in front of The Preacher.

"Yes, heal me. I'd heard my entire life that homosexuality is from Satan so I tried to reject those urges when they snuck up on me. I never thought I was possessed or anything like that—I just figured it was a cross I had to bear for a while, sort of a test I had to go through before Jesus would heal me. At first I just prayed that God would take it away, but when that didn't work I started fasting too."

"You fasted? When?" Mom asked.

"Just three or four times, during school lunch. The last

271

time I prayed to be healed, a feeling of peace swept over me. I called you right after." I turned to The Preacher. "In New York. When I almost spoke in tongues."

My words seemed to land in The Preacher's iced tea glass—he examined it carefully then took a swig.

"First I thought it was a sign that I'd been healed, you know, that God had taken the thorn away. I saw myself as this dirty vessel that the Spirit had washed clean. I was sure that I was straight at that point, but it didn't take long for those urges to come back and with them came thoughts of taking my own life."

Mom's eyes went wide. "Jake! Oh my god!"

My eyes were burning, but I fought back the tears. "You can't know how low I sank," I said, staring down at the table. "This thing was like an inoperable tumor for me. I now know sort of what Mamaw must've gone through with her cancer. Remember how she found this great peace at the end? She was actually comforting us."

"Mamaw was a God-fearing woman," The Preacher said, seeming to prefer the painful topic of his mother's death over the one at hand.

"Well, yeah, but there's just a peace that comes when you accept your fate. At least for me. I mean, Mamaw's fate was death but mine is just an unexpected way of life."

Bringing all my news out in the open made me feel a whole lot better. It was kind of like when you have food poisoning; you feel miserable until you force yourself to throw up. Once you do, it's almost like you were never sick in the first place. I was relieved to get all of this out of my gut. I'd always shared everything with my parents, but my thorn had seemed so awful and shameful—and something that could ruin my family's life—that I just kept it to myself.

And that's where I'd gone wrong.

The way forward was to stay close and share *everything*, and that went for Mom and Dad too. There was no reason for any of us to go walking around with some big burden when we had such a strong support network. If I could share this secret with them, they should certainly feel comfortable sharing anything with me. Phoebe had opened up about Richard, and that had brought us a lot closer together. Thinking of Phoebe reminded me of something she had said: ask your father about that scar on his wrist sometime. Maybe that Dr. Pepper bottle had been in the hand of another guy. Had The Preacher been in a gang or something? I decided I'd open that door a peek and if he wanted to share, he could. If not, that was okay too.

I straightened up in my chair. "Mom, Dad, this was the secret I kept from you. But I promise, no more secrets. They'll kill you. I want our family to be completely open with each other. I've told you my secret—are there any secrets you'd like to share with me?"

"Like what?" The Preacher asked.

I pushed the food around nonchalantly on my plate. "Anything at all."

My parents looked at each other for a moment.

"Is there something in particular you want to talk about?" Mom asked.

I suddenly wondered if this was such a brilliant idea after all. "Oh, nothing," I said, taking a bite of seven-layer salad. "Just wondering."

Mom put her fork down. "Jake, speak up. Something's on your mind, I can tell."

I shrugged like it was really nothing, but Mom was staring at me like a prosecuting attorney, waiting, so I turned to The Preacher. "Like, well, can you tell me more about what happened to your wrist?"

The Preacher put his fork down. "Who told you to ask that?"

I opened my mouth but nothing came out.

"Who?" The Preacher demanded.

I let out a sigh, knowing I had to come clean. "Aunt Phoebe just said—"

The Preacher glared at Mom. "Anna, you told *her* about that?"

Mom's hand flew to her mouth. "Preacher, it was a long time ago."

"I asked you not to tell *anyone*," he said.

"Honey, I'm sorry—really, it was ages ago," she said. "Before we were even married. I had to talk to someone about it. I haven't told anyone else and neither has she."

In my effort to bring us all back together, I'd only made it worse. I shook my head and wondered why I couldn't just keep my stupid mouth shut. "I just figured...never mind."

"You figured what?" The Preacher asked.

I cleared my throat. "It's just that—have you ever heard that quote, 'You're only as sick as your deepest darkest secret'? My secret nearly killed me, but once I started telling people, it lost its power completely. I never want y'all to get to such a dark place. I just want us to have a more open and honest relationship with each other."

He closed his eyes, pinched his nose, and let out a big sigh.

We all sat there silently at a complete loss. No one even moved.

"Jake, you once asked me about the summer before my senior year," The Preacher began, grimly.

"Henry, do you really want to—"

"Yes, I guess it's time the boy knows about his daddy." He took a deep breath. "The summer before my senior year of high school, Papaw sent me to a camp focused on the gifts of the Spirit because I hadn't yet spoken in tongues."

I'd never heard about this and had no idea where The Preacher was going with it.

"You just can't be the son of a Pentecostal preacher and not speak in tongues. You remember that line of his, 'Show me a Christian who don't speak in tongues and I'll show you a man who ain't Christian'? Well, by the end of the week, practically everybody in camp had spoken in tongues. Everybody except me."

"But I thought you *had* spoken in tongues." I could have sworn he'd said that.

"No, but I know all about it, believe you me. It was so hard to face Papaw when I got home."

Mom slid her chair back. She walked over and quietly squatted between The Preacher and me, one arm around each of us.

"For years I tried to be worthy of the gift—that's the reason I eventually pursued the ministry. But it never came."

The Preacher grabbed hold of Mom's hand.

How could he get so torn up over something so trivial? "Oh, Dad, that's not such a big deal—"

"It's a *huge* deal, Jake." The Preacher showed me the spider scar on his right wrist. "I tried to end my life."

I looked at that scar like I was seeing it for the first time. What kind of hell had The Preacher endured to do that to himself? All these years, I thought we had so little in common, yet we'd both experienced such absolute, unwavering despair that the emergency exit had seemed like the only way out. I wanted to protect him so he'd never have to hurt like that again. After all, no one, not even my wise, resolute, God-fearing father, was exempt from having a thorn, and I felt infinitely closer to him for that. "Could that be your thorn?"

"No, I was just a confused kid," he said.

"What if God knew that by withholding the gift of tongues you'd seek Him so earnestly that you'd end up pursuing the ministry? Don't you see that, Preacher? God needed you in the pulpit, and that was His way of getting you there. You're always saying that the Lord works in mysterious ways, right?"

The Preacher nodded but didn't look at me.

"It's kind of the same way my thorn forced me to search deep inside my soul to come to terms with my sexuality, something that seemed impossible at the time. That same kind of soul searching helped me figure out the path for my life.

It's all interconnected in a way that I'm just beginning to understand. And I now know deep down that, even though I didn't win an award, I'm meant to pursue journalism."

"Journalism? God revealed His will to you at that ceremony, clear as day. He wants you to be a preacher. You know that."

I wasn't taken aback by The Preacher's words in the least— I knew that was what he felt. He was simply speaking his truth. We were laying it all out on the table and my only regret was that we hadn't done this sooner. What had we been afraid of?

"Dad, I've thought a lot about that too, but I don't believe that putting out the fleece is the way to discern God's will. I mean, why would He give you a passion if He doesn't want you to pursue it? I believe that our passions are our callings in life, and mine's journalism."

"I've had enough sharing for one night," he said flatly, then stood and stared down at me. "You're preaching tomorrow. I—I don't care what you do after that."

As Dad left the room, Mom put her head down on the table and started sobbing.

I held her tight. "It's going to be all right, Mom. It's going to be all right." I wasn't sure I believed that myself, but I didn't know what else to say.

"Jake, did I coddle you too much?" she asked, wiping her nose.

"Are you kidding? You wrote the book on tough love. Remember when I missed the bus in second grade because I was piddling around, and you made me walk to school?"

"Did you ever miss it again?" she asked, a smile in her voice despite the tears.

"No, ma'am, or that time I poured syrup on the back doorstep?"

She chuckled. "I couldn't figure out why your new shoes were squeaking."

I smiled at her. "They weren't squeaking, they were sticking!"

She wiped her eyes. "You traipsed syrup everywhere."

"And you made me mop the entire house! I was only five!" I jokingly crossed my arms like I was still holding a grudge over it.

She laughed then rose to her feet.

After all that had gone down at dinner, I wasn't sure if my plans to hang out with Tracy were such a good idea. "Do you want me to stay in tonight?" I asked. "Tracy will understand."

"No—go and have a good time."

I stood and stroked her arm. "Really, I'm happy to stay."

She shook her head.

"Momma..." It just came out naturally, but in that moment I realized that—no matter what *anyone* thought—I'd always have a Momma.

She smiled and held my hand. "Yes, honey?"

"There's a question I've wanted to ask you all day but there's never been a good time—is it okay if I borrow Grandmother's hats?"

She pulled back, confused. "What in the world for?"

Poor Momma—she probably thought I was going to parade around in them. "It's sort of a surprise but one I know you'll like. Grandmother would've too."

"I guess. As long as you return them in the shape you found them."

I smiled real big. "I promise."

CHAPTER 25

The moment Tracy stepped out of the car I threw my arms around her. We really hadn't communicated much in the last six weeks, and I was almost as excited to see my best friend as I was my parents.

"I missed you so much, Jake. I didn't think you'd ever come home."

"I missed you too," I said, closing my eyes and nestling my head on the shoulder of her familiar red blouse. Tracy was big-boned with short, brown hair and a pretty face. She was the first person I'd seen all day who looked and acted the way she was supposed to. There was so much to tell her that I didn't even know where to begin.

She let go first. "I bet The Preacher's just crazy about your cool new haircut," she said sarcastically.

"Um, not exactly," I said with a smile, and then pointed at the canary yellow coupe she'd stepped out of. "Wow! So you got a new car?"

"Daddy gave it to me for senior year," she said, then tossed me the keys.

I jumped in and switched on the ignition; the car roared to life. "It's a five-speed too! Awesome!" I was fifteen the last time I drove Papaw's four-on-the-floor pickup and hoped I wouldn't make a complete fool of myself.

"Hey, wanna head out to the fire tower so we can really open her up?" she asked. "I haven't had the chance to break her in yet."

"Sure, but let's swing by the truck stop for an ice cream

first. We can say 'hi' to your cousin Kenny." I really wanted to make things right with him.

Tracy lifted her chin, suspiciously—probably because I'd only avoided Kenny in the past. "He just started at the Creamy Freeze."

"Even better," I said. "I could sure use a Creamy Freeze."

Tracy told me that things at home were still rough, but her parents were communicating more. That made me real happy even as I wondered whether I'd destroyed my own family unit.

At the Creamy Freeze, I pulled into a parking space a few spots away from a black Dodge pickup with a bumper sticker reading AMERICAN BY BIRTH, SOUTHERN BY THE GRACE OF GOD. I always got a kick out of Derrick's bumper sticker. Everyone was amazed that he and his best friend, Wade, managed to graduate from Tarsus High a few years back. They were always getting into trouble for skipping class or mouthing off or picking a fight. Derrick and Wade did everything together—they even dated the Reeves twins for a few weeks and dumped them on the same day. They were both now twenty-one and made a decent living at the sawmill.

Derrick and Wade sniggered between bites of their ice creams as they hurried through the parking lot toward the truck. I thought I heard Derrick say "homo" as he climbed in, but maybe I was hearing things.

But Tracy shook her head, so I guess I heard right. A small part of me wondered if they were talking about me and if my gayness now showed, until I looked over at the takeout window and saw Kenny. No guy around here wore a black dress shirt much less a black ruffled one.

Where I had once found Kenny's clothing choices somewhat embarrassing, I now admired him for blazing his own trail, like Julie. Of course, there was a big difference in that Kenny was called names and put down on a regular basis while Julie was off hanging with the cool crowd.

There was part of me that wanted to protect Kenny, but confronting Derrick was to confront Derrick *and Wade*, and that could end badly. I pointed my chin at Kenny. "When did he start working here?"

"Just this week. Things were getting a little rough for him at the truck stop."

"How so?"

"The new manager out there didn't take too kindly to Kenny's taste in clothes."

Kenny leaned out the window. "Hey, Jake! Hey, Tracy! What can I get y'all?"

For the first time, it was great to see him. "Two large Creamy Freezes," I said with a big smile. "Extra large if you've got 'em."

Kenny grabbed a couple of cones. "I like your new haircut, Jake"

I'd gotten pretty used to guys complimenting each other in New York, but not at home. "Thanks, Kenny."

The ice cream machine groaned as Kenny topped off the first cone.

I leaned over the counter. "Hey I, um, never congratulated you for winning that All-State Baton Twirling Challenge. That was huge, Kenny."

He turned his back to dip the cones in chocolate. "Oh, well, I'm giving all that up."

"Are you kidding? You're the baton-twirling guy. *Our* baton-twirling guy. If you quit, all we'd have left during football season is our crappy team. You're the one bright spot. You can't just up and quit—you'd be letting the whole school down."

My burst of enthusiasm surprised me and from the look on Tracy's face, her too. The thing was that Kenny and I were the only two kids in the entire school whose passions had been recognized at the state level. That, along with our shared sexuality (assuming he really was gay), bound us together somehow. We were part of the same tribe.

I felt Tracy staring at me. She had to be wondering how I could say all of this after keeping Kenny's article out of the paper.

Kenny turned and looked at me to see if I was serious or just another person poking fun at him. "You think so?" he said, finally.

"Absolutely!" I said. "Tracy, let's do a feature on Kenny for the first paper this year."

She looked at me like I had two heads. "Wow, I wish I'd thought of that."

Julie would've said the same thing! Am I just drawn to sassy rich girls? "What do you say, Kenny?"

He looked confused by my offer—probably because, I'd never been anything more than lukewarm to him in the past. "Well, okay. I guess so."

"Great! I'll do the interview myself if that's okay with Tracy." I was going to more than make up for being a jerk about the whole situation.

Kenny handed us two lopsided cones. "Sorry, but I'm still getting the swing of this."

We took our ice creams out to the cement picnic tables next to the entrance.

"What was that all about?" Tracy asked.

"What was what about?"

"You know what I mean. Back there with Kenny?"

I straightened up, pretending to be insulted. "What is this with you? Can't a guy change his mind?"

"I guess." She took a bite of her ice cream then looked like she was sizing me up. "Something's different about you."

"Don't let the hair fool you," I said, but of course she was right. She knew me so well but at the same time, she had no idea.

After our ice creams, we headed to the fire tower. As I drove, I obsessed over whether I should come out to her. If anyone in Tarsus was cool with homosexuality, it would be Tracy, but telling her might damage our relationship, since I suspected deep down she hoped for more than just my friendship.

That burr began to dig into my gut again. What was I doing to myself? Hadn't I had enough drama in the last couple of days, not to mention having to give the sermon tomorrow? I'd just keep it light tonight and come out to Tracy once things settled down a bit.

I obeyed the speed limit while in the town limits but opened up the Chevy once we were outside of Tarsus.

We passed tin-roofed chicken houses, cows grazing behind barbed wire on open pastures, and cornfields ready for harvest. As we traveled farther west, farmland gave way to woods filled with pine trees punctuated by the odd trailer home or run-down house. Outside one home, PECANS was painted in big white letters on a rotting plywood board leaning against a fence post.

We drove ten miles before reaching the tricky hairpin turns called "The Seven Sisters" (I don't know the exact origin of the name, but there were seven turns and they were, well, curvy.) By then, we were really in the sticks. Just past the final "sister," I came to a stop. This began the three-mile flat and relatively straight stretch called "the ridge," which ran along a hilltop just outside the jurisdiction of the local police.

"You sure you're okay if I open her up?"

"I asked you to, didn't I?" Tracy said.

This wasn't the first time we'd done this.

"Zero to sixty?" I asked.

"Let's go for a hundred."

"Cool!" As I revved the engine, she looked down at her watch. "Five, four, three, two, one, go!" she said.

I jerked my foot off the clutch. We cackled as the front wheels spun then jackhammered the pavement, launching the car forward.

Tracy let out a gleeful yell as the smell of burnt rubber filled the cabin.

I held tight to the steering wheel, which pulled left then

right, as the turbocharged engine threw us back in our seats. I shifted hard as the tachometer approached its 6,500 redline.

"Ten seconds," Tracy said.

I glanced down at the speedometer, "Seventy-five," I said, then threw the shifter into third. "Eighty-five...ninety-five...one-hundred!" I yelled then let off the gas and feathered the brakes.

"Eighteen seconds," Tracy said.

I shook my head. "I spun too much off the start line."

"Yeah, don't quit your day job, Mario," she said as she looked at the sky, which had turned a majestic blue. "Let's get to the fire tower before it's dark?"

We followed a steep, winding dirt road up to the old abandoned fire tower we'd first discovered last summer. Since then, we'd visited four or five times—it was a welcome break from the monotony of the bowling alley. The fire tower had sort of become our place.

We climbed the rickety wooden ladder to the tin-roofed lookout fifty feet above us. I hated the open-air climb but loved the view of the southernmost chain of the Appalachian Mountains.

Inside, the tower was like the treehouse I never had. It was all wood except for the low tin ceiling. A wall ran along three sides, but someone had removed a large swath of the fourth wall (perhaps a deer hunter to gain a better view of the forest below). I sat down on the plywood floor and inched my toes to the open edge and leaned back on my hands. Tracy plopped beside me with her legs dangling right off the side.

We sat quietly for a few minutes, taking in the oranges and yellows of the sunset and the soothing rustle of pines swaying in the breeze.

Tracy reached back and slapped my leg with the back of her hand. "You haven't told me a thing about New York City. Something major must've happened for you to be so doggone quiet about it."

It was an innocent enough question, but—between my

brush with suicide, my lost virginity, and my new *boy*friend—talking about New York was a freakin' minefield. Not to mention that she might be jealous as hell over Julie. "I don't even know where to begin," I said. And I didn't.

"Well, did you have fun? Any celebrity sightings? What was it like?"

"No celebrities. I don't know if I'd call my time there fun. It was certainly enlightening," I said, hedging. "Honestly, I was absolutely miserable for a big chunk of it."

"You really missed me that much?" She giggled.

"Of course, I missed you," I said, and instinctively reached out and touched her shoulder, but she seemed distant all of a sudden.

I pulled my hand back.

She looked out at the horizon. "We barely communicated the whole time you were gone. You say I'm your best friend, but it was like you just up and left and never looked back. Are you—are you mad at me?"

"Of course not. My time in New York was just overwhelming. Columbia really put us through the ringer."

"Let me guess: you finally threw caution to the wind and danced with some Yankee chick," she said. "That's who gave you that leather thing on your wrist, right? You certainly didn't have it when you left."

So that was what this weirdness with Tracy was about—she thought I'd fallen for a girl! For a split second, I considered telling her that I had in fact kissed a girl. That's what the old Jake might've done, but I was so over pretending.

"There was a girl at Columbia but we're just friends," I said with perfect truthfulness. Well, almost perfect since I did leave out the part about my boyfriend giving me the leather cuff. But it was hard enough just confessing to being close friends with another girl—it felt like I was two-timing Tracy or something.

"What's her name?" she asked, sounding crushed.

"Her name's Julie, but it's not what you think," I said.

"Jake, really, it's cool," she said, turning and smiling at me. "I bet she's really pretty."

"Yes, she is."

"Did you kiss her?" she asked, holding on to that same smile, but it was fraying around the corners.

I let out a big sigh, not liking where this was heading. "Yes, we made out once, but it was a big mistake."

"Why? You said she was pretty."

"I don't know," I lied, automatically slipping back into my old ways. Wasn't it obvious that I didn't want to talk about this? I suddenly resented her for putting me in this situation. "Well, I *do* know," I said, annoyed. "It just didn't work out, okay? Can we just leave it at that?"

"Wow, okay," she said, sounding extremely hurt. "I'm sorry for taking an interest in your life."

We just sat there in silence, like neither of us knew what to say. Of course, there was something to say, and it was up to me to say it. I just didn't want to: after going through so much hell in the last few weeks, I just wanted one stress-free night. Was that too much to ask?

Clearly it was.

Tracy had really pushed me into a corner. I knew her so well—this rift between us wasn't going away until I came clean. She'd give me the silent treatment, answering my questions with one-word responses, being unavailable to hang out, and basically making me feel abandoned and alone when I needed her now more than ever. I could easily imagine our final weeks of summer vacation being completely destroyed by this, which made me resent her even more.

"You want to know why it didn't work out with Julie?" I said like a brat, and then braced myself, knowing it was too late to turn back at that point. "It didn't work out because...because I'm gay. That's why." I couldn't believe I'd said the words and suddenly had that same falling sensation I'd experienced when I came out to my parents—like the entire forest had collapsed beneath me.

She stopped swinging her legs then stared at me for a moment as if trying to decide if I was serious. "You're so full of it, Jake," she said, finally.

I straightened up and looked her dead in the face. "Tracy, I'm gay. Why would I make that up?"

"Jake, I'm not falling for it."

I carefully pulled out my cell phone, then brought up the photo of Sam on Broadway. "This is Sam, my boyfriend. He's from L.A. He's actually cuter in person."

She took the phone and stared at the photo. "You're serious?"

I nodded. "He's the one who gave me this leather cuff."

She let out a long sigh and then handed back my phone. "I need a second to process this. I always knew you were different from other guys, but I didn't think you were *that* different." She laughed nervously. "You left here your old regular self and came home gay? When did you figure all this out?"

"It's hard to say exactly. I've had these feelings since I was thirteen but never acted on them until New York."

She suddenly glared at me, her eyes cold and hard. "You've known this for *four years* and you're just telling me now? How is it that I can tell you about my father's affair, but you hide important shit from me?"

"Tracy, I know, it's just that—"

"Don't you value our friendship?"

That brought tears to my eyes. Why did I keep important shit from Tracy? I hadn't even told her about the whole putting out the fleece debacle with The Preacher. I guess that as a PK, I've always felt that I had to keep a fortress around my issues and those of my family. After all, The Preacher's family needed to be Christ-like and drama-free to live up to the expectations of the congregation. But I now realized that by not sharing my burdens with Tracy, I had actually put some serious limitations on our friendship.

"Of course I do," I said. "It's just that, well, all my life,

I've been taught to live a Christ-like life and *turn away* from sin, so I tried not to even *think* about it much less *talk* about it. Of course, I prayed about it a lot."

"So what happened in New York that caused you to finally accept it?"

"That's a good question. Here in Tarsus, everyone views homosexuality as sinful. Can you imagine how awful it is to hear your own father stand behind the pulpit and preach that you're going to hell? That kept me in the closet for years, but in New York, most people view homosexuality as *normal*. After being around that kind of thinking for a few weeks, I began to question whether being gay was a sin after all. I mean, there's nothing in the Bible that even hints that Jesus was against it. So once I stopped viewing my sexuality as a sin, I quit turning away from it. So it's now a lot easier for me to talk about."

"Are you going to tell your parents?"

"I did. Last night."

"Oh my god," she said, visibly in awe. "How'd you do it?"

I shook my head then told her all about the clinic, the test, and the whole dumb drama.

Tracy covered her mouth. "Your father must've freaked!"

"Momma too."

Tracy shook her head. "Jake, I love you for who you are—straight, gay, or whatever. I'm just hurt that you didn't trust me enough to talk about it, even if you weren't sure what 'it' was. I don't want to make this all about me but..."

"Tracy, it won't happen again," I said emphatically. "No more secrets. Secrets will freakin' kill you. I know that now."

She leaned in and hugged me so fast, I thought we were both going off the edge.

"I love you, Tracy," I said, holding her tight.

"I love you, Jake."

After a few moments I said, "I have a big favor to ask of you. It's about my sermon tomorrow."

She pulled away. "What kind of favor?" she asked, warily.

"Don't worry. Actually, I think you're gonna love this."

She shrugged. "Sure. I'll always be here for you, Jake. Nothing could ever change that."

"Thank you. I'll always be here for you, too."

We sat with our arms around each other as the sky took on a deep shade of purple and the night wind grew cool on our faces. It was just like old times but without all the secrets.

CHAPTER 26

I woke up the next morning before the alarm went off. Someone had phoned our landline and there was no going back to sleep, especially after I spotted my freshly dry-cleaned suit hanging on my closet door: it was Fifth Sunday, 6:28 a.m. to be exact.

After showering and getting dressed, I walked into the kitchen and found Momma on her knees, wiping down the inside of our old rust-colored refrigerator. Salad dressing bottles, juice cartons, and leftovers were stacked on the counter and the refrigerator drawers and racks were laid out on towels, drying.

"What in the world…" I said to Momma's backside.

"I couldn't take this messy refrigerator one more day," she said, her voice muffled.

"Who called at the crack of dawn?"

"Mrs. Tate. They rushed Mr. Tate to the emergency room in the middle of the night. They think it's a heart attack."

"Is he going to be okay?"

"I don't know. The Preacher's there now."

"He's meeting us at church?"

"No, he ran out in his khakis. He'll come back home to change."

She finally leaned back, wiped her forehead, and looked up at me. "You're already dressed?"

"Yes, ma'am. If it's okay, I need to get to church early for my sermon. Mind if I borrow your car?"

"Sure. I'll get a ride with The Preacher. Just fill it up on your way home, okay? My credit card and keys are in my purse."

I backed Momma's minivan to the end of our driveway and, as silly as it sounds, pulled up Sam's photo on my phone as the cool blast of air conditioning washed over me.

I looked out at the street. Right took me to church. Left, to the interstate.

If I drove 500 miles a day, I'd be in Los Angeles by Wednesday. I had enough money for gas and food, but I'd have to sleep in the car. Sam would nearly collapse from shock when he opened his front door. He'd pick me up and I'd kiss him hard and say the words I wished I'd said back in New York: I love you, Sam Horowitz. Then maybe he'd say he loved me right back and we'd figure out a plan before his mom got home from work. Sure, there'd be sacrifices. Maybe I'd get a job waiting tables or perhaps his mom could hook me up as a proofreader at one of the movie studios. It was only for a year then we'd be off to college together.

I snapped out of my daydream with a groan, and headed for the church.

Once I got there, I threw myself into all the last minute preparations for the sermon and was running so far behind that I had to skip Sunday School. I finished up with just minutes to spare before the service, but that was enough time for me to get in a quick prayer and try to psych myself up for my appointment with the pulpit.

I waltzed into the sanctuary and spotted a sea of familiar faces. It was hot as blue blazes in there and looked like we'd be near our 312-seat capacity.

I could feel the bees stirring.

Someone tapped my shoulder. I turned around and saw Mrs. Roberts, my biggest fan and former babysitter, in her signature fuchsia lipstick. I threw my arms out and gave her a hug. I'd had a powwow with her husband and chairman of the deacons, Brother Roberts, right after I'd gotten to church that morning since I needed his assistance during my sermon. Brother and Mrs. Roberts were the same height, but he always kept his wiry hair long so he'd look taller. Everyone knew when she was mad at him because she'd wear high heels.

"Look at all these people—they came just to hear you, Jake!" she said.

Mrs. Roberts was just trying to encourage me. Attendance was pretty steady from Sunday to Sunday as long as my dad was preaching. He never announced when we were away because attendance would drop, impacting the collection dramatically. Even so, if one of my dad's sermon outlines wasn't in the bulletin when people got to church, some of them—who will go unnamed—would turn right around and leave. The only reason they were staying today was probably just to see if I'd blow this sermon like I blew the last one.

I checked in real quick with my school friends in the back two rows, then walked around the sanctuary, hugging on the older women who all made a big fuss over how much they'd missed me. Some asked about New York and a few, upon seeing my new hairstyle, asked if I'd lost my comb.

Momma sat down at the piano and began playing "Blessed Assurance," everyone's cue to begin quieting down. I took the spot next to Tracy, sitting toward the front of the sanctuary on the aisle just as we'd agreed. I was glad she was cool with her part in the sermon; I don't know who I would've asked if she'd said no.

Moments before the service was to begin, The Preacher appeared from a side door and took a seat in his oak pulpit chair on stage. He opened his Bible and studied the bulletin tucked neatly inside. I took the opportunity to study it myself, but I knew the drill: there were only four congregational hymns and the collection before I was to preach.

The songs we sang were like old friends to me: "Great Is Thy Faithfulness," "The Lilly of the Valley," "When the Roll is Called Up Yonder." I felt tears of joy as we sang the fourth hymn, "It Is Well," which summed up how I was trying to approach life despite all of its twists and turns:

When peace, like a river attendeth my way,
When sorrows like sea billows roll
Whatever my lot, thou hast taught me to say
It is well, it is well with my soul

Tracy elbowed me. I guess I was singing on the loud side. I smiled at her and toned it down a bit, especially on the last stanza when four deacons headed to the front of the church to take up the collection.

The Preacher called on Brother Roberts to lead us in prayer. That was kind of a reprieve since Brother Roberts's prayers are epic, and at 93 seconds, this one was pretty close to his all-time record of 112 seconds (I always time him).

As the deacons passed collection plates to each and every member of the congregation, Momma played "Bringing in the Sheaves." She kept an eye on the proceedings, finishing up the last bars of the hymn right as the deacons placed the collection plates, filled with checks and cash, on the oak offertory table next to the final model of the church complex. A new sign read "Construction Begins Next Spring!"

Knowing I was up next, I started shuffling my feet. Why did I always get nervous before a sermon? I could feel that army of bees getting into position at the back of my chest.

"You'll be great, Jake," Tracy whispered, grabbing my hand as if she could read my mind.

Her words caused the bees to scatter a little. I cupped her hand in mine and squeezed it tight. Like Momma told me years ago before my very first sermon, everyone gets nervous before speaking in public. Just take three deep breaths and let it out slowly.

I went to smile at Momma, but she had her head bowed in prayer. I couldn't help but wonder if she was praying for my performance or, more likely, that my gayness was just a phase.

The Preacher looked tired but wore a smile that seemed genuine, even to me. How many times had he stood up there acting all normal when he was falling to pieces inside? I wished he could've just stood there and shared with the whole congregation what our family was going through, but it wasn't that easy: he was our spiritual leader, and spiritual leaders were supposed to have solutions, not problems. At that moment, I'm sure he was thinking about me and questioning whether I was going to hell. After all, he wouldn't have preached that all these years if he didn't believe it. He might think differently about my salvation one day, but it was hard to imagine that he—or the One-Way Bible Church—would ever recognize gay people as anything but abominations.

There was no way to know what kind of emotional storm was going on inside of my parents now that they knew my secret. They could wind up in their own closets if they kept this to themselves. That's a real lonely way to live and why I had to do everything in my power to make sure that was not their future. I couldn't let them go to such a dark, lonely place.

The Preacher stepped up to the pulpit with his convincing smile and said, "As part of our Fifth Sunday Youth Service, I'm happy to once again present my son, Jake Powell."

He usually had a lot more than that to say on Fifth Sundays. Still, I was glad he called me his son—it would've been extra tough getting up there if he'd left that out. I wasn't worried that he was about to disown me, but then an awful thought hit me: many disowned kids probably never saw it coming.

I pushed that thought away and turned to Tracy. "When I wink at you—that'll be our signal, okay?" I asked, patting the bulge in my suit jacket pocket.

She nodded.

Only Tracy and Brother Roberts knew a little of what I was up to, but they were both sworn to secrecy.

I took a deep breath, then walked up the stairs to the

stage with my Bible and shook The Preacher's hand. He nodded at me but there was nothing behind his eyes—he just put one foot in front of the other, and then sat in the front pew.

The bees were swarming, but I was determined to breathe steady and stay focused.

The Preacher took a seat in the front row and opened his Bible. It dawned on me that every time he held his Bible like that, he couldn't help but see that scar, a constant reminder of his thorn.

I placed my Bible on the pulpit, next to the notecards The Preacher had written out.

My father had a real talent for making his sermons readily accessible, and this one was no exception. In it, he contrasted the Gospel of Christ to a Tootsie Roll, noting that the size, color and shape of the Tootsie Roll wrapper had changed over the years, but the recipe remained the same. Just like the Tootsie Roll wrapper, we could change the way we package the Gospel but the actual message never changed since the Bible was flawless, inerrant, and infallible. It was clearly a fundamentalist sermon but didn't go nearly far enough for my purposes that day.

My throat tightened as I thought back to my time in the gay clinic when I was waiting to take that HIV test. I remembered two of the vows I made before Sam and God that day.

One. To not get so caught up about what everyone else thought of me.

Two. To write my own editorials, which, as far as I was concerned, included sermons. I was so over delegating my point of view to my father or anyone else.

I put The Preacher's sermon aside, knowing what was on everyone's mind: would this kid crack under pressure like last time? Still, there were so many people pulling for me. All the warmth they were sending my way made me hopeful that this, the first sermon I had ever written, would go over well despite its more unconventional elements.

I paused for a moment knowing this stunt I was about to pull could put the final nail in my relationship with The Preacher. It was a huge chance but I didn't see any other way—if we were to continue to move forward as a family, I had to keep the conversation going. My father might be able to run away from the dinner table, but he'd have to sit and listen like everyone else in church.

Following The Preacher's lead, I started *my* "Back to Basics" sermon with the flawless, inerrant, and infallible Word of God, but I didn't compare it to a Tootsie Roll; I compared it to the Boeing 747 operations manual and how the pilots had to know all 971 lights, gauges and switches cold or they were liable to hit the wrong one and send themselves and all 440 passengers onboard plunging to their death.

The Preacher looked up, but didn't seem particularly alarmed. Yet.

I then described how the Bible was our operator's manual and much bigger than the 747 version because our souls were infinitely more complex than a jumbo jet. I emphasized that we also had to know our "user manual" cold, lest we wind up in hell. I paused, letting these words sink in. I hung my head and slowly shook it—like I'd just lost my beloved dog—then said in my loudest, most authoritative preacher voice, "I've had a burden on my heart for years that I'm now going to share with you."

A look of terror swept across The Preacher's face. Momma continued praying silently from the piano with her eyes closed.

Miss Ruby Smith, always on the lookout for trouble, leaned forward, her eyes magnified by those thick eyeglasses of hers. She probably thought I was about to confess to stealing from the offering plate or something.

I opened my Bible. "First Corinthians eleven. 'The head of every man is Christ, and the head of the woman is man. A man ought not to cover his head, since he is the image and glory of God; but the woman is the glory of man. For man did not come from woman, but woman from man; neither was man created for woman, but woman for man. For this reason, and because of the angels, the woman ought to have a sign of authority on her head.'" I slammed my palm down on the pulpit to punctuate "authority" then brought it up in a dismissive sweep.

At this point, The Preacher shook his head at me, clearly not amused by how off-script I was. I tried not to look down at the front row where he was sitting. "Folks, we've been treating God's Bible—our operator's manual—like a shopping cart: adding the passages we want to follow and simply ignoring the rest."

I nodded at Brother Roberts who signaled the other ushers. They walked up the aisles with large boxes filled with Grandmother Clarke's colorful hats, passing them out to the women in the congregation who smiled and seemed thrilled by the spectacle of it all.

There were purple, blue, yellow, and red hats in all shapes and sizes including fedoras, silk turbans, wool berets, and plumed derbies. The children especially loved the Russian fur hat. The audience laughed and chatted as the women swapped hats with each other.

Seeing Grandmother's hats everywhere, Momma gasped like she couldn't decide whether to laugh or cry. Brother Roberts tapped her on the shoulder and gave her a chocolate Indiana Jones hat that I had arranged for her to get. Of all the hats, it was the one I thought would look best on her. Momma put on the hat like it had once belonged to Cleopatra. She looked stunning as she smiled at me, but I kept a stern expression: she had no idea what I was up to.

I cleared my throat to silence the congregation. "First Corinthians instructs women to cover their heads in church. Otherwise, they disrespect the men of the congregation. Paul reminds us that women were created from and for men."

My entire sermon depended on someone refusing her hat—with all the attention Southern women give their hair, I figured there'd be bookoodles, but after scanning the sanctuary, only one woman was hatless: Miss Ruby Smith. She was sitting toward the front of the church with her teased white hair and those magnified blue eyes of hers. Miss Ruby was mean and ornery and the last person I wanted to pick on because she might put up a fight, but I had no choice.

"Miss Ruby," I called out, "you don't want a hat?"

She crinkled her nose and looked like she was sucking on a lemon drop. She shook her head no.

I signaled to a pink turbaned Tracy that it was time for her part in the sermon. Since Miss Ruby was involved, I was afraid Tracy would bail, but she stood and started making her way up to the pulpit like we'd agreed.

"But Corinthians instructs us that a woman's head must be shaved if she refuses to cover it."

My heart was racing as I took a cordless hair trimmer from my suit jacket, switched it on, and made a big show of handing it to Tracy. Tracy looked downright angry as she held the buzzing razor high and marched toward Miss Ruby. It was a real performance that created quite a ruckus in the sanctuary.

The Preacher raised a finger at me like I'd better get back in line quick.

Miss Ruby stood and stared Tracy down. "Have you lost your mind, Jake?" she shouted.

"Silence!" I said, slapping the pulpit. "The Apostle Paul said it is a shame for a woman to speak in church!"

Miss Ruby gathered her Bible and purse and stood to leave in a huff.

The Preacher jumped out of his seat and made a beeline for Tracy.

"I'm just trying to enforce God's word!" I said. "Won't you wear your pretty hat? You're dishonoring all the men in the congregation!"

The Preacher grabbed the razor from Tracy and switched it off. He tried to cover the awkwardness with a laugh. "Ruby, wait! Come back here. Jake's just playing with you."

She turned around hesitantly as I began to chuckle.

The congregation now stared at me expectantly, not knowing what could possibly come next.

"Folks, do you see what just happened?" I said. "Miss Ruby didn't care what the Bible said because she knows she's just as good as all you men here!"

"Better!" Miss Ruby shouted, as she sat back down.

The crowd laughed as one by one, the other women removed their hats. The air in the room suddenly lightened.

"That's right, Miss Ruby! Like Grandmother Clarke used to say, 'A good woman's better than a good man any day of the week!'"

Even Momma laughed out loud at that.

I raised my Bible above my head. "Who believes the Bible is alive? Can I get a show of hands?"

All hands went up.

"Then let's treat it that way as we apply the truths of the scriptures to the world we live in today. Hey, maybe one day we'll even see women standing behind One-Way pulpits. The possibilities are endless! So, who thinks all the women in the congregation should be quiet and wear hats?"

Brother Roberts raised his hand and smirked. Mrs. Roberts playfully hit him on the shoulder.

I pointed at Brother Roberts and said in a stage whisper, "Uh-oh! You better be careful, Brother Roberts, or she'll be wearing her highest heels next Sunday."

The whole congregation busted out laughing.

Momma looked at me with her face aglow and eyes sparkling. She started clapping.

Tracy clapped along with her, then Mrs. Roberts joined in.

Suddenly, I was beginning to feel bad for Tracy, Momma, and Mrs. Roberts, clapping all by themselves, but then Momma rose to her feet and continued clapping, only louder.

What the heck was going on?

Miss Ruby stood, plunked her purse down and joined in the clapping. Then, one by one, the women of the congregation rose to their feet, followed by the men.

For a moment, I was filled with a blinding light, like the sun had taken up residence right inside me. I never thought people would clap during my sermon—I wasn't even finished yet—and this was a standing ovation.

Then, I suddenly realized I wasn't alone on stage.

Dad's eyes narrowed at me.

I wished I could say that I didn't care, that it didn't affect me, that I just acted like he wasn't there, but that wouldn't be true. My dad's apparent disapproval reduced the light glowing inside me by half, but as it faded, I became aware of something even greater and much more enduring just beneath it. At that moment, I realized there were no longer two sides of me—the side that was acceptable and the side that was not. There was just me. And for the first time in four years—when I first realized I was gay—I actually felt…whole.

"Thank y'all," I said humbly. "Thank you so much."

When I finally stepped down, The Preacher raised his hands to quiet the congregation, "Okay, settle down everyone. The fun's over."

The applause died a little, but all eyes were on me as I walked down the center aisle and out the front door. I just wanted to be by myself so I could hold onto that light a little longer.

Of course, I couldn't just "come out" to the congregation until I had laid the proper groundwork, but this was a good first step.

I sat on the church steps with the late morning sun shining on my face. I had never felt closer to God than I did on that bright and glorious summer day. For years, I'd been swimming upstream, fighting against my very nature to be what I thought God wanted me to be, but I had grown to realize that He loves me just the way I am, and I could stop fighting.

I took out my cell phone and texted Sam, "I got a standing ovation!"

His reply was immediate: "Of course you did! You're a star!"

I pulled up a photo of Sam on the tiny screen, and immersed myself in those deep blue eyes of his. Maybe my parents *would* let him come during Christmas break. I could almost imagine holding his hand in church, or even making out with him in the back of the movie theater just like straight couples in town, or just hanging out at my house playing video games while my parents watched television in the den. I kept daydreaming about a life with Sam, then suddenly realized that the sun was no longer in my face.

Momma was staring down at me.

I jumped up like it had been a few years since I last saw her instead of a few minutes.

She reached out and hugged me tight. "That took a lot of gumption to get up there and say those things."

"Thanks for standing by me, Momma, and clapping and all."

"You may not realize it, but you stumbled onto a topic that is near and dear to a lot of women's hearts in town—the fact that we can't step behind the pulpit is just ridiculous. And I love that you used Grandmother's line, 'A good woman's better than a good man any day of the week.' She would've gotten a huge kick out of that."

"Did you see Miss Ruby's face when Tracy took that hair trimmer to her?"

"I don't know if that was brave or stupid." Momma laughed then noticed the picture of Sam on my phone.

I handed it to her, then led her down the steps. "You remember Sam? I like him so much. He's amazing, Momma, and so wise and caring. Well, in his own way. He stuck by my side during my darkest times in New York."

Momma nodded. "Yes, he's very handsome. He seemed very nice and his mom did too."

"Get this—she's some big movie executive so they have celebrities over and everything, not that Sam seems so wrapped up in all that. I'm not so sure about his father—sounds like he's not around much. I wish I could find a way to see him before school starts."

Momma handed back my phone. As we circled the church in silence, I noticed the labels that were slapped onto everything from the cars in the parking lot to the cover on the water meter to the sign in front of the church. I started thinking about how the world constantly slapped labels on me: PK, Bootette, boy preacher, editor, and, most recently, gay. Well, those labels don't capture me at all. I'm Jake Powell and I'm simply trying to live the best life I can. Out of billions of people on this earth, I am absolutely unique and exactly what God intended. The words of Jeremiah 1:5 came rushing into my head: "Before I formed you in the womb I knew you, before you were born I set you apart."

At that moment, I realized that there was no one else I'd rather be. It wasn't time to make that call to Aunt Phoebe—I wasn't at the point of seeing my gayness as a gift—but I no longer saw it as a curse either. And I was kind of excited to see where it would take me. After all, if I weren't gay, I never would've written that sermon, and I never would've fallen in love with Sam.

"I'd love for you and Dad to get to know Sam. I think you'd both really like him. In fact, the way he can get on his soapbox from time to time kind of reminds me of The Preacher. What do you think about him visiting at Christmas?"

"Honey, I'm sure he'd want to be with his own family at Christmas."

"He's Jewish so I don't think it really matters."

Momma let out a sigh. "Jake, honey, I just don't want you to get hurt. That's all."

"I'll be careful, Momma, but I want to be seen for who I am—not for who people want me to be. I told Tracy about me last night and she's totally cool with it."

In the distance, a lone bobwhite quail sang, "bob-white!" with a boundless pride of breed. I chuckled to myself—if Sam were a bird, he'd be a bobwhite. I'd been a bird with no song of my own but was certainly finding my voice now.

The front doors of the church opened, service was letting out.

Momma clucked her tongue. "The Preacher will be fit to be tied when he gets home. Let's role-play. You be The Preacher and I'll play you."

I gave her a big hug then looked her in the eye. "Momma, I've been role-playing my entire life. Trust me, I know where I stand on this. I don't need a rehearsal."

Acknowledgements

Katie Manglis, thank you for your support and enthusiasm every step of the way.

George Nicholson, thank you for being such an incredible agent and for your unwavering faith in me and in this novel.

Michael Carroll, David McConnell, Patrick Ryan, and Bob Smith, thank you for welcoming me into your awesome writing brotherhood.

Kellen Hertz, Michelle Koh, Melanie La Rosa, Karen Lawler, Julie Lynch, Luke Mayes, Betsy Nagler, Rebecca Penix-Tadsen, Evan Rubenstein, Samina Sami, Laszlo Santha, Gary Schwartz, and Ivan Weiss, thank you for being the best writing group ever and for your incredible feedback on my early drafts.

Courtney Bongiolatti, Bob Brooks, Tim Ceci, Mark DeGasperi, Stephanie Gunning, Martha Hughes, Nick Nicholson, Bill Pace, Staton Rabin, Erin Reilly, Vincent Robert, Marc Schector, William Thompson, and Liz Van Doren, you were critical people on my path to publication.

Osman Bol, Yvonne Borgogni, Hemant Chawla, Clayton Crawley, Rachel Elkinson, Mark Goodman, Nancy Hartley, Bruce MacAffer, Katie Manglis, Dr. Hal Taussig, and Tony Tyre, thank you for your expertise in areas I knew nothing about.

I would also like to thank Gina Adams, Jody Almengor, Gabriel Amor, Richard Anderman, Stephen Barr, Sandra Bellefleur, Cosimo Borgogni, Cary Brown, Kim Brown,

Robert Brown, John Campbell, Thomas Carroll, Michael Clinton, Tay Cooper, Ann Craig, John Crocker, Kevin Davis, Tom Devincentis, Janice Elkinson, Jessica Falvo, Cooper Fleishman, Philip Galanes, David Gale, Evan Galen, Jeff Gates, Tim Gibbs, Glenn Goldberg, Greg Gould, Novella Gray, Marta Hallett, Sharon Hardy, Barbara Haynes, Daniel Horowitz, Joe Hughes, Mike Johnson, Lisa Kapp, Jonas Karp, Ken Kuchin, Richard Lapin, Alan Levin, Mark Little, Dr. Ze'ev Levin, Paul Leyden, Talbot Logan, Norman Mallard, Dan Manjovi, Alan Markinson, Steve Markov, Doreen Massin, Caitlin McDonald, John McGinn, Lacey McNamara, Joyce McShane, Kate McShane, Bill Miller, Jay Moore, Patrick Murphy, Paul Murphy, Sue Ober, Clay Olsen, Holly Pettman, Stefanie Powers, Kay Pruett, Suzanne Ramos, Maddie Rice, Marc Rice, Patrick Rinn, John Rochester, Lauren Rosen, Les Rosen, Mark Rotenstreich, Brad Rothschild, Christopher Rowe, Randy Rupert, Chuck Santoro, David Schwarz, Craig Shirley, Diane Shirley, Erica Silverman, David Simanoff, Joey Smith, Mike Spencer, Buddy Stallings, Brent Taylor, Richard Tesler, Keisha Thom, Charles Tolbert, Jane Tully, Tommy Tune, Jason Wells, Kim Radetzki Wiese, Martin Wilson, Warren Wilson and Doug Wingo.

Finally, thank you to my editor and publisher, Don Weise, whose editorial expertise and passion for storytelling improved this book immensely.

About the Author

S. Chris Shirley is an award-winning writer/director and President of the Board of Lambda Literary Foundation. He graduated from Auburn University where he served as photo editor of *The Auburn Plainsman*. He later received a graduate degree from Columbia University and studied filmmaking at New York University. He was born and raised in Greenville, Alabama and now resides in Manhattan. *Playing by the Book* is his first novel. Visit him online at http://schrisshirley.com.

ENOCH PRATT
free LIBRARY

FEB 24 2015

ENOCH PRATT
RST
FREE LIBRARY

FEB 2 4 2015

CPSIA information can be obtained at www.ICGtesting.com
Printed in the USA
LVOW11s1554300914

406572LV00001B/233/P

9 781626 010710